DEA

"Really, Lindy," Stella said. "I hope you packed better school lunches than you did that. Well, no matter. I have a surprise for dessert."

Lindy groaned.

"Crème brûlée. My specialty." Stella laid out silverware and a linen napkin, flipped the top off the container and arranged the contents on a plate. "Chicken salad, anyone? Made with water chestnuts and three different peppers." She sat down and began to eat with relish while she chatted about a party she had catered the weekend before.

The microwave beeped.

"Black bean soup?"

Lindy watched Stella dig into her soup. After a few bites, she paused, spoon in the air, and made a face. "I must have been daydreaming when I put this batch together." She got up and put the bowl next to the sink.

"And now for the *pièce de résistance.*" She reached into the fridge. "My crème brû—"

She groaned and fell against the counter. The bowl she was holding toppled over. Her face went slack for a moment; then a horrible grimace spasmed across her features. She grabbed her stomach and lurched forward. . . .

Books by Shelley Freydont

BACKSTAGE MURDER

HIGH SEAS MURDER

MIDSUMMER MURDER

HALLOWEEN MURDER

A MERRY LITTLE MURDER

Published by Kensington Publishing Corporation

A Lindy Haggerty Mystery

HALLOWEEN MURDER

SHELLEY FREYDONT

KENSINGTON BOOKS
Kensington Publishing corp.
http://www.kensingtonbooks.com

KENSINGTON BOOKS are published by

Kensington Publishing Corp.
850 Third Avenue
New York, NY 10022

All Kensington Titles, Imprints, and Distributed Lines are available at special quantity discounts for bulk purchases for sales promotions, premiums, fund-raising, and educational or institutional use. Special book excerpts or customized printings can also be created to fit specific needs. For details, write or phone the office of the Kensington special sales manager: Kensington Publishing Corp., 850 Third Avenue, New York, NY 10022, attn: Special Sales Department, Phone: 1-800-221-2647.

First Kensington Hardcover Printing: September 2002
First Kensington Paperback Printing: September 2003

10 9 8 7 6 5 4 3 2 1

Printed in the United States of America

Acknowledgments

John Scognamiglio,
my editor

Evan Marshall,
my agent

Carolyn Hancock,
who said,
"You should write a mystery."
and then made sure that I did

Kathleen Sayles,
RN, BSN, CCRN

Burke Pearson, Nicole St. John,
John and Sandra Scarry,
who know about writing

The librarians at the Ridgewood
and Ho-Ho-Kus libraries,
ever helpful

My family, near and far,
patient, supportive, believing

Chapter One

Lindy Haggerty lifted the tailgate of her station wagon. Sixty pounds of Irish Setter jumped inside, circled twice and flopped down on the floor.

"Good dog, Bruno." Lindy tossed in a bag of clothes destined for the cleaners and closed the hatch.

When she opened the door to the driver's side, Bruno was sitting upright in the passenger's seat, staring intently out the window.

"Very clever," she said, sliding into the car. "I suppose Cliff lets you sit in the front."

Bruno snuffled against the window. His nose left a smudge across the glass.

"Well, your halcyon college days are over—at least for the next week. So it's into the back for you."

Bruno turned his head, ears drooping.

"Get."

He scrambled over the gear shift and stretched out on the backseat.

"And tomorrow, you're going to the groomer's. Honestly,

most college students bring home dirty laundry—I get dirty dog."

Bruno's tail thumped in reply.

Lindy had returned from Europe two days before to find Bruno waiting eagerly at the back door, a roll of shredded toilet paper in his mouth, and a note on the kitchen table. "Mom. Gone to a seminar in Boston. Can you dog-sit for a few days? A few weeks? Thanks. Love, Cliff."

"How is it," she asked over her shoulder as she pulled out of the driveway and onto the country road, "that I started out with a husband and two kids and ended up with you?" Cliff at college, Annie in Switzerland, and Glen—she had seen her husband for two days in the last two months. The only reason she had seen him at all was because she had detoured after her work in Spain to fly to Paris, where he was consultant to a multinational telecommunications firm. He hadn't been glad to see her.

Pushing that memory aside, she turned her attention back to Bruno. "Now, there are a few things we need to get straight. The Van Cleef farm and church is a historical site. That means no digging up plants, no marking territory on the shrubbery and absolutely no squatting, except in the woods, out of sight. And you'll have to stay in the car while I'm at the board meeting." She glanced in the rearview mirror. Bruno was asleep.

She slowed to the twenty-five mile an hour speed limit as she crossed the town line and drove along Main Street. It was crowded with cars, traffic brought to a standstill while people attempted to parallel park along the curbs. Quaint shops lined the brick sidewalks, their "to code" green awnings unfurled in the crisp sunlight. Display windows were decorated in the orange, gold and brown colors of autumn. Nothing so gauche as a skeleton or a witch in sight. A perfect, politically correct village of old wealth, upwardly mobile parents and exceptional children. People with money to burn and a need for "appropriate" family entertainment.

Which was the reason Lindy was headed to the scene of

the Mischief Night Marathon on an early October morning, jet-lagged and feeling lonely.

The brain child of Mary Elisabeth Porter and Juvenile Detective Judd Dillman, the marathon would include haunted hayrides, ghost stories, games, food booths and a plethora of other theme-related activities. The proceeds would be used for the completion of the Van Cleef historical restoration and a new teen center to be housed in the church annex.

In a weak moment, Lindy had agreed to direct the Frightmare Follies variety show.

Since Annie and the Porters' youngest son, James, had been in the same class at school, the Porters and Lindy had served on many of the same committees. Mary Elisabeth had always been the consummate organizer. Howard had the clout to get things done. Lindy was better with ironing out details and troubleshooting. Over the years, the three of them had helped raise considerable money for local charities and community projects.

So when Mary Elisabeth, sounding uncharacteristically tired and frazzled, called the previous evening, asking Lindy to be her assistant for the entire event, Lindy didn't have the heart to say no. And she needed something besides the Follies and Bruno to keep her busy until she returned to work in November.

At the far edge of town, a mall sprawled across the bulldozed countryside. Being banned from the village proper, it encroached as closely as possible, its asphalt parking lot stopping two feet short of the town boundaries.

On the opposite side of the road was the Van Cleef property. Fortunately, it lay within the town borders and had thus far escaped the bulldozer. But there were plenty of others who desired this piece of prime real estate.

Lindy turned into the driveway. A wide graveled parking area separated the house from the Old Reformed Church. A macadam parking strip ran lengthwise between the church and the road. Behind them, twenty acres of woods rose into gentle foothills.

Lindy stopped the Volvo in front of the stone and clapboard farmhouse. Mary Elisabeth was waiting on the porch beneath a gable of white gingerbread fretwork.

"Stay," Lindy commanded in a low voice and got out of the car. Bruno lunged after her but only managed to get his nose through the opening at the top of the window.

Lindy rolled her eyes. He had gotten worse since living with Cliff, and he hadn't been that obedient to begin with, despite several attempts at doggie school.

Mary Elisabeth came down the steps to meet her. A few years older than Lindy, she was, as always, perfectly coifed and color coordinated, from her padded, plum-colored jacket trimmed in matching fur to her subtle mauve eye shadow. But as she drew nearer, Lindy noticed that beneath her eyes were circles of nearly the same color. Mary Elisabeth was losing sleep over this one.

"I owe you big time," said Mary Elisabeth, giving Lindy a light hug.

She's lost weight, too, thought Lindy, glad now that she had agreed to help. Good cause or not, Mary Elisabeth was working too hard for the money.

"Come on in. Not everyone is here yet. Father Andrews is in the dining room and I think I heard Stella in the kitchen."

"Where else?" said Lindy.

"Where else, indeed?" Stella Rasmussen appeared in the doorway to the kitchen, holding a large white bakery box. Her more than full figure took up the entire space. A single parent with three rambunctious children, Stella still found time to run a catering business, coach Little League baseball and volunteer for almost every important event that required food.

"Oh, no," said Lindy. "Please tell me those aren't your lemon tarts."

"They're not my lemon tarts," said Stella dutifully, then grinned. "They're my apple fritters."

Lindy groaned. "Is coffee made?"

"Just finished brewing. Janey's bringing it out."

"Does she need help?" asked Mary Elisabeth.

Stella shook her head, tight curls bobbing. "This is one of her better days." She turned to Lindy. "You've been gone. Just try not to look shocked when you see her."

"That bad?"

"That bad. She's already turned in her resignation to the high school."

"She's been a fixture there for thirty years. What will the English department do without her?"

"They've already hired her replacement."

"You're kidding." Lindy glanced toward the kitchen. "Who?"

"You'll meet her in a few minutes. She's not shy."

"But she is good," added Mary Elisabeth. "Even if her methods aren't the same as Janey's."

"Anything else I should know?" asked Lindy as she followed Mary Elisabeth and Stella into the dining room.

"Just wait," said Stella over her shoulder. She plunked the box down on the polished table.

At the other end, Father Andrews was asleep, hands folded over his stomach, chin tucked into his ecumenical collar, his white-fringed pate shiny in the morning sun. He awoke with a start as the box hit the table.

"Must have dozed off," he mumbled and pushed himself to his feet.

"Hello, Father Andrews," said Lindy. "It's good to see you."

"Welcome to the fold, Lindy. We were afraid we had lost you to the wide world."

Lindy smiled, momentarily distracted by the aroma that wafted from the box Stella had just opened.

"Ah, Stella's fritters. A heavenly delight."

Stella laughed. "Or a sinful temptation." She handed a plate to the retired priest.

Just then, Janey Horowitz brought in the coffee tray. Lindy was glad Stella had warned her. She wouldn't have recognized Janey if she hadn't. Diagnosed with cancer less than a year ago, Janey had declared that she was a survivor. It was obvious now that she wouldn't be. Her once thick gray hair was thin and cut short. Her skin hugged bones that seemed too frail to support her weight.

Stella flashed Lindy a look as she took the tray from Janey and placed it on the table.

"Lindy. What a surprise." Janey looked up, her eyes at least still bright and sparkling blue. "How are Cliff and Annie?"

Lindy swallowed. "Fine. Cliff is at the university, and Annie plays for the Swiss Conservatory Orchestra. They'll be pleased to know you asked about them."

Janey smiled and lowered herself into a chair.

Lindy barely managed an answering smile before she had to turn away.

"Okay, who's for coffee, who's for tea?" asked Stella, bustling around the tray while Lindy composed herself. She passed a cup down to Father Andrews, while the others helped themselves to the crisp, sugar-coated fritters.

More committee members began to arrive, and the next few minutes were dedicated to laughter, conversation and the passing out of cups and saucers and apple fritters.

After a few minutes, Mary Elisabeth carried her coffee to the head of the table. She slipped out of her jacket, draped it over the back of her chair and sat down. "I'd like to call the meeting to order. I believe we have a quorum."

The others quickly took their seats. Stella motioned Lindy to a chair beside her.

"Judd can't make today's meeting, but he'll be in later this morning. Bryan Morrison, president of the Teen Council, is in school," Mary Elisabeth paused to explain to Lindy. "The council is in charge of the hayride, and Bryan is our liaison. So we're only missing Derrick, Melanie and Evelyn. I'm sure they'll be here any minute now."

The last three names were new to Lindy, and one that she did expect was conspicuously missing.

"What about Howard?" she asked.

"Howard has had to withdraw from the committee," said Mary Elisabeth.

Stella nudged Lindy under the table. "Tell you later," she whispered.

"First I'd like to announce that Lindy has offered to be co-coordinator, so feel free to call on her as well as me for any help you need."

Lindy acknowledged the familiar faces around the table. *Not exactly true*, she thought. Mary Elisabeth had done some major arm twisting, and they probably knew it.

"Let's hear first from our committee chairs, and then we need to discuss the latest development with the Gospel of Galilee Church."

There were disgruntled murmurs throughout the room.

"Are they performing in the Follies?" asked Lindy, hoping against hope that they weren't.

"Now, there's an idea." The statement was followed by a petite young woman who crossed the room and leaned over the box of fritters. Green spiked hair pointed across the table. One ear was lined with silver earrings, and a matching stud pierced her nose. Her boyish figure was poured into a pair of faded jeans, torn at the knees. Beneath a distressed leather jacket, she wore a T-shirt short enough to display her navel ring as she reached into the box.

"I don't think we've met," she said, taking an appraising look at Lindy. "Melanie Grant."

"My replacement," Janey added in a voice as thin as it was quiet.

Stella lowered her chin and raised an eyebrow toward Lindy.

"Lindy Graham, I mean Haggerty," said Lindy, disconcerted. How on earth had anyone convinced their conservative school board to hire this creature?

"Lindy is rehearsal director for the Jeremy Ash Dance Company when she's away from home," explained Mary Elisabeth. "Graham is her stage name."

"Jeremy Ash. Cool," said Melanie, who snared a fritter and took a seat next to Father Andrews. She rested one foot on the upholstered dining chair that Lindy guessed was original Duncan Phyfe. Her bare knee sat above the table surface like an uninvited guest. Lindy could only wonder what Father Andrews thought of such a spectacle. Fortunately, he seemed to have dozed off again.

Mary Elisabeth glanced toward the door. "Ah, there you are, Evelyn."

A tall African-American woman strode into the room and took her place in the empty chair to the other side of Lindy. She nodded to Lindy. Lindy nodded back. She had no idea who the woman was.

"Sorry I'm late." Evelyn released the single button of her tweed jacket, reached into a buttery leather handbag and pulled out paper and pen.

Lindy made a note to dress better for the next meeting. Her corduroys and cable-knit sweater were definitely out of place. She ran her hand over her hair. Too long and probably sticking out by now. There hadn't been time to get it cut since she came home. She and Bruno would both get coifed tomorrow.

Stella pressed her foot under the table. "Evelyn is in charge of cleanup," she whispered.

Lindy blinked. The only black woman on the committee in charge of cleanup. Definitely not PC.

The meeting proceeded with status reports from games, exhibits and food. A schedule of events was passed around the table. On a second page, a map showed the designated areas for each activity.

"Things seem to be in good shape," she commented.

Mary Elisabeth looked at the others. "Let's take a minute to bring Lindy up to speed." She took a long breath. "Since Father Andrews appears to be asleep, let me just quickly say that we're in deep shit."

"What's happened?" asked Lindy, wondering why Mary Elisabeth hadn't mentioned any problems the night before.

"Where to begin? I can't remember how much had happened before you left town." She made it sound like an accusation. "You may know that Howard"—she paused on her husband's name and then continued—"Howard persuaded Englebert Van Cleef to bequeath this land to the town. The stipulation was that it be restored to its original condition and maintained as a historic site. What we didn't realize until recently was the time restrictions involved. The restoration committee has to raise the necessary funds by the new year or forfeit it back to the Van Cleef estate."

"And how realistic is that?" asked Lindy.

"Well, it's possible if the marathon is a major success and inspires some substantial last-minute donations."

"Sounds like we had better plan on a major success."

"That's where the shit comes in," volunteered Melanie.

Father Andrews opened one eye and scowled at her.

Mary Elisabeth pushed back the sleeves of her sweater and leaned forward on her elbows. "We have run into a few snags." She looked at Melanie. "I may as well lay it out for Lindy."

Melanie's lips tightened. Her lipstick was blue-black.

"Melanie's new theater group is performing scenes from *The Crucible*. Some of the parents are concerned."

"About *The Crucible*?" asked Lindy. "It's a staple of high school drama programs."

"It isn't the play. It's my kids," said Melanie.

Didn't take her long to become possessive, thought Lindy. She darted a look at Janey. Her lips were pursed, but she was looking at her cup of tea, not at Melanie.

"They're losers. According to Bryan, King of the Council."

"Now, Melanie," said Janey, her voice wavering. "You can't play favorites with your students."

"Even though their parents, the principal and everyone else does?" Melanie's dark eyes flashed with anger.

The others looked uncomfortable; a few disgusted. The new teacher was not winning any friends. Most of them were the parents she was maligning.

Mary Elisabeth broke in. "Melanie is working with a group of 'at-risk' teens. And having an excellent success. We may choose to ignore the fact that drugs and crime have come to the suburbs. But recently there has been a sharp increase in teen arrests. Judd is working overtime. Melanie was very successful in turning at-risk kids around in her last teaching position, and we're lucky to have her." She cast a kind but warning look toward Janey. "However, as usual, there are a few nervous parents."

Melanie opened her mouth to protest.

Mary Elisabeth cut her off. "Only a few, and no one in this room. But at the moment, that isn't our main concern. The Gospel of Galilee Church is threatening to picket the event."

"Can they do that?" asked Stella.

"If granted a permit, and that seems likely." Mary Elisabeth leaned forward and spoke to Lindy. "It's a fundamentalist sect. Led by some charismatic madman. We had never even heard of them until last week. They're accusing us of devil worship."

"That's ridiculous," said Lindy.

"Not entirely," said Father Andrews. "Actually there has been some concern among the local clergy about a community-sponsored celebration of Halloween. Most are sitting on the clerical fence at the moment." He smiled ruefully. "I'm not one of those. The incorporation of pagan custom has always been the prerogative of the church. It's the public endorsement of witches, devils and Freddy Kreugers that makes them squeamish."

"I had no idea. It seems so harmless and fun."

"One would think so," said Mary Elisabeth. "But this—this Brother Bartholomew is all hellfire and damnation. We must consider the best way to approach them."

"I haven't been successful in changing their minds," admitted Father Andrews.

"I don't believe anyone could influence that Brother Bartholomew," said Stella. "They could cause trouble."

"True," said Father Andrews. "And if they do decide to incite ill feeling, we'll lose a lot of support."

"Is there any chance they could be reconciled? Convinced that we have no religious intent?" asked Lindy.

"I don't have great hopes, but I'm willing to meet with their leader again."

"Thank you, Father. We'll leave it to you." Mary Elisabeth began gathering the papers that had collected in front of her. "If there's no further business, I suggest we adjourn. I'd like to show Lindy the setup."

As the others began leaving the room, Mary Elisabeth joined Lindy and Stella at their side of the table. "Well?"

"I think this should keep me busy." Lindy held up her notebook and the list of things she had offered to do.

"I guess now you can see why I coerced you into assisting me," said Mary Elisabeth.

"Because I'm an expert in pumpkin painting?"

"Because you're an expert in a lot of things." The tone of Mary Elisabeth's answer made Lindy's skin prickle. "Not only in fund-raising, though we have been a successful team in the past. But I'm afraid we're going to need your expertise"—she paused—"in other areas as well."

Lindy flushed. Stella avoided her glance. Had they heard about her "meddling" in police investigations? Glen would have a fit if he thought it was public knowledge. Just because he was never home didn't mean he didn't care about his standing in the community. She swallowed hard.

"I'll help in any way I can, of course," she said. "But—"

She was interrupted by a crash from above their heads.

"Oh, dear," said Mary Elisabeth. "I hope T.J. hasn't fallen through the floorboards again. Excuse me. I'll be right back." She rushed from the room.

"T.J.?"

"T. J. Renquith," said Stella. "Neither rain, nor sleet nor Brother Bart can stop the intrepid restorer. He plans to work right through the festivities and woe to anyone who gets in his way."

Lindy stood up. "Walk me outside. I need to check on Bruno, but I've got a million questions."

"I bet you do." Stella hoisted herself out of her chair.

Chapter Two

They walked across the porch and down the newly grouted steps. Bruno scrambled back and forth across the seats, then barked and lunged against the window of the Volvo.

"My upholstery," moaned Lindy and ran to open the door. Bruno jumped out and headed toward the yew bushes in front of the house.

"Remember what I said," she called after him.

Bruno lifted his leg.

Lindy rolled her eyes and turned to Stella. "Okay, quick before Mary Elisabeth gets back. What's going on?"

"For starters, she's left Howard."

"I don't believe it. They've seemed so happy lately."

"That's what everyone thought, but the day after James left for Perdue, she moved into an apartment and started divorce procedings."

"But why?"

"Fallon came back."

"Again?"

"Yep. Pushing thirty and still hasn't found herself. So she did what she always does. Came home to suck up to Daddy and to make Mary Elisabeth's life miserable. I guess it was the final straw. Howard is in shock—hurt and angry. He had no idea of what was in the wind. But then, he never could see past his daughter."

No, he couldn't, thought Lindy. Fallon Porter was Howard's daughter from his first marriage. She had been an unruly and defiant child, resentful of her stepmother and terrifying her half brothers with malicious pranks. She was the one thing in life on which Howard and Mary Elisabeth couldn't agree. And now she had wrecked their marriage.

"She didn't tell me before I left. She didn't even say anything last night when she called."

"She was probably embarrassed. It's hard to face your friends and wonder whether they'll take your side or his."

Spoken from experience, thought Lindy.

Stella shook herself. "You're here. That's what counts. She needs our support. Are you going to be able to handle the extra work?"

"Sure. I'll call one of the guys in the company to direct the Follies. I'll give him an honorarium—keep him off the unemployment line for the next few weeks."

"Must be nice to have money to throw around." Stella headed for a white van. "How do you like my new set of wheels?"

Against the shiny white side of the van, black iridescent letters spelled out *Stella by Starlight Caterers*.

"The catering business must be booming. Very chic."

Stella chortled. "But not quite as chic as that." She gestured to a car parked next to the van. A black Jaguar, XKG convertible, polished to a glaring shine.

"Who does that belong to?"

"Derrick Justin," drawled Stella.

"Mary Elisabeth mentioned him. But he wasn't at the meeting."

"Derrick doesn't do meetings. Just lunches *and* a few of the local ladies, if you ask me."

"Who is he?"

"Our *artiste* in residence. Fallon's residence to be precise. He's part of the straw that finished off the marriage."

"All right. Tell me everything."

Stella glanced at her wristwatch, a battered man's Timex. "In a nutshell . . . While Fallon was extricating herself from her latest failed marriage, she got her hooks into Derrick. She brought him home to Daddy, and now he's got his hooks into us. In less than two months, he's managed to make himself indispensable to the powers that be—through their wives, mainly. Lords it over the marathon committee like it was his idea, which it wasn't. Is always around, pushing his 'concept' for the evening down everyone's throats. Doesn't do a damn thing but snap a few pictures and get in the way, if you ask me. The only thing he's actually *done* is introduce Melanie to the school superintendent."

"Jeez," said Lindy. "I wondered where they had dug her up."

"She's good, looks aside. I think that's something she cultivates just to upset the adults. The kids eat it up."

"An interesting little *ménage à trois*," said Lindy.

"Oh, hon, it doesn't stop at the *trois,* or I don't know my apple fritters." Stella looked at her watch again. "I've got a delivery to make."

She climbed into the front seat and lowered the window. "I'll call you tonight for a gossip fest." She wobbled her hand from side to side in a queenly wave and gunned the engine. Seconds later she screeched onto the main road and was out of sight.

Lindy turned back to the house. Mary Elisabeth was still inside, which was just as well. She needed time to digest Stella's bombshell about the divorce. It was so senseless. Their marriage had survived the turbulent Fallon years, only to fall apart now that Fallon was gone.

But Fallon was never really gone. She had flunked out of college, married and divorced twice, tried modeling, acting and innumerable other careers that ended in the same way—with Fallon on the doorstep.

Talk about children at risk. But Fallon was no longer a child.

How awful for this to happen now, just when Mary Elisabeth and Howard were planning to have each other to themselves. And how must Howard feel to be rejected by the person he had loved for so many years and thought loved him?

She quickly clamped her mind shut on that thought. Fortunately there was nothing wrong with her marriage, even if it was carried on long distance. Glen might be an absentee husband, but they were still together.

Enough of this, she thought. There was work to be done. She reached into the Volvo for her cell phone and punched in Rebo's number. It was picked up after the fourth ring; she started to leave her message.

"Heh-o."

"Rebo?"

"O ahn."

"Juan, is that you?"

"Ess."

"What's the matter?"

A groan. Something that sounded like "yummy."

The sound of laughter and a "Hello?"

"Rebo, it's Lindy."

"Lindelicious. What's up?"

"What's wrong with Juan?"

"Had two wisdom teeth extracted. I keep telling him not to answer the phone. He'll scare away my other boyfriends, but . . . Ouch!"

"Maybe this isn't a good time."

"All times are good times with you. Anyway I was just balancing my checkbook."

"That's why I'm calling."

"About my checkbook? Not much to talk about. I think I've only got a zero or two left."

"In that case, how would you like a little work for the next couple of weeks?"

"Paying work?"

"It's in Jersey."

"I can do Jersey. What is it?"

She explained about the marathon and how she needed someone to direct the variety show. "The next two Friday nights and Saturday mornings and a couple of evenings next week. All the acts are local and amateur, real amateur. The dress rehearsal is on the twenty-seventh, a Saturday morning, and the show is on Mischief Night."

"Frightmare Follies," said Rebo. "I think I can find a part for Juan. Ouch."

"You can stay over at my house, if you want. The trains run pretty regularly. I can pick you up at the station."

"That's okay. Juan has a car."

"Great. Why don't you come tomorrow and check out the site. It's in an old church. The first rehearsal is on Friday." She gave him directions.

"Be there with bells on."

I certainly hope not, she thought. She hung up and looked for Bruno. She searched the yew bushes around the porch, then looked across the gravel to the Old Reformed Church. It was constructed of roughly hewn sandstone and topped by a steep shingled roof edged in gingerbread woodwork similar to that of the farmhouse.

A sagging, one-story clapboard addition jutted out from the far side. This was the proposed site of the new teen center. The church dated from 1732, but the annex couldn't be over forty or fifty years old and was in terrible disrepair. Lindy doubted that T. J. Renquith would care about its preservation.

She perused the hawthorn bushes that grew alongside the church until she caught sight of a shaggy red rump. A spray of dirt sailed through the air and settled on the church steps.

"Bruno, no!"

Bruno's head appeared from the shrubbery. He pricked his ears, then took off toward the back of the church.

She hurried over to survey the damage. The hole was already six inches deep. With an exasperated sigh, she scuffed the dirt back into the hole, tamped it down with her foot and went to find the culprit.

There was no sign of Bruno when she reached the back of the church. But there were plenty of places for him to get into trouble. The area was being used as storage and dumping ground for the restoration. Stacks of new lumber were piled head high. Nearby, a whole landscape of cast-off furniture, appliances, rusted pipes and rotten timber rose even higher. The back door of the church was propped open with the bowl of a marble baptismal font. The pedestal lay nearby on the ground, a sight that was bound to raise the ire of the infamous Brother Bart if he were to see it. And a dangerous place for man and beast. There was a lot of work to do if they were to make the farm safe for the marathon.

She picked her way cautiously past a velvet couch, the legs missing and the plush nibbled by years of resident mice, then squeezed between an old bedspring and a dismantled pew. She stepped into a shadowy glade. Beneath a canopy of gnarled branches, a rusted wrought-iron fence enclosed a scattering of lichen-covered gravestones. Holding her breath, she scooted past the neglected cemetery and stopped at the edge of a dirt road that led through the woods.

"Bruno," she called. She peered down the road where wooden spikes topped by red flags marked the route of the haunted hayride. *Perfect*. It would pass right by the old cemetery. She wondered what the teenagers had planned. Ghosts? A headless horseman? The Texas chain-saw murderer? It had been years since Lindy, Glen and the kids had all piled into the car and driven to the Platts' farm for Halloween. But the Platt farm was now the mall across the street, and there hadn't been a haunted hayride in years.

This would be fun. Just what the town needed. And it would prevent the Van Cleef farm from going the way of the Platts'.

A flash of red fur darted into the road; Bruno gamboled around her. She reached for his collar, but he vaulted away and disappeared again. She crossed the road and followed him down a path that led through the woods. She saw the outline of a flat-roofed stone building, half hidden in the trees, and heard the sound of rushing water. She stepped from the path to take a closer look. It was an old spring-house. A trampled patch of grass lay in front of a heavy wooden door. The door was secured with a shiny new pad-lock.

Good, she thought. One less thing to worry about. But there were other unused outbuildings on the property. She made a mental note to check their stability and make sure they were all padlocked. The marathon didn't need any accidents.

A few yards away, a brook flowed rapidly toward the Hackensack River. Close to the shore, the water was clear enough to see the bottom, but farther out, the stream dropped off into darkness. Thinking of another stream, another time, she made a note to cordon off the perimeters of the fair.

Bruno bounded out of the shrubbery, slid across a patch of mud that sloped down to the brook and splashed into the water. He stopped long enough to give her an expectant look, then took off downstream.

"That's the last time you go off the leash," she yelled and added the car wash to her list of things to do.

The bank was overgrown with brambles, making it impossible to go after him. She had to backtrack along the road until she came to a place where she could see the water. The air was suddenly cooler.

Had they made contingency plans in case of bad weather?

An old horse bridge spanned the brook where it turned sharply to the east. She stopped beside it and looked down the eroded bank to where Bruno stood, belly deep in the stream.

"Get out of there," she called. She picked up a stick and threw it toward him. "Fetch." It landed with a splash and floated away.

"Bruno, come. Mary Elisabeth is waiting for me. How about a treat?"

Bruno stayed frozen in the water, tail extended, body taut. Then Lindy heard the low growl. He must have something cornered under the bridge.

"Bruno," she pleaded. "Don't make me ruin my good boots pulling you out of there. Leave that poor animal alone."

Bruno continued to growl. She was close enough to see the fur bristling on his neck.

"Whatever it is, it isn't worth it," she threatened. She grabbed one of the support beams and scooted down the bank where rainwater had cut a gully next to the bridge. She tiptoed through mud and loose pebbles to the edge of the water, keeping one eye out for whatever was beneath the bridge. Surely it was too late in the year for snakes.

"Damn it. Get out of that stream right now."

Bruno stood his ground.

She stepped onto a flat rock and reached for him. Her foot slipped into the water. She could feel her sock soaking up the chill.

Bruno's growl became louder. Her other foot slid from the rock. Consigning her boots to the Goodwill bin, she splashed through the water, skirting the bridge and whatever was lurking there, and grabbed Bruno by the collar.

He felt rigid beside her.

She peered beneath the bridge. Erosion had carved a cavern into the bank. Foam and detritus were entangled in a tracery of bare roots and rocked against the bridge supports. It was dark and murky, but there were no animals, just sticks, leaves, plastic bags and a larger bundle—a garbage bag or a piece of tarp.

"You dingbat dog. It's just a bunch of trash." She pulled at his collar. He broke free and lunged forward. He clamped his teeth on the mass of debris and tried to drag it from beneath the bridge, but it was stuck fast. He wrestled with it until there was a rip and part of the bundle freed itself. Slowly, it turned over in the water. A pale globe rose to the surface. A face, bloated and unreal, stared out from the shadows.

Lindy screamed and skittered backward. Then she stopped, heart pounding, feeling like a fool.

"Jeez, Bruno. What a couple of ditzes." She laughed unsteadily. "It's a dummy. They must have already started setting up for the hayride. At least it wasn't the chain-saw murderer. Now, *that* would have been scary."

Bruno whined.

"Yes, you're a good dog. You found him, but he isn't real." She reached over and tugged at a piece of jacket sleeve. "See?"

A hand popped to the surface.

Lindy fell onto her butt with a splash and sat there. Bruno jumped across her. Wet fur slapped against her face. He bared his teeth and growled.

"Shit," she whispered. "Shit." She knew it was a surgical glove filled with birdseed, but it looked like a real hand—a hand with hairy fingers and a pinkie ring.

The teenagers had outdone themselves. This was the stuff of nightmares. They'd have to post a parental warning sign for the hayride.

Bruno's head snapped toward the opposite shore and he began to bark.

On a ridge, at the far side of the brook, stood the figure of a man. It towered over the landscape. A giant, robed in a brown monk's cassock. Wisps of white beard spread across the front and down his chest. Stalks of plants seemed to spring out of the fabric. He gripped a gnarled wooden staff.

Lindy marveled at the ingenuity of the teenagers. He looked so real.

The head turned. Lindy blinked and cursed her overactive imagination. The head moved again, and then the entire figure. Lindy's feet began to make running movements, but she was stuck on her butt in the water.

She watched him come to life, testing stiff, inhuman legs. And suddenly he was lumbering down the slope.

Somebody whimpered. She hoped it was Bruno.

At the edge of the stream, he paused and jabbed the staff into the mud. He leaned over, pulled the cassock over his head and dropped it on the ground. When he stood up again, he was wearing a red flannel shirt and denim coveralls. The Grim Reaper meets Deliverance.

Lindy jumped to her feet and stood dripping and shivering as she watched him step slowly into the water, using the staff to steady himself.

This was no apparition, but a man. She felt relief, then embarrassment. She wondered why he didn't use the bridge. It was only a few feet away. She pointed toward it; for some reason, she couldn't find her voice. She watched as he waded into the middle of the stream, while the water swept about his thighs. He didn't seem to notice the swiftness of the current.

Bruno stood between them, so intent on protecting her that he nearly pushed her over.

The man forded the stream, but stopped when he was still ankle deep in water. He regarded her with deep-set eyes beneath shaggy black brows. Then he looked to where the dummy thumped against the bridge.

"It isn't real, is it?" she asked, wondering if the words had come out aloud.

"Looks to be." He waded closer and slid his walking stick beneath the jacket. One sharp yank and it tore free of the bridge. With a grunt, he used the stick to push it into the deepest part of the current.

"No!" Lindy lunged forward.

The man raised his hand. The power of the gesture stopped her cold.

"He's on a journey." His words were deep and seemed to echo through her bones. "Who are we to stand in his way?"

He turned, and they both watched the mass of brown wool drift silently downstream, then sink beneath the surface as it rounded the bend. When it was out of sight, he began to retrace his path across the brook.

"Wait," Lindy cried after him.

He didn't stop.

She scrambled up the bank and stepped onto the bridge, meaning to follow him.

"No," he thundered. He turned and lifted his stick.

Lindy froze.

He swung the tip of it toward the bridge. "Rotten." He turned away and continued across the stream. When he reached the far side, he picked up the cassock and disappeared into the trees.

Lindy stared after him until she wasn't sure if he had really been there or not.

Bruno nudged her thigh. Her hand went automatically to his head. Then she dropped down and wrapped her arms around his neck.

"Let's get out of here."

Bruno took off at a full run, Lindy close behind, wet corduroys slapping at her legs.

Chapter Three

Lindy burst into the house. She barely had time to notice the man standing next to Mary Elisabeth before he shrieked, "Not on the Aubusson!" and propelled her backward onto the porch.

Mary Elisabeth followed them out. "What on earth happened to you?"

Lindy started to speak, but was stopped by a high-pitched voice. "I knew it, I knew it," the man exclaimed. "How can I possibly get any work done when I'm constantly being undermined. Howard was crazy when he agreed to let you use this site. You're ruining everything." He slapped an open palm to his freckled forehead and rested it there while he shook thinning red hair at them.

"T.J. You're overwrought."

"Overwrought? You bet I am. I'm being sabotaged at every step. And who told Casanova he had full run of the place? Who does he think he is? I swear, if he crosses me one more time—" He groaned. "This is impossible!" He turned on his heel, tripped over Bruno, then stalked back into the house.

"Don't let T.J. intimidate you. He tends to be a little high-strung," said Mary Elisabeth. "Why are you all wet?"

"I fell into the stream."

"Come around to the back. You can dry off in the kitchen."

"First I have to make a phone call."

"There's an extension in the hall. Oh, here's Judd."

A white, town-issued Taurus came to a stop in front of them. Judd Dillman grinned through the open window.

"A bit brisk for a swim, isn't it?"

"Thank God, Judd. I need to talk to you."

Judd opened the door and unfolded to his full six feet, three inches. He was all bones and sinew with dark, closely cropped hair and malleable features that could change from a smile to a frown with comical swiftness. He had been head of the juvenile division for ten years, was hep enough to gain the trust of the local teenagers, and big enough to make sure they stayed out of trouble.

"If you're worried about the men's kick line—we've already agreed to be in the Follies. It took us long enough to learn the steps for the scholarship show last spring. Might as well get some use out of them."

"It's not about the kick line. I need to show you something."

Judd's face performed its acrobatic change from smile to frown, but it was Mary Elisabeth who asked, "Lindy, is anything wrong?"

"Just another little snag," she said. There was no reason to upset Mary Elisabeth if she was mistaken about what she had seen. She had enough to worry about already. "Nothing that Judd and I can't handle. We'll be right back."

Lindy took Judd's sleeve and pulled him across the drive, leaving Mary Elisabeth frowning after them. As soon as they reached the back of the church, she started to run.

"Hurry."

"Where're you off to?" Judd sprinted after her. "Hold up a minute. Where's the fire?"

She got as far as the bridge before she felt a hand clamp down on her shoulder.

"Before I go chasing you all over town, could you give me a hint about what's got you in a tizzy?"

Lindy took a deep breath, knowing she would probably sound like an idiot. "Just listen and try not to get upset. Okay?"

"I can probably do that."

"I'm not sure what I just saw, but I think we need to call the police."

"I am the police." He was trying not to smile.

"I know. I mean the—" She couldn't think of the name. "The grown-up police. I mean, homicide or something."

The smile turned to a frown. "Maybe you should start at the beginning."

Lindy took a deep breath. "Bruno found a body down in the stream. At first I thought it was a dummy. You know, some ghoulish scene for the hayride."

Judd shook his head. "It's two weeks away. They're still in the planning stages."

"That's what I was afraid of. And besides, when I got a closer look at it—well, it looked too real to be a dummy."

"Damn. No offense, but I hope you're wrong. We don't need any more adverse publicity about the marathon. A dead man could finish us. Show me where it is."

"That's a problem." Lindy swallowed. "He's gone. He's probably halfway to the ocean by now."

Judd whistled, then scratched his head. When he looked up, his eyes were twinkling. "A little early for trick or treat, isn't it?"

"I know what you're thinking. And I hope you're right. But just hear me out. Whatever it was, dummy or human, it was caught up on the bridge. Then suddenly, this strange man appeared out of nowhere and pushed it out into the current. He shouldn't have done that. You're not supposed to touch anything. Of course, it might not be anything. But even so—he said it was real, too, and that it was on a journey." She knew she was beginning to babble.

Fortunately Judd stopped her. "Well, at least I can guess who the strange man might be. Big, tall guy with long white hair and a beard?"

Lindy nodded.

"Adam Crabtree."

"The storyteller?"

"Uh-huh. He lives in a cottage on the property. Bit of a recluse when he isn't entertaining the masses. And it sounds just like something he would say." Judd looked toward the bridge. "He thought it was real?"

"That's what he said."

"Well, show me where it was."

She climbed down the bank, Judd following, and pointed to where the face had floated to the surface.

Judd pulled a flashlight off his belt and shined it beneath the bridge.

"Nothing there now, but I guess we'd better report it, just in case. Hopefully, it'll turn up in another county. We really don't need trouble like this."

They returned to the house and Lindy waited by the police car while Judd radioed the station for the homicide team.

"What do we say to Mary Elisabeth?" asked Lindy as soon as he signed off. "I don't want to upset her."

"Upset me about what?" While they had been intent on the radio call, Mary Elisabeth had come up beside the police car.

Judd quickly took her hands. "Just a possible accident down by the bridge."

Lindy watched the color drain from Mary Elisabeth's face.

"Who? Did you call an ambulance? What do you mean, possible accident? Was there an accident or not?"

"Now, Mary Elisabeth, calm down. I'm going to tell you

the whole thing while we're waiting for the detectives to arrive."

"Detectives?"

"In the kitchen, over a cup of coffee." Judd took each of them by the arm.

"We'll have to go in the back door," said Lindy. "I can't drip on the Aubusson."

"Whatever you say." He led them around the house, past a double cellar door with a Keep Out sign nailed across it and up a set of wooden steps to the back porch.

Two doors led into the house. One was boarded over. Mary Elisabeth searched through a ring of keys and opened the other one.

Bruno bolted from beneath the porch and dashed past them into the kitchen. His nails clicked across the linoleum floor. He headed straight for the rectangular Formica table, squeezed between two metal chairs, and curled up beneath it.

"I hope T.J. won't have a fit when he finds out that we're in here," said Lindy.

"Don't worry," said Mary Elisabeth. "The kitchen has to be entirely restored, which is the only reason we're able to make full use of it."

T.J. had his work cut out for him, thought Lindy. The topmost layer of linoleum had curled up in the corners. Exploratory cuts in various places across the floor revealed several layers of older linoleum. The stove was '70s avocado green. A bulky refrigerator with rounded edges and pockmarked enamel rattled and buzzed in the corner. On the far wall, a door led to the main hall; on the nearest wall, three doors were boarded over.

Judd poured coffee from an urn that sat on the wooden counter. They took their mugs to the table and sat down.

"Now, what about this accident?" asked Mary Elisabeth.

Judd cleared his throat. "A possible drowning victim."

"Oh, dear God. Is it anyone we know?"

"We're not exactly certain," began Judd.

Mary Elisabeth's eyes widened in horror.

"Now, don't let your imagination run wild. He's no longer there. That's why we haven't been able to identify him."

"Him?" Mary Elisabeth looked toward Lindy.

"Yes, a man in a sports jacket." The grisly image sprang into her mind. She shivered.

The door from the hallway squeaked open. Evelyn Grimes paused long enough to acknowledge them, then crossed to the coffeepot.

What's she still doing here? wondered Lindy. The other committee members had left right after the meeting, and Evelyn's work didn't even begin until the marathon was over.

Judd glanced at Lindy and Mary Elisabeth. His meaning was clear.

There was a moment of uncomfortable silence while Evelyn joined them at the table.

"I'm not interrupting anything, am I?" Her eyes took in Lindy's bedraggled clothing.

Never one to lose her head, Mary Elisabeth said, "Judd and Lindy were just discussing the men's contribution to the Follies."

"Oh?" Evelyn's curiosity shifted to Judd. "And what do the men contribute?"

A flush crept up Judd's neck and he fiddled with his coffee cup. "Well . . . each spring the parents put on a review for the scholarship fund. It's a tradition that the Police Athletic League ends the show with a kick line." He tugged at his collar. "We've volunteered to repeat it for the marathon."

"A kick line," said Evelyn. The hint of a smile played at her lips. "All in the line of duty, I assume."

"Yes, ma'am. We live to serve." Judd was bright red by now. It was one thing to act zany for the scholarship fund, but another to try to explain it to a stranger. He was spared further elucidation by the sound of tires on gravel.

Judd jumped to his feet. "Excuse me, ladies. Uh, could you join me for a minute, Lindy?"

She quickly followed him out, but not before she saw

Evelyn's eyes flit from Judd back to her. She was no longer amused, but curious and something more—suspicious.

Judd and Lindy watched from a distance as two detectives searched around the bridge, took a few pictures, then climbed up the bank. It didn't seem to take very long. Judd stared at the ground, his hands stuffed into the pockets of his khaki trousers.

"Nothing much there," said one of the detectives. "We'll take a look downstream. See if it snagged up. Then we'll call the next township and tell them to be on the lookout. If nothing turns up, I guess we'll have to drag the brook." He started to say more, but only shook his head and rejoined his partner.

"He didn't seem too enthusiastic," said Lindy, trying to catch Judd's eye. Getting no response, she went on. "You'd think a homicide detective would be glad to get an occasional homicide. He can't have too much work in this area."

"He and the rest of the squad have had plenty of work, thanks to me." Judd shrugged. His angular shoulders lifted to his ears. "I've had to borrow just about every man on the force, for all the good it's done me. Haven't turned up a damn thing, and they're beginning to think I've developed paranoia."

"Mary Elisabeth said you'd been working overtime. What's up?"

Judd started walking toward the house. "I always wanted to be a juvie cop. I thought if I could get to them before they became hardened criminals, I could really make a difference."

Lindy reached up and touched his shoulder. "You *are* making a difference."

"They're winning."

"Who?"

"The bad guys. And I can't even figure out who they are."

"Hey, this doesn't sound like the Detective Judd Dillman

I know. Think of all the kids you've turned around. And all the problems you nipped in the bud. I remember you showing up at my door with Cliff a few times."

"For being in the park after curfew. I'm out of my element with this new thing."

"What new thing?"

He stopped suddenly and scowled, his eyebrows dipping to a point at his nose. "I've arrested more teens in the last three months than I did in the whole of last year."

"Is that good or bad?"

"Bad. There's a new influx of drugs: grass, coke, Ecstasy, new designer drugs that didn't have names before this summer. Can't figure out where they're coming from, but I know where they're going—high school kids and younger. I picked up four twelve-year-olds last night. So loaded they couldn't even run. I've pulled every favor, borrowed every available man, and we still come up empty-handed."

"I'm sorry, Judd. I had no idea."

"Of course you didn't," Judd said viciously. "Because we don't have a drug problem here, not in this town, and by the time we get our heads out of the sand, it'll be too late to stop it."

They had come to the graveled drive and Judd stopped at his Taurus. He gave her a smile that barely registered before it was gone. "Sorry to unload on you. I haven't had much sleep lately."

And I just added one more worry to your list, thought Lindy. "We all believe in you, Judd." It was a corny thing to say, and it had anything but the reassuring effect she intended.

"I wish I did." He opened the door and folded himself into the driver's seat. "Tell Mary Elisabeth that there's no cause for alarm. I'll try to get back tomorrow."

He closed the door and drove away, just as a powder-blue Trans Am entered the parking lot. The mane of red-gold hair behind the wheel was unmistakable. Fallon Porter was making what had to be a surprise appearance.

That's all we need, thought Lindy, waiting stoically for the car to stop.

The door swung open and a pair of high-heeled boots appeared, followed by designer jeans enclosing long, thin legs. Fallon lifted her fingers through her hair and tossed her head. Then she reached back inside the car and brought out a large cup of Starbucks coffee.

She glanced around the lot until her eyes rested on the black XKG, then walked toward Lindy. Everything about her was perfectly done, the makeup, the gold jewelry, the long-sleeved apricot silk shirt, opened at the neck and showing the edge of a lacy bra. She was thinner than usual.

Anorexic, said the mother in Lindy. *Not your problem*, she cautioned herself.

Fallon cast a distasteful look at Lindy's clothes.

"Fell into the stream," said Lindy.

Fallon didn't comment, merely wrinkled her nose.

Mary Elisabeth must have seen the car, because she was walking purposefully down the porch steps, followed closely by Evelyn.

"What are you doing here, Fallon?" Mary Elisabeth's demeanor was unruffled, but her words were clipped.

"Just brought Derrick his latte." Fallon smiled innocently and looked around. "Where is he?"

"In the house talking to T.J., I believe."

"Oh, good, I'll just run along." She stepped past them, walking on her toes to keep her heels from sinking into the gravel. "Oh, I almost forgot." She reached into her jeans pocket and pulled out a piece of paper. "Daddy sent a check for the restoration."

"That's very generous of him." Mary Elisabeth reached for it, but Fallon snatched it back.

"First you have to put me on the marathon committee."

Mary Elisabeth's hand dropped. "I'm afraid all the committees have been filled."

"Too bad." Fallon shook her head; her hair caught the sunlight. "Because Daddy said if you didn't let me be on the committee, he's going to buy the land and give it to me for a wedding present." She sighed theatrically. It was obvious why she had never gotten a job as an actress.

A faint blush spread across Mary Elisabeth's cheekbones.

Lindy interceded. "Getting married again?" She hoped she sounded as catty as she intended.

Fallon was oblivious to innuendo, however. "To Derrick. We'll live in the house, I suppose, though it does need a lot of work. Derrick can turn the church into an art gallery and photographic studio. He has such vision. That's probably why he's talking to T.J." She tossed her hair and gave them a coy look. "Since there's no place left on the committee, I guess I'll just tear up this check. Daddy *will* be disappointed." Another sigh.

Mary Elisabeth slowly took the check. "I wouldn't want to disappoint Howard. You can be Derrick's assistant."

"Okay. Well, I'd better hurry before his latte gets cold. Toodles."

"Toodles?" said Evelyn as soon as Fallon had walked away.

Mary Elisabeth was staring at the check. "Why would Howard do such a nasty thing?"

Evelyn and Lindy looked over her shoulder.

"It's for ten dollars," said Lindy unnecessarily.

"He must really hate me."

"Hurt, not hate," said Lindy and slipped her arm around Mary Elisabeth's waist.

The three of them looked toward the porch, where Fallon posed against a column. "Just kidding," she called and waved another check in their direction.

Lindy rushed to collect it before Mary Elisabeth could be further humiliated. Fallon dropped the check just as Lindy reached for it, and she had to snatch in from the air. Fallon strolled into the house, laughing.

Mary Elisabeth took the check without comment. She glanced at it as if against her will, and the breath caught in her throat. Then she held it out for the other two to see.

Lindy had to count the zeros twice before the amount sank in. Fifty thousand dollars.

"Impressive," said Evelyn.

Mary Elisabeth gave a quick shake of her head and turned away. "I'm sorry, Lindy, we'll have to go over the plans in the morning. I have . . . an appointment." She walked across the gravel and around the side of the church without another word.

A few minutes later, Mary Elisabeth's Lincoln drove out of the lot and turned toward town.

"Well, I have things to do, too," said Lindy. "See you tomorrow." She went to retrieve Bruno from the kitchen, leaving Evelyn alone in the parking lot.

Chapter Four

Lindy headed straight for Shady Oaks Kennels and Dog Grooming. She knew they wouldn't be able to get to Bruno today, but if she were lucky, they'd keep him overnight and get to him first thing the next morning.

She was in luck.

"If he looks anything like you do," said the proprietor, Joe Liefman, "I'd better keep him. But you'll have to leave him overnight."

"We had an adventure down by the stream."

"Then I'll give him a tick dip as well. Tomorrow at five okay?"

"Sure."

"And you'd better give yourself a good tick check as well."

"I plan to. Thanks, Joe."

Joe followed her out to the car and pulled a whining Bruno out of the back. "Hey, fella. You haven't forgotten your old friend, have you?" He slid his hand out of his pants pocket and dropped a kibble into Bruno's mouth. A quick slurp and Bruno was following him happily into the kennel.

That accomplished, Lindy drove to the cleaners and the car wash. No reason to put it off until tomorrow. It looked as if her dance card was filling up.

It was almost four o'clock before she stopped the Volvo at her own door and climbed out. She stripped out of her clothes in the laundry room and went upstairs to shower.

She spent the next hour nibbling on a salad and organizing the notes she had taken during the meeting. She itched to call Judd to see if the body had turned up, but resisted. She had already caused him enough extra work.

At five o'clock, she poured a glass of the wine that she had brought home from Spain, grabbed a jacket and went to sit on the terrace.

The sun was already setting, the days getting shorter as autumn marched toward winter. In two weeks they would lose another hour of twilight when they went off daylight saving time. It was already too cold to comfortably enjoy the view. She had been away for the entire summer and most of the fall.

Leaves blanketed the lawn and perennial borders. The dried stalks of plants stood brittle against the encroaching shadows. At the far end of a brick path, the dry rectangle of an aborted vegetable garden scarred the yellowing grass. She should probably have it sodded over. She hadn't had time to tend vegetables since she returned to work a year and a half ago.

She could almost taste the sweet, firm tomatoes that had overwhelmed them that first summer. She had planted ten seedlings, expecting half of them to die or get eaten by deer. Not only had they survived, but all had yielded bumper crops. They had eaten raw tomatoes, grilled tomatoes, stewed tomatoes; had canned, frozen and given away tomatoes. By the end of summer they had just let them rot on the ground.

She was hit by an unexpected pang of regret. This yard had seen so many happy times, and a few wild ones. It didn't hold up well in this quiet. Her throat tightened as an unaccountable sadness swept over her.

Must be the Spanish wine, she thought. She took a last

look around; then, turning her back on the yard and the memories it evoked, she went inside.

She was surprised at the number of blinking lights waiting on her answering machine. She had forgotten to look at it when she returned home that afternoon. It was a habit she had gotten out of while on tour, living in hotels, spending days and nights in the theater where anyone who needed to talk to you just yelled over the music.

She pressed the retrieve button and sat down at the table to listen.

Stella had called to chat during a break in her deliveries. The cleaner had called to say one of her jackets needed a repair. There were two telemarketing calls. And a request from a charity. Her friend and co-worker, Biddy McFee, had left a message that she and Jeremy had arrived at the booking conference in Chicago and she'd call again that night. There were no messages from Glen—there hadn't been for the three days she had been home.

She looked at the kitchen clock. Six hours later in Paris. It was almost midnight there. She might wake him up. She didn't care. She felt lonely and depressed. She wouldn't tell him about finding the maybe-body. He would be angry. Well, he could be angry; she needed to talk.

He didn't answer. She left a message to call her. She thought about phoning Mary Elisabeth to see if she were okay and realized that she didn't have her new number. A call to information told her that the number was unlisted. She tried the hotel in Chicago. Neither Jeremy nor Biddy were in their rooms.

She did smile for a second, wondering how long into their new relationship it would be before Lindy lost her roommate, and Jeremy and Biddy started sharing a hotel room. With Jeremy's track record, it might be a long time.

There was only one other person she felt like talking to. She hadn't called him since she returned home. It always took her a few days to get up the courage. He never called her first.

But she couldn't go crying to Bill just because she missed her husband. Especially since things were suddenly unclear about what was happening with Glen. And she certainly couldn't tell Bill about the body. She didn't feel like getting yelled at by either of the men in her life.

She poured another glass of wine and sat down to read the mail. The phone rang.

"At last," she said and reached for the receiver.

It was a telemarketer.

She didn't wait to hear the spiel but hung up on the "Hello, I'm with—"

She did a load of wash. She wandered around the kitchen, restacking piles of mail, adjusting dish towels, keeping one ear out for the telephone. Then she paced from the side door to the back door until it was eight o'clock.

It was two o'clock in Paris. He wouldn't be calling tonight.

The telephone rang. She snatched it up on the second ring.

"Hello."

"Hi, It's me."

"Oh, hi, Biddy."

"Gee, such excitement."

"I was hoping it was Glen."

"Where is he? In the field?" Biddy laughed.

"Probably."

"He's always in the field. Honestly, people will think he's a farmer."

"So how's it going there?"

"Great. There are a lot of booking agents and local organizations here. Maybe we're going to rebound from the money crunch."

"That would be great." Touring had dried up for dance companies in the last few years. There was too little money to go around, and most companies were too expensive for smaller communities.

"Jeremy's working like there was no tomorrow."

"I hope you're mixing a little pleasure with your business."

"Some. Chicago is already cold as all get out, not that we've had a minute to leave the hotel. But we're having a good time."

"I notice you're staying in separate rooms."

"We're not having that good of a time. Yet."

Lindy rolled her eyes. It had taken Biddy announcing her resignation as business manager to make Jeremy realize his feelings toward her. He was taking his sweet time about acting on them. He had good reasons for being cautious, but it was exasperating. Especially for Biddy.

"Well, hope springs eternal."

"It does. Actually—" Biddy hesitated.

"What?"

"He was kind of making rumblings about spending a week in Mazatlan after the conference. Me and him, I mean." She laughed. "He didn't actually ask me if I wanted to go, but he's working on it."

"That's great."

"You don't sound like it's great. Is something the matter?"

"Not really. I'm working on a fund-raiser."

"That is depressing."

"Rebo's going to help."

"That's good. Are you worried about Glen?"

Jeez. Biddy had managed to pinpoint something she hadn't even admitted to herself, and she was a thousand miles away. But Biddy had always known how to read her when they had been dancers together, and again after Lindy had come to work for Jeremy after a twelve-year retirement.

"I guess."

"What is it? You aren't moving to Paris, are you?"

"No. But I did offer. When I went there after Spain."

Biddy growled over the phone.

"I know. I would have less to do there, and I wouldn't see Glen any more than I do now. I know the drill. You've run it by me often enough."

"I just don't think you should give up your life because he's got a new job."

"I think that's what wives do."

"Remind me of that if I ever start getting any stupid ideas."

"Well, it's academic. He doesn't want me to move to Paris."

"Good."

"Why?"

"Why is it good?"

"Why doesn't he want me to come to Paris? He wasn't even glad to see me for two days. He avoided me almost the whole time I was there. He was so—I don't know, distant."

She could almost see Biddy twisting a strand of hair at the other end of the line. She always played with her hair when she was thinking or upset.

"I don't guess you want to hear my views on marriage?"

"I have them memorized. I'll just say them to myself and save you the nickel." Lindy laughed and then shocked herself and Biddy when the laughter turned to tears.

"I'll come home right after the conference."

"No. I'm just tired. You and Jeremy have a good time. I'm going to be up to my eyeballs in this Mischief Night thing anyway."

"Call Bill."

It was a tempting thought. But not very flattering for Bill. Everyone already called him the boyfriend wannabe, thanks to Rebo. He wasn't. Or if he was, he had only hinted at it. But he was a good friend. He was always there for her; she couldn't say the same for herself. She only called him when she felt like having lunch or when she was in trouble.

"Are you still there?"

"Sorry. Hey, listen. Give Jeremy my love. And have a great

time in Mazatlan. Try to get into the same hotel room. I could use a little vicarious excitement."

"You'll be the first to know. But really, I'd just as soon come home."

"No way, pal. Have a blast."

Lindy hung up the phone, angry with herself for breaking down in front of Biddy. Not that they hadn't shared a bucket of tears before. But it wasn't fair when it looked like Biddy was finally getting her love life on track. She would just have to brazen this out by herself.

On second thought, what was wrong with lunch in the City? She punched in Bill's number before she could change her mind.

"Brandecker." Lindy moved the receiver away from her ear. Years after leaving the NYPD to teach criminology at John Jay College in Manhattan, Bill still answered the phone like a detective. His voice was resonant, and though not loud, it seemed to thunder throughout a room, or over a telephone wire.

"Hi. It's Lindy."

"Welcome back. How was Spain?"

"Fine."

"I thought you might take a few days off before you came home."

So had she. "No. There's a fund-raiser I'm working on." She gave him the condensed version of the marathon. "But I thought we might have lunch some day this week."

There was silence on the other end.

Lindy felt the first flutter of panic. Maybe she was going to be rejected by everyone she cared for.

"I can't," he said finally.

"Oh, well, it was just a suggestion." She hoped he couldn't hear the disappointment in her voice. Better to get off the phone before he was forced to think up excuses.

"I have departmental reorganization meetings all week."

"No big deal. Some other time."

"Is something wrong?"

"Of course not." God was she really that transparent?

"How about dinner Wednesday night?"

Dinner? He had never invited her to dinner. There were certain things that never came up in their relationship. Dinner was one of them. They were friends, nothing more. Dinner held too many connotations.

"Unless you're busy."

"No." Why should having dinner be any different from having lunch?

"I teach a seminar Thursday night, and on Friday I have to go to Connecticut to pick up my nephews."

"You have nephews?"

Not that she should be surprised. Bill never volunteered much about his life. She knew he had been married before. His wife was the reason he had left the police force. She had divorced him anyway. This past summer, he had told her he had a son. In another twenty years, she might have a half-formed picture of the man.

"My sister Sharon's kids. Will and Randall. Sharon's married to Patrick O'Dell. You remember him."

As if she could forget the police chief in charge of the investigation that nearly destroyed the company. "Of course."

"Dell's taking a retraining course at the academy, and Sharon has to take my mother to visit her sister in Portland. She's not well. So I volunteered to keep the kids."

"That should be fun."

"For a whole week."

"Yikes. No wonder you can't have lunch."

Bill laughed. "I'm kind of out of my element. So it's got to be dinner Wednesday, or wait for a couple of weeks and hope I survive it."

"Wednesday, then."

They agreed to meet at an Upper West Side restaurant and Lindy said good-bye. She finished her glass of wine, and this time it left a rosy glow.

Hell, she had a date.

* * *

The luminescent numbers on the bedside clock read 2:46. Lindy turned over for the fiftieth time in the last hour. It had been stupid to go to bed at 9:30. And now she was paying for it.

She plumped her pillow, pulled up the comforter, and kicked it off again. Finally she got up.

She padded down the hall past the office, past Cliff's room, past Annie's, past the den with its television and stacks of video games and down the stairs to the kitchen. Outside the window was unrelieved darkness. Even in the daylight, she couldn't see their nearest neighbor. "Wooded estates" was how the property had been advertised when she and Glen had bought the house fourteen years ago. Lindy had loved the little federal houses in town. But there had been nothing little about Glen's plans for his family.

And now Lindy was rattling around a silent, sprawling house with five bedrooms and four baths she didn't need. Not to mention the guest wing and the family room where Glen held communion with a big-screen television and surround sound on his few visits home.

Maybe it was time to sell and move into something smaller. But even as she thought it, she knew the kids would never go for it, even though they no longer lived there. Glen would never go for it, even though *he*—there was a noise just outside the window.

Lindy skittered back into the hallway.

Hell, what was wrong with her? She had never been afraid to stay alone in the house. There was a state-of-the-art alarm system—which she had forgotten to set. Well, she never set it, did she? She lived in a safe neighborhood in a safe town.

She hurried back upstairs glancing over her shoulder, jumped into bed and pulled the covers over her head.

Chapter Five

The next morning Lindy called Glen's Paris office. She was informed by his secretary, in impeccable English though Lindy had spoken French, that Mr. Haggerty was out of the office. No, he couldn't be reached. He was "in the field." The secretary would relay the message.

Next she called The Upper Cut and begged for a morning appointment. Fifteen minutes later, after discovering the overturned trash can and the remains of a raccoon's late-night snack, she was speeding into town.

Lindy had been going to Jeanette for so long that she could get in and out of the chair in less than thirty minutes, if there was no late-breaking gossip to hold them up.

Jeanette had no sooner snapped the plastic apron around Lindy's neck than she said, "I guess you heard about Howard and Mary Elisabeth Porter."

"I've been out of town," said Lindy, not wanting to encourage speculation about her friends.

"Well . . ."

When she left, hair shorn to a barber cut above her ears and not much longer everywhere else, Lindy had the full scoop on the latest breakup. How much was true and how much gross exaggeration, she didn't even begin to try to unravel. Some she dismissed out of hand. Mary Elisabeth crying, "Fallon or me," and Howard telling her to get out. Or Howard banging on Mary Elisabeth's door in the middle of the night, begging her to come home.

Lindy did her duty and tried to squelch the most outrageous scenarios, especially after the topic had caught the attention of several of the other patrons. She assured them that it was an amicable separation, even though she knew it wasn't, and it was obvious that none of the others believed her.

On the way to the marathon, she took a detour to the pumpkin farm to confirm their order. She could have done it over the phone, but after her solitary evening, she had decided that a few festive decorations might dispel the gloom at home.

The Maddens owned one of the few working farms in the area, but its survival depended largely on the overpriced vegetables, baked goods and country crafts that the Madden clan sold from its Country Emporium.

Lindy walked past bins of shiny, polished apples and water-sprayed produce and pushed open the swinging doors that led to the back room. Several men and women were busy cutting off the outer leaves of lettuces, picking through Mexican strawberries, and wielding pushcarts of imported root crops across the slab of concrete that was being hosed down by Cy Madden, Jr.

Cy was seventy years old if he was a day, still tanned from working the fields, if growing slightly soft from riding mechanized farm machinery. He greeted Lindy with a "Howdy," wiped his hands on his overalls and shook hers with enthusiasm.

"Pumpkins are right on schedule and we have some beauts this year. Steady rain with lots of sun in between. Want to take a look?"

"Sure," she said and followed him out the back door and into a nearby field. They chatted about the merits of the different sizes, shapes and colors of pumpkins, then went back inside to check over the order form.

"The store is looking great," she said.

"Yup." Cy looked around as if he were slightly dismayed by what he saw. Then he shook his head. "Chilean sweet onions. Australian star fruits. Organic field greens. Hell, when I was a kid, only poor people ate dandelion greens." He dipped his hand into the colorful leaves and dropped them back into the basket. "Nine dollars a pound. Go figure."

Lindy smiled. Yuppie cuisine had been good for business, and Cy knew it, even if he did like putting on that homespun act. He walked her to the door, past jars of local honey, wreaths of dried flowers, and packages of herbal tea with hand-printed labels.

Lindy stopped as a familiar name caught her attention. Crabtree's Moon Mist tea.

"Crabtree. Is that a local product?"

"Yup. We're not the only folks that have had to adapt to the times. Adam Crabtree makes all these teas, though my niece Betsy does the labels."

"Adam Crabtree," she mused. "The storyteller who lives over on the Van Cleef property?"

"That's the one. I expect you'll be seeing some of him while you're making preparations for the marathon. When he was in the other day, he said that Janey Horowitz had talked him into doing ghost stories that night. The man's a true entrepreneur. Have to be to live the way he does."

Lindy's eyes scanned over the other teas, all hand-collected herbal mixtures with curative properties. Teas for the immune system, digestive complaints, skin irritations, depression, anxiety.

"How does he get past the FDA?"

"Herbs aren't regulated the same way as other foodstuffs. He has a food handler's license. And none of the herbs he uses are dangerous. Want to try some?"

"I don't think so," said Lindy. "Comfrey, slippery elm, nettles? Ugh."

"Good for sore throats, or so they say. Myself, I take a couple of Fisherman's Friends. But people swear by him. He has a private client list about yea long. The man may be a recluse, but he knows which side his bread is buttered on."

They stopped by an outside stall, where Lindy selected several pumpkins, a bag of gourds, and two bundles of cornstalks. Cy loaded up the back of the station wagon and slammed down the hatch.

"Figure I'll send the truck over on Monday, next week. Two of my boys will unload 'em for you if you have somebody there to direct them." He waved her good-bye.

She drove back to the highway, thinking about Adam Crabtree and his herbal remedies. She had to smile at her initial reaction to his Monk's cassock sprouting plants. He must have been collecting herbs, and the plants she had seen were merely stuffed into pockets. The cassock probably protected his clothing from burrs, pollen and forest parasites.

But really. "He's on a journey." Well, he was now, thanks to Adam Crabtree. Maybe he had known all along that it was a dummy and was just pulling her leg. It would be just like a storyteller to capitalize on her imagination.

She hoped she hadn't caused too much strife among Judd and the rest of the police force. Especially if it turned out to be a hoax.

Instead of turning into the Van Cleef farm, she continued along the road. She had offered to take an updated schedule to Crabtree, and this was as good a time as any. Of course, she had an ulterior motive when she volunteered. She wanted to know what he had said to the police without having to bother an already harassed Judd, and she had a few questions of her own.

She took the northern fork of the highway. When the odometer read two miles, she slowed down and began looking for the turnoff to Adam's cabin.

A stone wall ran along the road. In places the stones had fallen to the ground; in others, vines completely concealed the wall's existence. At last she found an opening where the macadam ran into the woods beneath an arch of overgrown trees. She turned the Volvo into the drive.

Twenty feet later the pavement ended, and she bumped onto a rutted dirt road. It twisted through the trees, then narrowed to a lane, barely wide enough for the station wagon to pass. Lindy winced as branches scraped against the side of her car. She stopped at a wooden bridge that spanned a rivulet of brackish water.

Not willing to risk her station wagon, she pulled off to the side and continued over the bridge on foot. The last blaze of autumn canopied her way. Dried leaves rustled beneath her feet.

She would have missed the cottage if the lane hadn't ended abruptly at a wall of bushes. She paused at the No Trespassing sign tied around a maple tree.

She hadn't considered what reception she would receive from Adam Crabtree. She hoped it wouldn't be a shotgun. She slipped out of her jacket. It was brown suede, but beneath it, she was wearing a multicolored sweater she had bought in Equador. No mistaking this for a wild animal or camouflaged hunter.

She continued down a poorly marked path until she stepped into a clearing. A white shingled cottage with a railed front porch stood in the center. On one side, a trellis supported a vine of morning glories. The leaves were beginning to die back, but there were still a few blue flowers that had opened to the sun earlier that morning. Two windows flanked the door, their shutters painted a deep green. *Real shutters*, thought Lindy, that could be closed over the windows to keep out the elements—or prying strangers?

A thin trail of smoke wafted from the chimney, and the smell of burning wood was sharp in the air.

Knee-high grass surrounded the cottage, disturbed only by a narrow footpath that led to the porch steps. Lindy followed it to the front door and knocked. No answer. She knocked again, then called, "Mr. Crabtree?"

Still no answer. She briefly considered slipping the schedule underneath the door, but only briefly. The schedule had only been an excuse for talking to Crabtree, whether he wanted to talk or not.

She went back down the steps and looked around the yard. There were several wooden outbuildings nearby. A gray pickup was parked next to one of them. The body was battered and had rusted in several places, but the tires were new and oversized. Crabtree would need them if he tried to navigate that road after a snowstorm.

She called again, then walked toward the nearest shed. To her right, gardens were neatly laid out in square plots. Although most of the plants had died back, she could still see the original designs. One was concentric squares, a mulched walk separating the plants with a break in each square to allow the gardener to reach the innermost planting. Next to it was a complicated serpentine arrangement of late-blooming monkshood, polygonam and goldenrod. Beyond it, rows of cabbages, broccoli and lettuce were still flourishing. And beyond them, a greenhouse filled with plants. Gray-green bushes separated each of the plantings, and when Lindy brushed past them, the heavy scent of lavender filled the air.

She stopped at the first shed. It was unpainted wood, weathered to a gray taupe that upscale neighborhoods tried to recreate with expensive paints and faux finishes.

There was no answer to her knock, but there was a window. She put her hands to the glass and peered inside.

It was a small room with a low ceiling. Bunches of drying plants hung from the exposed beams. Wooden shelves held jars and boxes. Beneath them a work table was covered with dried plants and a pair of heavy shears. Crabtree's workshop. But no Adam Crabtree.

She continued past a woodpile that rose nearly to the roof of the cottage and stopped in front of another outbuilding, this one made of the same stone as the wall along the highway. Some of them had probably been usurped from the wall itself.

There was no window in this building, so she tried the door. It creaked inward and she stepped inside.

"Mr. Crabtree?" Her voice wavered in the dark interior. The air was several degrees colder than the outside. There was just enough light coming through the door to make out a circle of stones laid out on the floor. She shivered, as an unexpected sense of dread overcame her. She gave herself a mental kick. It must have been the talk about *The Crucible* and Brother Bart and his accusations of devil worship that made her skittish. It was just a smokehouse. And the rocks were where the fire was laid.

She backed out, closed the door, and retraced her steps. The gardens stretched before her, laid out with almost mathematical precision, like a patchwork quilt. Each square, a different pattern. *With its own personality*, she thought, then wondered where the thought had come from.

She was about to give up and leave the paper in his door, when Adam Crabtree appeared on the crest of the ridge that ran behind the house. Dressed once again in a brown cassock, he seemed to materialize from nowhere.

Lindy took an involuntary step backward. She couldn't help but think that he had done that on purpose—a natural streak of theatricality that probably served him well in his recounting of local ghost stories and historical tales of intrigue.

The man sure knew how to make an entrance. He stood, feet spread beneath his robe, wild beard lifting in the breeze as if it had a life of its own. His face turned toward her, powerful—mesmerizing. And though he was too far away to see his expression, he held her riveted. Then he began to wind down the slope, brushing the weeds and stalks of dried grasses aside like Moses parting the Red Sea. It was very effective. He was sure to be a hit on Mischief Night.

He stopped when he was right in front of her and glowered down at the paper she held in her hand.

She thrust it forward. "Mary Elisabeth wanted you to have the new schedule."

He took the paper without a word. She opened her hand. "I'm Lindy Haggerty, Mary Elisabeth's assistant."

Adam Crabtree stuck the paper into one of the oversized pockets, then crossed his arms. He was a recluse, Lindy reminded herself. Maybe he didn't like to be touched. She dropped her hand.

"We sort of met at the stream, remember?"

Was that a nod? Encouraged, she went on. "I talked to the police. I told them I wasn't sure if it was really a body or a dummy for the hayride. Did they talk to you?"

"They came."

Not exactly an answer to her question, but before she could ask another, he walked past her and up the front steps.

"Mr. Crabtree," she called after him.

He paused with his hand on the doorknob. "Adam," he said and went inside, closing the door behind him. Lindy stared after him, then stood in the yard expecting him to reappear. But he didn't, and after a few anxious minutes, she admitted defeat. She wouldn't be seeing any more of the recluse on that visit.

Chapter Six

Lindy was still brooding about her abrupt dismissal when she pulled into the Van Cleef driveway a few minutes later.

Stella, dressed in a red knit pants suit, was unloading the catering van. "Just in time," she said, as she lifted two white boxes off the floor of the van. "I brought some pumpkin cheesecake tarts to test out on the gang."

Lindy opened the door for her, then followed her into the kitchen.

Janey looked up from where she was sitting at the table. A brown paper bag and a wicker basket for steeping tea were placed in front of her. Lindy recognized the label from the ones at the Maddens' store. Janey smiled, but Lindy could tell it had taken an effort. This must not be one of her good days.

She should be resting, she thought, then realized how ridiculous that was. Janey probably needed to stay busy in order to keep her mind and spirits off the inevitable.

The kettle began to whistle. Janey started to push herself out of her chair.

"I'll get it," volunteered Stella. She poured boiling water into a mug and set it on the table in front of Janey.

Janey attempted to place the basket in the cup, but it flipped over and fell onto the table. Dried leaves and twigs spilled out. She tsked and began wiping the contents back into the basket. With shaking hands, she managed to balance it on the cup rim.

Lindy realized that she had been holding her breath as she watched. She exhaled.

Stella placed miniature cheesecakes on a serving platter and offered one to Janey. Janey shook her head. Lindy took one. It looked incredibly rich, but she had been expecting more of Stella's delicacies and had foregone breakfast.

Stella helped herself with a chuckle. "Just want to see if they're still as good as when I made them last night."

The kitchen door swung open, and Evelyn strode in, followed by Fallon and a man who had to be Derrick Justin.

He was slightly built with thin, finely honed features, and dark, overlong hair that curled over his brow. He was wearing a billowing blue shirt. His concept of a Romantic artist, no doubt. His dark eyes flashed with amusement.

Evelyn went straight to the coffee urn, ignoring the other two.

"It's your job," said Fallon. "That place is a mess and I want it cleaned up this afternoon." Her voice was shrill. Evidently this conversation had been going on for a while.

Evelyn carried her coffee to the table and perused the cheesecakes. "These look wonderful," she said to Stella. She plucked one off the plate and placed it on a napkin.

Stella lifted a tart to her mouth to hide her grin.

"See how long you stay on this committee, if you don't do what I tell you." Fallon planted both hands on her hips and stared angrily at Evelyn.

Evelyn bit into the cheesecake. "Delicious," she said.

"Listen, you—"

Derrick came up behind Fallon and slipped both arms around her waist. She melted against him. "I'm sure Evey will do all she can to help us out." He crinkled his eyes at Evelyn, then led Fallon out of the kitchen.

"Evey, my foot," said Evelyn as soon as the door closed behind them. "Men have died for less."

Lindy didn't doubt it, if Evelyn's expression was any indication of how she felt.

Stella burst out laughing. "Great tactics, Evelyn. Maybe if we all act like she's invisible, she'll finally disappear for good."

"What was that about?" asked Lindy.

"Fallon seems to think it's my responsibility to get rid of that pile of garbage behind the church. They want to pitch a tent for extra dressing rooms."

"They should have a dumpster. It will have to be carted away."

"I tried to explain that. But she would have none of it. What a little priss pot."

Janey reached a bony finger along the table. "She can also be vindictive, Evelyn. Don't underestimate her."

Evelyn looked mildly surprised. "Don't worry about me. As they say, I can take care of myself."

"Still . . ."

"Janey had her in senior English; she knows whereof she speaks," explained Stella.

"That was one of the worst years of my life," Janey agreed, then looked embarrassed.

Not as bad as this one, thought Lindy.

"Well, she can clean up her own mess," said Evelyn. "They shouldn't have dragged all that junk out of the church. T.J.'s the only person authorized to make decisions on what is to be thrown out."

"That isn't T.J.'s doing?" asked Lindy.

Evelyn shook her head. "Fallon and Derrick had a cleaning spree last weekend. T.J. is livid."

"But Fallon wasn't even on the committee last weekend," said Janey.

"Since when did that stop the beast?" asked Stella.

"You know," said Lindy, turning to Evelyn, "I don't think we've met officially."

"Oh, I'm sorry. Mary Elisabeth has told me so much about you that I feel like we're old friends."

Lindy smiled weakly. She hoped Mary Elisabeth hadn't been recounting her murder escapades. After all, Evelyn was a stranger, and she might be prone to gossip.

"Mary Elisabeth and I live in the same apartment complex. We met one day taking out our garbage."

"And no good deed goes unpunished," said Stella, reaching for another cheesecake. "She was bound to snag you for a committee. Caught you with one little Hefty bag and you didn't stand a chance."

"She is rather persuasive," said Evelyn, "but I had just moved to the community and it seemed like a good way to meet people. I volunteered."

Stella grinned. "Sure you did."

"You just moved here? I wondered why we hadn't served on a committee together," said Lindy.

Evelyn said nothing.

"Come from the City?"

"Yes."

"Commuter?" asked Stella.

"I work at home."

They waited for her to elaborate. Finally, she said, "I'm a consultant."

The woman was no conversationalist. Maybe she was shy. No, Lindy didn't believe that, not after watching the way she handled Fallon and Derrick.

Janey was studying Evelyn over the rim of her cup. She seemed to have roused a bit since they had begun asking Evelyn about her background, though she asked no questions herself.

Lindy groped around for something to continue the conversation. She was curious about Evelyn, but mostly she wanted to keep Janey's mind off the pain that was obviously bothering her that morning.

"What does your husband do?"

Stella snorted. "Lindy, how un-PC."

"I apologize to the feminists of the world. I was just making conversation."

"Actually, I live alone."

"Right on, sister." Stella raised a fat fist in the air.

"Oh, Stella." Janey tittered behind her hand.

"It must be those red bell-bottoms you're wearing," said Lindy.

Stella grimaced. "They're not bell-bottoms. Or at least they weren't until last week. The girls did the wash for my birthday. The entire load came out pink, and my new pants came out bell-bottoms."

Janey looked at the clock. "I wonder where Mary Elisabeth is. I have a doctor's appointment." Her lips thinned.

"You go ahead," said Lindy.

"I think I'd better. It's a waste of time, really. Adam's teas give me more peace of mind, and that's about all anybody can do. But I don't want to hurt the young man's feelings." Janey folded the top of the little bag and put it in the cabinet.

The others fell silent after she had left.

"Where *is* Mary Elisabeth?" asked Lindy.

"At the bank," said Stella. "Wanted to deposit Howard's check before he had a chance to change his mind."

"She was going to explain the booth placement to me." Lindy pulled the map of booth sites from her bag and placed her empty cup in the sink.

"I can show you around," said Stella and hurried Lindy out the door.

They had just reached the porch when an ancient Chevy belched to a stop in front of them. The door opened and Rebo climbed out of the driver's side.

"Lindelicious." He grinned a row of white teeth at her.

Stella grinned even wider.

"This is Juan's car?" asked Lindy, coming down the steps to meet him.

"Uh-huh. The Black Beauty." He struck a pose. "The *other* Black Beauty."

"I'll say," muttered Stella under her breath.

Most of the car was black. The front fender was a matte red, and the bumper was wired into place. A piece of cellophane was taped over one of the headlights. The remains of an antenna stuck up from the hood, a raccoon tail tied to the top. There was a hula dancer on the dashboard.

Lindy shook her head. "Well, you won't take anybody by surprise."

Rebo scratched at the red bandanna he always wore around his shaved head. "Yeah. I noticed that. Juan was supposed to change the spark plugs, but his face is swollen into pig's eyes. Not a pretty sight. And definitely a drawback for detail work."

"You must be Rebo," said Stella.

"In the flesh." Rebo kowtowed. "And you must be Stella of the Starlight. Lindy told me about your fritters." He waggled his eyebrows.

Stella guffawed, setting off a chain reaction along her midsection. "Did she tell you about the body?"

Rebo swiveled his head toward Lindy and gave her a deadpan look. "There's a body?"

"Not anymore."

"Lindisaster. You weren't going to hold out on me, were you?"

"She was just going to show me where she found it," said Stella.

"I thought we were looking at the site map. And how did you know about the body?"

Stella shrugged. "Guess I overheard Mary Elisabeth and Evelyn talking about it."

"Evelyn knows, too?"

"What body?" asked Rebo.

"I'm not supposed to discuss it." Though it seemed academic at this point, and Rebo did have a right to know what he was getting into.

"Hell, 'fess up," said Stella. "Everybody will know before the day is out. Was it really a dead man? How do you do these things?"

"It wasn't me," said Lindy. "It was Bruno. And we're not sure it was real. Adam Crabtree pushed him out into the brook and he floated away."

"So that's why you offered to take the schedule to him. Going to do a little sleuthing?"

"No!"

"Are you going to tell me about the body?" Rebo asked.

Lindy sighed. "After Stella shows me what goes where."

"And then you'll show us where you found it?" asked Stella.

"Oh, all right, but you'll have to keep it to yourselves."

"Mum's the word." Stella took the map and began reciting at breakneck speed. "The area between the church and house is designated as younger children activities. They'll start construction this weekend and we'll have to park across the street at the mall." She pointed to several of the little boxes outlined on the map. "These are for game booths, those are for exhibits, the historical society, the genealogical society, New Age paraphernalia—we couldn't really leave them out. The food booths are over there between the church and the highway." She pointed across the drive where the narrow strip of asphalt ran the length of the church and continued without taking a breath. "Tables and chairs for real eating. A few candied apple, cotton candy, and hot dog kiosks will be positioned strategically throughout the rest of the fair. You can leave all the food stuff to me."

"Great."

"The Police Athletic League and the Jaycees are in charge of setup. Though from the way things have been going, it might just be the Jaycees. Johnston's Electric is rigging generators and light boxes. Porta Pottys are here and here. Now show us where you found the body."

Lindy held the map at arm's length and squinted. "Fortune Telling?"

"Lisa Conway as Madame Glosky."

"I thought she was pregnant with twins."

"She is. Let's just hope they don't come early."

Lindy tried to ignore the glint in Rebo's eye. "Hmm, Madame Glosky. Maybe *she'll* tell me about the body."

"Oh, hell, come on." Lindy looked at the map again. "I think we can get there if we go this way."

They followed a path that ran behind Madame Glosky's tent site. Several hundred yards from the back of the farmhouse they came to another clearing. A massive stone fireplace stood in the center surrounded by circles of rock seating.

"Wow," said Lindy. "I had no idea this was here."

"It was the summer kitchen, according to T.J. Now, the site of the bonfire and Adam's ghost stories. The hayride starts out at the back of the house, goes along the stream then loops back around to the front of the church. You can see the stakes marking the route through the trees there."

"That's where we're going," said Lindy.

Stella didn't wait but headed to the far side of the fireplace and thrashed through the underbrush, Rebo on her heels. By the time Lindy caught up to them, they were standing in the middle of the road. Rebo was peering into the trees, hands on his hips.

Stella was bent over, her hands braced on her knees, breathing hard. "Gotta start getting more exercise," she huffed.

"Where's the bridge?" asked Lindy, trying to orient herself.

Stella pointed. "Right over there." The bridge was less than fifty feet from where they were standing.

"I didn't realize it was so close to the house."

"The brook curves around the property," said Stella. "Come on."

"Hold on a sec, Lindiscovery. I want the whole blow by blow first."

Lindy told him about finding the body and about Adam Crabtree pushing it away. "He said he was on a journey and who were we to stop him."

"Very new age, or old hippie," said Rebo. "Which is it?"

"A little of both, I think."

"So lead on, Macduff."

The three of them advanced toward the bridge. Lindy and Rebo stopped when they were several yards away. Stella marched ahead.

"I don't think you're supposed to disturb the scene," said Lindy.

"I don't see any of that yellow tape they're supposed to put up. So it must be all right." Stella lumbered down the bank, dislodging an avalanche of pebbles. She peered beneath the bridge. "Spooky."

"Yes, it was," said Lindy, climbing down behind her. "I thought it was a dummy for the hayride. See." She pointed up to the road. "It runs right past here."

Rebo moved them aside and bent down to take a look. "He was just lying there?" His eyes rounded to comic proportions.

"Yep, along with a bunch of trash," said Lindy.

"And you let him just float away?"

"I couldn't help it. It all happened so fast."

"Aren't bodies supposed to sink to the bottom?" asked Stella.

Lindy and Rebo looked at each other.

"It's shallow right here," said Lindy. "But he did seem to start sinking after he drifted away. Oh, God, you don't think he's still out there, do you?"

Rebo shook his head. "Nah, the current probably carried him downstream."

"Good."

"Guess you were glad to see him go."

Lindy winced. "Actually, everybody was. Nobody wants the marathon involved in a suspicious death. Even the police seemed relieved that it had 'journeyed' out of their territory."

"Think he fell off the bridge?"

"Judd said he probably floated from upstream somewhere, maybe even from New York. That's where the brook starts."

Rebo squatted down and stuck his hand in the brook. "In six inches of water?"

"It's close to five feet at the center."

"How tall was this dead guy?"

"Over five feet. But there's no place around here to fall in. The other bank slopes to the edge and this side is covered with underbrush except at the springhouse."

"Springhouse, huh? Like where they stored sides of beef, you mean?"

Lindy nodded.

"Next stop, springhouse." He climbed up the bank and leaned back to hoist Stella up the side.

"Brains and brawn," said Stella. "I think we're gonna do just fine." She took off in the direction of the springhouse, Rebo at her side. Lindy reluctantly followed.

Stella pulled up sharp and Lindy plowed into her.

"What the hell is he doing out here?" Stella pointed into the woods where a man squatted in a pile of leaves. "Hey, T.J. Did the plumbing in the house back up?"

"Very funny." The restorer stood up, turned slowly in a circle scanning the underbrush, then scribbled in a little notebook.

"Okay. We give up. What are you doing?"

"Calculating." Mumbling to himself, he wandered back into the trees.

"Weird," said Rebo.

"In a word," agreed Stella. "Come on. The springhouse is over here." She veered off into the trees and stopped in front of the padlocked door. "Can you imagine schlepping food from here to the kitchen? Give me Kwiki Mart any day."

An expletive exploded from behind them. T.J.'s head appeared from the other side of the springhouse. "Damn those kids. If they don't stop throwing their garbage out back here, I'll, I'll—" He broke off and began gathering up cast-off potato chip bags, soda cans and other signs of partying. "If I've told Melanie once, I've told her a thousand times."

"Well, I think I've seen enough," said Lindy, backing away. "Shall we leave him to it?"

"You scared of that little pipsqueak?" asked Rebo as T.J. stormed away. "Uh-oh." He knelt down by the water. "Looks like what's-her-name's kids are doing more than eating down here." He held out his hand. A small brown bottle rolled along his palm.

"What's that?" asked Lindy.

Rebo screwed up his face, then tossed the bottle over his shoulder into the stream. "Just something on a journey and nothing you want to tell Judd, the J.D., about." He took a last look. "You know, Lindenial, even if the guy had a heart attack and fell in, he wouldn't float away. Unless—" He gave her a pointed look.

"He had help," said Lindy.

"Damn, you two are frightening," said Stella. "Whose idea was this anyway?"

Rebo and Lindy gave her a look.

"Teatime," she said brightly. "I have some chocolate macaroons in the van."

Chapter Seven

On their way back to the parking lot, they passed the hayride committee, carrying lumber and tools into the woods.

"School must be out," said Lindy. "The Teen Council is in charge of the hayride," she explained to Rebo. "Those guys"—she pointed to a group going toward the church—"are in the drama group. They're doing scenes from *The Crucible*. They'll perform at six and the Follies begins at eight. So you'll have a fast turnaround. I'll take you over to the church to see what the setup is."

"And ne'er the twain shall meet," said Rebo.

"You picked up on that, huh? The drama group are at-risk teens; the council is made up of high achievers. They don't seem to get along."

"Like the Jets and the Sharks?"

Lindy shivered. "Let's hope not."

"Oops," said Rebo. "Trouble in River City."

Beyond the group of low-slung pants and oversized tees, Fallon and Evelyn were at a standoff in the middle of the gravel. Evelyn turned away. Fallon grabbed her arm. With a flick of her elbow, Evelyn sent Fallon stumbling backward.

"Oh, Lord, here we go again." Stella hurried toward the two women.

"Don't think Mary Elisabeth will stick up for you," yelled Fallon. "They'll never accept you. Just look at them—look at yourself."

Stella stepped between them. "That's uncalled for, Fallon. And a lie."

"Get out of my way, fatty."

Stella raised her hand. "That's right, you little brat. So get out of here before I sit on you, and you turn into a designer pancake." She took a threatening step forward.

Fallon jumped back, hesitated for a moment, then stalked away.

Lindy looked on with satisfaction as her heels sank into the gravel. Those shoes would never be the same.

"Thanks for intervening," said Evelyn. "It's hard to believe she made it to adulthood with that vicious attitude."

"Only the body made it to adulthood," said Stella. "The rest of her is stuck in obnoxious adolescence. Hard enough to take from an adolescent."

"I don't suppose we could get rid of her somehow," said Lindy.

Evelyn raised an eyebrow.

"I didn't mean anything drastic," said Lindy, thinking about the body she had found. "A world cruise, maybe. I'd donate to the cause."

"Frankly, my dears, I would consider something more drastic," said Stella. "I've just about had it with her. And Mary Elisabeth doesn't need any more stress right now. Damn, that girl pisses me off."

Evelyn stuck out her hand to Rebo. "Evelyn Grimes—and you are?"

"The other token." He flashed his teeth at her.

"Rebo," warned Lindy in a tight aside.

"Glad to meet you," he said, unperturbed. "I stopped at

the deli in town. Got a turkey on white bread." He faced Lindy, waiting theatrically for her reaction.

"You should have asked for tongue on pumpernickel," said Evelyn.

Lindy couldn't decide if she was attempting a joke or an insult. Her delivery was as bland as Rebo's white bread. "Come on, I'll show you around the church." She dragged him away.

Four students sat on the steps. Curls of smoke drifted upward from their cigarettes. When they saw Lindy and Rebo, they dropped them on the ground and shuffled inside.

Lindy stopped to grind out the burning stubs.

"So this is the scene of the Follies." Rebo gave the facade the once-over. "Not bad. I got some ideas after I stopped laughing over the lineup. *Danse Macabre*? They're really going to use Day-Glo tombstones?"

Lindy nodded. "Miss Carole Anne's School of Dance."

"Brrr. I can hardly wait. If they need an understudy, we can wrap Juan up with gauze. His face would scare the pants off the audience. Can we go in? I want to try out some things for the men's kick line."

Oh, Lord, thought Lindy. "Just remember, they're policemen," she said, hurrying after him.

"Hey, I can do policemen."

Lindy groaned out loud and ushered him inside.

The church was long and narrow, paneled with dark wood. A vaulted ceiling rose into shadows. Arched windows lined the sides. The panes were thick amber glass; no scenes from the scriptures here. Sconces lined the walls and cast the same yellow light as the windows.

The air was chilled. Lindy pulled out her notebook and made a note to check on the heating capabilities. Then she made a note to call Larry Briggs, who had done the lighting and sound for the scholarship review. The play might be able to get by with the available lighting in the church, but the Follies would need to be enhanced.

A plywood platform had been constructed over the chancel steps and extended past the pulpit and lectern. The front row of pews had been removed to make room for the stage.

Lindy looked around with satisfaction. The church made a wonderful little theater, even though there were no wings and all entrances and exits had to be made through the choir loft or down the center aisle. And it was a perfect space for performing *The Crucible*.

A group of young people huddled around two space heaters that glowed red at the back of the makeshift stage. Melanie directed from a stool at the front of the center aisle.

"All right. Let's take it from Act One. Claudia, start where Abigail and Mercy are trying to convince Mary to stop pretending and wake up."

"Yo, Mama," said Rebo under his breath. "I think she musta got lost."

"She's the new English teacher."

"You're shitting me." He wandered off to study the interior, and Lindy settled onto a pew to watch the rehearsal.

A girl moved away from the heater, pushing lank blond hair behind her ear. She ambled to the center of the platform and pulled a script out of the pocket of a denim jacket covered with patches of rock bands.

"Without the book. You were supposed to know your lines by today."

The girl mumbled something.

Melanie put her hands on her hips. "Try moving your lips when you talk. It might sound like English."

The girl looked sullenly at the floor and rifled through the book.

There were a few smirks among the other teens, which were quickly erased when Melanie's eyes scanned the group.

"Well?"

"I was too busy," said the girl, puckering her lips with exaggeration.

"Well, there's always Meals on Wheels." Melanie sighed. "Oh, that's right. You had your license revoked. Maybe you can volunteer for Community Clean Up. Get a pair of work gloves if you want to keep those nails."

The girl glanced down at inch-long, black-polished fingernails. Then she shoved her script back into her pocket.

"Places," said Melanie.

Rebo sat down near the front and leaned forward on his elbows. Melanie cast a cursory look in his direction before turning her attention back to the stage.

A girl lay back between two chairs positioned to represent a bed. Claudia and another girl huddled together and looked down at her. Claudia gave the girl on the chair a shake. The girl's head hit the back of the chair, and Claudia giggled.

Melanie stood up. "Oh, yes, it is funny, isn't it? You're about to hang because Mary claims you drank blood."

Claudia made a face. "That's stupid."

"Sure it is. But guess what. Stupid things happen. And Abigail and Mercy—you and Val"—she pointed to Claudia and the girl next to her—"are going to take the rap for it. Sound familiar?"

Claudia glared down at Mary, who sprawled across the chairs looking defiant. "I guess she would know."

"It's not my fault you're such a fuck-up," said the girl who was playing Mary.

There was an intake of breath from behind Lindy, and she turned to see Janey grasping the back of the pew.

"Sit here," she whispered and moved over to make room. Janey sat down and put her hand to her mouth.

"Is that right, Val? Is Mary out to get you? Does she want Abigail to take the rap for her?"

Val, a short, chunky girl with frizzy red hair, looked confused.

"Well, is she?"

"I don't know," Val mumbled.

"Sure you do. It's happened before, hasn't it? Probably will happen again. We all know it. You know it. What—?"

"I didn't do anything," yelled Val. "You can't prove that I did."

Janey moved forward in her seat. "What is Melanie doing?"

She's walking a fine line, thought Lindy.

"We don't have to prove it," said Claudia. "Everybody knows about it, don't they, Dina?"

"It wasn't me," said the girl on the chair.

"Well, it wasn't me," said Claudia.

They both looked at Val.

"Oh, no, you don't. Stay away from me." Val pulled her script out of her pocket and threw it on the floor. She bounded off the stage and ran past Melanie toward the exit.

Melanie grabbed her by the back of her jacket.

Val tried to push her away. "Leave me alone. Leave me alone." Melanie wrapped both arms around the girl while she struggled.

Janey tried to stand. "I'm going to stop this right now."

Lindy touched her arm and Janey slumped back.

Melanie looked over Val's head at the other two girls. "So if it wasn't you and it wasn't Claudia, who was it, Dina?"

The girl on the chair stuck out her chin. "How should I know?"

"Won't anybody tell the truth?" asked Melanie. She began guiding Val back to the group. She stopped when she was center stage and turned Val to face the others. "Who knows? Is Val guilty?" Val pulled away and stood defiantly facing them. They looked away.

"How about you, Kenny?" asked Melanie.

A boy stood up from the floor. He was almost six feet tall, skinny, and wearing pants that looked like they might fall to the ground if he exhaled. He blew a strand of hair out of his face and crossed his arms without answering.

"Well, if she isn't guilty, who is?"

Kenny shrugged, not looking at her.

"Kenny," Val pleaded.

Kenny didn't move.

"Darien?" asked Melanie.

No answer from a dark-skinned Indian boy.

"Jeff?"

Jeff gave her a guarded look from where he was perched on the communion rail. He pointed across the room. "Kenny."

"What the hell?" Kenny looked confused; then his lips curled into a slow smile. "Darien."

"Me? It was Carl."

"Like hell it was." A head popped up from the choir loft. "What the hell are we talking about anyway?"

"If you weren't sleeping, you'd know, shit-head," said Darien.

"You're the shit-head."

"No, Jeff's the shit-head," said Claudia, then burst out laughing.

"No, Kenny is," said Dina from the chair.

They all began pointing and laughing and name calling. Melanie joined in the fun.

"I don't understand," whispered Janey. "This isn't English. I'm going to die and I'm leaving my children to this."

Melanie walked to the front of the stage, laughing and wiping her eyes. Then she stopped and turned toward them. Lindy saw her ribs expand in an intake of breath. "And now you're all going to die." Her words echoed into the rafters and snowballed to the back of the church where Lindy and Janey sat.

The laughter broke off to dead silence. One by one they turned to watch Melanie. They weren't getting the joke.

Lindy risked a glance toward Janey. She was sitting stiffly on the pew. One hand gripped the pew in front of her.

"You're going to die," Melanie repeated. "Die. Everyone of you who was accused of being a shit-head. You're going to die. Just because someone pointed the finger at you."

"That isn't fair," said Carl.

"Since when is life fair?"

"You can say that again," mumbled Kenny.

"But you don't die just because someone calls you a name," said Dina.

"No?" Melanie looked around the stage, pausing on each face. Then she snatched Val's script off the floor and shook it at them. "These people did."

"It's just a play."

"But it really happened. If you had read the play notes, you would have known that."

"They all died just because someone called them witches?" Val wiped her nose across her sleeve.

"Yeah."

"That's stupid."

"Tell it to the Jews," said Kenny.

"You're right, Kenny," said Melanie. "It happens time and time again. Why?"

Kenny looked taken aback. "I don't know. 'Cause they were mean." His eyes narrowed. "Or 'cause they were scared."

"Yeah," said Claudia. "Accuse somebody else before they accuse you." She looked at Dina. "Like we were just doing."

"But that was just for kicks," said Carl.

"Pretty high stakes for a game, don't you think?" Melanie turned away from them. No one moved until she was back on her stool.

"Okay, Claudia. Mary's game is going to get you killed. Hung or pressed or dunked to death. You're scared. What are you going to do about it?"

Claudia reached for Mary. This time when she shook Dina, Dina stayed limp in her hands. The lines weren't perfect, but the feeling was clear. No one laughed. Those sitting around the side of the stage were focused intently on the action.

A few minutes later, Kenny made his entrance as John Proctor. Val and Dina exited and Claudia turned a flirtatious smile on him.

It was more like a scene at the mall than a serving girl attempting seduction of a stalwart New England farmer. But when Kenny called her a child, Claudia's face flashed with sudden disappointment. And a few lines later, when she defamed Elizabeth, Proctor's wife, Kenny's anger was real.

"Okay, let's take a break," said Melanie. "That was good. Very good."

The cast relaxed. Talking broke out among the group, and several of the teens headed toward the back door.

"Just a cigarette break," Kenny said to Melanie as he passed. "I need it."

"Those children shouldn't be smoking," said Janey. Both hands were white-knuckled on the pew in front of them.

Lindy agreed, but she also knew teenagers. She had raised two herself. A lot of them smoked, and she sympathized with Kenny's need against her better judgment.

"Let's get some tea," she said. She looked around for Rebo, but he was deep in conversation with the new English teacher.

Lindy helped Janey out of the church and down the steps. The group lounging there shifted uncomfortably. Kenny dropped his cigarette to the ground.

Janey pursed her lips, her eyes filled with disapproval. He kicked the cigarette butt away, then took her arm.

Janey commanded her own kind of clout, thought Lindy, as she watched them walk toward the house. It might be old-fashioned, but she still had something to offer. It was too bad she and Melanie couldn't work together. She would be gone all too soon.

"Hmm, shit-head symbolism. It works for me," said Rebo, coming up behind her.

Evelyn, not Melanie, was with him. She must have been watching the rehearsal, too.

"Yeah, it works for me, too," agreed Lindy. "But it's hard on Janey."

"She's concerned for her students, as she should be," said Evelyn. "Melanie is playing a dangerous game."

"I don't think it's a game with Melanie," said Lindy.

"No." Evelyn paused to watch Kenny come down the steps of the farmhouse and stop to light another cigarette. "I wonder if she knows what she's doing." She walked down the steps and nodded to Kenny as they passed in the driveway.

"Brrr," said Rebo. "Think she knows something we don't?"

"It's a distinct possibility. She doesn't say much, but when she does, I always get the feeling that she's thinking more than she's letting on. And she's always around."

"So what's her story?"

"Beats me. She knows a lot more about us than we do about her."

"Hmm. You think she does that on purpose?"

"Yeah, I think she does. But why?"

Rebo decided to stay overnight, ostensibly because he heard a strange ping coming from the Black Beauty, but Lindy knew that the hamburgers weren't the only things that would be grilled for dinner.

She picked up Bruno at the groomer's, while the Chevy grumbled and belched in the parking space beside her. Then Rebo followed her home and parked behind her in the driveway.

As soon as she opened the car door, Bruno bounded into the shrubbery.

"Don't you dare get dirty," she yelled after him.

He stopped to anoint an azalea bush and then dashed toward Rebo, who was trying to climb out of his car.

"Down, down, damn Spot," he grumbled.

Finding a friend who understood him, Bruno cavorted and pranced with delight.

Rebo rolled his eyes.

"I never use the garage," Lindy said. "It's too much trouble."

"Your car looks clean to me, except for those weeds in the back."

"Those aren't weeds. They're cornstalks. I'm going to decorate the porch with them."

Rebo flipped up the tailgate and peered inside. "Terribly tasteful," he said. Then he grinned. "I'll help."

They hauled pumpkins, gourds, and cornstalks to the front of the house while Bruno tried to walk between Rebo's feet.

Rebo leaned a bundle of cornstalks on each side of the door. Lindy stood back and tried to think of a nice tableau of pumpkins and gourds.

She frowned. "I guess I'm not in the mood for festive Halloween decorations."

"Could be your choice of decorations, or could be the floater you found."

She arranged the pumpkins in front of the cornstalks and stood back. Boring. She cocked her head to the side. Still boring.

"Boring," Rebo said out loud. "What you need is some of those plastic skeletons they have in the costume shop on Christopher Street." He moved his hands in front of his face like a movie director. "Yeah. About twenty would do the trick. We can place them along the walk in Kama Sutra positions. Get some of those little pumpkin bags that you put candles in to light the way. The trick or treaters will love it."

Lindy threw up her hands and went inside to make the burgers.

Over dinner, she filled him in on the details of the "floater," as Rebo insisted on calling the drowned man. She told him about the committee members. How Mary Elisabeth and Howard's divorce affected the marathon. About Adam Crabtree's herbal remedies. She explained the nature of the bequest, what T.J. was doing there, how Fallon was a thorn in everybody's side, about Derrick and his "concept," though she had never figured out what the concept was.

They were loading the dishwasher, when the telephone rang. Rebo was closest. He answered it and immediately started chatting.

"Glen?" she mouthed.

"Biddy," he mouthed back. He shooed her away.

"Don't tell her about the body," she whispered. "I don't want her to worry."

"Oh, that's just Lindy telling me not to tell you about the body."

"Rebo." She tried to grab the phone, but he jumped away and took it into the mud room. She followed.

"No really. It's okay," he said. "I've got it under control. Go get laid in Mazatlan."

"Rebo," cried Lindy again.

Rebo jerked the phone from his ear. "Stereo chastisement. Now, there's a 'concept.'"

Lindy wrestled the phone away. She spent the next ten minutes assuring Biddy that the drowning was an accident and she didn't need to cancel her trip to Mazatlan.

"And how did Rebo find out about Mazatlan?" asked Biddy.

"*I* didn't tell him."

Rebo shrugged.

"Oops, gotta go," said Biddy. "Jeremy's at the door. We're having dinner with some potential sponsors. I'll call tomorrow." She hung up.

"How *did* you know about Mazatlan?" asked Lindy as she hung up the phone.

"Saw him looking at travel brochures in the airport." Rebo yawned. "It's getting late. Where do I sleep?"

Lindy opened her mouth, then closed it. "You can have Annie's room," she said and led him up the stairs.

Chapter Eight

Emergency meeting. Lindy hung up the phone and snuggled back under the covers. Emergency meetings were as common as scheduled meetings when it came to fund-raisers. Something unexpected was always turning up, and with this fund-raiser they had more than the normal share of variables.

She pushed the covers off and sat up. Maybe Judd had found out something about the drowned man. Maybe there really was an emergency.

She pulled on a T-shirt and padded down the hall to Annie's room.

Rebo was stretched out on the single bed, surrounded by frilly pillows and stuffed animals that Annie had never quite outgrown. Lindy felt a pang just seeing that room occupied, even by a muscular, adult dancer. Rebo was something of a black beauty himself.

He opened one eye.

"Emergency meeting," said Lindy. "Go back to sleep. I'll leave you a map."

"Nuh-huh," he croaked back at her. "I can do emergencies." He sat up.

Lindy took an appreciative look at his finely developed muscles before going downstairs to make coffee and a couple of sandwiches for lunch.

Forty minutes later, she saw the reason for the emergency.

There must have been fifteen of them lined up along the road in front of the mall parking lot. It was a chilling sight: young women and old, clean-cut men in polyester pants, and old men in suits. There were children, who should have been in school instead of standing by the side of a busy highway, holding plump teddy bears, paper crosses pinned to their fur. They were all dressed in shades of brown and beige. Drab colors that clashed in spite of the sameness of the hue.

They carried hand-lettered signs. *Devil's Marathon* with a red circle and slash painted over the words. *Down with Devil Worship*, *Evil Walks Among You*, and one that made Lindy gasp with surprise: *Marathon=Death.*

Had they heard about the drowning? Judd was supposed to keep it quiet.

She turned too quickly into the Van Cleef parking lot, and gravel spurted out from her tires as shouts rose up behind her. She got out of the car and stood with her hands on her hips as she looked across the road. All their attention was focused on her, fists shaking in the air, their cries unintelligible as they coalesced into one angry hum.

She wondered which one was Brother Bart.

Rebo pulled the Chevy in beside her and leaned out the window. "Your fan club?"

"Brother Bart and the Gospel of Galilee Church."

"That's a joke, right?"

Lindy shook her head.

Rebo got out of his car and followed her across the drive. She could hear him humming "Onward Christian Soldiers" under his breath as they went into the house.

The dining room was packed. Extra chairs had been brought in to accommodate the overflow. Judd caught her eye from across the room. It was a small movement, but the downward quirk of his mouth told her the news wasn't good.

She introduced Rebo as the director of the Follies, then walked over to the sideboard and poured herself a cup of black coffee. This morning the white box contained oatmeal, raisin and macadamia nut muffins. She didn't take one.

Rebo took two and went to stand next to Melanie at the back of the room.

Lindy sat down next to Derrick Justin, who raised his cafe latte in hello. Fallon was sitting on his other side. Next to her, Father Andrews snored quietly. Even T.J. was present, perched on a stool behind Mary Elisabeth's right shoulder.

Mary Elisabeth called the meeting to order. She was wearing gray slacks and a turtleneck sweater in tones of gray and heather blue. A classic look that unfortunately brought out the hollows in her cheeks.

"The town has granted a permit for the Gospel of Galilee Church to picket, as you no doubt have seen. They have to remain on the opposite side of the road, but that's almost worse than being on the premises. Everyone who drives by or goes to the mall will see them."

"Will we have to cancel?"

The question was met by outcries from around the room.

"We can't cancel now."

"There are two more weeks before Mischief Night. Maybe they'll lose interest by then."

"We don't even know who this Brother Bartholomew is."

"And what about that sign *Marathon=Death*? Is that a threat?"

"Please, everyone," cried Mary Elisabeth over the din that had broken out. "Let's proceed in an orderly fashion."

The room became quiet.

She looked about until her eyes rested on Father Andrews. His head drooped on his chest.

"If someone will wake Father Andrews, we'll find out what Brother Bart had to say."

Fallon snickered and lifted her elbow. Before she could

poke him in the ribs, which it was obvious she was about to do, Father Andrews opened his eyes.

"I'm afraid I've failed," he said. "Brother Bartholomew intends to fight us with everything he has. Hopefully within the bounds of the law."

"We'll see to that," volunteered Judd.

"I should hope that as a purported man of God, he won't make that necessary. However . . ." Either Father Andrews closed his eyes to think or he had drifted off again. Fallon took the opportunity to elbow him.

"You needn't do that, my dear. I was merely thinking." Father Andrews turned a beatific smile on her.

Fallon flushed. Derrick smirked into his coffee cup.

The rest of them waited to hear what he was thinking about.

"Do you have any suggestions?" Mary Elisabeth prompted.

Father Andrews rubbed his chin. "I don't relish being the one to cast the first stone, but has anyone investigated this gospel church?"

"You mean there might be something illegal about them?"

"I'm suggesting that they may not be what they appear. I don't like what I've been hearing *about* them and *from* them. Some of the clergy in town are concerned. They've been renting space in the basement of the Baptist Church, but the Baptists have canceled their lease. They'll need another place to meet."

"If you're suggesting that they want my church, they can forget it," said T.J.

"Your church?" demanded Fallon, jumping to her feet. Derrick pulled her back to her seat.

"The Old Reformed Church," amended T.J. in icy politeness.

"I've heard nothing that points to that as an option they're considering. However, I have been wondering if they might have motives that don't include our moral salvation." Father Andrews blushed a bright pink. "I don't want to be the cause of dissension, but—"

There were supressed smiles around the room. In his younger days, Father Andrews had been a political activist, marched against the Vietnam War and espoused the limited use of birth control, much to the dismay of the diocese. He had been summoned before the church council more than once for his outspoken views.

"Perhaps it would behoove us to do a background check. I tried to do a little questioning on my own, but Brother Bartholomew was either defensive or evasive. Little is known about them except that they came from the City. They are recruiting young families and single men and women at an alarming rate. Not that we should complain; our flocks are dwindling these days. But I wonder . . ."

"I'll check with New York and see if they have a rap sheet on them," said Judd. "Do you think there might be brainwashing involved?"

Father Andrews pursed his lips. "I wouldn't go so far as to say that. I have no proof. But at the risk of sounding unchristian, there's something not quite right about them. My opinion of course."

"We'll check it out," said Judd.

"Is there any other discussion?" asked Mary Elisabeth. "I think we should have a vote on whether to continue with our plans."

"A vote isn't necessary," broke in Derrick. "I can't believe you would let a little thing like this interfere with something so important."

"We all understand its importance, I assure you," said Mary Elisabeth. "Most of us have lived in this town for a very long time."

Fallon stood up again. "Derrick is just as concerned as any of you. And he knows better than all of you how to make the marathon a success."

Derrick smiled and pulled her back down.

"Well, you do," Fallon insisted.

"If there's no further discussion—"

"Just one thing." It was T.J. All eyes turned to him. He

cleared his throat. "Something has come up. Uh—" He ran his tongue over his lips. "With the restoration, I mean—I must really insist—"

"Spit it out, man," laughed Derrick.

T.J. narrowed his eyes. His voice lowered. "New discoveries have been made in the course of the restoration. It may be necessary to restrict access to additional parts of the property."

"What parts of the property?" asked Mary Elisabeth.

"At the moment, it appears that the summer kitchen and part of the hayride route may be involved. I'll know better in a few days."

"But that's where Adam is telling his ghost stories," argued Janey.

"Is that what you were doing in the woods?" asked Stella. "There can't be enough left of that old kitchen to warrant reconstruction. It's been used for campfires and weenie roasts for years. There's probably not one original stone left unturned, so to speak."

"I believe we've strayed from the point," said Judd. "As I understand it, the restoration is confined to the house, the church and possibly the outbuildings, not the grounds." He looked to Mary Elisabeth for confirmation.

"I'm afraid I don't know. Howard was our legal advisor. Perhaps someone could find out and report back at our next meeting."

"There are two weeks left," said Stella. "Let's not throw a wrench in the works. I move that we continue with the preparations for the marathon."

"But . . ." said T.J .

"I second the motion," said Judd.

"But . . ."

"All in favor?"

The vote was unanimous, except for one abstention by T.J., and the meeting adjourned.

Judd stopped Lindy at the door. "I'd like to talk to you and Mary Elisabeth. In her office."

She looked at Rebo.

"You go ahead. I'll be at the church."

Father Andrews stopped as he passed them. "I think I'll go across the road and have another talk with Brother Bartholomew."

"Do you think that's a good idea, Father?" asked Judd. "Maybe I should check them out first."

"I could go with him," volunteered Rebo.

Father Andrews looked mystified. "I'm not sure that would be a good idea."

"What?" Rebo looked down. He was wearing black parachute pants, a faded Marilyn Manson T-shirt and a brown bomber jacket. He touched his ear. "Is it the earring? I can take it off."

"On second thought," said Father Andrews, "I'd be glad of your company." Eyes twinkling, he motioned Rebo out of the room.

"I wonder what he's up to?" said Judd as he watched them leave.

Lindy followed him to the sunporch, where Mary Elisabeth was waiting. He closed the door.

"The body has been located. By the Passaic County police, I'm relieved to say. They'll be taking charge of the investigation."

"So it really was a man?" asked Lindy.

"Yes, unfortunately."

"Do they know how he died? It was an accident, wasn't it?"

"It's nearly impossible to tell with a drowning. And the body was so beat up by the time they discovered it, that they'll have to do a full autopsy before they can even begin to determine what happened. Officially, he isn't our problem, but as you've probably guessed, there's been a leak. I think that's what the sign was about."

"And if they know—" began Lindy.

"Pretty soon everyone else will," said Judd. "Thank God for Adam Crabtree. At least we won't have the onus of the investigation."

"Since we have enough trouble already," said Mary Elisabeth.

"Now, Mary Elisabeth, everything will turn out all right. The Passaic police will make an ID, we'll run a check on old Brother Bart and gang and T.J. will find whatever he thinks he's discovered long before Mischief Night."

"They haven't identified him?" asked Lindy.

"Not yet. No identification was found on him. No wallet, nothing. They're running his prints through AFIS but that could take a few days."

"But what about his poor family?"

"No one around here has filed a missing persons report. My guess is he's from up north somewhere, and the current washed him down."

Lindy thought that might be wishful thinking on Judd's part.

"But it was an accident?" asked Mary Elisabeth. She had gone pale beneath her makeup.

Judd leaned against the edge of the desk. "Probably. It will be treated as a homicide until cause of death can be determined. If it can be determined."

"Homicide?"

"Just a technical term for death under questionable circumstances. Nothing to worry about."

"I'm not worried," said Mary Elisabeth.

"Good. You shouldn't be. But let's keep this to ourselves for now. The details will come out soon enough."

"Stella and Evelyn already know," said Lindy. "And Rebo. I thought he should know what he was getting into."

Judd gave her a reproachful look.

"I didn't tell Evelyn and Stella. And actually, Stella told Rebo. I just explained what happened."

"Evelyn guessed something was wrong," said Mary Elisabeth. "I don't think I told her, but somehow she learned what had happened. I guess from me."

"Well, no harm done. It was bound to get out sooner or later." Judd stood up. "But the less speculation, the better."

"Don't worry. I'd like to forget the whole thing," said Lindy.

"Good."

"But what about Adam Crabtree?"

"We talked to him first thing. Didn't have much to say. I don't think we need to worry about him blabbing."

"Isn't it illegal to move a body?"

"Only if it's a crime scene. Well, I gotta be going." Judd nodded and took his leave.

Mary Elisabeth let out a sigh as soon as the door closed behind him. She picked up a pen and began toying with it, avoiding Lindy's eyes. Lindy shifted uncomfortably. This was the first time they had really been alone. She didn't want to talk about the body. She knew she should say something about the divorce, but she dreaded that topic almost as much. She took a deep breath.

"Stella told me about you and Howard. I'm so sorry."

Mary Elisabeth nodded but continued to play with the pen.

"I know Fallon has always been a problem, but—"

"You don't know what it's like. Howard is a stranger when she's around. I just can't live like that anymore."

"But you love him, and he loves you."

"It isn't enough. Fallon will always be first with him. I could live with that, if she weren't so destructive, but she's always done everything she could to drive us apart."

"But he's never let her succeed."

"Until now." Mary Elisabeth stabbed the pen tip into the blotter.

"He sent that check," said Lindy. "I think he's trying to tell you something."

"Just as a bribe to make me put Fallon on a committee." Mary Elisabeth gasped. "The check. I forgot to deposit it."

"I thought that's where you were yesterday morning."

"I meant to go, but I had another appointment, and with this drowning business—I forgot. I'd better take it to the bank now." She took her purse from the drawer and stood up. "Someone needs to call Howard about the terms of the restoration. I don't think I could talk to him just now. Would you mind terribly?"

"I'd be glad to," said Lindy, though talking to a friend reeling from divorce was the last thing she wanted to do. "I'll call him."

She waited until the door closed behind Mary Elisabeth, then shifted the Rolodex around and found Howard's office number. She used Mary Elisabeth's private line to make the call.

Howard's secretary put her through, unlike some secretaries she could think of, and she made an appointment to see him the following day. The conversation was brief. Howard's words were stilted and cautious. It was apparent that he didn't want to see her, but he couldn't deny her a business appointment.

She wasn't looking forward to it, either. But Stella's statement about choosing sides had stuck in her mind, and she was determined to remain friends with both Mary Elisabeth and Howard, in spite of their estrangement.

Chapter Nine

Lindy emerged from the sunporch just in time to see Evelyn enter the house and go into the kitchen. She paused for a discreet moment, then followed.

Evelyn was sitting alone at the table. She looked up when Lindy entered.

"We missed you at the meeting," Lindy said as she crossed to the coffee urn.

"I couldn't make it. I was swamped with work." She motioned Lindy to join her at the table.

Right, thought Lindy. Consulting. That was a handy catch word for just about anything. She took her cup to the table and sat down. "Did you happen to see Judd when you came in?"

"I just got here. He was already gone."

"They found the body in Passaic County."

Evelyn lifted an eyebrow.

Lindy gave her a look. "I know you know what happened. Judd asked us not to talk about it."

"I have no intention of discussing it. I think we should let the matter rest."

Just the slightest stress on the "we," but as always, her tone of voice put Lindy on the defensive. Was Evelyn privy to her past history?

The kitchen door swung open and Janey entered, followed by Rebo carrying a cardboard box filled with paper. He dropped it on the table.

"Flyers for the marathon," Janey explained. "I thought I would fold and address them here. Your friend was kind enough to carry them in for me." She put the kettle on and took her tea-making equipment out of the cupboard.

Lindy picked up one of the flyers. "They're nice," she said. She handed it to Evelyn, trying to defrost the chilly atmosphere that had descended between them.

"Mmm," said Evelyn.

"Derrick designed them," said Janey. "Though if you ask me, the ones Bryan Morrison designed were better. There's a mock-up on the bottom, if you want to see it."

Lindy rifled through the flyers and found the one designed by Bryan. It was much better than Derrick's and captured the spirit of the evening perfectly. "This is great. Why didn't they use it?"

"They were going to until Derrick came up with his 'concept,' and one of the ladies on the committee insisted we use his idea. Typical." The water began to boil. Janey spent the next few minutes busy with tea preparations.

Lindy returned Bryan's design to the box. "I saw some of Adam Crabtree's teas at the Madden farm. There certainly were a lot of varieties to choose from."

"Adam's so clever," Janey agreed. "This one is for purifying the blood. He's given me others to help me sleep, for energy, to help with the pain." She paused, looking embarrassed. "I don't know what I would do without him. He's been a godsend. And not just to me. He's helped so many people. If he decided to market them, he could make a fortune. But of course Adam doesn't care about money."

"Everyone cares about money," said Evelyn.

"A young thing like you shouldn't be so jaded," said Janey.

This won a half smile from Evelyn.

Janey sat down and began folding the flyers. Lindy joined in, then Rebo, and finally Evelyn.

"Did you go with Father Andrews?" asked Lindy.

Rebo tossed a folded flyer onto the table and reached for another. "The man's an avenging angel in sheep's clothing. Not that it did any good." He grinned. "He was being very tactful, until one of the little snot-noses asked if I was the devil, 'cause Brother Bart said the devil was black."

Evelyn made an undignified sound in her throat.

Rebo slanted her a look. "Thought you'd like that. Anyway, the politic padre went ballistic, in a Christian way, of course. Said the role of the church was to spread love, not distrust. Then he threatened the little weasel."

"He threatened Brother Bartholomew?"

"Well, what do you call it when you ask someone to uphold the precepts of the universal church, and that someone raises his fist to you, and you grab it and twist his arm behind his back, saying the arm of the Lord is longer than man's?"

"I'd call that a salutary reminder," said Janey and smiled with genuine amusement.

"Father Andrews actually did that?" asked Lindy.

"Yep. And that's when I came to the rescue." He flexed his biceps.

"Okay, out with it," said Lindy.

"The mob was advancing on us when I delivered my vilest gypsy curse, did a little hand-jive thing, and told them I was Old Blackie. Then I ordered them to leave the marathon alone."

"You'd better watch your back," said Evelyn.

"That's what the padre said, but while we were making a strategic retreat, Brother Bart was doing some fancy back-pedaling of his own. I figure by the time he's dug himself out of that hole, the marathon will be over."

They fell into silence, broken only by the folding and stacking of flyers. As the finished stack became larger, other sounds began drifting from the other side of the wall.

"Do I hear the Van Cleef ghost?" asked Rebo. He got up to listen at one of the barricaded doors. "Where does this lead to?"

"Canning porch, servants' staircase, and inside door to the cellar, but they're off limits," said Evelyn without looking up from her folding.

"Oh, yeah?" Rebo began rattling the board nailed across the door.

"No," said Lindy. "T.J. will have a coronary."

"What do think he's found?"

"Evidence that George Washington slept here?" she surmised, only half facetiously.

"Or at least one of the many women he slept with may have slept here," offered Evelyn.

"I hope he doesn't turn up evidence that the Van Cleefs were British sympathizers. That wouldn't do," said Janey.

They continued to speculate on the historical significance of T.J.'s new discovery while they folded and stacked.

The box was empty when Stella came in. "Lunchtime, girls, and Rebo."

Lindy looked up at the wall clock. It was already past one. They were surrounded by piles of tri-fold papers.

Lindy and Evelyn stuffed them back into the box and Rebo moved it aside.

Stella disappeared into the refrigerator and came out with a Tupperware container. "Don't tell me none of you brought lunch."

"I'll have you know I had the foresight to make sandwiches," said Lindy. She rummaged in her bag until she found the paper lunch bag, buried beneath her wallet and address book. "A little the worse for wear, I'm afraid." She pulled out a misshapen sandwich and handed it to Rebo.

"Looks like Salvador Dali made this," he said.

"Sorry."

He took a bite. "Deelish."

Stella shook her head in mock consternation. "Really, Lindy. I hope you packed better school lunches than you did that. You should look around for an old lunch pail." She looked at Evelyn.

"I had a late breakfast."

"I ate at home," said Janey.

"Well, no matter. I have a surprise for dessert."

Lindy groaned.

"Crème brûlée. My specialty." Stella laid out silverware and a linen napkin, flipped the top off the container and arranged the contents on a plate. "Chicken salad, anyone? Made with water chestnuts and three different peppers." She sat down and began to eat with relish, while she chatted about a party she had catered the weekend before.

The microwave beeped.

"Black bean soup?"

They all watched Stella dig into her soup. After a few bites, she paused, spoon in the air and made a face. "I must have been daydreaming when I put this batch together." She got up and put the bowl next to the sink.

"And now for the *piéce de resistance*." She reached into the fridge. "My crème brû—"

She groaned and fell against the counter. The bowl she was holding toppled over. Her face went slack for a moment; then a horrible grimace spasmed across her features. She grabbed her stomach and lurched forward. Her body heaved and she vomited into the sink, then toppled to the ground.

"Call 911," ordered Evelyn.

Lindy ran from the room to the hall phone.

When she returned, Stella had been sick again. Rebo was cleaning up the floor around her, while Janey held a pan near her head. Evelyn was putting Stella's dishes into a paper bag.

Stella lay in a fetal position on the floor. Spasms wracked her body, and she vomited into the bowl Janey held.

At last they heard the sirens of the ambulance in the driveway. In a matter of minutes, the emergency squad had examined Stella and strapped her onto a gurney. Evelyn handed the paper bag she had packed with Stella's Tupperware to one of the EMT's, talking urgently as they wheeled Stella toward the ambulance.

They watched from the door as the ambulance pulled away, siren blaring. Janey clung to Lindy's arm, her frail fingers cutting into Lindy's flesh. Lindy absently patted her hand.

When the ambulance was out of sight, Evelyn turned and walked back into the house. Lindy, Janey and Rebo followed.

The kitchen was vile smelling. Rebo opened the window and porch door to dispel the odor. Janey began rinsing the sink. Lindy picked up the crème brûlée that lay on its side on the counter and started to return it to the fridge. A piece of paper was taped to the top.

"What's this?" She put down the bowl and ripped the paper away.

"Some kind of instructions?" asked Rebo.

"Somebody's idea of a joke," said Lindy. "And not very funny."

"Let me see." Evelyn pulled it from Lindy's fingers and read:

"There once was a lady who sat
Wrapped up in the folds of her fat
She scared off her fella
Too bad for old Stella
And that was the sad end of that"

"Oh, dear," said Janey and pressed her hand to her chest. "That's awful. Who would do such a horrible thing?"

"Has the bowl been here all morning?" asked Evelyn, moving to peer inside the refrigerator.

Lindy shrugged. "I guess so. We were all at the meeting. Stella must have put it in before that."

"Does she have any enemies?" asked Rebo.

"Everyone likes Stella," said Janey.

"Not everyone," said Evelyn. She picked up the paper and slid it into her pocket. "I'm going to the hospital. I'll call as soon as I know anything." She paused at the door and frowned at them. "Someone has a lot to answer for." Without waiting for a response, she slipped out the door and closed it behind her.

"I think I'll take a little rest," said Janey.

Chapter Ten

Lindy and Rebo walked Janey to the parlor and settled her into a wing chair. Lindy was only half paying attention. Evelyn's last words were rattling in her brain. *Someone has a lot to answer for.*

She tucked a brightly colored afghan around Janey's legs. "I'll let you know as soon as we hear from the hospital." Janey closed her eyes and immediately fell asleep, sitting upright, ankles primly crossed, hands folded in her lap. Her face was so transparent that she looked lifeless.

They tiptoed away and went to sit on the front porch.

"Evelyn thinks someone poisoned Stella," said Lindy.

"I picked up on that. Didn't take her long to reach that conclusion, did it? And the way she had those containers ready to go to the hospital. Is she a nurse or something?"

"She says she's a consultant."

"What does she consult?"

"Nobody seems to know."

"She acts suspicious, if you ask me."

"It's just the way she is," said Lindy. "Kind of hard to get to know."

"She was the only one not at the meeting." Rebo raised both eyebrows.

"Jeez, you have a devious mind, but you're right. She *was* the only one not there."

"Floaters and poisoners. Hell, who needs the movies when I've got you?" He was smiling, but his voice was serious.

Mary Elisabeth's Lincoln pulled into the parking lot, and they went to meet her. Fallon and Derrick, carrying the ubiquitous Starbucks cup, came from the back of the church at the same time. Derrick jogged up the church steps, and Fallon clambered after him. They disappeared inside.

"It's absolutely ridiculous the way she fawns on him," said Mary Elisabeth. "The man is probably stewed on caffeine. Not that he doesn't deserve whatever he gets. And now they're in there annoying Melanie. Derrick kibitzing and making useless suggestions, while Fallon hovers over him making sure he doesn't pay more attention to Melanie than he does to her. Stupid child."

"Mary Elisabeth, Stella's been taken to the hospital," said Lindy. "Evelyn is with her."

The telephone rang from the house, and the three of them rushed inside, Mary Elisabeth asking questions as they went.

Lindy picked up the receiver.

"It's Evelyn. Stella's okay. They had to pump her stomach, and she's been checked into the hospital overnight. I called a neighbor to watch the children."

"What was it?" asked Lindy.

"Are there people within hearing distance? Just say yes or no."

"Yes."

"Just say that it was food poisoning. The soup contained a dangerous amount of *Cephaelis ipecacuanha*."

Lindy couldn't even begin to pronounce the name, but she recognized part of it. She shielded the receiver with her hand and lowered her voice. "Is that like ipecac?"

"Yes, but it will take further analysis before they know whether it was the over-the-counter kind or emetine, an alkaloid extracted directly from the plant itself."

Good Lord, thought Lindy. Did ipecac plants grow around here? Her mind flashed on the bag of herbal tea in Janey's purse, then on the image of Adam Crabtree's teas lined up on the Maddens' shelf. "You don't really think that—"

"I don't think Stella put it into her own soup. Which means someone else did. In large enough quantities to be fatal."

"But—"

"But I don't think you should talk about it." Evelyn hung up.

Then why tell me about it? Perplexed, Lindy replaced the receiver and turned to see Janey standing in the doorway, supporting herself on the frame.

"How is Stella?"

"Just a case of food poisoning," said Lindy, chafing at the lie. "She's going to be fine."

Rebo narrowed his eyes at her, but didn't say anything.

"The limerick," whispered Janey. "It was a warning." She swayed on her feet.

Lindy reached to steady her, but Janey waved her away.

"What is she talking about?" asked Mary Elisabeth.

"Just a silly joke that someone played on Stella," said Lindy. "I really think you should go home, Janey."

Janey hesitated. She seemed confused.

And who isn't, thought Lindy.

"I'll drive you," said Mary Elisabeth.

"I'll be glad to," said Lindy. "It's on my way. And I have to get going anyway. Are you coming, Rebo?"

"I think I'll stay here and sit in on Melanie's rehearsal, but I'll walk you outside."

He helped Janey to the Volvo. As soon as she was safely stowed inside, he turned to Lindy. "What the hell is going on?"

"Someone put ipecac in Stella's food," she whispered. "They don't know whether it was the kind that you buy at the drugstore or from a plant."

"You mean, like did the pole-vaulting storyteller suddenly take up cooking?"

"And if he did—"

"Do the floater and the spewer have something in common?"

"The fl—the drowned man was probably not even from around here."

"Betcha he was."

Lindy got into the car and Rebo slammed the door. "I've got to go back to the city tonight. Are you going to be okay?"

"Of course. Anyway, I'm going to the city, too."

"Hmm. Can I guess—"

"Nope." She backed up and drove away before he could guess. But when she looked in the rearview mirror, he was grinning and doing a mating dance in the parking lot.

They were silent as Lindy navigated the narrow streets of downtown and stopped in front of Janey's shingled Cape Cod. It was painted a light yellow with sky-blue shutters. The front yard was small, but had once been a lovely garden. Now the grass was brown, and weeds choked the perennials beds. Overgrown hemlocks and yews grew along the driveway.

Janey made no move to get out of the car. Lindy was about to get out and open the door for her, when Janey spoke.

"Why didn't you want me to say anything about the limerick?"

Lindy contemplated the steering wheel, avoiding Jane's eyes. "I'm not sure. I just know that Evelyn didn't want to worry Mary Elisabeth. I didn't mean to cut you off so rudely."

Janey's mouth curved into a tired smile. "My dear, I've spent thirty years teaching high school students. That wasn't even close to rude."

"Still—"

"Evelyn thinks someone poisoned Stella's food, doesn't she?"

Lindy shrugged.

"You're not very good at dissimulating, Lindy."

"I really don't know what Evelyn thinks, but she seems to have a plan."

"She certainly took control of the situation, didn't she?" said Janey.

"Yes, she did. Do you know what she really does for a living?"

"You know as much about her as I do. She's not a very open person."

"No, she isn't."

"Adam doesn't use poisonous herbs in his teas. If that's what Evelyn's thinking, she can forget it." Janey frowned. "Or if she thinks I would do something so heinous—"

"I'm sure she's thinking no such thing," managed Lindy, startled by the non sequitur.

Exhaustion passed across Janey's face. "An interesting syntax, Lindy, but if you'll excuse me, I'm really feeling a bit tired. No need to see me to the door. I can manage."

Lindy watched her climb stiffly out of the car and waited until she was inside. Then she drove home ruminating on the astuteness of the dying English teacher and the odd happenings at the Van Cleef farm.

Bill was sitting at the bar when Lindy walked into Paparelle's at eight o'clock that evening. She recognized him immediately even though the lighting was muted. She smiled, thinking of all the times she had seen him in half-light. But she had come to know that face whether she could see it distinctly or not. The clear blue eyes, the hair cut short at the sides and longer on top. He brushed it away from his forehead, but it never stayed in place. It was one of the few hints at the passion that lay beneath his subdued exterior.

He looked up and saw her, his smile a flash of white teeth above a black sweater and gray jacket. He looked good.

She smiled back and crossed to where he was sitting. He stood up and leaned over to kiss her cheek.

"Hi," she said. He smelled good. He felt good, too.

"Hi, yourself." He moved away. "Our table's ready." He led her toward the dining area.

Paparelle's was one of Bill's favorite restaurants. Quiet, small, with plenty of space between the tables, good food, and an extensive wine list.

The maitre d' pulled Lindy's chair back and spoke to Bill. "We have an excellent Sole in Escabeche tonight. Sautéed and laced with a lemon-orange sauce, a dash of tabasco and coriander. Very piquante. Very delicious."

Bill raised his eyebrows to Lindy.

"Sounds wonderful."

The maitre d' snapped his fingers at a waiter who brought over an ice bucket and poured out two glasses of white wine.

Bill lifted his glass. Lindy lifted hers. They drank, looking across the table at each other.

"I brought you a bottle of wine from Spain," said Lindy. "But I forgot to bring it."

Bill's eyes twinkled.

"What?"

"Nothing. I've missed you."

"You have?" Well, at least somebody had.

"Yep."

There was a moment of silence while they got used to each other's company. It wasn't awkward, just . . . hesitant.

By the time the waiter brought their salads, they were chatting congenially. About Lindy's tour, Bill's nephews, Rebo and the marathon.

She wanted to tell Bill what had happened in the few days she had been home. About the drowned man, about Stella, about Glen not calling. She told him about Biddy and Jeremy instead.

"He'll get around to it," said Bill. "Better to be careful in the beginning. They've waited this long—" He didn't finish the statement because the waiter came to remove their salad plates. She hoped he would finish what he had been about to say. That was the only way she really found out about his feelings, by gleaning them out of ordinary conversation.

He didn't continue, but lifted his wineglass. "Good—dry, but not too thin."

Lindy watched him return the glass to the table. His long fingers elegant. His movement refined. Bill enjoyed good wine, good food. He was a cultured man. A cultured man with a quick temper. An athletic man who could hold his own in a fight.

His ex-wife had been an actress who longed for better things. How could it get better than this man who sat across from her? She hoped the dentist she had married was worth it.

"What?"

She was startled out of her ruminations and embarrassed by the turn her thoughts had taken. "Uh, I was just wondering how you stay in such good shape."

He grinned, that open smile he had. "I hit the gym every morning and the handball court three times a week. One thing about leaving the police force, I don't have time to sit around the donut shop."

"Do you miss it?"

"Sometimes. What have you been up to besides the marathon?"

A neat change of subject, as always when he didn't want to discuss himself. His powers of deflection were finely honed.

"Not much." She took time to cut a piece of tender fish.

"Must be something."

She looked up in surprise. "Why do you say that?"

"You barely touched your salad, and you've cut four pieces of sole without eating any of them."

"Oh." She speared the fish and popped it into her mouth.

"Might as well come clean. What's happened?"

She swallowed. "Something has happened, but after we decided to have dinner."

"What does that have to do with it?"

"I don't want you to think I only call you when I need help."

"Okay, I won't. What happened?" He leaned forward on both elbows.

She told him about Stella and the limerick.

"It sounds like a vicious prank. At least there's no body," he said, relieved.

"Well . . ."

He lowered his forehead to his hand, then quirked his head, looking at her sideways. "Is there?"

"I don't want to be yelled at."

He stifled what was probably an expletive. "I'll try to stay calm."

She told him about the drowned man and how Adam Crabtree pushed him into the stream.

"So that's it. I wondered why you called."

"That's not why I called."

"Do you want coffee?"

"Dammit, Bill."

He waited, one eyebrow raised.

She wanted to say that she called because she had missed him, too. That she enjoyed his company. That she wanted to see him for himself. But that would be admitting too much. Might send their friendship hurtling into something that would eventually kill it.

"Sure, coffee's fine."

They drank in silence.

"Please don't be mad at me."

He pushed his chair back. "I'm not mad."

The waiter hurried over with the check and placed it at Bill's elbow.

Lindy reached for it. "My treat. After all, I asked you."

Bill slid it out of her reach. "Afraid it will look like a date?"

He placed his credit card inside the folder and summoned the waiter. He didn't look at her, but the irony in his words hit the mark. He was angry, and he had every right to be. They walked in silence to the garage where she had left her car.

While they were waiting to cross 74th Street, he pulled her into a hug. "I'm sorry I'm prickly tonight. I'm preoccupied with having my nephews here for such a long time. I'm not used to kids."

Because his own son had been raised by another man. It was enough to make her hate dentists. She gave him a squeeze. They stood that way while the light changed to Walk, Don't Walk, and back again. She felt safe and cared for—and needy and sad. God, she was a lousy friend. Here she was so worried about her own problems that she hadn't even considered his.

"I'm sure you'll be fine." She laughed. "Uncle Bill. I like that."

"Will you be all right with your marathon?" His smile was open and generous again. She had been forgiven.

She nodded. "I have a feeling I'll be seeing a lot more of Rebo than is strictly necessary for the Follies."

They waited, arm in arm, for the garage attendant to bring her car. Bill held the door while she got in.

"I thought I might take the boys to the zoo on Sunday. Would you be interested in coming along?"

"Think you might need backup?"

He grinned. "Yep."

"I'd love to."

"I'll call you on Saturday with the details. And Lindy, if you run into any more bodies, call me."

"Thanks."

He closed the door, and she drove up Amsterdam Avenue feeling reprieved and just a little lonely.

Chapter Eleven

The marathon was turning into a full-time job. It was only nine-thirty when Lindy passed the picketers and turned into the farmhouse grounds the next morning. There were fewer of them today, and Lindy was glad to see that most of them were adults.

It was early and there were only two cars in the lot: Mary Elisabeth's Lincoln and Father Andrews's Volkswagen. She parked the Volvo and, ignoring the angry shouts from across the road, hurried into the house.

She met Mary Elisabeth coming out of the dining room. "Have you seen Father Andrews?"

"His car is here," said Lindy.

"I know. He was supposed to meet me, but I can't find him." Mary Elisabeth wrung her hands. "I hope he isn't across the road trying to talk sense into those people. I don't trust them."

"I didn't see him when I drove by. Maybe he's at the church."

Mary Elisabeth shook her head, her eyes worried. "I

looked there first. He often goes in to reflect or pray. But he wasn't there."

"The kitchen?"

Mary Elisabeth crossed the hall without a word, Lindy close behind. One of the barricaded doors stood open, the wooden plank propped against the wall. Lindy stopped and peered inside. A shadow loomed out at her and she stumbled backward.

"I told you to stay—" T.J. stepped through the door, raising a hand encased in a heavy work glove. His hair was filled with dust and cobwebs, and his face was streaked with muddy sweat. "Oh, it's you."

Lindy peered past his shoulder, trying to get a look at what was beyond the door. He glanced behind him and slammed it shut.

"We were just looking for Father Andrews," said Mary Elisabeth.

"He was here earlier," said T.J. "He must be around somewhere. He said he was meeting you."

A muffled cry sounded from somewhere inside the house.

"What was that?" Lindy rushed out into the hall, followed by Mary Elisabeth and T.J. Sounds of a struggle came from the parlor. As soon as she stepped inside, Lindy saw the source of the commotion. The wing chair had been turned toward the window. The crocheted afghan writhed ghostlike from the other side. It took a moment for her to realize that the afghan was covering a figure, a seated figure, twisting against—ropes? He was tied to the chair. She bolted forward.

"Father Andrews?"

"Good Lord," gasped Mary Elisabeth from behind her.

T.J. was already grappling with the knot. He yanked the rope away, and Lindy pulled the afghan from Father Andrews's head.

Father Andrews sputtered and looked at her, owl-eyed. "What's this?" His voice was sleepy and confused.

Lindy was too astounded to speak.

"Someone tied you to the chair," said T.J. coming around to face the priest. "And with my rope. Of all the nerve."

"Must have dozed off." Father Andrews rubbed his eyes and pushed himself to his feet. He looked at the rope T.J. was holding and then at the afghan that Lindy was mechanically folding into a ball. "What a strange thing for someone to do," he said. "Some kind of joke, I suppose."

"Joke?" said T.J. "Who did this?"

Father Andrews blinked at him. "I have no idea. I must have been sleeping too soundly." He smiled apologetically. "The infirmities of old age."

"Absolute rot, Father. If you got more sleep, you wouldn't be so tired all the time."

"I'm sure you're right, Mary Elisabeth."

"What's that?" asked T.J., pointing to the afghan.

Lindy looked down. A square of paper was crumpled between the folds of wool. A shiver ran across her back. She stared at it, reluctant to touch it. Especially if it was what she thought it was.

T.J. reached across her and snatched it from the afghan. He smoothed it out and began to read, his voice curious at first and then becoming angry.

"There was an old priest drowned in sleep
Which kept him from thinking too deep
You might think his snoozin'
Would be quite amusin'
A sheperd who can't keep his sheep"

He looked from Lindy to Father Andrews.

Father Andrews blushed pink. "I suppose I do sleep too much."

"Nonsense," said Mary Elisabeth. "Just wait until I get my hands on the person who did this."

"It was merely a salutary reminder of my duties here on earth."

"Bull—" Mary Elisabeth's hand went to her mouth. "You

do more than anyone I know. Hospitals and prisons and hospice work. Then you spend night after night at that homeless shelter. You're exhausted. You should let someone help you."

"I'd gladly accept help, but people are busy, the clergy is spread thin. Those unfortunates need to know someone cares about them."

Mary Elisabeth started to protest.

Father Andrews patted her shoulder. "My job is to make the world a better place. And it won't be a better place until there's a place for everyone."

"The world won't be a better place until people stop playing these selfish, infantile, malicious pranks." T.J. crumpled the paper in disgust.

"I think we should keep that." Lindy tugged it out of his hand and put it in her jacket pocket. "Listen, I have to meet with Howard. I just stopped by to find out if you had any other questions."

Mary Elisabeth looked startled. "No, just what we talked about yesterday. I think that covers it."

"Are you sure you don't want to go with me?"

"No. I'll—just stay here and, um, talk to Father Andrews."

"Then I'll report back after lunch. Will Evelyn be here? I need to talk to her, too."

"She was going to the hospital this morning, then come by later. I'll tell her to wait for you." She hesitated. "Lindy?"

"Yes?"

"Nothing."

Lindy squeezed Mary Elisabeth's arm. "It will be all right. I'll be back in a couple of hours."

Howard Porter's law office was on the second floor of a downtown storefront, above a Danish bedding boutique and a Korean nail salon. Lindy had to circle the block twice before she found a place to park.

A woman carrying several shopping bags stopped at an

SUV, and Lindy pulled up behind it. She waited while the woman deposited her packages onto the roof and began searching a voluminous handbag for her keys. She had to keep brushing her hair out of her face in order to see, but finally came up with a key ring. She blipped the alarm system off and blipped the car doors open, then began loading her items into the backseat.

Lindy drummed her fingers impatiently on the steering wheel. The woman had to know she was waiting, but she made no pretense of hurrying. She got behind the wheel and sat, while Lindy fumed. This delay was going to make her late, and she didn't want to keep Howard waiting. She was uncertain of her reception as it was.

The woman proceeded to apply lipstick, looking into the rearview mirror. She fluffed her hair, then put her cell phone to her ear. *This is why people go to the mall*, Lindy thought. There were always plenty of parking places at the mall.

Finally the brake lights came on. After a few interminable seconds, the woman began to inch the SUV back and forth attempting to get out of the space. Lindy was tempted to get out and help her.

Jersey drivers, she thought. The woman had plenty of room to get out. If she drove a normal car, she would be able to see over the hood.

At last the car drove away and Lindy parallel parked with the speed of a New York cab driver. She grabbed her bag and raced across the street, stopping traffic with her hand.

She took the stairs two at a time, then paused outside the door to catch her breath. Putting on a smile she didn't feel, she opened the door.

The outer office was painted in a creamy blue with darker carpeting. Prints of seascapes hung along one wall above a leather couch. A coffee table held stacks of magazines.

Howard's secretary looked up from her Dictaphone and raised plucked eyebrows in welcome.

"Lindy Haggerty to see Mr. Porter."

The secretary announced her over the intercom. "Go right in. Mr. Porter is expecting you." She pointed to one of several doors to her left.

Howard rose and came from behind his desk when she entered. He was a slightly built man of average height. Gray wiry curls were cropped close to his scalp. His face was thin, today unusually so, and heavy bags draped his mild brown eyes.

"Lindy," he said formally and held out his hand.

She shook it, but leaned into him and kissed his cheek. "How are you?"

"Fine. Please have a seat." He motioned to the chair in front of the desk and returned to his own. "I understand you have some questions concerning the restoration guidelines."

Lindy swallowed. This was going to be harder than she thought. It was clear that Howard was going to treat her as a client instead of a friend. She began explaining their concerns.

"I'll have Ms. Holcart bring in the bequest agreement." He pressed the intercom and made the request. Then he looked at his desk. "I may as well tell you that I am no longer offering my services to the committee *gratis*. I'll read it over as a favor to you, but after that, I wash my hands of the business."

"Howard."

"If the committee doesn't come up with the stipulated funds by January first, the property will revert back to the estate. And subsequently to Adam Crabtree. It will remain in probate for quite some time, I can assure you. But it will be his, eventually. He can live there, sell it, burn it to the ground for all I care."

Ms. Holcart entered at that moment carrying a manila folder and placed it on his desk. She turned to Lindy. "Would you care for coffee or tea?"

"No. No, thank you," she stammered, hardly believing that this was the same man she had known for years.

Ms. Holcart left them, and Howard opened the folder with nervous hands. He kept his eyes on the contract for a few moments while Lindy studied his face. She had expected him to be angry and hurt. But it went much deeper than that. Howard was near the breaking point. He found the paragraph and read it in a precise, expressionless voice.

"In other words," said Lindy, struggling for composure. "If T.J. were to find original structures on the grounds, they would be included in the restoration?"

"That's correct. Now if you'll excuse me, I'm very busy. If you find that you have any more questions, one of the other partners will be able to assist you, but they will expect a consultation fee." He stood up. "Good-bye."

She fumbled for her bag, shaken by his rudeness. He was dismissing her as if she were an exasperating client. "I'll have Ms. Holcart bill this half hour to Glen's and my account." She stood up.

If she had slapped him, he couldn't have shown more shock. He turned abruptly and stared out the window.

"Howard," she said moving closer. "We all care about you and Mary Elisabeth very much. Talk to her. Things can still work out."

"She walked out on me. Without warning. She used me and now she doesn't need me."

"Oh, Howard, you know that it isn't true. Mary Elisabeth loves you. She's very unhappy."

"Then why did she leave?"

This had gotten more intense that she had planned, but it was too late to back down now. She chose her words carefully. "I know she was looking forward to having you all to herself, now that the kids are gone." She waited, wondering if he understood the unspoken meaning.

"But Fallon came back." His voice held such a tone of finality that Lindy's stomach flipped over. He turned from the window. "She's my only daughter. Her mother died when she was ten years old. I'm all she has left. I can't turn her away.

If Mary Elisabeth could just be more understanding. More patient. I'm sure she'll get herself together. She just needs another chance."

"She says you're going to buy the Van Cleef farm and give it to her as a wedding present. She and Derrick are planning to live there."

Howard looked at her incredulously. "That's ridiculous," he said finally. "I'm not buying her that farm. I don't know what gave her such an idea. I don't want to have anything to do with it. And I'll go to hell before that little twerp gets his hands on her trust fund." He frowned. "She thinks I'm going to buy it for her?"

"That's what she said. The day she brought your check. I don't know why she wants to—Howard, what is it? Are you all right? Shall I call Ms. Holcart?"

Howard shook his head and ran a hand across his face. "I'm all right." He didn't look all right. His face was colorless. "You said that . . . Fallon brought the check?"

"Yes. So that Mary Elisabeth would have to put her on the committee."

"Did you see it?"

"The check? Yes. It's quite generous." Especially from someone who had washed his hands of the marathon.

"How much was it for?"

"For fifty thousand," she said slowly. "Howard, are you sure you're okay?"

"I didn't write it. I just got off the phone with Mary Elisabeth. The bank had called. I accused her of forging the check."

"Didn't she tell you?"

"I hung up on her." His eyes widened and he blinked several times, then he slumped back against the window sill. Good Lord, the man was going to cry.

Lindy averted her eyes. She shouldn't have gotten involved. And she was so angry with Fallon that it was hard to sympathize with Howard. Well, it was too late now. In for a penny in for a pound.

"Fallon forged that check, Howard. It was a bribe. And Mary Elisabeth endured the humiliation in front of her friends so that you wouldn't be hurt. You're not being fair. Fallon doesn't care about the marathon. She and Derrick have their own plans for the Van Cleef farm."

"Why? What could she possibly want with that property?"

Lindy clenched her teeth. She shouldn't be drawn into this. She knew that old saying about killing the messenger. The words came out anyway. "Because she's jealous. She's always been jealous. She's made Mary Elisabeth's life miserable, but she endured it for you. She needs you as much as Fallon does. You're being unreasonable. Just talk to her. Doesn't she deserve at least that?" She clamped her hand over her mouth and backed away. "Howard, I'm sorry. I shouldn't have said that."

He shook his head. "It's too late for talk." He got to his feet and began gathering papers. "If you'll excuse me."

Lindy walked slowly, sadly out of the office.

She stood on the sidewalk, shaking. She should never have gotten involved. It had done absolutely nothing, except upset Howard. And how was she to face Mary Elisabeth after what had just transpired? At least she could tell her that she had straightened out the misunderstanding about the check. Misunderstanding. What an insipid word for such a horrible situation.

She needed time to calm down before returning to the farm. She started to go into a nearby coffee bar, but after looking at the name, she opted for Bagel's Bounty, several doors away.

She ordered a cappuccino and a sesame bagel and sat down at a table by the window. She was already sick of the marathon, and the real work hadn't even begun. This was absolutely the last committee she'd serve on. Always rife with petty jealousies, power struggles, frazzled nerves—and now this. Better just to ask for donations and stay at home. Not that the idea of home was too appealing at the moment.

She jumped when she saw a face peering in at her from the window. Evelyn hurried inside and sat down.

"Mary Elisabeth sent me to stop you."

"Too late."

"It wouldn't have been if your cell phone had been turned on."

"Well, at least he's been disabused about who forged the check. It was Fallon."

"Mary Elisabeth came to the same conclusion. She thinks Howard knew that Fallon forged his name, and he's using it as an excuse to destroy the marathon, because he's angry with her. She actually went so far as to say that he would sabotage the event and give the property to Fallon, just to get back at her."

"This is getting totally out of hand," said Lindy. "Howard has no intention of buying the property. He said he'd go to hell before he let Fallon marry Derrick. Though if you ask me, he's in hell already."

"Well, Mary Elisabeth doesn't know that. When I left she was on her way to ream out Fallon."

"God, I hate committees."

Evelyn gave her a considering look. "I visited Stella at the hospital this morning. She's pretty wiped out but they're letting her go home this afternoon. Mary Elisabeth told me about Father Andrews. Do you have the limerick?"

"In my pocket."

"May I see it?"

"Sure." Lindy pushed it across the table.

Evelyn looked up. "Shepherd is misspelled." She showed the limerick to Lindy.

"You're right. I didn't notice before."

"I'd like to keep this."

"Why?"

Evelyn didn't answer, but slipped the paper into the outside pocket of her handbag.

Lindy narrowed her eyes. "Do you have a theory?"

Evelyn looked at her with surprise. "About what?"

"About who wrote those."

"I have no idea. Tell me about the drowning victim you found."

"Judd told me not to talk about it."

"Judd is up to his eyeballs in work. He's relieved that they found the body in another county."

"How did you—"

Evelyn cut off her question with a brusque movement of her hand. "It was obvious from his expression of relief yesterday. But he's right. You shouldn't talk about it."

Lindy frowned. Evelyn seemed to be taking charge again. Everything about the woman set off alarm bells in her head. "Who are you?" she blurted.

"Just a committee member who wants things to succeed. It isn't easy for someone like me to be accepted in a town like this. Mary Elisabeth was kind to me. I'd like to help her out. And we can help her best by not getting into trouble. That's all."

Trouble? She had no intention of getting into trouble. But she understood Evelyn's desire to protect Mary Elisabeth. Mary Elisabeth inspired loyalty. She nodded her understanding.

"In that case, I think we should get back to the farmhouse," said Evelyn. "At least we can relieve Mary Elisabeth's mind about the check."

Lindy followed her out, still confused by Evelyn's behavior. Her insistence on taking the limericks, asking about the body, then not pressing Lindy for information. Did she think the two were related? And that bit about staying out of trouble. Had it been a warning not to meddle? Something didn't add up when it came to Evelyn Grimes.

It wasn't until she had pulled onto Main Street that it hit her. Evelyn couldn't have seen Judd's reaction to the body being found. She hadn't arrived at the farmhouse until after he had left.

Chapter Twelve

Rebo was sitting on the hood of the Black Beauty when Lindy pulled to a stop in the church parking lot a few minutes later. A rental van pulled into the slot next to her at the same time and three people jumped out. Lindy did a double take. Three people she knew. She shuddered to think how Rebo had managed to get the company costumer, production manager and lead dancer to work for free. No doubt he had told them the whole story.

She threw open the door to the Volvo and went to meet them. "Hi, guys. What brings you here?"

Rose Laughton stretched her arms out and yawned. She was close to six feet and all muscle. Today her strawberry-blond hair was pulled back into a thick ponytail, which was stuck through the opening of a Mets baseball cap. Rose was the best costumer in the business, wielded a mean needle and thread and, by her own admission, was good with feathers. She was also a good friend to have in a crisis.

"Nothing like a day in the country," she said.

"You too, Peter?" asked Lindy, turning a suspicious eye on the stage manager.

Peter's dark eyes flashed with embarrassment. He lifted one shoulder in a shrug. "Rebo twisted Mieko's arm, and she twisted mine."

Mieko Jones's face was expressionless. It always was except when she was performing. It had taken a good year before Lindy had learned to read the subtle body language that revealed her true feelings. She seemed relaxed today as she sauntered over and stood next to Peter; the top of her head barely reached his shoulder. Standing together, they were strikingly exotic. Peter, tall with jet-black hair and piercing, almost black eyes. Mieko, small and deceptively fragile looking, with oriental features beneath lustrous blue-black, shoulder-length hair.

Lindy wondered how Mieko had twisted Peter's arm. Was there something going on between the two of them? She smiled at the thought.

"Let's get a move on," said Rebo enthusiastically. He began shooing the others toward the church. "I've got a few things I want to try out."

They met Melanie coming down the church steps. "I thought I heard somebody. Thank God you're here," she said.

"Chill, my little green goddess. I've brought Rose and Peter to take care of your every costuming and production need." Rebo made the introductions. "And Mieko to take care of everything else."

"I hope it involves dry ice," said Melanie. "Derrick's having a truckload delivered next week. He and Fallon are inside, figuring out how to use it for *The Crucible*."

"Dry ice?" Peter looked disgusted. "Nobody uses dry ice anymore. Too messy and unreliable. If you want smoke, I'll bring out an Electralite."

"I don't want smoke," said Melanie. "I want them out of here."

"No prob, Mint Julep." Rebo shoved Rose toward the door and said in a stage aside, "Handy with a needle and a whiz at Aikido. His skinny white ass will be writing 'Surrender Dorothy' across the sky before you can click your heels together."

Melanie laughed. "I'm tempted. But actually I thought you were my cast. There's standardized testing all this week. Some of them had an early day and said they would come over to run some scenes."

"They went thataway," said Rebo, flicking his thumb in the air. "Saw them heading into the trees while I was waiting for the troops."

"Damn. I'll be right back." Melanie walked around the side of the church. Halfway to the back she broke into a run.

"Uh-oh," said Rebo and took off after her. The others followed automatically.

When they caught up to her, she was standing at the cemetery, peering up and down the road. She cut Rebo a sharp glance, a combination of fury and indecision.

"Try the springhouse," he said. It was the most subdued statement Lindy could remember hearing from him.

Melanie took off again, the others trotting after her. They had just reached the path to the springhouse when a giggle erupted from somewhere within the trees. Melanie froze, throwing her hands out to stop the others. Her head darted from side to side as she listened. Then she advanced more slowly down the path.

She stopped at the edge of the clearing and motioned for them to be quiet. A cluster of teenagers were huddled close together, sheltered by the stone wall of the building. Smoke curled up from the group. Lindy watched Darien inhale deeply from a cigarette and pass it to Val. Not a cigarette, Lindy amended. A joint.

"Damn it! Damn it!" cried Melanie and crashed through the underbrush to where the teens were standing.

Their heads jerked up, the faces etched in panic. Val tossed the joint toward the stream. It landed in a pile of dried leaves, which immediately began to smolder. Carl backed up, looking furtively about him. Darien reached into his pants pocket. Melanie tackled him, knocking him to the ground.

"Melanie. Stop!" yelled Lindy.

Rebo's hand closed around her arm. "Leave her alone."

"But she can get prosecuted for using physical force on a minor."

"I don't think anybody will be telling."

Melanie struggled with the boy until she pulled a plastic sandwich bag from his pocket. Then she hauled him to his feet. "Where did you get this?"

Darien shrugged and looked away. She shook him. He lunged for the Baggie. She grabbed him by the shirt front and held the Baggie over her head, out of reach. She turned to Val, then to Carl. "Where did this come from?"

They stared sullenly at the ground.

"Shall I show this to Judd? Tell him you broke your parole, Carl? Is that what you want? They'll send you to juvie hall this time. Want to know what they do with innocent suburban white boys in juvie?"

Apprehension replaced Carl's defiance. "Bought it from some kid," he said.

"Not good enough. Try again."

"I don't know his name."

"Empty your pockets, all of you."

"You can't do that," said Val.

"Watch me." Melanie grabbed Val's jacket. The pocket ripped away at the seam and a tube of lipstick and a pack of gum fell to the ground.

"I'll tell what you did," said Val, holding the pocket flap against her jacket. "My parents will sue."

"Good idea. Why don't we call Judd and tell him I tore your pocket. He can call your parents." Darien made another grab for the Baggie, but Melanie's foot slashed out across his legs. His knees buckled and he fell back onto his butt.

Lindy's chest tightened. Melanie would be sued six ways to Sunday if this got out.

"Who's got their cell phone? Let's call right now. Judd can be here in ten minutes." Melanie frowned, then put her finger to her chin, as if thinking. "Who's your understudy, Val? I think this is your third offense, too." She smiled suddenly. "At least I'll have plenty of time to replace you in the play. But it's kind of too bad, isn't it? The girls' correctional facilities are even worse than the boys. They'll probably cut off your hair while you're sleeping." She paused. "Or worse."

Val stared at her in horror. "Please, Melanie, please."

Melanie returned her look, then gave one to Darien. She stopped on Carl. Carl's eyes were filled with fear.

Melanie was going too far. Lindy wrenched free of Rebo and stepped forward.

Melanie threw out her arm and stopped her. "You think I'll let her come to your rescue? You poor misunderstood children? Think I'll let your parents take you home and buy you a new TV or car because that mean Miss Grant hurt your feelings? Think they can buy your way out of jail forever? And when they come up against a judge that wants to nail your ass, or when they just get fed up with you . . ." The sentence went unfinished, the ensuing silence more threatening than any verbal threat would have been. The three teens didn't move. They hardly seemed to take a breath.

When Melanie spoke again, her voice was soft, lower in pitch, the delivery chilling. "You know how much they like rich kids in jail? A lot—a real lot."

"It was just some kid," Darien blurted out, his voice shrill with panic. "I don't know his name. He doesn't even live in town. Honest."

"Please," sobbed Val. "He sells outside of Geno's Pizza. That's the only time we ever see him."

"What else does he sell?"

"Mainly grass and coke." Carl's voice was low and resigned.

"I'm going to have him picked up."

"You can't," cried Val. "We'll be in big trouble."

"You're already in big trouble." Melanie fingered the bag. "Can he name names?"

Val looked at the ground.

"You don't use your fucking credit cards, do you?"

"Of course not," muttered Darien.

"Then it's his word against yours?"

They all nodded.

Melanie looked at them for a long time—the air so thick with recrimination that even Lindy felt guilty. Then slowly Melanie walked to the stream. Keeping her eyes fixed on the group, she opened the Baggie and poured the contents out into the water. When it was empty, she threw in the bag.

Lindy thought of the sandwich bags among the debris under the bridge. God, was she naive.

"Get back to the church. Know your lines before rehearsal starts this afternoon. You'll spend tomorrow cleaning the choir loft and polishing the pews. I'll ask Father Andrews to supervise."

One of them groaned.

Melanie turned on them. "Which one of you doesn't want to clean the church tomorrow?"

No one said a word.

"That's what I thought. Get going."

Carl pulled Darien to his feet, and the three teenagers walked slowly back to the church.

"Hey," called Melanie.

They stopped, but didn't turn around.

"Just remember. You didn't get away with this." She stared after them until they were out of sight. Her hands were clenched into fists at her side.

Everyone spun around when the applause began. Derrick Justin stepped out from behind a tree. "Bravo, Melanie. That'll learn the little assholes." His face was a study in amusement.

He walked past the others, ignoring them, and stopped close to Melanie. He ran his hands down her arms. "I love watching you in action, babe."

Melanie pushed him away. "Get out of here, Derrick. Get the fuck out."

Derrick's smile of amusement broadened into a grin. "She scares me shitless."

"I'll show him shitless," muttered Rose.

Melanie raised her fist, and Derrick threw up his arms to shield his face. He was laughing.

"I'm going, I'm going." He flashed them a grin. "She's a beast, but you gotta love her."

"Now!" screamed Melanie.

Lindy could feel Rose poised for attack. "I think you'd better leave," she said.

"I think you're right." Derrick backed up a few paces, winked at Lindy, then glanced past her shoulder. "Fallon, doll. I wondered where you had gotten to." He brushed passed Lindy and strolled casually toward Fallon, who waited impatiently on the path behind them. He clasped her around the waist and began to guide her away.

She glared at Melanie over his shoulder. "You'd be nothing without Derrick," she screamed. "Nothing, do you hear?"

"Come on, honey. Melanie didn't mean anything. She understands I was just kidding her. We go back a long way." Derrick gave Melanie an insinuating smile.

"No. I'm the one who understands you." Fallon's boot heel must have sunk into the soil, because she swayed backward. Derrick caught her by the arm and pulled her close.

"You do. You do." He put his arm around her and started toward the road. Lindy could hear his laughter long after the two of them were out of sight.

Melanie dropped to the ground and buried her face in her hands. Rebo sat down beside her and put his arm around her shoulders.

If she keeps expending this amount of energy on her students, thought Lindy, *she'll be burned out before the year is out. And then where will these kids be?*

"Who was that sleazebag?" asked Rose.

"Derrick Justin, resident *artiste* and conceptual scuz bucket."

"And Fallon is the daughter, right?" asked Peter.

"God, how much did Rebo tell you guys?"

"Just enough to get us to work for free," said Rose. "Let's leave Rebo to shore up Wonder Woman and go someplace where we can talk."

Before they could leave, Melanie pushed Rebo away and jumped up. "You don't understand. It's happening again." She gulped back a sob. "It's happening again. Only now I know what to do about it."

She began walking quickly back toward the church, then broke into a run. Rebo rolled his eyes and followed her.

"And to think, I won't even miss the soaps," said Rose.

Peter shuddered. "That brought back a few memories."

Mieko tilted her head.

"I wasn't always the responsible person I am now."

One side of Mieko's mouth twitched, her response to Peter's sense of humor. *They were made for each other*, thought Lindy.

Rebo was waiting for them on the church steps. He was frowning. "She slammed the door in my face," he said as they gathered around him.

"Judd needs to know about this," said Lindy.

"I promised Melanie we wouldn't say anything to the police." Rebo threw up his hands. "Then she slammed the door in my face anyway."

"But—"

"She's planning something that ain't quite kosher. She's one scary mama." He shook himself. " I think we've got what they call a 'situation' on our hands. But we can't get to the bottom of it until we get her to trust us."

"And how long do you think that'll be?"

"I don't know, but the four of us are going in there and make ourselves real useful, and real trustworthy. And you're not going to say anything about this until we know more. Come on troops. Welcome to Nightmare Marathon."

Lindy watched her four friends go into the church, Rebo's arm draped over Rose's shoulders, Peter and Mieko following behind, not touching. Lindy didn't envy them. She had the distinct feeling that Melanie wouldn't welcome their interference.

"Have a blast," she said and left them to it.

Chapter Thirteen

Lindy spent a restless, sleepless night and woke up the next morning with a headache. Glen had finally called her back. They had argued. When Biddy called a few minutes later, she had cried—again. Then she had to convince Biddy not to come home on the next flight. Lindy had drunk too much wine, while her insecurity about her marriage turned to anger. Then she drank too much water because the wine made her thirsty, and spent half the night getting up to go to the bathroom.

She stood in the shower until the water ran cold, put conditioner on her hair instead of shampoo and forgot to shave her legs. Bruno bolted out the door when she tried to leave and refused to come inside. The gas light came on halfway to the farm, and she had to wait in line at the gas station. And now she had to deal with dead bodies and drug-using teenagers, limerick-writing poisoners and neurotic daughters, divorcing friends and depressed juvenile detectives.

Fund-raising was just too damned much work.

Her mental whining turned to alarm when she saw Judd's Taurus parked outside the farmhouse. She rushed inside and pushed open the door to the dining room. Judd and Mary Elisabeth were sitting at the table.

"Where is everybody?" she asked.

"I told Evelyn and Janey to come at eleven," said Mary Elisabeth. "Judd wanted to speak to us first."

Lindy glanced at Judd. His flexible mouth drooped nearly to his jawline. She lowered herself into the nearest chair and waited.

"They've identified the body. His name was Earl Koopes. He was a private detective from Suffern."

Lindy relaxed. "Suffern is in New York."

Judd went through a series of facial gymnastics before he said, "His car was found in the woods near here."

Lindy felt a ripple of unease. "How near?"

"Near enough to involve the marathon. That's why I wanted to talk to you and Mary Elisabeth. They'll get a warrant to search his files. See if they can find out who he was working for. But it will take some time, and time is something we don't have."

"You think someone hired him to investigate the marathon?" Lindy asked.

"Could be. But everything related to the marathon has been cleared through legal channels, so what I'm thinking is, uh—" He rubbed his jaw and looked uncomfortable.

"He was investigating someone who is involved with the marathon," said Lindy.

"Well, yeah," he agreed.

Mary Elisabeth flinched. Her face was pallid. "That isn't possible. I can't think of anyone who would be the subject of an investigation. One of the new members? Melanie? Evelyn? Der—" She broke off and her hand went to her mouth.

"No call to get upset, Mary Elisabeth. I know what you're thinking, and I think you know how unlikely that is." Judd unfolded himself from the chair and went to stand beside her. He looked at Lindy. "I'd like you to show me again where you found the body. Go over it one more time. Maybe remember something you didn't remember the first time."

He looked apologetic. “You were in shock, and, well, I wasn’t taking you real seriously.”

“I’ll go, too,” said Mary Elisabeth.

Judd rested his hand on her shoulder. “No need. Your committee members will be showing up pretty soon. I don’t guess I need to tell you not to mention this to them. No reason to get people all excited. And if somebody is being tailed, or was being tailed, at any rate, I’d just as soon they don’t find out that we’re onto them. We’ll be back in a few minutes.”

He escorted Lindy to the door. As soon as they were outside, she asked, “Who could have hired the detective? We’ve known all these people for years.”

“Lindy, you wouldn’t believe what goes on behind closed doors in this town. It just looks real good on the outside. Doesn’t mean we don’t have some real rotten folks living among us.”

“Janey? Stella? Father Andrews? Give me a break.” She stopped. “Me?” The idea was ludicrous. “Mary Elisabeth’s right. If it does involve the marathon, it must be one of the new people.”

“Morning, Evelyn,” he said over her head. “I believe Mary Elisabeth is waiting for you.”

Evelyn dipped her chin and went inside.

Lindy watched until the door closed behind her, then ran to catch up to Judd who had continued to walk away from the house. “What do you know about her?” she asked.

“Evelyn? Moved here in the middle of September. Seems nice enough.”

“I wonder. She took the note that was attached to Father Andrews as well as the one left for Stella. Oh! You do know about Father Andrews?”

“Yeah. Sounds like something a kid would pull. Not very nice. But hell, I’ve seen a lot worse.”

“And what about Fallon and Derrick? She’s just come back, with the boy toy in tow. We don’t know a thing about him, do we?”

"We know he's got the powers-to-be, or at least their wives, snowed. And he has elbowed his way into anything that's going on. I don't like the man. That's a fact. Doesn't mean he's up to no good."

"But a jealous husband might have him watched if he thought he was, uh, consorting with his wife." Lindy stopped suddenly. "Or his daughter." Surely Howard hadn't hired the detective. Was that what Mary Elisabeth was afraid of?

"Well, if I find him doing more than consorting on this property, he'll still be trying to find the ground when he reaches the state line." Judd nodded sharply, driving the point home.

"You're not the first one to express that sentiment," she agreed, picturing a blue sky with "Surrender Dorothy" scrawled across it. She started to mention Melanie, then remembered Rebo's promise. She needed to talk to the woman and get her to agree to confide in Judd.

"Now that I think about it," she said, "there's an inordinate number of newcomers on this committee."

"Let's not go looking for trouble, Lindy, since it seems to find us easily enough. Just keep your wits about you."

"Don't I usually?"

Judd smiled and for a second the worry disappeared from his face. "Usually. And you do have good powers of observation. I can't be around as much as I'd like. I'm not asking you to spy on anybody. In fact, I'm ordering you not to. Just keep your eyes and ears open.

"We need the marathon to be a success. I don't care one way or the other about keeping it up as a museum, but I do want that teen center. We've been turned down on every property that was within our reach. People either object to the noise, or the extra traffic, or the kind of kids it would attract. People are damn selfish and that's a fact."

They had come to the bridge, and Lindy was surprised to see a team of detectives in and around the water.

"I didn't see their cars."

"I didn't want to upset Mary Elisabeth or the others. They parked up at Adam Crabtree's place."

"And what does he have to say about all this?"

"Not much, but then Adam doesn't have a whole lot to say about anything. Except when he's storytelling. Says he was out gathering herbs when he saw you fall in the water. Came down to see if you needed help."

"But he told you he pushed the body into the brook?"

"Yeah. Said he was just trying to get a better look and the body floated away." Judd stopped her before she could express an opinion about Adam Crabtree. "I guess he thought he was doing us a favor, or maybe he didn't want a bunch of people snooping around asking questions. He's a private man."

"Or maybe he hired the detective and doesn't want anyone to find out. He's next in line for this property."

"Yeah, but he doesn't want it. He's the one who suggested turning it into a historical site in the first place. Too much responsibility. He's happy just to have a place to live and to be left alone."

"Are there any other potential heirs?"

"They're running a standard check, but nobody's turned up so far."

They stopped to watch the search team move along the shoreline. Two men knelt in the water beneath the bridge. One was taking pictures.

"Hey, Paul," called Judd.

The other man stood up and looked in their direction. He was short and stocky and was wearing green waders. Lindy recognized him from the high school scholarship committee.

"Find anything?" asked Judd.

Paul shook his head. "I don't expect to. Too much water, too many days."

"Can we come down?"

"Sure. This quadrant's been photoed and cleared. Took some casts, but there were more tracks than you could shake a stick at. A damn dog or something."

Bruno, thought Lindy, chagrined. And me, not to mention Stella and Rebo. Adam Crabtree had stood in the water. Was that significant? But he had already admitted to being on the scene.

Judd helped Lindy down the bank. Paul took her hand and she jumped to the bottom.

"This is Lindy Haggerty. She found the body initially."

Paul nodded. He took a notebook out of a jacket that was hanging on a tree limb. "I'm acquainted with Mrs. Haggerty." He turned to Lindy. "Okay. Show me where you were standing, and describe what happened before Crabtree helped with the vanishing act."

Lindy moved close to the water's edge. "About here, I think. Bruno found something under the bridge. Those are probably his pawprints. I thought he had cornered an animal. But then he got a piece of jacket in his mouth and it tore away from the bridge. His head bobbed up—the man's, I mean." She swallowed, determined to stay calm even as the bloated face appeared in her mind. "I thought it was a dummy."

"The hayride runs past here," explained Judd.

"So I was going to show Bruno that it wasn't real. I yanked at the sleeve and this hand popped up. It had hairy fingers, and a ring on the little finger. Let's see. He must have been floating on his stomach, because I didn't see anything but a mass of garbage at first. Bruno . . ." She closed her eyes trying to remember the scene. "His left side must have been hung up on the bridge, because when Bruno pulled him away, he flipped over on his back and that's when I saw the face. Dark hair, I think. Hard to tell because it was wet. A brown sports jacket. The face was too, you know, to tell."

"Pretty accurate description of our man. Which way was he headed?"

"Before Adam?"

"Yeah. Was his head toward the shore or away?"

"Away. His head was pointing downstream."

He turned to Judd. "Too much activity to know if he went in here, but it seems unlikely. Couldn't have fallen off the bridge and ended up where he did. The bank isn't steep enough anywhere around here for him to have fallen in and knocked himself out. Must've happened upstream somewhere, and the bridge snagged him on his way down. The brook makes a big turn just below here. I've got some men checking. Not likely that they'll find anything."

Several seconds elapsed before Lindy's understanding caught up. "He was knocked out?"

Paul hooked his thumbs in his belt. "I bet you sure kept 'em hopping on those homicide cases. But don't get too excited. His skull was cracked, but it could have happened when he fell. At this point, there's no reason to think this was anything other than an accident. We may know more when the full postmortem comes back. We'll ask some questions. See if anybody saw anything, but it isn't our investigation. We'll pass on anything we learn to Passaic."

Lindy felt Judd stiffen. "I sure would like it, Paul, if you didn't have to involve the marathon. We're having enough troubles as it is."

Paul shook his head. "Listen to yourself, Judd. You know the SOP."

He asked Lindy a few more questions, then flipped his notebook closed. "Well, I guess that's about all," he said and returned it to his pocket.

Judd helped Lindy back up the bank. She could feel his dejection as she came to stand beside him.

"Judd," Paul called. "Get some sleep, go fishing. Just let me do my job."

Judd thrust his hands into his pockets and began to walk away.

"What was he talking about? Going fishing?"

"Aw, heck. Everyone's kinda p.o.'ed at me right now. They think I'm overreacting to the drug problem. And that my involvement with the marathon is taking me away from my work and causing them more." He ran a hand over his face. "Sometimes it seems like nothing goes right."

"What's SOP stand for?"

"Standard Operating Procedure. Which means they're not going to cut me any slack on this one."

They walked along the road, not speaking.

"Does everybody know about me and, uh, that other stuff?"

"Just about." He cleared his throat, then blurted, "Aw, hell, Lindy, things like that come in over the wire. The first time, no one made the connection. But by that cruise you did, we had wised up to the Graham-Haggerty thing."

"But the trial was in Florida and the crime happened in the ocean."

"Yeah, but one of the victims was a New Yorker. It's a small world."

Too small, she thought. Now we have another dead New Yorker. She sighed. "Glen'll kill me."

"What Glen doesn't know won't hurt him. Your secret's safe with the local PD."

Lindy's stomach sank. The whole town probably knew about her "indulging in disaster," as Glen referred to it, and were laughing up their sleeves at her.

"But I'm warning you, don't go stirring up any mischief. I want to gloss over this as quickly as possible. Get it cleared up before the marathon."

They had come to the springhouse, and Lindy was again tempted to tell Judd about the drugs.

Drugs. She turned to Judd. "Show me where they found the car."

"Like hell, I will. You think you can find clues that Paul's team can't?"

"I wouldn't presume, but if we know where he fell into the water, we might have an idea why. And who."

Judd's face modeled itself into a frown. "I don't get you."

"Just satisfy my curiosity, okay?"

"Come on." He led her past the springhouse, and she began to hear activity from somewhere in the trees.

"Does the road go in there?"

"Not this one. They found the car down a trail that cuts off from the road to Adam Crabtree's place. It's on this side of the brook, but this is as close as we can get from here. Anyway, they're still actively searching."

"But I can't see the car."

He caught her by the elbow and moved her over. "Look there." He pointed beyond them. She saw flashes of uniforms moving through the trees and the top of a tan car. She looked back in the direction of the springhouse. Had he been hired to watch the teenagers?

"Now, come on," said Judd and guided her across the road. "You don't want to mess up any more evidence."

"It wasn't my fault," she protested. "How was I to know there was a body there?"

They skirted the cemetery. The garbage and cast-offs had been removed from the back of the church and only the piles of lumber remained. She wondered if T.J. had given his permission to have it hauled away.

"Derrick and Fallon were here last weekend."

"How do you know that? What were they doing here?"

"Evelyn said they had started cleaning out the church, and T.J. was mad about it. Fallon was trying to get her to cart the garbage away. Maybe they saw something."

"I'll tell Paul. He's in charge of our end of the investigation. Go on back to the house and try to reassure Mary Elisabeth. She's not holding up so well."

"Will do."

"And don't say anything about all this."

"Just one more thing, Judd."

"Uh-huh."

"You're juvie, right?"

"Yeah, and what am I doing investigating a drowning? Nothing official. I'm just kibitzing."

Lindy smiled.

"What?"

"I have a friend who says that. He's an ex-cop. Still enjoys the chase."

"Wish I could say the same for me. I'm not enjoying much of anything but failure and bad opinions."

"Hang in there," she said and watched him walked away.

Chapter Fourteen

Stella was the last person Lindy expected to see that morning. But she was sitting with Janey at the kitchen table, looking pallid but otherwise okay. Lindy sat down. "How are you?"

"I've been better. But if one person makes a comment about me not knowing the difference between ipecac and cooking sherry, I'll clobber them."

"No one would dare," said Lindy. "Someone played a nasty trick on you. You heard about Father Andrews?"

"I heard. Must be one of those damned teenagers. Just like something they would do. Lucky for them that ipecac didn't kill me."

Janey opened her mouth, but Stella interrupted.

"I know that most of them are good kids. But it only takes one rotten apple." She lifted her cup and drained it. She made a face. "That has to be the nastiest-tasting brew I ever drank. Maybe I could suggest some things to make Adam's restoratives more palatable."

Mary Elisabeth stuck her head in the door. "Everything all right?"

"Just hunky-dory," said Stella.

"Fine," said Lindy and gave Mary Elisabeth a thumbs-up. "Oh, I do need the party rental invoice. I think we're going to need more canopies for the play area. I meant to ask for it this morning, but with everything else, it slipped my mind."

"I have it here." Mary Elisabeth placed her briefcase on the table and flipped it open. Her eyes widened. The top of the briefcase prevented Lindy from seeing whatever she was staring at, but she had an idea. So did the others.

"What is it?" Stella asked.

Mary Elisabeth brought out a square piece of paper.

"Oh Lord, not another one," said Janey.

Lindy took it from Mary Elisabeth's clenched fist and read it to the others.

"There was an old bag on a throne
Whose vanity turned men to stone
But her lofty gaze
Turned into a haze
When she went to answer the phone"

"Damn," said Stella.

The telephone rang in Mary Elisabeth's office.

The four women jumped.

"Ridiculous," said Mary Elisabeth. "A coincidence. But I'm going to get to the bottom of this. Today."

Janey stood up, visibly shaken. "What are you planning to do? You can't accuse someone without having proof."

"I wouldn't think of it. You should know me better than that." Her eyes met Janey's; then she turned and walked out of the room.

Janey stared at the door. "I think—I'll be right back." Using the tabletop as support, she moved toward the door.

Lindy turned to Stella as soon as Janey was out of the room. "What was that all about? Is something going on between those two that I didn't pick up on? Do you think Janey suspects someone? That bit about having proof. One of her students? It would be just like her to try to protect them."

"That limerick wasn't about Janey's students." Stella slumped back in her chair. "Damn."

"Stella, what is it? There almost seemed to be a challenge between the two of them."

"I think it was because of the line about turning men to stone."

"I don't get it."

"It happened a long time ago. When your kids were still in grammar school."

"What?"

Stella pushed her teacup aside and leaned on her elbows. "The year that Fallon was a senior, Mary Elisabeth and Howard were having a rough time of it. Nothing was going right. Fallon was worse than usual, and they were arguing a lot. I guess Mary Elisabeth thought that Fallon should get professional help, and Howard was being stubborn. We were all waiting for things to blow up.

"Then somehow, a rumor got started about Janey and Howard. She was paying a lot of attention to Fallon at school. The half-wit actually made A's in Janey's class. Can you imagine? Anyway, you know how people jump to conclusions. It was hogwash, of course, and it gradually died away without doing any lasting harm. But it was tense for a while."

"How awful," said Lindy.

"It was the A's that did it, I guess. Some people figured Janey was doing it because of Howard. Total bullshit. Mary Elisabeth never believed it."

A metallic clatter brought them to their feet, and they ran toward the door. T.J. barreled down the stairs and skidded to a halt in front of them.

"What have you people done now?" he wheezed. His head whirred around. "Damnation."

"Mary Elisabeth," said Stella. She pushed her way into the parlor, T.J. and Lindy close behind.

The door to the sunporch was open. An aluminum pail

lay at Mary Elisabeth's feet. Mary Elisabeth stood like a statue on the threshold. She was drenched with water. Wet spaghetti covered her hair and shoulders and clung to the back of her jacket and skirt. Water puddled around her shoes.

Janey was standing a few feet away.

"Jesus H. Christ," yelled T.J. and bolted forward. He fell to his knees, scooped up spaghetti and water off the floor, and dumped them back into the bucket. "I need a mop, quick."

"Screw the mop," said Stella and began pulling strands of pasta from Mary Elisabeth's hair.

Mary Elisabeth didn't move or say a word, merely stared into her office. Lindy looked inside. No one was there. Nothing looked out of the ordinary.

Janey took a faltering step and reached toward Mary Elisabeth. "I—I—" She didn't seem to be able to continue.

Mary Elisabeth finally moved. "What is it, Janey? Are you all right?" Her voice was kind. She was perfectly composed in spite of the water that dripped down her face and the remnants of pasta stuck to her collar.

"I know the source of those limericks." Janey reached for the back of a chair to steady herself. "All three of them. I thought they seemed familiar, but it wasn't until this one—" She looked sadly about her. "But it couldn't be—I'm sure none of them would—"

Mary Elisabeth took both of Janey's hands in hers. "You have to tell us what you suspect."

Janey shook her head in stiff little jerks.

"These are not harmless jokes," said Lindy.

"Spenser," Janey said, then fell silent.

"Spenser who?" asked Lindy.

"Edmund Spenser. *The Fairie Queen.* It's a poem about the seven deadly sins." Janey glanced at Mary Elisabeth. "My senior English class studies it every year. I have them write their own poems based on them. They inevitably come up with silly limericks of this sort. They've been doing it for years. It doesn't do any harm and it keeps them interested in poetry." Her eyes lit briefly with memory, then sobered. "None of them would resort to such malicious acts as this. I know it."

Mary Elisabeth looked doubtful. "Which of the students working on the marathon are in your English class this year?"

"I can't believe any of them would do such a thing."

"Janey, please. We won't accuse anyone, but maybe they can help us find out who is doing this. The kids working on the hayride? Someone in Melanie's group?"

Janey put her fingers to her lips. "Bryan Morrison, Tolliver Ames, Jake and Steffy Adamson, Kenny Stackhowser, Darien Ghandami, Jeff Linden and Valerie Combs. I think that's it."

Lindy recognized the last four from Melanie's group.

Mary Elisabeth squeezed Janey's hand. "I'm going home to change. When Bryan arrives this afternoon, we'll ask him to help us get to the bottom of this. I hope you'll be able to be here."

"Let me know when you find out who did this," said T.J. "I'll strangle the kid myself. And you can add another thousand bucks to the restoration total. That's how much it will cost to have this carpet cleaned professionally."

Mary Elisabeth merely nodded in his direction and, still dripping, walked out of the house.

Bryan Morrison was summoned to the sunporch as soon as he arrived that afternoon. There were no signs of spaghetti or water, but Lindy glanced above her head as she walked through the door.

Mary Elisabeth, freshly changed and apparently calm, asked Bryan to be seated.

He looked around, suddenly uneasy. Even a model teenager tended to get suspicious when he was called before his elders.

Dining chairs had been squeezed into the tiny room.

Three of them were occupied by Janey, Stella and Evelyn. Bryan sat down in the remaining chair. Lindy went to sit on the windowsill.

Mary Elisabeth sat down behind her desk. "Bryan, as president of the Teen Council, we hope that you will be able to help us."

Bryan shifted his weight and relaxed. "Of course. That's my job," he said good-naturedly.

Mary Elisabeth cleared her throat. "We have been the targets of several practical jokes. Just silly things for the most part. They were all accompanied by limericks which Janey tells us are based on the seven deadly sins."

Bryan turned pale.

"I'm sure they were not intended to harm, but they must stop." She handed him the slip of paper that she had received that morning.

He read it over quickly. "Oh, yeah. Some of the kids make these up and pass them around." He looked at Janey. "It's just a joke. I mean. Hey. Just shows you how interested they are."

"That's what I told Mary Elisabeth," said Janey.

"And I'm sure none of the guys would do anything to hurt the marathon. The teen center is really important to us." Janey smiled her triumph.

"I'm sure that's true, Bryan," said Mary Elisabeth. "But someone is being malicious. I don't know how to get to the bottom of this without your help."

Bryan's face clouded over. "I'll talk to the others, but if you ask me, you should be questioning those losers in Melanie's group."

"Bryan!" exclaimed Janey.

"I'm sorry, Ms. Horowitz, but they *are* losers. They're always in trouble. Maybe they don't want the teen center. They probably wouldn't come anyway. I know Kenny and Jeff and Val are in your—I mean, Melanie's, English class. And that other kid, what's his name?"

"Darien Ghandami," said Janey.

"Yeah, Darien. If somebody from class is writing those limericks, it must be one of them. I can ask them for you."

"That won't be necessary," said Mary Elisabeth. "I'll have Melanie handle it. If you could just ask those participating in the hayride, I'd very much appreciate it."

"Sure thing, Ms. Porter. Anything else?"

"No, Bryan, thank you."

"Sure." Bryan got up, quirked a smile at Janey and went outside.

"Well," said Mary Elisabeth, leaning back in her chair, "I suppose we had better go ask Melanie what her group has been up to."

"Oh," said Janey. "It's so unfair. Everyone expects them to get into trouble. And unfortunately, most kids live up to your expectations of them. Isn't there some other way?"

Mary Elisabeth stood up. "I'm afraid not, and the sooner we approach them, the sooner we'll find the culprit."

The five of them went to the church. *Like a tribunal of inquisitors*, thought Lindy. She was relieved to see the Black Beauty parked in its usual place. She was even more relieved to see Rebo standing beside Melanie at the edge of the stage.

Mary Elisabeth went ahead of the others and whispered something into Melanie's ear. Melanie stopped the rehearsal.

"Mrs. Porter would like to ask us some questions. Come sit down."

She motioned the teens forward. They immediately dropped out of character and shuffled toward her, hands shoved into their pockets.

Janey jutted out her chin and went to join Mary Elisabeth and Melanie. Lindy and Stella started to follow, but Evelyn stopped them. "Too confrontational."

Mary Elisabeth began explaining about the pranks and how they were related to the Spenser limericks. "Do any of you know anything about this?"

Sullen expressions turned to scowls. Eyes darted around, looking at anything other than the woman who was speaking.

They look guilty, thought Lindy.

"I need an answer."

Even as she heard the words, Lindy knew that Mary Elisabeth was using the wrong technique. It sounded as if she expected them to be guilty and most likely she did.

"Screw this," Darien muttered.

"Darien, shut up," said Melanie.

"Screw you."

"Darien Ghandami, don't you dare use that kind of language," said Janey.

Darien chewed on his lower lip and mumbled, "Sorry."

"I think I can speak for all of my—Melanie's—students. They didn't have anything to do with those pranks. They're good kids."

"Thanks," said Melanie.

Janey's face lit momentarily.

"Is that true?" asked Mary Elisabeth.

Darien scowled at her. "I didn't have anything to do with it."

"Neither did I," said Kenny. "But I don't expect you to believe me."

"Well, I didn't do it. I have more important things to do than write stupid limericks," said Val.

"Yeah," said Jeff. "Go ask Bryan. His bunch are so-o-o good at English. They could probably write a few good limericks in their sleep."

"We've already talked to Bryan. He's going to ask those who are working on the hayride."

"I bet." Kenny glowered at Melanie. "I knew this was stupid. They're just looking for a way to get rid of us. They probably wrote that shit themselves, and now they're going to make it look like we did it." He threw up his hands. "What's the point?"

He pushed past the others and strode toward the door.

"Kenny," Melanie yelled. She turned on Mary Elisabeth. "Damn it. See what you've done. I'm telling you this once and for all. My kids didn't have anything to do with it. You're looking in the wrong place." She hurried down the aisle, stopped halfway and called back to the stage. "Stay put. Got it? I'm going to find Kenny. If one of you is gone when we get back—"

She didn't have to say anything else. The group melted back into the shadows of the chancel. Rebo walked casually toward the back door.

"It could be anybody," said Janey. "Those limericks have been going around for at least fifteen years. I have a folder full of the best ones." She looked sheepish. "Some of them are amazingly good—for limericks."

"That doesn't help to narrow the field any," said Evelyn. "We may have just shot ourselves in the foot. Whoever it is will be more careful in the future."

"You mean you think there'll be more?" asked Lindy.

"There are *seven* deadly sins," said Evelyn.

The sound of a gunshot exploded from the driveway. Everyone froze in horror, except Evelyn, who grabbed her side and raced for the back door.

Janey clutched Lindy's arm. "Surely not," she pleaded. "Please, no."

Rebo was grinning when he and Melanie returned to the church dragging a belligerent Kenny Stackhowser with them.

"Tried to hot-wire the Beauty." He cuffed Kenny on the back of the head. "She only responds to a gentle touch, my man. I'll show you some moves after the rehearsal."

"I'm not doing the dumb play, and I don't care about your dumb car."

"Oh, yeah, you are doing this dumb play," said Claudia. "We've all worked too hard learning these stupid lines for you to screw it up."

"Bite it," said Kenny and threw himself full length on the nearest pew.

"Melanie. You have to make him." Val's voice climbed up the octave.

Melanie said nothing. The cast peered out at her.

"It isn't fair," whined Val.

Still Melanie said nothing.

Come on, thought Lindy. *Don't let them down now*.

"You're just going to let him ruin the play?" Carl's deep voice was a painful contrast to Val's.

"Then we'll do it without him. He's not the only John Proctor in town." Claudia turned on Melanie. "We'll do it without *you*, if we have to."

Darien moved center stage. "I'll learn his fu—stupid part. Where's a script?"

Carl tossed a book toward him. "We're on page twenty-seven. And don't act like some dumb pothead guru. Proctor's a new England farmer. Everybody respects him, got it?"

"Sure, I got it. Do I look like I got shit for brains?"

"Ignore him, Darien. Stand here." Claudia pulled him stage right. She pointed to a place in the script.

Darien cleared his throat.

Melanie slipped quietly off the stool and came to stand beside Rebo.

"Cool move, Mama."

"Whew," said Melanie.

The pew creaked behind them. Kenny ambled past, hands in his pockets, looking at the floor. He walked onto the stage without pausing. He snatched the script from Darien's hand and pushed him out of the way.

Claudia gave him the cue.

"Two for two," said Melanie under her breath and walked slowly back to the stage.

"Not a bad day's work," said Lindy, coming to stand beside Rebo.

"Now, if we could just get rid of the vamp in the corner." He cut his eyes to the right.

Fallon sat at the far end of the pew, arms draped across

the back, legs stretched out together, looking like a pose from *Elle*.

"If you figure out a way, I'll help."

"You're on."

The Follies participants began arriving at seven.

"A motley crew," said Rebo. He looked down at the list of acts. "Mind if I rearrange some of these?"

"Not at all. It's your baby."

"In that case, I think we'll start with a C-section." He stood up and introduced himself. "Can I have the three witches from *Macbeth*?"

It took three hours, but by ten o'clock, all the acts had been given a slot in the performance and had run through their bits. The men's kick line came last. Only two-thirds of the original cast were there. They muddled through the steps.

"Sorry, but Judd had an emergency call. Had to take some of the guys with him," they explained as soon as the music ended.

Rebo dismissed them and called the morning rehearsal for ten o'clock.

"Okay, this'll work," he said as he sprawled on a pew next to Lindy. "Those tombstones aren't so bad. I think I'll use them to backdrop the witches. But *nomine patre*. Those were the chubbiest skeletons I ever saw. What do you feed these kids?"

"At least they're wearing black."

"Yeah, but did they have to use fluorescent paint? When they bend over, the bones disappear into their tummies." He straightened up. "How about this? We borrow some of those old robes and candelabras from *Carmina Burana*. Do you think Jeremy will mind? I mean, it's not like we're ever going to do *that* piece again."

They both fell silent for a second remembering the ill-fated ballet.

"I thought we could dress up the ushers in the robes and

they can do some ghoul schtick with the candelabras. Real spooky."

Lindy shuddered in response. The candelabras were spooky all right; in fact, one of them had been lethal. She wasn't sure if Jeremy would want them used again.

"Call him and ask," she said.

"Yeah." He jumped up. "And bats, flying bats, yeah." He wandered away looking into the rafters.

She grabbed her bag and stood up. "I'm leaving. It's been a long day."

"You go ahead," he said, waving over his shoulder. "I've gotta go back to the City. See you tomorrow."

She left him standing in the pulpit, talking to himself.

Chapter Fifteen

Lindy arrived early on Saturday morning. After the fiasco with the drama group, she wanted to talk to Bryan without an audience. They needed to get to the bottom of these limericks before things got really out of hand.

The area in front of the house had been roped off and parking was limited to the side of the church. The grounds were already filled with workers. The Jaycees were busy pounding stakes into the gravel. Lumber was being hauled from a flatbed truck and dumped at strategic places in the yard. T.J. leaned out of a second-story window yelling at everyone to stay away from the house. Fallon and Derrick sat on the porch railing, head to head. A cardboard Starbucks cup sat on the balustrade between them.

Lindy passed by the crew that was raking the ground around the outdoor fireplace and struck off through the trees in search of Bryan.

It was a lovely walk, even though it would soon be transformed into ghoulish tableaus for Mischief Night. She felt bad about leaving Bruno at home. He had looked so forlorn when she had shut him in the kitchen that morning, that she almost broke down and brought him with her. But this was no place for a dog today.

The sounds of activity drifted away and the silence became poignant. The air was crisp and invigorating, the shelter of the trees relaxing. Gradually, the quiet was interrupted by the sounds of activity ahead. She picked up her pace, looking about her for the teenagers. She stopped next to an old oak tree whose branches spread above the road, blocking the sun.

"Bryan?"

No answer. Just a gust of wind that rustled the leaves. Then a sudden whoosh from behind her and something heavy sailed past her head. She spun around just in time to see the thing swinging back at her. Instinctively, she jumped out of the way as it barely missed her shoulder. Then she watched, arms akimbo, as a burlap bag rocked back and forth and finally came to a stop. It hung limply from a rope that was tied to a limb somewhere above her.

There was laughter in the trees and she looked up. Two grinning faces peered down at her through the branches.

"Had you going there for a minute, didn't we Mrs. H.?" Jake Adamson straddled the limb, his legs dangling on either side.

"It works, Bryan," called the other boy, whom she recognized as Tollie Ames. He took a minute to reposition a wooden platform in the crook of the tree, then shimmied out to the limb where Jake was sitting.

Bryan Morrison stepped out of the woods. He looked at the bag, then up to the boys in the tree. "You sure you didn't have to help it along, Tollie?"

"Didn't touch it." Tollie grabbed hold of the limb and swung himself to the ground. Jake jumped down behind him.

The three boys stood grinning at Lindy.

"Pretty scary, guys."

"And the beauty of it is, we don't even have to sit in the tree all night," said Jake. "Bryan designed a lever at the bottom that drops the floor and releases the hanged man. All we have to do is replace it before the next ride."

Bryan gave the bundle a push. "Well, it works with the gunny sack anyway. But I think it will work even better when we get the real thing in place. The extra weight will help."

"You're not planning to use a person, are you?"

"No, ma'am. It'll be a dummy. I just have to get the distribution of weight right, so that it keeps swinging long enough for the wagon to pass."

"I had no idea you were so mechanically minded."

"He's a real genius," said Jake. "Draws up the plans and everything."

"It's nothing," said Bryan.

"He even designed a great flyer for the marathon, but they went with Derrick's idea."

"It was no big deal," said Bryan. "Oh, I talked to the council about the limericks."

"We didn't do it," said Tollie. "We're all on the council to encourage dialogue, not promote bad feelings."

"Thanks for telling me, guys," said Lindy. "We didn't really think it was one of you. Keep an ear out, will you?"

"Sure thing," said Bryan. "But like I said, you should talk to Melanie's los—kids."

"We did. They denied it, too."

The looks the three boys gave her let her know exactly what they felt about that.

"Thanks." She left them hauling the gunny sack back onto the platform.

She had just recrossed the outdoor kitchen when the sound of raised voices came from the back of the house. She rushed to see what was wrong. T.J. and Derrick stood nose to nose in front of the cellar door. Fallon stood behind Derrick, pressed so closely that the three of them looked like a human sandwich.

"I don't care who the hell you are," yelled T.J. "You can't store it in the cellar."

"Give it a rest, T.J. It's just a cellar."

"You can't store dry ice in the cellar. You can't use the cellar at all. I'm working in there. And besides, it's dangerous. You have to store it where there's proper ventilation."

"But the cellar's convenient." Fallon looked daggers at T.J. "Derrick wants it there. So too bad."

T.J. crossed his arms. "In case you've forgotten, I am in charge of the restoration. You're all here on my good graces. So don't push me."

"In case you've forgotten, it was my father that hired you."

"She's got you there, T.J."

"Shut up, Derrick. You may have charmed half the women in this town, but you haven't done one damn useful thing that I can see. So you can take your dry ice and—"

"He has, too. You're just jealous. And if you want to keep your job, you'll—"

"Fallon, darling—" Derrick began.

"You're a spoiled brat, Fallon. You always have been. Take your boy toy and get the hell away from my house."

"Your house? We'll just see about that."

T.J.'s eyes widened. His mouth opened but no words came out.

"Don't push your luck, buddy." Derrick smiled at him, but there was nothing friendly in it.

T.J. took a deep breath and spoke through clenched teeth. "I'm telling you once more. You can't use the cellar. If the gases build up, they can cause an explosion." He turned angry eyes on Fallon. "Is that what you want? To blow up the whole house?"

"Only if you were in it."

T.J. inhaled sharply and started to shake. Lindy marched forward. It was time for an executive decision, before the restorer gave himself a coronary. But before she reached them, T.J. threw back his head and laughed uproariously.

Fallon clenched her fists and stepped toward him. Derrick slipped his arm around her and pulled her away.

"You have that cellar ready by Wednesday, or else," screamed Fallon. Then Derrick hauled her around the side of the house and they were out of sight.

"What was that all about?" asked Lindy.

T.J.'s face was blotched with patches of red. "The idiot has ordered a truckload of dry ice. For what, I can't imagine. Howard should never have allowed the marathon to be held here. If the crowds don't destroy everything, those two will."

"Howard okayed it? I thought the property belonged to the town."

T.J. snorted. "Not until the town proves it can afford the restoration and maintenance. In the meantime, Howard is the executor. Whatever he says goes. He also has first refusal on any plans for selling it."

Howard had mentioned none of this in their meeting. Not even when she told him what Fallon had said about him buying it for her. Had he been totally honest with her?

"You think Fallon's threats are real?"

"As of now. But if I find what I think I'm going to find, it will be out of all of our hands, including Howard's."

"What do you think you'll find?"

T.J. smiled enigmatically. "I'm not telling until I'm sure. But what a coup it will be." Suddenly mollified, he strolled away, leaving Lindy staring in bewilderment.

The witches from *Macbeth* were just beginning their trio when Lindy slipped into a pew next to Mieko. "Wow. What a transformation."

Black drapes were swagged from the rafters and pulled back behind the pulpits. They were attached to the walls by gray, plaster-of-Paris gargoyles. Rose's doing, Lindy was certain. The outlines of cardboard tombstones dotted the stage. Two papier-mâché boulders sat to each side of a black plastic cauldron, which must have come from the party store. It looked like it should be holding trick-or-treat candy not a noxious, bubbling brew. The witches had brought their own props.

Peter had rigged two lighting trees and light suffused the chancel stage. He sat at a card table at the back of the church, a portable light board in front of him. A tape deck rested on the floor at his feet.

"You brought all this stuff from the City?" asked Lindy

"Most of it. Each act brought their own props, and the sound system belongs to the high school. It's a little outdated." As always, Mieko's face and voice showed no emotion. Today her elbows were relaxed by her side; her eyes, though almond-shaped, were fully open. Mieko was having a good time.

"How much is this going to cost me?" asked Lindy. Not that it mattered. She had already planned to add to Rebo's honorarium to include pay for the others.

"Nothing," said Mieko. "Peter was owed some favors around town. He called them in. We may have to rent some sound equipment, but Peter can probably find someone to loan that to him, too."

Lindy smiled. She loved these people; she loved her job. Part of her was glad that Glen didn't want her to move to Paris. She would hate to lose all of this.

The witches ended their trio and the lights dimmed. Just as the lights faded to black, a blue aura emanated from the front of the stage. The outlines of the tombstones glowed purple, and Day-Glo lettering appeared on the fronts. Peter had managed to rig up black light for Miss Carole Anne's graveyard.

Lindy chuckled as she read the memorials. *RIP, Here Lies Ralph. G.I. Died*. The dance school students must have made the gravestones themselves. The music of Saint-Saëns' *Danse Macabre* began. Nothing happened.

Rebo's voice boomed through the darkness. "Where are the da—darling little skeletons? Miss Carole Anne, where are your dancers?"

A head popped up from one of the tombstones. Miss Carole Anne stood to her full height. Someone giggled.

"We're having a little trouble getting them into place," she said apologetically.

"Then let's preset them before the witches. Can they stay still that long?"

"I think so."

"Okay, put them in their places, and we'll take it from the end of the witches' trio."

The witches returned to the stage while Miss Carole Anne arranged her skeletons behind the tombstones.

"Ready?"

"No," came Peter's disembodied voice from the back. "Hold on a minute while I rewind this thing."

"I think I'll go help." Mieko crawled over Lindy's knees and disappeared into the darkness.

A few minutes later, the witches left the stage, carrying their cauldron with them. *Danse Macabre* began again. One by one, heads popped up from behind the tombstones and the skeletons began waving their arms.

Cute, thought Lindy. The audience will love them, and all their friends will yell and cheer. This could work.

Rebo sat down beside her and rolled his eyes. "This is what you did for twelve years of retirement?"

"It was for a good cause."

"No cause could be that good."

"You're not going to wig out on me, are you?"

Rebo looked at her incredulously. "I don't do wig. This is a challenge." He got up with a flourish and yelled, "Eddie Poe, are you in place for your recitation?"

Lindy sat blissfully alone in the kitchen. She had made it through an hour of the Follies rehearsal, but *she* had wigged out when things came to a standstill while Mieko, as Queen of the Bats, placed her charges. None of the bats was over five years old, and a few got lost on their way down the aisle to the stage. It was mayhem, as it should be a week and a half before a performance. The Follies was right on schedule—but the marathon itself was in trouble.

She reached for her notebook. It was times like this that she missed Biddy most. Biddy could always come up with a different slant to a problem. But Biddy was with Jeremy. Would probably go to Mexico with him. Well, good for her. This was Lindy's problem. It didn't even involve the company, just her friends and neighbors. But that wasn't exactly true. Rebo and the others had come riding in like the cavalry. They were her real family and friends.

This would really be the last time she'd ever volunteer for anything, but she still had to get through this. She drew four columns on the page. At the top of the first three she wrote *Detective, Fundamentalists, Teenagers*. At the top of the fourth, she put down *Limericks*. Then she studied her four categories.

Could the limericks be linked to the detective? They had only started after Lindy had found the body. Maybe the person had taken matters into their own hands. But for what possible reason? Why not just hire another detective?

Brother Bart's group was obsessed with sin, but they weren't allowed on the property.

The teenagers? She didn't think so. They had been in school when the incidents had occurred. And teenagers would be more likely to e-mail nasty limericks than rig annoying sabotages.

Seven deadly sins, but only three limericks—so far. Did someone plan to deliver a limerick a day until all seven were accounted for? And then what? Would it all be over, or would they just start on something else? The ten commandments? The twelve days of Christmas?

She reigned in her thoughts.

Three limericks—three board members. Stella, poisoned with ipecac. Ipecac could be bought in any drugstore or health food store. She wrote down A. Crabtree and put a question mark by his name. Accompanied by the limerick about . . .

What were the seven deadly sins anyway? She didn't remember Edmund Spenser's poem, though she did remember the year Cliff was in Janey's English class. Had he been upstairs in his room writing limericks when he should have been studying?

She tried to remember the words that Stella had received—folds of fat. *Gluttony*, that was one. *Idleness*, Father Andrews's amusin' snoozin'. *Vanity*, Mary Elisabeth. The writer had even used the word in the poem.

That was three. The other four were . . . She searched her mind. *Envy, Greed* and—*Lechery*? *Anger*?

She wrote them all down, leaving a space after each. It didn't make sense. Stella's joy was in feeding others. Father Andrews wasn't idle, just overworked. And if Mary Elisabeth seemed a bit proud, she had also done her share of philanthropy. Were the limericks really directed at the individual members of the committee? (Of which you are one, she reminded herself.) Or against the marathon as a whole?

There was a lot more tied up with this event than a few limericks and pranks, she was beginning to realize. There were people with axes to grind. Who wanted the property. And she bet there were a lot of unknown players.

She poured a cup of coffee and drank it while frowning at the notes she had written.

"Oh, there you are. You'd better come quick." Mieko stood in the open door. She appeared perfectly calm. It was her stiff elbows that drew Lindy to her feet and had her running to the church.

Chapter Sixteen

A crowd was gathered outside. A patrol car and Judd's white Taurus were parked in front of the church, engines running. Around them stood the teenagers from the council and the drama group. An invisible line divided them. Rebo, Rose and Peter stood on the church steps, Fallon and Derrick in the doorway. Melanie was arguing with Judd, Janey by her side. Behind them, Kenny stood between two policemen, his chin thrust forward, his eyes defiant.

Lindy pushed through the group. Mary Elisabeth wasn't around; that left her in charge. "What's this about, Judd?"

Judd's face was harsh with exhaustion. "Valerie Combs O.D.'d last night."

Lindy stared at him. "Val? Is she dead?"

"No, but she hasn't come to yet. There may be brain damage."

"But why do you have Kenny under guard?"

"Her parents said that she told them she was meeting him to go to a movie. I need to take him in to answer some questions."

Melanie grabbed his sleeve. "Judd, you can't do this. You're humiliating him in front of his peers."

"Melanie, if he's responsible for giving that girl drugs, I'm going to do more than humiliate him. I'm going to put him away."

"He didn't. Kenny wouldn't hurt anybody."

"Beat the daylights out of his stepfather, broke his nose and three ribs. What do you call that?"

"But he's clean."

"Doesn't mean he isn't selling. If it's any consolation, I'm just as disappointed as you." He turned back to the group. "If anybody has anything to say, I'll hear it. If you want anonymity, you can call me. I'll be at the station until eight o'clock." He nodded to the policemen, who guided Kenny to the patrol car and pushed him into the back seat.

Kenny didn't put up a fight or look for help. Melanie ran toward the car. One of the officers stopped her.

"Kenny, defend yourself," she yelled around him.

Kenny didn't respond, just stared at the back of the front seat.

The patrolmen got into the car and began backing away. Melanie ran alongside holding the door handle. "I believe in you, Kenny," she yelled. The patrol car sped up, and the handle was yanked from her hand. Judd slowed down as he passed her, but she turned angrily away and walked slowly back to the others.

The drama group stood apart, looking anywhere but at Melanie or each other. The Teen Council stood across from them, their pointed stares a harsh contrast to the shifting glances of the drama group.

Anger, distrust, fear pulsed in the air.

"Losers," someone muttered. The drama group shuffled nervously.

"Druggies," came another accusation.

"You've wrecked everything. I hope you're satisfied." Bryan Morrison stood feet apart, fists clenched.

Lindy stepped between the two groups. "Now just a minute, Bryan. I know this is very upsetting, but nothing has been proven against Kenny. And it certainly doesn't mean any of the others were involved. Let's try to stay calm."

"While they destroy everything we've worked so hard for?"

"They haven't destroyed it. Think what you're saying. What was all that talk about establishing dialogue?"

"It's too late now."

"Scumbag losers!" A boy from the council lunged across the space that separated the two groups and tackled Jeff. Jeff staggered back. Carl grabbed the boy and threw him into the dirt. Jake Adamson swung a punch that caught Carl in the face. Darien and Dina threw themselves at Jake, and Steffy joined the fray. Fighting broke out among the others. Bryan hesitated, then entered the melee.

"Stop it," screamed Lindy, but no one was listening. She was aware of Peter and Rebo running down the steps. Then they disappeared into the fighting. Rose bounded across the gravel. She pulled Dina and Steffy apart and shoved them toward their respective sides. Then she lifted Darien by the back of his T-shirt and tossed him toward Dina.

Melanie stood unmoving as the dust literally flew about her.

In a few long minutes, it was over. Rebo, Rose and Peter hauled the last of the fighters to their feet and sent them stumbling away.

"Jesus," Darien exclaimed. He looked down, then fell to his knees. "I didn't touch her, I swear."

Janey lay at his feet. She struggled to get up. "I just got pushed. I'm all right. Could someone give me a hand?"

Everyone stepped forward, then stopped, eyeing each other with contempt.

Melanie was the one who reached for her hand and helped her toward the steps of the church.

No one else moved.

Lindy held her breath, waiting to see what Melanie would do. *Turn around*, she thought. *Just turn around and give them a sign. Please, Melanie, don't reject them now.*

Slowly Melanie turned around.

"Come on," she said and went inside.

The church was quiet. Melanie sat in the front pew, looking out the window. Janey sat beside her. The group huddled at the edge of the stage, misery etched in their faces.

Claudia, dusty and disheveled, sat clasping her knees. Jeff stood with one arm resting against the pulpit, his face hidden. Carl rocked back and forth on his heels. Dina leaned back against Darien, but he stood up and moved away.

Lindy and Rebo stood at the back of the aisle, not daring to break the tension-filled atmosphere.

"Why doesn't Melanie say something?" whispered Lindy.

Rebo took a slow breath. "Damned if I know."

Carl slammed his fist into his palm. "Kenny's wrecked it for everybody."

Jeff's hand tightened on the pulpit.

"He never got high," said Dina. "He wouldn't give drugs to Val."

"Yeah, like we're going to believe anything you say." Darien crossed his arms and glared at her.

"How were we to know he was selling? He never talks about anything." Claudia choked back a sob. "What if she dies? He'll be a murderer."

"Shut up," said Jeff.

Claudia flinched as if he had struck her. "They'll blame us," she whimpered.

Jeff pushed himself from the pulpit and glared at the group. "'Then we'll burn together.'"

Melanie's head jerked toward him. Even Lindy recognized the line from the play.

"What?" said Claudia.

"I said, half-wit, that we'll burn together. Or are you too chickenshit to stand up for a friend?"

"I wouldn't exactly call him a friend," said Carl.

"No? You did last week."

Carl looked away.

Lindy felt the door open behind her. The members of the Teen Council stopped just inside.

"Oh, shit," said Rebo. "This is going to get ugly."

"He was always in trouble," said Claudia. "You heard Judd. He beat up his own father."

Jeff snorted. "Don't you see what they're doing? We've been doing this damn play for a week and you still don't get it, do you?"

Claudia looked confused.

"Get what?" asked Dina.

"That you're losers."

Everyone looked to the back of the church.

Bryan Morrison stood at the head of the other teenagers. His head snapped around. "Who said that?"

No one answered.

Jeff laughed harshly. "Better to be losers than to be like you."

Bryan started walking forward, the group following close behind him.

Lindy and Rebo blocked the way.

Bryan looked past them to Jeff. "I'm sorry, Mrs. H. But we need to get this out in the open. I've had training in peer counseling."

Rebo shrugged and let him pass, then turned to watch him, effectively stopping the others. "Peer counseling, my ass," he said to Lindy. "He reminds me of that kid on those *Leave It to Beaver* reruns. You know the one. 'Good Evening, Mrs. Cleaver.' "

The imitation was perfect.

"Eddie Haskell."

"Yeah, that's who Bryan Morrison reminds me of."

Bryan walked to the end of the aisle.

"What is it you don't like about us?" he asked. His tone was perfectly modulated and nonconfrontational. A technique he must have learned at his training session, Lindy thought.

"Don't pull that peer-counseling shit with me, Bryan," said Jeff. "Save it for when you run for Congress."

"I think we should talk about how Kenny's behavior has impacted on the future of the teen center," answered Bryan.

"I think you'd better get out of here, before I do some impacting on you."

Bryan took a step back, his diplomacy shaken.

Jeff took his advantage. "So take your appropriate behavior and shove it. You're a bunch of spineless wonders."

"At least we don't beat up our own fathers," jeered someone behind Lindy.

"Yeah?" returned Jeff. "So maybe you don't have a stepfather that beats the crap out of your mother. Lucky you."

"Mr. Gainer would never beat his wife," said Bryan.

Jeff snorted.

"I don't believe it."

"Of course not. But Mr. Fine Upstanding Citizen, Paragon of the Community, comes home every night, belts back his drug of choice—scotch, I believe—and slugs Kenny's mother a few times. Nothing she doesn't deserve, I'm sure." Jeff paused long enough to take a harsh breath. "But Kenny, fool that he is, doesn't realize that this is the way 'good' men treat their wives, so he tries to stop him. And Mr. Gainer, upstanding asshole that *he* is, calls the cops and says Kenny's acting violent and ple-e-e-ese come take him away." Jeff's fist slammed onto the edge of the pulpit. "And does his mom stick up for him? Shit, no. Cause she's just as snowed by Mr. Big Shot as everyone else is. And if she just lies low for a few days, nobody will see the black eye she's got."

"I don't believe it," repeated Bryan, his voice wavering.

"*You* don't have to. But Kenny does. Night after night."

"If that's true, why didn't Kenny tell someone?"

"Because he's a bigger chump than all of you. Afraid of what people will say about his mom. That they'll snub her. Oh, God, you people make me sick. So say or do whatever you came to do and get the hell out. But don't give me any of your 'open dialogue' bullshit. We've got a play to rehearse, and quite frankly, I'd just as soon take my chances with the hypocrites of Salem."

Jeff turned toward the altar and raised his arms. All eyes were riveted on his back. "'An invisible crime,'" he intoned and began to laugh.

The sound echoed above them, then ricocheted against the walls.

Bryan backed down the aisle. Then he turned and with a quick look of confusion at Lindy, he led the rest of the council out of the church.

"Shit," said Rebo under his breath. "These kids are intense."

Lindy wrapped cold arms across her chest. "This is getting way past the limerick stage."

Jeff wheeled around. "I didn't say any of that stuff. And I'll deny it if anybody says I did." He jerked his head away. "Shit. Kenny'll never forgive me."

"Why didn't Kenny confide in someone?" It was Janey who had spoken, and for a moment Jeff could only stare at her.

"I—I didn't know you were there, Ms. Horowitz."

"You didn't answer my question, Jeff."

Jeff scuffed his shoe along the floor in the universal teenage sign for embarrassment. "He confided in *me*. And now I've screwed that up, too."

"You didn't 'screw up,' Jeff. I think it was very brave of you to stand up for Kenny."

Jeff lowered his head.

"Well," said Melanie, getting up from the pew as if nothing had happened. "Shall we get back to the play?"

"You know something?" said Claudia, turning to Jeff. "I think I get it now. You just pulled a John Proctor, right?"

Lindy and Rebo left them discussing whether John Proctor was a hero or a "sap."

"Melanie didn't exactly jump on the bandwagon about Jeff's bravery, did she?" asked Lindy as they walked outside.

"Definitely a hedge."

"She puts an incredible amount of energy into those kids; badgers and cajoles them, then suddenly she pulls away and you don't know if she's regrouping, giving up or whether it's another technique in her varied repertoire. One minute she's threatening them, and the next she's sticking up for them. It's hard to tell how she really feels."

"Yeah. She's a deep 'un as they say somewhere or other."

They stepped out into the waning light, just in time to see Derrick helping Fallon into his Jaguar. She was clinging to him so tightly that he had to pull her hands away in order to close the door. He rushed to the driver's side. Then he saw Lindy.

"Fallon's not feeling well. I'm taking her home."

Lindy peered into the car. Fallon was curved into a ball in the front seat. "Maybe you should call a doctor."

"No. No. She gets like this all the time. Nerves or something. She'll be fine." He jumped into the car and drove away.

Lindy sighed. "I hope she isn't seriously ill, but I wouldn't mind her being indisposed for a few days. I wonder if I should call Mary Elisabeth and tell her."

"I'd go home if I were you," said Rebo. "That's where I'm going. Gotta get back to the crack addicts and serial killers where it's safe." He slapped his cheek. "These wholesome communities scare the shit out of me."

Lindy took his advice and headed for the parking lot. As far as she knew, the council was back working on its hayride and the drama group was putting in understudies for Kenny and Val. Half-constructed booths had been deserted for the night. There were only a few cars left in the lot.

The Gospel of Galilee Church was still camped out on the side of the road, dining on fried chicken from one of the fast-food chains. She waved good night, knowing they couldn't see her in the growing darkness. She hummed *Danse Macabre* as she drove, speeding up the tempo with each phrase until the tune was unrecognizable.

God, she was glad to be out of there. The marathon had taken on a life of its own, but it was a double life, one meant to do good and one that was opening wounds no one had expected. She wondered which side would be the survivor.

Lindy stretched out along the couch in the family room and turned the page of her book, a copy of *The Crucible* she had found in a box in the attic. She had meant to scan through it while she was waiting for Glen to call. Now it was late, and she was immersed in the story of the Salem witch trials. It was horrific, the deaths of so many innocent people because of the pranks of a few wicked children.

The page she was reading grew blurry as John Proctor confessed his sins in hopes of exonerating himself and his wife, Elizabeth. But he refused to accuse his neighbors, thus sealing his fate to death by hanging.

The play ended with Elizabeth, alone on stage, saved by the husband whose fidelity she had doubted. Lindy closed the book and threw it across the room. She glanced at the phone. She was suddenly afraid of what she might discover if Glen did call.

Damn, she should have chosen a nice cozy mystery. Those murders were never too gruesome. Sometimes they were even funny. But there was nothing funny about what had happened in Salem, and there was nothing funny about what was happening at the Van Cleef farm.

A detective was dead. Stella poisoned. Anonymous limericks. Val overdosed on drugs. Kenny arrested. At least, she had never had to face that problem with Cliff and Annie. They were good kids.

She stood up and began to pace, disgusted by her thoughts. She sounded just like Bryan and the council. Janey was right about kids living up to your expectations. Kids weren't good or bad, they became that way. Was Kenny bad because he tried to protect his mother? Was that the kind of person who would sell drugs to a friend? And they did do drugs, she had seen them with her own eyes. Would their presence reflect badly on the marathon?

At least there had been no more limericks. With all the angst between the two groups of teenagers, there hadn't been time. Or maybe they had taken Mary Elisabeth's words to heart.

The telephone rang. She snatched it up.

"Hello."

"Hi. It's Bill."

"Oh."

There was silence, and Lindy knew she must have sounded disappointed. "What a day," she said, trying to erase the sound of that "Oh."

She heard squeals and shrieks in the background. "Sounds like you've had a day of it, too."

"It's been energetic," said Bill. He sounded tired. "Do you still want to go to the zoo? Don't feel obligated."

"Are you kidding? I can't wait." Was she overdoing the enthusiasm? A knee-jerk reaction because she was afraid she had hurt his feelings? And why all this second guessing? She did want to go to the zoo. It would be relaxing after the zoo she had been in for the last few days. And she was curious to see Bill in the role of uncle.

"I'll meet you there. What time?"

Cries of "Uncle Bill, Uncle Bill" drowned out his answer. "The boys are excited. Would ten-thirty be too early?"

"Fine."

"Okay. See you then."

"Good-bye, Uncle Bill." She laughed and hung up the phone.

Chapter Seventeen

Lindy awoke to the rumble of thunder. Outside her window the sky was dark gray and the rain came down in sheets. Her first thought was of the zoo; she sighed with disappointment. Then she remembered the half-finished booths at the Marathon and jumped out of bed.

While coffee brewed, she called Mary Elisabeth; there was no answer. Over the blare of Sunday morning cartoons, Stella's daughter shouted that Stella was at work, but she didn't know where that was. Next, she called Bill. More cartoons.

"Hang on a minute," he said. The noise level decreased. "I guess the zoo is out."

"Too bad," Lindy agreed. "I was looking forward to it."

"Me, too."

There was a moment where neither spoke.

"What are you and the boys going to do?"

"God only knows. They've been awake since six. I've watched three hours of alien-zapping cartoons. They've made a fort over the couch using every sheet and towel in the closet and half the books in my office. That was after Will was up half the night crying that he wanted to go home." He sighed. "It's getting a little crowded."

"Why don't you take in a movie?"

"Can't find anything under PG-13 that isn't a cartoon. They nixed the museum and Broadway. They're afraid of the subways. Hate bagels. Christ. Manhattan has something for everyone, and I can't figure out a thing to do."

"Poor Uncle Bill."

"I am," he said. "God, I really am." There was a crash in the background. "Christ. I have to go." Bill hung up the phone.

Lindy smiled sympathetically. His good intentions were getting the better of him. She poured herself a cup of coffee, listening to the rain. The house was quiet and peaceful. Or at least it should have been, but after the noise of Stella's kids and Bill's nephews, it just seemed lonely. These walls could stand to hear the patter of little feet again. For an afternoon anyway.

She picked up the phone and punched redial.

"Bring them out here," she said as soon as Bill answered.

"To New Jersey?"

"I know it sounds stupid when they have Manhattan at their fingertips. But they're boys. My house is huge. They can play with Bruno. I have a basement filled with Cliff's old toys, and a pool table—and if it stops raining, there's the yard."

"You really mean it?"

"Sure. I just have to go over to the farm and make sure everything is tarped over. It should take less than an hour. And later we can drink the bottle of wine I brought you from Spain."

"We're on our way."

"Remember how to get here?"

"Yes. You're sure you don't mind?"

"I don't mind; it'll be fun." And it would give her a chance to be a real friend for a change.

Judd and two others from the setup crew had just finished covering the construction when she arrived at the marathon site. A landscape of amorphous tarps and plastic drop cloths littered the ground behind them. As soon as their tools were thrown into the back of a pickup, his two helpers jumped in and drove away, honking as they turned out of the driveway. Judd came over to her car.

"Looks like I'm just in time," said Lindy.

"Just in time to unlock the house and let me clean up," said Judd. "I'm on call."

"Okay, but you'll have to go around to the kitchen. I'll go through the house and let you in. Lucky for you, Mary Elisabeth had the foresight to give me an extra set of keys."

"I thought she'd be here, but I'm glad she didn't get out in this weather."

Lindy inserted the key into the lock, but the door wasn't locked. She wondered why T.J. hadn't told Judd the house was open. But when she saw the Aubusson carpet and remembered T.J.'s reaction to her dripping on it, she was even more surprised that he hadn't locked *and* bolted the door.

She took off her shoes and threw her rain poncho onto the porch. Then she listened for signs of working. "T.J. It's Lindy. I'm letting Judd into the kitchen. We won't drip on anything."

She waited for an answer and hearing nothing, she hurried down the hall.

Judd had taken off his slicker and was shaking it with a vengeance when Lindy opened the kitchen door.

"It's getting cold." He let the screen door slam behind him and threw his slicker over the back of a chair.

"I'll make you a cup of coffee, but what you should probably have is some of Adam Crabtree's slippery elm tea."

Judd's face went through a series of contortions. "Coffee'll be fine."

He changed out of his shoes and washed his hands and face at the sink, while Lindy made coffee. She became aware of scraping sounds behind the closed-off doors, quiet at first, but becoming increasingly louder.

"Lord, what's that racket?" Judd asked.

"T.J.'s been doing something in that back stairway for days. He won't let anybody take a look."

"I've never known anybody to get so excited about broken-down old buildings as T.J. Been that way ever since he was a kid."

"He's from around here?" Lindy took a milk carton from the fridge and shook it. "Enough left for a couple of cups."

"Sure. He grew up here. Then he went off to Rhode Island or somewhere and came back with a string of degrees and a portfolio like you've never seen. Adam took one look and said he was the man for the job." Judd's mouth quirked up. "What he actually said, I believe, was 'Fine.' "

They both laughed, but stopped when the scraping turned to pounding.

"What the hell's he doing in there?"

Lindy shrugged.

"Let's peek." Judd tiptoed over to the boarded door. Winking conspiratorially at Lindy, he slipped a long finger beneath the barricade. It held fast.

Muffled cries came from the other side.

Judd pressed his ear to the door and listened. "Holy roller! I think he's stuck in there." He grabbed the board with both hands and yanked. The nails screamed as it pulled away from the wood.

Judd groped on the inside of the door, looking for a light switch. "See if you can find a flashlight." He disappeared through the doorway.

Lindy rummaged through the kitchen, opening and closing drawers until she found a flashlight. She carried it over to the door and followed Judd through the opening.

She shined the light up and down the stairway until she found him. He was feeling his way along the wall, balanced precariously on a flight of steep steps.

"Be careful," she said.

"Shh." He listened for a second, then called out, "Stay where you are, so I can find you."

"What is it?" Lindy asked, though already she was beginning to recognize T.J.'s voice. "Where is he?"

"He's stuck on the other side of the wall."

"But there's nothing there but the outside wall."

"Tell that to T.J." Judd banged on the wall. "T.J., are you okay?"

He was answered by a burst of yelling.

"Stay calm," Judd called. "We'll get you out, but I can't tell where you are. Knock twice if you can hear me."

There were two knocks.

"Okay, just keep knocking at regular intervals until I can trace the sound."

Judd knocked on the wall, and there was an answering knock, only this time lower than the one before.

"What the hell's he doing?" Judd took a step down. The treads were so narrow that he had to stand sideways.

The knock came again, this time lower.

"He's leading us to the cellar," said Lindy.

Judd took the flashlight. It cast bizarre shadows on the walls as he sidestepped down the stairs. Lindy followed two steps behind him, hands pressed against each wall for balance.

When she got to the bottom, Judd pushed the flashlight into her hand. "Stand back." He threw himself against the cellar door. It splintered and he fell into darkness.

She stepped inside behind him and shined the light around. The cellar walls were carved from dirt and rock. The floor above was supported by timbers. She could hear shouts and banging. They were loud, but hollow sounding, and seemed to come from the same level as the cellar. But that was impossible; the room was empty, except for an ancient furnace.

Judd began to prowl the space, knees bent and his head tucked down because the ceiling was too low for him to stand upright. Lindy focused the beam of light on his hunched figure. Finally he seemed to zero in on the location of the knocks. He squeezed behind the furnace.

"Damnedest thing I ever saw." His voice echoed from the darkness.

Lindy peered around the furnace. A cast-iron door, barely wide enough to squeeze through, appeared from the earthen walls. It was locked from the cellar side. Judd threw the bolt back and pulled the door open. It creaked on its hinges. T.J. tumbled out onto the ground.

Lindy gasped and jumped back; then she shined the flashlight on his face. His hair was wild and covered with cobwebs. His eyes were two white orbs in a black, dusty face, his mouth a stiff, pink O.

Judd dragged him out from behind the furnace. "Hell's bells," he said. "You look like something out of a minstrel show."

"I . . . I . . . I've been in there for hours—all night—I could have died. I could have—" He broke off.

Judd peered over his head into the door. "What's in there?"

T.J. pursed his lips together and tried to bar the door with his body. Judd started to move him aside.

"Wait," said T.J. He chewed on his lip for a second, then said, "It's a secret passage."

Judd guffawed. "You lose your mind while you were cooped up in there?"

"No, I did not lose my mind. There are two sets of staircases. I noticed the discrepancy when I was making my initial measurements. I've been clearing out the second one for days."

"Okay, tell us the rest upstairs. This place is giving me the creeps."

They helped T.J. up the stairs and into the kitchen. He looked worse in the light of day.

"How did you get locked in there?" asked Lindy.

"I was in the second stairway, and suddenly the door slammed and the lights went out. That was around midnight. And I've been there ever since."

"Hear anybody?" asked Judd.

"No, but somebody locked me in." T.J.'s voice was piercing.

"Yeah. Unless you know how a bolt lock locked itself, I'd say that was a safe assumption."

"Not from the cellar. From the upstairs closet." T.J.'s eyes widened. Lindy didn't know whether to laugh or scream. Before she could do either, T.J. was running out the door. "If anything has been damaged—" he yelled as he ran up the central staircase, unaware of the dirt and dust he was dropping on the runner.

T.J. took the last three stairs in one leap and disappeared into the back bedroom. When Judd and Lindy entered, the room was empty except for a fine layer of dust, a ladder and a box of tools. An extension cord lay across the floor. It had been pulled out of the socket.

The other end led to the door of a closet that jutted out into the room. There were rummaging noises coming from inside. They both looked through the door. T.J. was on his haunches inspecting the interior wall. The plaster had been chipped away to reveal an opening to what looked like a laundry chute. It was padlocked shut.

"Locked," he said over his shoulder. "I could have died in there."

Judd grinned. "Somebody would have found you tomorrow morning. You were making enough racket."

"But who would lock you in?" asked Lindy.

Judd picked a square of paper off the floor, holding it by one corner. His eyebrows rose nearly to his hairline.

Lindy leaned against the doorjamb and sighed. "I thought we were through with those."

"You sure you didn't see or hear anybody?"

"I'm sure." T.J. frowned. "They're after my discovery." He blinked several times; then his eyes focused on the paper Judd was holding. A low growl came from his throat. He reached for the paper.

Judd snatched it back. "We'll read it just as soon as I get a Baggie to put it in. It's a long shot, but I'll check it for prints and see if anything comes up on file. You never know."

They followed Judd to the kitchen and sat at the table, watching expectantly while he opened a box of sandwich bags. He snapped one open, slipped the paper inside and pressed out the air.

"Now then." He placed it on the table, then reached into his breast pocket and brought out a pair of reading glasses. He blew on the lens and polished them with a dish cloth.

"Judd," Lindy urged. "You're milking this a little too much."

Judd's face fell. "Sorry, But I don't usually get such an attentive audience." He sat down and began to read:

"There was a redhead on a farm
Whose greediness brought him to harm
He dug day and night
Out of everyone's sight
So he couldn't sound the alarm"

"I'll be damned," he said, scratching his head.

"Greed," said Lindy.

"I'm not greedy," huffed T.J. "My work will benefit history and won't make me one damned penny. Of all the nerve."

Judd hushed him with a look. "Why don't you tell us what you're in such a lather to find. Maybe that'll give us a clue as to what's happening here."

T.J. folded his arms and scowled.

Judd cocked his head and gave one of his 'I can last longer than you can so you might as well tell me' looks that he was famous for.

"I'll have to swear you to secrecy."

"T.J." Lindy and Judd chorused together.

"Oh, all right. The underground railroad."

They looked at him blankly.

"The underground railroad," he repeated. He gave them an impatient look. "The Civil War? Runaway slaves?" He spread both hands out in exasperation.

"I didn't think Jersey had any underground railroads," said Judd.

T.J. jumped up. "That's just the point. New Jersey has never been fully credited with the work we did to free the slaves. It had a reputation for playing both sides of the war because of all the industry located here. Only a few stops have been discovered, and except for the one in Paterson, they were much farther west. If this turns out to be a safe house, history will have to be rewritten."

"Okay, just calm down for a minute. What kind of evidence have you found?"

T.J. shifted uncomfortably. It was obvious he didn't want to let them in on the details of his research. Finally, he sighed. "That door in the cellar. It's cast iron."

"Yeah?" said Judd

"It goes to the hidden staircase, not to the servants' stairs." T.J. put up a hand to cut off any interruptions. "They run side by side until they reach ground level. After that, the second one veers off to the left. Didn't you notice how far away the two doors are from each other? The cast-iron door was added much later, probably early twentieth century. I think the second staircase originally led directly into a tunnel down to the brook. It's been filled in, but I know the signs." T.J. began to pace as his excitement grew. "I haven't been able to plot the course yet. It probably comes out at the springhouse. The slaves could be hidden there until a boat could pick them up—"

"But the stream flows southeast, not north."

T.J. waved Judd's comment aside. "They probably only went as far as the nearest road. These things sometimes involved a lot of backtracking." He broke into a wide pink grin. "Imagine what finding the tunnel will mean. There might even be evidence in the tunnel itself, but it's very time-consuming work and I'm only one man—"

"And unfortunately, so am I. This is real interesting, but I've got to get to work, and I think it's time we got to the bottom of these pranks. They're getting nastier. I'm going to take this by the station, and I want you to stay out of that stairway and the cellar unless there are people around."

"Sure. Sure. But remember, this is in confidence." T.J. reached for a cup and poured coffee into it. "Don't tell anybody." He glared at Lindy and at Judd.

"No problem," they said.

Judd grabbed his slicker and went out into the rain.

Lindy jumped up. "Lord, I've got company coming. Will you be okay?"

T.J. was pacing, drinking coffee and mumbling to himself. "Sure, go ahead." He waved distractedly, but Lindy was already gone.

Chapter Eighteen

Some hostess, she thought. She had meant to get home long before Bill arrived with the boys. But how was she to know they were going to get waylaid by a nasty limerick and a history-changing tunnel?

She had just dumped her shoes and poncho in the mud room when she heard Bill's Honda pull into the driveway. She grabbed a pair of clogs and raced to the front door. She dropped them on the foyer tile, slipped her feet into them and went out to meet them.

She waited on the stoop, whooping air and trying to look like Martha Stewart.

Two small boys jumped out of the back seat and scrambled up the brick walk, followed by Bill looking a little worse for wear. They came to an abrupt halt, eyes wide. Bruno lunged past Lindy, tail wagging madly.

Damn, she had forgotten about Bruno.

"Bruno, down." She clomped after him. The younger of the boys had grabbed Bill's leg and was trying to climb up it. Bill swung him to his hip, where he clung tightly to Bill's neck and buried his face in his shoulder.

Unperturbed, Bruno planted both paws on Bill's chest and licked his face. Lindy grabbed his collar and pulled him away. Two wet paw prints stood out on Bill's blue flannel shirt.

"Sorry," said Lindy. She tucked her head to see the boy Bill was holding. "Bruno's just a big dope. He likes to play." The boy peeked out at her.

"See, Will, he won't hurt you. Good boy." His brother had knelt on the wet bricks and was letting Bruno lick his face. "It tickles." He laughed delightedly.

Will slid down Bill's side and took a tentative step toward Bruno. "Does he bite?"

"Nope. Doesn't even growl." *Unless he finds a dead body*. She quickly erased that thought.

Bruno barked. Will jumped.

Bill took Will by the hand and walked him over to Bruno. He knelt down before Bruno had a chance to jump and scratched behind his ears. Bruno snuffled with pleasure.

Another conquest, as usual. Bill had a way with people, women especially, and evidently with children and animals, too.

Will stretched an unsteady hand toward Bruno's head. Bruno took the opportunity to give it a lick. Will laughed.

Bill stood up and grinned at her.

"What?"

His grin widened.

Will stood up, too. "How come your face is dirty? Uncle Bill made us wash ours before we came."

Lindy touched her cheek. Dried mud flaked down her sweatshirt. "I was having an adventure. I haven't had time to wash my face."

"What kind of adventure?"

"Well . . ." She glanced at Bill. "I'll tell you all about it when we're inside."

Will fell in step with her. "How come your pumpkins don't have faces?"

Lindy looked at her artful arrangement. Why didn't her pumpkins have faces?

"I have so many that I knew I would need help. How are you at pumpkin carving?"

His mouth puckered. He had Bill's mouth, thin-lipped, but expressive. "Mama won't let me use a knife. But I can draw the pictures and you can cut them out."

"Huh?" She brought her mind back to the pumpkins. "That's a good idea. Maybe Uncle Bill would be nice enough to bring them inside."

Bill handed two of the smaller ones to Randall and the smallest one to Will. He carried the largest ones himself.

As soon as the pumpkins had been deposited on the kitchen table, Bill made the formal introductions. Randall, dark-haired and stocky, was a miniature version of his father, Patrick O'Dell. "I'm ten," he announced. Will shook hands solemnly. He was finer boned than Randall, and though only eight, Lindy thought he might someday surpass his brother in height.

"Do you really have a pool table?" asked Randall.

"Uh-huh. Would you like to play?"

Both boys beamed, and Lindy took them down to the basement.

"You sure have a big house," said Will.

Bill racked the balls and showed them how to use the cues. Bruno rested his snout on the table edge and barked when Bill broke the balls.

"Want some coffee?" Lindy asked.

"Do I ever." They left the boys happily knocking balls around the table.

"So what adventure did you have this morning?"

"Sure you want to know?"

"No, but tell me."

She explained about T.J being locked in the hidden staircase, how he expected to find a tunnel. She found herself recounting all the limerick episodes. "So there are three more to go. Honestly, it's always something. I don't know why I keep volunteering. It's just tempers, egos and territorial spats. All your worst diva nightmares rolled into one."

"Sounds like my reorganization meetings this week," said Bill. "It's surprising how violent a group of criminologists can get over class scheduling."

She nodded sympathetically. "This committee should be getting along well. Most of us have worked together before and have pretty much ironed out the kinks. We know where not to go with each other. But there are several new members. They do not get along. Plus there's the Gospel of Galilee Church picketing across the street." She saw the look on Bill's face and explained. "They think celebrating Halloween is devil worship.

"T.J., the restorer, treats the house like an overprotective mother. Mary Elisabeth's stepdaughter and her boyfriend get in everybody's way and Fallon even forged a check to the marathon."

Bill was smiling. "Sounds like you have your hands full."

Lindy rolled her eyes. "And then there's the drowned man. It turns out that he's a detective. They found his car nearby. Judd thinks he might have been investigating someone working on the marathon."

Bill's smile vanished. "That doesn't sound good. Are you safe working there?"

"Rebo showed up with Peter, Rose and Mieko, and they've been there ever since."

"What drowned man?" Will's eyes were huge with curiosity as he pressed against the door frame, half hidden from view.

"What has your mother told you about eavesdropping?" asked Bill.

"What drowned man? Hey, Randall," called Will. "Lindy found a drowned man."

Bill groaned.

Randall appeared in the doorway followed by Bruno. "Wow, was that the adventure you had?"

"Uh . . ." Lindy slanted a glance at Bill. "There's a carnival for Mischief Night," she hedged, trying to distract them from the drowned man. "There's going to be a haunted hayride with all kinds of spooky things along the way. A dummy that swings out over the road, and a headless horseman, and a chain saw—" She quickly edited herself. "And a bunch of kids dressed up really scary."

"The Texas Chain Saw Murderer?" asked Randall. "Oh, boy. I lo-o-ove him. Daddy rented the tape one night, but Mama made us turn it off. I didn't get to see how it ended."

"And there'll also be apple dunking and fortune telling and pumpkin painting," Lindy enumerated in an effort to get away from the chain saw murderer.

"Can we go to the carnival, Uncle Bill? I really, really want to see the chain saw murderer." Randall turned to Lindy. "Does it really work? Is he going to turn the saw on? It's so cool. You see, it starts with a close-up of his hands starting the saw. Then he stomps right at the camera and then—Will started crying and Mama came in and yelled at Daddy."

A smile tugged at the corners of Bill's mouth.

"I did not," said Will.

"Did, too. Can we go, please?" Randall cast pleading eyes at Bill.

Bill wrestled him into his lap and started tickling him. "You little manipulator. Don't you bat those baby browns at me."

Will took a step into the kitchen and stood watching. A look from Bill and he was in his lap, too. The three of them tickled and poked and made muscles at each other.

Lindy bit her lip. Bill must have been a good father. He had been divorced when his son, Stephen, was seven, about Will's age. She had guessed from the few things he had said that it wasn't amicable, for his ex-wife had not been cooperative about visitation rights. She wondered how he felt playing with his nephews.

Now that Bill had deflected their attention from the

marathon, Lindy sent them to the storage closet looking for Cliff's old LEGOs. While the three of them built, she made pizza from the kits she had bought from the marching band. Pepperoni and extra cheese for the boys, and another, more upscale one for Bill and her.

After lunch, Bill took the boys and Bruno outside with a dog-chewed Frisbee. Lindy stood at the kitchen window watching the orange disk float through the air, Bruno diving after every catch. The rain started again, and the boys came in to draw faces on the pumpkins. When the pumpkins were covered with black magic marker, she sent them to search through the stash of videotapes for a movie to watch.

Lindy was sponging off the table when she felt Will beside her.

"Bored?" she asked.

Will shrugged. "Uncle Bill isn't very good at playing."

"Sure he is, he's just a little out of practice." She looked over Will's head. Bill was standing in the doorway.

"Randall's waiting for you to start *Space Balls.*"

Will ran past him to the family room, yelling, "Wait for me" down the hall.

"He's right. I'm lousy at playing."

"What did your mother tell you about eavesdropping?"

"Too many years as a detective. Are you planning to carve those pumpkins?"

While Bill spread newspapers over the table surface, Lindy searched the drawers for the pumpkin-carving knives.

"State of the art equipment," said Bill, flicking at the stainless steel tip of the serrated knife. "I thought they were supposed to have orange plastic handles."

"Glen sent away for these. Only the best for the Haggerty pumpkins."

She sat down and the next few minutes passed in companionable silence, accompanied by the sound of the knives as they sawed through pumpkin flesh. Lindy poured glasses of wine and set them on the table. She brushed a pumpkin seed off Bill's cheek.

They drank and carved and chatted until the table was heaped with pumpkin guts, and six ghoulish faces were lined up in a row. Lindy put votive candles in each one and they carried them to the front porch. It was already dark though it was only a little after five o'clock.

Bill called the boys while Lindy lit the candles. She stood back as faces danced from the darkness.

"Wow, cool," exclaimed Randall.

Will had once again wrapped himself around Bill's leg. Bill's hand rested gently on his shoulder.

Lindy felt a pang of something. Sadness? Regret? Sentimentality? She shook it off. "Pretty neat, huh, guys?"

"Can we come back tomorrow?" asked Randall.

"Randall," said Bill.

"Please."

"You're welcome anytime," said Lindy and realized that she meant it.

"Go finish cleaning up your mess," said Bill. "It's time we were going."

The boys ran off.

"Thanks for having us. They take a lot of energy."

"If you want to bring them out again, it's fine. I can take them with me to the farm. There's lots of things for boys to do." She paused. "If you think it's safe."

"Can we, Uncle Bill? Please?"

"Damn," said Bill. "Where did you two come from?"

"Uncle Bill said a dirty word." Will giggled.

"We'll see."

He gathered up shoes and socks, sweatshirts and coats. Lindy packed a box of old toys and comics to send with them. She snuffed out the candles of two pumpkins and put them in the back seat with the boys.

She watched them drive away and stayed on the porch until the taillights of the Honda disappeared over the hill. She walked back inside. The house seemed too quiet after the day they had just had. Bruno was asleep on the couch in the family room. She picked up an old ninja turtle that had been missed during the cleanup. Michelangelo? Leonardo?

She smiled, remembering the day Cliff had come home from school and seriously announced that the ninja turtles had painters named after them.

She poured out the last of the wine and looked around at the kitchen. A house should be filled with noise and activity, she thought. She sat down at the table and wondered how long it had been since she and Glen carved a pumpkin together. Or if they ever had. When had they last enjoyed just doing nothing?

She reached for the phone. When the answering machine came on, she slammed down the receiver, rested her head on the table and cried.

Chapter Nineteen

"This is absolutely outrageous. T.J. could have been seriously injured." Mary Elisabeth slapped her hand down on the kitchen table just as Lindy opened the door. "Can't you find out who's doing these things?"

"Me?" asked Lindy, still befuddled by a sleepless night, worrying about her marriage and the marathon.

"I'm sorry. I know this isn't your problem, but—"

"It's everyone's problem," said Stella.

"It isn't the children," Janey insisted.

"I thought it would end once we confronted them," Mary Elisabeth continued as if Janey hadn't spoken. "Perhaps it would be better if we asked Melanie to postpone her play and present it at another time."

"No." Janey upset her cup in her agitation. Stella grabbed a paper towel and began mopping up the liquid.

"Let's be sure before we do anything so drastic," said Lindy. "All of the limericks and pranks have been aimed at members of the committee. As if someone had a personal vendetta. Why would kids who are depending on the marathon do such a thing?"

"And they wouldn't hire a private detective, would they?"

Everyone stared at Evelyn.

"What does the detective have to do with this?" asked Mary Elisabeth.

"And how did you know he was a detective?" asked Lindy. Judd had insisted on silence concerning the body. Now it seemed everyone was going to know.

"Judd explained it to me when he asked me to verify seeing Fallon and Derrick here last weekend."

"I just thought they might have seen something," Lindy said defensively. She didn't know why she always reacted that way to Evelyn. The woman's manner was calm, to the point of calculation. But it rankled.

"They were here last weekend?" asked Mary Elisabeth. Her face was a mixture of surprise and annoyance. "They had no right to be here." She stopped talking and drummed her fingernails on the table.

"Okay, let's think this thing through," said Lindy. "There were three limericks during the week. Gluttony." She shot an apologetic look toward Stella. "Idleness and Pride. They were all delivered during the day, while we were here and when the kids were in school."

"If they were in school," said Stella.

Lindy remembered the day they had caught Val and the boys by the springhouse. But they had been more intent on getting high than anything else.

"T.J. was locked in the staircase on Saturday night. And we all know how teenagers run wild on the weekends."

"You're wrong, Stella." Janey looked close to tears. "Please just trust me on this. It isn't one of the students."

"Do you know who it is?" asked Evelyn.

Janey bit her lip and shook her head. She seemed to shrink inside the white cardigan that was draped over her shoulders.

Evelyn eyed Lindy. "Where is the limerick that was left for T.J.?"

"Judd took it. He thought he might be able to lift prints from it."

"A long shot," said Evelyn.

"That's what Judd said."

"Do you remember it?"

Lindy deliberated before she answered. It seemed like the only way to figure out who the culprit was would be to work as a team. She tried to conjure up the words on the paper. "There was a redhead on a farm. Whose greediness—um—whose greediness brought him harm." She glanced at Janey. "I'd never have made it in your English class."

"That's okay, dear, you're doing fine."

Lindy closed her eyes, concentrating. "He worked night and day . . . no, day and night, something out of sight and he couldn't raise the alarm, or words to that effect." She opened her eyes. "Greed. That was the fourth one."

She reached into her bag for her notebook and opened to the page she had written on Saturday. "Gluttony, Idleness, Pride and Greed. Four deadly sins. That makes three left. Maybe we can second-guess whoever wrote them."

"Yeah, and bag the little devils when they try it again," said Stella with the first real enthusiasm she had shown since her return from the hospital.

Evelyn reached inside her purse and extracted a piece of paper. She dropped it onto the table. "Two left. I got this last Tuesday. You might as well read it aloud."

Mary Elisabeth picked it up.

"There once was an uppity blackie
No better than any old lackey
Her anger was hidden
But came out unbidden
Her manners will always be tacky"

"Oh, Evelyn, why didn't you say something? This is awful."

"Good Lord," said Stella. "I hope you didn't think that's how we feel."

"Frankly, I wasn't sure. I thought at the time that one of you sent it. That I wasn't welcome on the committee."

Lindy raised a metaphoric eyebrow. "Was it accompanied by a prank?" she asked.

"Someone let the air out of my back tires."

Stella laughed. "Sorry, Evelyn, it isn't funny, but hon, if we didn't want you around, we certainly wouldn't have taken out your only means of transportation."

"It seemed odd, but cruelty isn't always thought out in advance."

"Okay," said Lindy. "We have *two* left." She consulted her notes. "Envy and Lechery, right?" She looked to Janey for confirmation. Janey's eyes were brimming with unshed tears. "Janey?" she asked quietly.

Janey fumbled in her lap for her napkin and blotted her eyes. "*One* more." Her words were muffled by the linen.

They all turned to gape at her.

"This morning," she said, not looking at them. "It was taped to the bag of tea that I leave in the cabinet."

"You didn't drink any of it, did you?" Lindy looked down at the half-empty cup and started to move it away.

"I threw the bag in the trash. Adam was kind enough to bring me a new bag. Such a dear man."

From the corner of her eye, Lindy saw Evelyn open the cabinet beneath the sink where the trash can was kept.

"Don't tell me you've been out flirting with somebody's husband," laughed Stella, then the comprehension of what she had just said suffused her face. "Oh—I mean—it's so totally ridiculous." She wound to a stop.

Lindy darted her a sympathetic look. In her attempt to make light of the situation, Stella had stumbled onto the one subject that was taboo.

"I would never do such a thing, never," said Janey. "Never."

"Of course you wouldn't," said Mary Elisabeth.

Then it has to be Envy, thought Lindy. She dreaded to think what the limerick said. To anyone who was dying, envy of the living must be overwhelming. Please heaven the note writer hadn't said so.

"May we see it?" asked Evelyn.

"I can't," said Janey.

Evelyn waited. Stella shot Lindy a nervous look.

Finally, Mary Elisabeth pulled a chair next to Janey and sat down. "It's all right, Janey. We'll read it together."

Janey reached slowly into the pocket of her sweater, then handed her the note. The others watched as Mary Elisabeth's face drained of color.

Janey hiccuped, suppressing a sob. Evelyn eased the note from Mary Elisabeth's fingers.

Lindy's first thought was to snatch it away. Not let this stranger read whatever had so upset her two friends.

But Evelyn didn't read it aloud. She perused it, then handed it to Stella. Lindy watched Stella's face change from shock to outrage. She started to speak, but Evelyn stopped her with a brusque shake of her head. Stella passed the note to Lindy.

She didn't want to know what was written there, but she didn't have a choice. She forced herself to look at the paper:

There was an old crone who loved Howard
Who saduced him the day that it showered
Now she is dying
And nobody's crying
Her envy, not her, got deflowered

It was horrible. She slid the note back toward Janey without looking at her.

"It isn't true," Janey said. She crumpled the paper and shoved it into the pocket of her sweater. "None of it. You must believe me." Her words were for Mary Elisabeth. The others became uncomfortable voyeurs.

Mary Elisabeth didn't answer. Her eyes were focused on some invisible spot on the table.

"It was Saturday afternoon. I was in the square downtown. It began to rain and suddenly Howard was there, unfurling a black umbrella. We took shelter under the band shell. He told me he was out shopping with Fallon. He asked me about school and I asked him about work. Then it stopped raining, and we went our separate ways. That's the truth." Her voice was feeble, but intense. "I swear it."

Mary Elisabeth continued to stare at the table.

"You mean this refers to an actual event?" asked Lindy.

Janey nodded.

"But the rest of the limericks are general or allude to things in the present." An idea was forming in Lindy's mind.

"You have to believe me." Janey grasped Mary Elisabeth's hand. "Mary Elisabeth, please."

Lindy sighed with relief when Mary Elisabeth squeezed the hand that held hers.

"Who knew about that afternoon?" Evelyn asked.

"Only Howard," said Janey.

"Howard would never write limericks," said Mary Elisabeth, her voice filled with indignation.

"Fallon?" suggested Lindy. "Howard might have told her that he ran into Janey that day."

"It's Fallon," said Janey. "I'm sorry, but I know it's Fallon." She lifted her eyes to the others. They were red-rimmed and sunken. "This is Fallon's work. She could never keep her meter straight, even with something as simple as a limerick. Anapestic—two shorts and a long. But she never bothered to find the words that would fit. Or even spell them correctly." She sighed, the school teacher in her taking over momentarily. "Saduced. Really."

"There was another misspelling," said Lindy.

"Shepherd in the one left for Father Andrews," Evelyn and Lindy said at the same time.

"S-h-e-p-e-r-d," said Janey.

They both looked at her in astonishment.

"How did you know?"

"It's a common mistake. Fallon always had difficulty with words that had silent consonants in them."

Lindy's mind was racing far beyond limericks. What would possess a girl to remember such an insignificant meeting all these years? Had she really feared that her father was having an affair with Janey? Or worse, had she known it wasn't true but had started those rumors about Janey and Howard herself? To hurt Mary Elisabeth? It had taken ten years, but Fallon had finally managed to get back at her stepmother. Anger boiled up inside her. Lindy wanted to shake the little witch until her teeth rattled.

"Well, that makes me feel a lot better," said Stella, attempting a laugh. "And come to think of it, Evelyn got the first limerick right after her fight with Fallon over the church garbage."

"And Father Andrews after she poked him in the ribs," agreed Lindy. "And Mary Elisabeth after she accused her of forging the check. And T.J. after banning the dry ice from the cellar."

"That leaves one sin," said Stella. "And one member of the inner circle." She looked at Lindy.

"Me?" she asked, as the meaning of Stella's words gradually sank in. She was the only one who had not yet received a limerick, and the only sin left was Lechery. "That would be a stretch, even for Fallon."

"Hell, I'd be flattered if I were you," said Stella.

"Well, I'm not." Lindy stood up. "I suggest we talk to Fallon."

They didn't have far to look. Derrick was striding across the parking lot, Fallon hurrying to keep up. "But I want you to." Her voice rose stridently in the air. Derrick looked annoyed.

Lindy slowed down. The four other women drew up behind her.

"What do you think is going on?" asked Stella.

Derrick stopped when he saw that he was being observed. His look of disgust changed to one of amusement.

"Ah, the ladies of the marathon." He took a casual step toward them, leaving Fallon glaring after him. "You know, that would make an excellent title of a painting or a play."

"Put a lid on it, Derrick. We have business with Fallon." Stella bulldozed past him. The others followed. Derrick fell in line behind them, but took his stand next to Fallon once they had come to a stop in front of her.

Fallon tossed her hair and looked down her nose at them. Mary Elisabeth stepped toward her, and she moved closer to Derrick.

"You're no longer welcome here, Fallon. Take this poor excuse for a man and get out."

"Mary Elisabeth, I'm hurt." Derrick put his hand over his heart and hung his head à la Byron.

"How dare you," sputtered Fallon. "I'll tell Daddy."

"Go right ahead. I'm sure he would be interested in knowing what you've been up to."

"And what have you been up to now, my darling?" asked Derrick, dropping his misunderstood artist pose and smiling nervously.

"Nothing."

"That isn't true, Fallon," said Mary Elisabeth. "You've been playing horrid tricks and leaving nasty limericks all week. I won't have any more of it. Take your threats and your forged checks and your—coffee off this property and don't come back."

"You can't make me, and when Daddy finds out what you've done, he'll buy all of this for me."

"Give it up, Fallon," said Lindy. "Howard has no intention of buying this property for you. And we have no intention of letting you wreak havoc with the marathon."

She noticed Derrick's quick frown at Fallon, before it became a smile again. "Lindy, give the girl a chance to defend herself."

"She has thirty seconds."

Fallon's face distorted with anger. "You think you're so smart, Ms. Busybody. You're the one they should get rid of. You found the body. Wait until people find out about that. They won't dare bring their little kiddies to a marathon where somebody was murdered."

"You wouldn't dare," said Mary Elisabeth, her voice tight.

"Oh, wouldn't I? You think you can have everything you want. What about me? You never did like me, because Daddy loved me more. I hate you."

Mary Elisabeth took a step forward, and Lindy was afraid she was going to hit the girl.

It was Janey who slapped Fallon across the face. The sound cracked in the air, and a welt immediately rose on Fallon's skin.

"I'll have you arrested," Fallon whimpered and rubbed her cheek.

"No, you won't. I should have done that ten years ago. I thought I was making progress with you. I rationalized those A's and gave you the benefit of the doubt. But it was wasted on you. If you had only shown as much industriousness to your studies as you did to malice, you could have gone to any college you wanted."

"You only wanted to please Daddy."

"That's a bold-faced lie and you know it. My students were my life. You were a student. Even after you started those rumors, I thought you could change, that I could help you. But I was lying to myself. I was afraid. Afraid of your threats and your blackmail. It wasn't my envy or adulterous intentions that flowered that year. It was my cowardice." Janey took a ragged breath. "Well, it's over. That, at least, is over."

She stepped back and stumbled. Lindy grabbed her by the waist. She seemed weightless.

"We'd better leave before you make matters worse." Derrick was smiling, but he dragged Fallon none too gently toward the church parking lot.

"I'll make you pay," she screamed. "I know something you don't know," she taunted.

Lindy rolled her eyes. The woman was a raving lunatic.

Derrick pushed Fallon into the front seat of his Jaguar and strode quickly back to where they were standing. "I had no idea about the limericks, I just wanted you to know that.

She won't cause any more trouble. I'll come back and we can discuss this without"—he flicked his head in the direction of the Jaguar—"any distractions." He winked at them and hurried back to his car.

"Why, that little—" Stella cut her eyes to Janey and censored herself. "Let's get you inside, hon."

Lindy pulled Evelyn aside as the others went up the steps.

"I saw you take Janey's tea from the trash. What are you going to do?"

"I'm going to ask Judd to have it tested." She smiled suddenly. "Did you think I was destroying evidence?"

The question brought gooseflesh to Lindy's arms. "Of course not. I just wondered why you were being so secretive about it."

This time it was Evelyn who looked disconcerted. She didn't answer the semi-veiled accusation, merely turned and followed the others into the house.

While Mary Elisabeth put on water for tea, Stella fussed over Janey, and Lindy and Evelyn quietly eyed each other from opposite sides of the room.

"I'll get your tea," said Stella, opening the cupboard. "Oh, you threw that bag out. Do you have more?"

"There's some in my purse," said Janey. "If you'll just hand it to me." She seemed barely able to sit upright.

Evelyn and Stella both reached for Janey's purse.

"I'll get it," said Lindy. She moved the purse away from Evelyn and opened it. There were two brown bags inside. She pulled out one.

Janey leaned forward on her chair. "Not that one. The other one with the gold label." She nodded when Lindy brought out the second bag, then slumped back. "Such a dear man," she murmured.

Stella brought mugs of coffee to the table. "Damn. I should have made something for a snack. I believe I'm getting my appetite back."

They sat silently after that, drinking coffee, while Janey steeped her tea.

After a few minutes, Mary Elisabeth pushed her chair back. “I have work to do.” She left the kitchen.

Evelyn moved toward the door, but Lindy got there first. “I’ll go see if there’s anything I can help her with.”

She went into the hall, feeling Evelyn’s eyes on her back.

Chapter Twenty

"She said 'murdered.' " Mary Elisabeth sat at her desk on the sunporch, staring at the blotter on the desktop.

Lindy closed the door. She had hoped Fallon's word choice had gone unnoticed. "She was just being overly dramatic, I'm sure. Trying to get the last dig in."

Mary Elisabeth shook her head. It was a small movement. Almost indiscernible.

Lindy sat down. She couldn't think of anything to say.

"I think Howard hired that detective," said Mary Elisabeth.

"Why on earth would he do that?"

"To sabotage the marathon. He hates me, and who can blame him? I think he would do anything to get back at me."

"Mary Elisabeth, you're not being fair. He's hurt and angry, but he loves you."

Mary Elisabeth fought to control her mouth before she said, "Or to spy on Derrick and Fallon. And—" She stopped.

"And what?"

"What if one of them killed the man?"

Lindy stared at her. She hadn't realized how close to the edge Mary Elisabeth had come. She leaned over the desk and touched her hand. "Fallon is disturbed. That's become obvious. But she isn't homicidal."

"You don't know—" Mary Elisabeth broke off again.

"Don't know what?" asked Lindy with a growing sense of apprehension.

"Why—why I left."

Lindy waited. She shouldn't encourage Mary Elisabeth to talk. She didn't know that she wanted to be privy to such intimate troubles.

"Howard had taken James to Purdue and was returning home late that night. I was in my sewing room. I'd bought some lovely antique silk to make—" An embarrassed laugh erupted from her throat. "She came in. She was acting stranger than usual. Prowling around, touching everything. Her eyes were, I don't know, odd-looking. For the first time, I was frightened of her. I tried to ignore her, pretended to be absorbed in what I was doing. She came to stand over me. Watching me. I could hear her breathing. Then suddenly she grabbed my scissors and tried to stab me. I managed to push her away. I don't know how. I ran to the bedroom and locked myself in."

Mary Elisabeth looked at Lindy for the first time since she had begun talking. "Now do you see why I had to leave?"

"What I don't see is why Howard would continue to treat her like an irresponsible child after something like that. She needs professional help."

"I didn't tell him."

"But—"

"I couldn't, not then, and not now. If Fallon had to be institutionalized, Howard would never forgive me. Even though I know it's over for us, I still can't bring myself to tell him." Mary Elisabeth leaned forward and lowered her voice. "There's something that nobody knows—about Howard."

Lindy's eyes widened.

"You heard Fallon's threat."

Oh no, Lindy thought. *No family skeletons.*

But Mary Elisabeth didn't give her time to protest. "Howard's first wife was emotionally unstable. We had been married several years before he found the courage to tell me how she died. He was afraid I wouldn't love him, the ridiculous man. One night they had a terrible fight. She threatened to kill herself. Then she stormed out of the house and drove her car over a cliff." Mary Elisabeth's voice wavered. "It's the kind of thing you see on one of those made-for-TV movies. But it really happened. He's petrified that Fallon will show signs of the same instability."

"She has," Lindy murmured.

Mary Elisabeth didn't seem to hear her. "So he's always given her anything she wanted, let her do anything, just so she would be happy. Oh, I know that probably wasn't the way to help her, but he was so desperate. The few times we sent her to a therapist, she made awful threats, so we didn't make her go back. Our doctor even prescribed drugs, but she said they made her fat and refused to take them. She's always been selfish and destructive, but it seems like since she's been back this time, it's gotten worse. We're—Howard's losing the battle. She's acting more irrationally than ever."

Lindy thought of the forged check, the limericks, the way she followed Derrick around with that ridiculous cup of coffee. Her spoiled-child routine would be comical if it weren't so destructive.

"And if she does tell everyone about his past, it will devastate him."

"I think you underestimate Howard. Please talk to him."

Mary Elisabeth shook her head.

"If Fallon has become violent, and considering what she did to Stella and you it looks like she has, don't you think you have to take that responsibility? Won't Howard be more devastated if she really hurts somebody? Whether you tell him or Fallon's own actions do, he's going to need you more than ever."

Lindy's last word was punctuated by the unmistakable backfire of Juan's Black Beauty. She felt a surge of relief. "Mary Elisabeth. Call him. Please." She fled outside.

Rebo and Rose were getting out of the front seat. Peter and Mieko got out of the back.

"Hey, what are you guys doing here?"

"Coming back from lunch," said Rebo.

"You're not even supposed to be here today," she said, though she was glad to see them.

Peter, Rose and Mieko stood together, looking blandly innocent. Since Mieko never showed her feelings, Lindy beetled her eyes at Rose. Rose took a deep, satisfied breath. Lindy cut her off before she could start expounding the benefits of country air. She knew what they were up to.

Rebo waved his hands in the air. "I'm on a creative roll. When the muse speaks."

"You sound like Derrick."

"I'll just shoot myself now."

"Don't do anything drastic. I think we've seen the last of those two."

"Botticelli boy and Vampirella?"

"Got it in one. Fallon wrote the limericks. Mary Elisabeth gave both of them the heave-ho this morning." She smiled. "So you really didn't have to give up another day off."

"And miss the latest installment of *As the Marathon Turns*? No way." Rebo opened the trunk and began handing things to Peter. He eyed her over a pile of leather and hardware.

"What's all that stuff?"

"Fly harnesses."

"Oh, no. You can't fly those children. I don't think we have enough insurance even if their parents agreed, which they won't. It's too dangerous."

"That's what Peter said, so we're going to fly Mieko." Rebo bared his teeth. "She signed a waiver, but we had to buy her lunch first."

Lindy looked at Mieko. No reaction. It must be fine with her.

"And you?" she asked Rose. "Have an urge to play Peter Pan?"

"I don't trust the beams to support her weight," said Peter.

"Thank God for that."

"I'm just here to take a few nips and tucks on the costumes. Try to upgrade this musicale from suburban kitsch to not-quite-ready-for-prime-time."

"Don't step on any toes. People around here get their feelings hurt easily."

"Would I do that?"

Of course, she would. But nobody would dare say so.

Lindy followed them inside, offering up a prayer of thanks for having such friends.

Melanie was standing in the center aisle, looking into the rafters. She turned when they came in. "You did this?" she asked Peter.

They all looked up to where she was pointing. Since Saturday, Peter had rigged fly wires and installed a motor-driven winch to drive the apparatus.

"Is it a problem?" he asked, instantly guarded.

"It's fabulous. Just don't let my kids get near it. They'll all want rides."

"Yeah," said Rebo. "The flying witches of Salem. Now, there's a concept. Oops, I said the 'c' word."

"You're incredible," Lindy said to Peter.

Peter smiled, something he was doing more of these days. She wondered if Mieko had anything to do with that.

"I padded the beam before I clamped the guide rails. That way the fly wires won't scratch it. The only problem is that Mieko will have to sit up there during the first part of the performance. There's no way to get her up during the show."

"How long is that?" asked Lindy.

"If she goes up at half hour, it'll be about forty-five minutes in all." Peter fastened Mieko into the harness. "Now remember what I told you."

She dipped her chin.

Rebo turned on the winch. Peter held her steady as she rose into the air. "We'll just lift you up and down until you get the hang of it. Are you okay?"

"Yes," came the reply from above them.

"You won't hear the noise of the motor over the music," explained Peter as he watched Mieko hover above them. "I'm going to pull up the lower wire," he called. "It will tilt your back so it looks like you're flying."

Mieko's "okay" was an echo.

Peter took the controls from Rebo, and Mieko began to shift in the air. She spread her arms.

"It's like flying," she said.

"It is flying, my little bird of prey," said Rebo.

Peter lowered the back of the harness until she was upright in the air. "Try to land on your feet. Rebo will spot you."

They watched her descend slowly to the floor. Four sets of hands reached out to steady her landing.

A loud "Bravo" resounded from the back of the church. Derrick Justin walked toward them. "Excellent."

Lindy stepped forward. She was getting sick of his surprise appearances. He was worse than Adam Crabtree. "What are you doing here?"

"I just came by to apologize to your friends for Fallon's behavior this morning and to clear up the misunderstanding with the committee. I really had no idea what the girl was up to. But inadvertently, I might have caused it." He put on a repentant face. His acting wasn't much better than Fallon's. "I mentioned that she might do something to influence the committee. I meant something positive, but she must have misconstrued my meaning. She's not the brightest bulb on the tree."

She couldn't be, thought Lindy. Not if Fallon thought this specimen was worth all that cloying devotion.

"I'm really not the one to speak to, Derrick. If you feel the need to explain, I suggest you talk to Mary Elisabeth." Lindy turned her back to him. She saw the expression on Melanie's face and added hurriedly, "If you'll excuse us, we're really busy."

She waited until she heard the door close. "What did he want to apologize for?"

"He and the *enfant terrible* were here this morning," said Rose. "She wanted him to fly."

"Yikes."

"Not to worry. Peter let them have it." Rose snapped her teeth together. "They got the point."

"She's flying high enough for both of them, if you ask me," said Rebo.

Lindy turned a startled gaze on him.

"Definitely *Valley of the Dolls* material." He flicked his eyes toward Melanie, who had moved away from the group.

"If Fallon is on medication, the wrong dosage might account for her erratic behavior," said Lindy.

"Uh, hold that thought." Rebo walked away. He headed directly to Melanie and said something in an insistent whisper. Melanie shook her head. He wrapped his fingers around her upper arm, but she broke away and began sorting through play books. Rebo threw up his hands and stalked back to Lindy.

"What was that about?"

Rebo scowled over her head. She knew he was watching Melanie.

"Unfortunately, my lips are sealed. For the time being, anyway." He dropped onto a pew and turned his back to her.

Soon afterwards, the drama group, or what was left of it, began to arrive. They dragged in and slumped dejectedly around the stage.

There was no Kenny and no Val and no understudies. *Not a good sign*, thought Lindy. And not a good time or place to ask Melanie what she intended to do about the play.

"I think I'll go home," she said to Rebo. "I need a break."

"Uh-huh," he said distractedly.

She squinted her eyes at him. "No comment?"

"Uh-uh." He walked her to the door.

"Well, at least Derrick's car is gone, but take this just in case." She unhooked a key from the key ring Mary Elisabeth had given her and handed it to him. "Be sure to lock up whenever you leave. We don't need any more surprises."

He turned the key over in his hand and started to speak. Then he put the key in his pocket.

"What?" asked Lindy.

"I was just thinking how nice it would be to see that asshole fly." He gave her a two-finger salute and went back inside.

Taking that as good-bye, she got into the Volvo and headed home.

As soon as she fed Bruno and picked up the newspaper he had shredded to punish her for being left alone all day, Lindy called Bill's number. Now that the source of the limericks had been exposed, she thought it would be safe to invite the boys to spend the day. And besides, she wanted to see how his day had gone.

"Brandecker residence. Who's calling, please?"

"Randall, is that you?"

"Hi, Lindy. It's boring here. Have they started on the chain saw—"

"Hi. He's not supposed to answer the phone."

"Well, he did it very well. You sound a bit frazzled."

"A bit."

"Things not going so great?"

"I'm trying, but they had to sit in my office with a grad student while I taught. It was only a few hours, but they were not happy. Now they're bouncing off the walls after being cooped up all day. If Sharon doesn't get back by the end of the week, I'll have to take time off."

"Is that likely?"

"My aunt's condition is worse. My mother doesn't want to leave her, and Sharon doesn't think she should leave my mother. And I don't know shit about the new math. You could say that things are a bit of a disaster."

"Well, I can't help with the new math, but I can with the other. Fallon Porter has been sending the limericks. Mary Elisabeth kicked her off the committee and off the property today. So it would be safe if you want to bring the boys out tomorrow before your classes."

"I couldn't ask you to do that. My day is spread out tomorrow. I start at ten and don't finish until four-thirty."

"Piece of cake. Can you get them here?"

"Yes, but are you sure you don't mind?"

"Not at all."

She heard Bill talking to the boys, then squeals of delight, and loud thank-you's in the background. She'd have to say something to them about not hurting their uncle's feelings. After all, he was doing the best he could under the circumstances.

She hung up and started on a grocery list. Chips, soda, cookies. All the things she used to buy.

The phone rang. She picked it up, stuffed it between her ear and shoulder and kept writing.

"Hello."

"It's Glen."

She stopped writing. Was he still mad at her? Her stomach clenched.

"Hi."

"I've been calling you all day. Where were you?"

She glanced at the answering machine. Three blinks.

"Working on the marathon. I told you."

"Well, you were in such a hurry to talk; now you don't even return my calls."

"I'm sorry. I just got home."

"I don't need this crap, Lindy."

She swallowed the sudden ache in her throat. "What crap?" she asked slowly.

"You never being home."

"You're the one in Paris."

"You know what I mean."

"No. I don't. I came to visit you. You ignored me. I offered to move there, but you said no. I don't know what you want me to do."

"Just stop pressuring me."

She was having a hard time hearing past the roaring in her ears. "Okay, I won't call so much. Is that it? I just miss you, but I can wait for Thanksgiving."

"I won't be able to come back for Thanksgiving. Things are too busy here."

"Christmas?"

"I don't know. It depends."

"There's someone else, isn't there?" She hadn't meant to say it. She hadn't even known she was thinking it. It came out before she could stop it. And now it was too late to take it back.

There was silence on the other end of the line and she knew. She concentrated on the waves of heat that roiled through her stomach.

"No. Of course there isn't anyone else."

But she knew. His response had taken too long. How had this happened to them? They had been happy just this summer. Hadn't they? Had it all been a lie?

"Glen?" She could hardly form the word.

"Look, I don't have time to talk about this now. I'll call you tomorrow or the next day."

Lindy listened to the dial tone after he hung up. She couldn't quite bring herself to put down the receiver, as if hanging up would cut the final ties that held their marriage together.

Finally, she slammed it down, tears blinding her eyes. She crumpled up the grocery list and threw it on the floor. He had called her and then didn't have time to talk. She couldn't believe it. She forced herself to take even breaths while she paced back and forth across the kitchen, and Bruno whined. Then she stood staring out the window until he nudged her thigh. He was holding the crumpled grocery list in his mouth.

"You're right, boy. Let's go to the store."

Chapter Twenty-one

Will and Randall stood at the mud room door, faces pressed to the panes of glass. Lindy grabbed Bruno by the collar and opened the door. Randall dove forward, Bruno broke loose and they rolled together into the kitchen. Will stood next to Bill, not quite sure about letting him go, and Lindy felt her first pang of misgiving. What if she had a homesick boy on her hands all day?

Bill nudged him forward.

"Hi, Will. I was just about to give Bruno a treat. Let's go find the dog biscuits." Will followed her uncertainly into the kitchen, glancing back at Bill. Bill stepped inside and dropped two backpacks on the floor.

Lindy gave Will the box of dog biscuits and whistled. Bruno came bounding over.

"Are you sure you're up for this?" asked Bill.

"They'll be fine."

"Call me if they get to be too much."

"Okay, don't worry."

"There's a change of clothes and their school books in

their packs. I'll be back around six o'clock, depending on traffic. I'd better get going."

He cast an uneasy glance toward the boys. They were busy stuffing dog biscuits into Bruno's mouth. Bruno was in doggy heaven.

"Bye, fellas," said Bill.

"Bye," they called, not even looking in their uncle's direction.

"See you tonight," said Lindy and pushed him out the door.

Within a few minutes they were heading for the marathon, loaded down with backpacks, snacks, and a bag of outdoor games and sporting equipment.

"How come Bruno can't come?" asked Will.

"He gets too dirty."

"We could give him a bath."

"Will they be working on the chain saw murderer today?" asked Randall.

"Is it really a farm?"

"What are we going to have for lunch?"

And so it went all the way to the marathon.

"Cool. Who's that?" asked Randall.

The Gospel of Galilee Church congregation had doubled in size. Today they were marching back and forth along the highway. There were a few new signs, but the one that lifted the hairs on the back of her neck read: *One dead. Who will be next?*

So, the word had gotten out about the detective. She would have to call the publicity chairperson and find out if it had made the papers. Then begin damage control.

"They're just some people who don't want us to have the marathon."

"Why don't they want you to have the marathon?"

"Don't they like Halloween?"

The nice thing about the barrage of questions was that they didn't give her time to answer.

She managed to complete most of her calls from her cell phone while she watched Will and Randall explore the grounds and scout out the hayride route. Later, they oversaw the unloading of used couches, tables, chairs and stereo equipment into the church annex.

At eleven, the Manhattan contingent arrived.

"Yo, if it ain't Frick and Frack," said Rebo when Lindy introduced the boys. Then he engaged them in a complicated two-handed jive handshake that doubled them over with giggles.

At noon, they went to McDonald's, their first and only choice for lunch.

"Uncle Bill won't take us to McDonald's. He only eats weird stuff," said Randall.

"Yuck," agreed Will.

After lunch, they stopped by the church and watched Mieko fly. Randall wanted to try it, but Lindy put her foot down. She left them with Rose, hanging fake spider webbing from the wall sconces.

Lindy had forgotten how exhausting keeping up with kids could be. She headed for the kitchen for a much-needed cup of coffee. Janey was addressing flyers at the table. Stella perused a pile of invoices.

"We missed you at the library last night," said Janey.

"Library?"

"Adam presents *Tales from the Revolutionary War* on Monday nights."

"Oh," said Lindy.

"Evelyn was there," said Stella. "Bent his ear after the talk. We were dying to know what they were saying, but couldn't figure out how to eavesdrop without being seen."

"That's why you missed me, right?"

Stella and Janey both nodded.

"Well, why didn't you just ask her?"

"We did," said Stella. "She said she was interested in history."

"Sounds reasonable."

"We think she's up to something."

Great. Now everybody was on the sleuthing bandwagon.

"Ever notice how she's always around when something's happening?"

"We're all around all the time," Lindy said, though she silently agreed with them.

"But she's on cleanup. She doesn't even need to show her face until after the marathon's over," said Stella with an arch look to Janey.

"But the limericks are finished," Lindy reminded them.

"But the body isn't. Guess you didn't see this week's local."

"I wondered at the new sign across the street. What did the paper say?"

"How about, *Mysterious death at Van Cleef farm.*"

"Damn," said Lindy. "Any details?"

"Just that it was being investigated as death under unknown circumstances. Mary Elisabeth has been fielding calls from reporters and concerned citizens since eight this morning."

"And here I was having a delightful day." Delightful, if you discounted her marriage on the rocks. "I should have know it wouldn't last."

"We think Evelyn knows something about it," continued Stella.

"Judd already talked to her."

"Yeah, but what did she tell him?"

"We want you to find out," said Janey. "It's—it's important."

Lindy frowned. Then she looked at Stella for an explanation. Stella looked blank.

"Well, I'll see what I can do. Right now, though, I have to check on the boys." She gave them a brief explanation about Will and Randall and went to the church, wondering at this sudden interest in Evelyn.

"They're with Rose and Peter and the hanged man," said Rebo. "I guess Bryan is having some trouble getting the bugger to swing, and he heard that Peter had a fly rig."

The drama group came in as she left the church.

"How's Val?" she asked.

"They won't let us see her," said Claudia. "Her parents are going to send her to rehab. They won't even let her finish the play before she goes."

"That's too bad. What about Kenny?"

"They let him go. But he's pretty bummed. I hope he comes back."

"So do I."

Lindy watched them file into the church and wished there was something she could do to help. If Judd could just find the new source of drugs, and get the teen center opened, they might have a chance of getting themselves together. That was what Judd was hoping, too. Even though they both knew that it would just be a matter of time until a new dealer moved in, and the temptation began again.

She found Will and Randall sitting on the ground at the base of the hangman's tree. Rose was looking up into the branches, where Peter and Bryan were doing something to a pair of overalls.

"Bryan's letting us stuff the hands," explained Randall enthusiastically. There was a half-filled gunny sack between him and Will, and a growing pile of birdseed on the ground.

"It's hard to get it inside the fingers," said Will.

"Then he's going to show us where the chain saw murderer is going to chase the wagon."

"Cool, guys. But you were supposed to do some homework today."

"We already did," said Randall. "Mieko helped us. She made it fun."

"That's great, but we have to leave soon. Bill is picking you up at six."

Their bright faces changed to frowns.

"Can we come back tomorrow, please?"

"It's okay with me. We'll ask Bill. As soon as you're finished with the Chain Saw Man, meet me at the house." She left them happily throwing birdseed at each other.

* * *

Rebo and Melanie were anything but happy. Lindy could tell that as soon as she stepped out of the woods and saw them, nose to nose on the church steps. She wasn't sure what was going on between those two, but she bet it wasn't an argument over rehearsal schedules. She hurried over to referee.

"Problems?" she asked.

Rebo looked at Melanie before answering. "Major."

Melanie glared at him.

"Let's see if we can work this out."

"Good idea, but not here." Rebo grabbed Melanie by the arm and led them around the annex. He stopped as soon as they got to the parking lot.

"What's this about?" asked Lindy.

Rebo turned to face Melanie, hands on his hips. "Tell her. She's not one of them." He grimaced. "Well, she is, but she's also one of us."

Melanie pressed her lips together.

"It's about who's selling drugs to these kids," said Rebo.

"You promised," cried Melanie.

"You gotta take a chance, my verdant vixen. We can deal with this, but you gotta lay it out for Lindy. They'll listen to her."

Melanie leaned against a parked car and crossed her arms. She glowered at Rebo, then took a deep breath. Her words, when they came, were spoken to the ground.

"This has happened before," she said. "The same way that it's happening now."

"Elucidate, my little green goddess," Rebo prompted.

"Where I was working before—it was a new program. Kids were sent to me in the evenings to keep them off the street. Things were going great. I was making a lot of headway. They were clean. I thought. Then one kid showed up stoned, and then another. I didn't realize what was happening at first. By the time I did, it was too late. Everything fell apart."

"Tell her when this went down."

Melanie pushed away from the car. "After I met Derrick. It was at some educational bash. I was on display as their big success story—the teacher who had turned the school around. Derrick acted really interested in the program; he even came to the school to see what I was doing. He flattered me and kept coming back. Then the drugs started."

"You think that Derrick introduced drugs to the group?"

"Well, he wasn't the first. But things were changing. The kids were straightening out—until he came." She sniffed. "After that, the school dropped the program, and the kids got sent back to detention or jail instead of to the drama group. I lost my job and became a pariah. Derrick said he could get me another job, that he believed in me.

"I didn't make the connection until it started happening here. He's using me to get to the students, but I can't prove it. None of the kids will talk. I think most of them are still clean, but after what happened to Val . . ."

"God, it makes perfect sense," said Lindy. "The increase of drugs here also coincided with Derrick's arrival in town. We've got to stop this. You have to talk to Judd."

"I can't," said Melanie. "I already confronted Derrick. He just laughed and said that if anyone was in a position to sell drugs to teens, it was me. And everybody would know it."

"The bastard was threatening her."

"Sounds like it," agreed Lindy. "But Judd will understand. He'll be able to help."

"No," said Melanie. "It's my word against Derrick's, and who are they going to believe? He's conned this whole town. And if they get rid of me, who's going to protect my kids?"

The statement sounded very much like what Janey had said about leaving her kids to Melanie. Two women who cared so intensely, at odds with each other, and being undermined by an insidious drug dealer.

"So what do you suggest?"

"I need concrete evidence. I've got to find his stash."

Lindy let out her breath. "Any ideas where to look?"

Melanie considered for a moment. "I think it's here on the farm."

"That's really crazy," said Rebo.

"Or very bold," said Lindy. "That could be why he's courting Fallon—to get his hands on the farm. Strategically located, especially after they finish the new teen center."

The other two looked at her.

She shrugged. "It's possible. In fact, it's very probable."

Rebo slapped his head. "Oh, great. How many acres is it?"

"Twenty plus," said Lindy. "But I have an idea of where to start looking. Derrick and T.J. were arguing over where to store the dry ice. Derrick was adamant about using the cellar, not the springhouse, where T.J. suggested. Maybe we should look there first."

"But T.J. padlocked it before we started rehearsing here," said Melanie.

"Or Derrick did," said Lindy.

"Well, there's one way to find out," said Rebo.

"Ask T.J.," said Lindy.

"Break into the springhouse, tonight."

"Asking would be much simpler."

"Sure, but if it wasn't T.J., he'll throw a hissy fit, and we don't want anyone to know what we're up to until we find the stash—or not."

"And if we do?" asked Lindy.

"Then you can call Judd, and we'll tell him that Melanie helped us find it. That way she'll be off the hook, and Judd can do his investigating."

"I suppose you're right."

"So deep-six Frick and Frack and meet us back here at midnight."

Lindy sighed. It sounded awfully theatrical, but if Rebo wanted to search the springhouse, they would search the springhouse. He had been right before. He had found the cave where a frightened sixteen-year-old had been hiding from the man who wanted to kill him.

"All right, midnight," she said.

"Thanks," said Melanie.

Bill called at six. He was stuck in bumper-to-bumper traffic on the Henry Hudson Parkway. Lindy fed the boys dinner. Tacos. At least they'd get lettuce and tomatoes that way.

Bill finally showed up at eight o'clock.

"Sorry," he said. "There was a four-car accident on the Cross Bronx, and a semi was overturned on the ramp to the bridge."

He declined Lindy's invitation to come in, but he couldn't get the boys to leave until he promised to bring them back the following morning.

"If I had known they were going to have such a good time, they could have slept over and you wouldn't have to make the trip again," said Lindy.

"I like making the trip." He kissed her cheek and herded the boys into the car.

Four hours later, dressed in jeans and sweatshirt, Lindy drove back to the Van Cleef farm. Melanie and Rebo were waiting in the parking strip. As soon as she turned off the engine, Rebo pulled her out of the car and into the shadows cast by the annex.

"T.J. was just outside rummaging in the toolshed," he said.

"He lives here," Lindy reminded him. "He's probably working late."

"And he might be looking for this." He held up a crowbar.

"Yikes. What are you planning to do with that?"

"Snap the lock off, unless you have a key."

"No."

"Then let's go." Rebo crept to the back of the church. Melanie followed him. Lindy brought up the rear.

We look like The Three Stooges, she thought.

Melanie hadn't said a word, and Lindy wondered if she had changed her mind about trusting them.

They walked single file down the dirt road, their way lit by a plump moon. But as soon as they stepped into the trees, the moonlight was snuffed out and they stumbled down the path holding on to the back of the person in front of them to keep from getting lost. They had to feel their way along the edge of the springhouse. When they finally reached the door, Melanie pulled a flashlight out of her jacket pocket and shined it on the lock—where the lock had been.

There was no padlock on the door now.

"What the hell?" Melanie stared at the other two in confusion, then rushed inside. Lindy and Rebo crowded through the door while Melanie shined the flashlight frantically in all directions. "There's nothing here," she cried.

"But I bet there was, and dreamboat removed it while we were sitting around speculating."

"Damn, damn." She kept shifting the flashlight, determined to find something.

"Let's be organized about this," said Lindy. "Shine it in the far corner and we'll search along the base of the walls. Maybe they overlooked something."

But after a few minutes of fruitless searching, they had to admit that nothing had been left behind. They dragged Melanie back outside.

"Now what do we do?" she asked.

"It's gone," said a voice from the darkness.

They all yelped and grabbed for each other. Adam Crabtree stepped from the trees. He was wearing an old plaid jacket and hunting cap with earflaps that stuck out over his ears.

Lindy found her voice first. "What's gone?"

"Whatever it was."

"There *was* something here," murmured Melanie.

"What did they take and who were they?" asked Lindy.

"Don't know."

Adam Crabtree's penchant for showing up unexpectedly and then milking the scene was beginning to irritate her. "Mr. Crabtree, what exactly did you see?"

"Two men putting boxes in a boat."

"When?" the three asked together.

"Last night."

"What did they look like?" asked Lindy.

"Too dark to tell."

"And the boxes?"

"Not big, not little. They're gone. Good riddance." He looked past them to the dark waters of the brook.

"You're wrong," Melanie began.

Lindy knew the futility of trying to get Adam Crabtree to cooperate. He hadn't helped with the detective either. Then a thought occurred to her.

"Melanie, did you hire the detective?"

"What detective?"

Jeez. Melanie had never been around when they were discussing the drowning. Could she really not have heard the speculations about the dead man? She was an acting teacher, but her ignorance seemed genuine.

"The man who drowned was a detective."

Melanie looked bewildered. Adam Crabtree looked totally unconcerned.

"Mr. Crabtree, please. Do you know what happened to the detective? He might have been investigating someone connected to the marathon. Someone who's very dangerous."

Crabtree said nothing.

"Someone is selling drugs to children. The detective might have been on to whoever it was. Might have seen what was stored in the springhouse. And someone killed him. You've got to help us. The man is evil." Lindy stopped, the shrillness of her voice echoing in her ears. "Please."

"Evil is merely the other side of the same reality." With that he turned and disappeared back into the darkness.

"I'll reality him," said Rebo, starting to go after him.

"Don't bother," said Lindy, close to tears. "He's determined not to get involved. I don't think anything will change his mind."

Melanie groaned. "It's hopeless. God, what have I done?"

"You've tried to stop a drug pusher," said Lindy.

"I brought him with me. Now they'll fire me and he'll be free to prey on these kids."

"No way, doll face. We'll figure out something."

"No. It's my problem. I brought it and I have to get rid of it. He won the first time, but now I know what to do. He won't get away with it again."

"Yeah, well, cool, but just remember you gotta be in it to win it."

"Meaning?" asked Melanie.

"It means, if you pop Derrick Justin and fry for it, who's going to protect the little darlings from the next guy?"

Chapter Twenty-two

A delivery truck was parked outside the farmhouse when Lindy and the boys arrived the next morning. T.J. was standing on tiptoe, leaning into the cab window.

"Well, take it back," he said.

"I can't take it back. You people ordered it. Now show me where to unload it."

"What's the problem?" asked Lindy, coming to stand by T.J.

"Derrick's dry ice," he said contemptuously.

The truck driver thrust a clipboard at her. "You in charge here?"

"Yes." She perused the yellow delivery order. "That's a lot of dry ice," she said.

"So where do you want I should leave it?"

She looked at T.J. "Think we can find something to do with it? Pack ice cream or something? Maybe Bryan can use it for the hayride."

"Dry ice. Oh, boy," said Randall. "If you pour hot water on it, it smokes."

"And if you touch it, it burns you," Lindy reminded him.

T.J. ran his hand across his hair. "I guess you can use the springhouse. A few more days shouldn't matter. But I'm warning you. If I find that I need access to it, I'll dump the stuff in the stream."

"Fair enough." She directed the driver around the house to the road to the springhouse. She and the boys headed for the shortcut by the cemetery.

"Keep the door open," T.J. called after her. "For ventilation. Maybe it will melt. Maybe somebody will steal it."

Lindy stopped. "Isn't the springhouse locked?"

"No. Why would I lock it? It's empty."

Well, that answered that. Derrick must have kept it locked until he removed whatever had been hidden there. The night before the dry ice was delivered. And since Derrick was the one who had ordered it . . . it was circumstantial, she knew. Bill had explained the term to her.

On second thought, maybe storing it in the springhouse wasn't such a good idea. There might be residual evidence of drugs. But she couldn't broach the subject with Judd. Even if he found something, there was no way to connect it to Derrick, and it would only alienate Melanie. Maybe even cast suspicion on her.

And if the door had to remain open, what would keep the curious out? She looked toward Will and Randall. This was definitely not a good idea.

The truck pulled to a stop behind them. The driver jerked his chin in the direction of the springhouse. "That where it's going?"

Lindy nodded.

He grumbled and backed the truck into the path. He jumped down from the cab, pulling on heavy gloves, and began to unload blocks of dry ice onto a hand trolley.

"Are you sure you can't take this back?" she asked.

"You've paid for it, and I'm leaving it here." He maneuvered the load down the path, muttering under his breath. The boys ran after him.

"Stay out of the way," she cautioned them.

She stood by the truck, watching the cart bounce toward the springhouse. In a few minutes the driver returned with the empty handcart.

"Should have gotten a smaller storage area. It's gonna sublimate pretty fast in there."

Good, she thought. *Let it sublimate, the faster the better.*

When the truck was empty, she signed the work order and called to Will and Randall. They came running up the path. They had managed to get muddy and wet during the twenty minutes it had taken to unload the dry ice.

"Come on, boys, let's get rid of some of that dirt." She scurried them up the path and along the road toward the farmhouse.

The boys raced for the kitchen. As soon as they had washed hands and faces, they dove into the pastry box that sat on the table, while Lindy pulled off their wet shoes and socks. Somebody had bought milk, and she poured two glasses. She cut up slices of an apple and placed them on a plate.

"We don't like the peels," said Randall, stuffing something flaky and chocolate into his mouth. She peeled the slices. They disappeared along with the chocolate.

"When you guys are finished, I'll show you where the pumpkin-painting booth is going to be. You can help me measure out the space."

"What about lunch?" Randall's face was smeared with chocolate and milk. "McDonald's. Okay?"

"First we have to do a little work."

The boys cleared the table, and Lindy quickly washed up the dishes. She took the boys outside.

"When is Bryan coming?" asked Randall. "We've got to get the hanging man ready. He's testing it tomorrow night. He said we could ride on the wagon. Okay?"

"We'll have to ask Bill. He probably misses you guys."

"Couldn't he come, too?" asked Will.

"He has to work, but maybe he can get here in time for the test ride."

"Cool," said Randall.

"Do you think he'll get scared?" asked Will.

Lindy gave him a reassuring smile, the mother in her reading between the lines. "Maybe, a little. But you'll have each other, so it won't be so scary."

"You can come, too," said Randall magnanimously.

"Thanks. I might do that."

She pulled a retractable tape measure from her jeans pocket. "Okay, Randall. You stand here and hold the end of the tape. Will and I are going to pull it out to that corner."

She and Will walked backward and the tape lengthened. When they were nearly to the corner Randall started jerking the end up and down. "It's a snake. It's a snake."

Will dropped his end of the tape and skittered back.

"Crybaby, crybaby," yelled Randall.

Will *was* about to cry.

"Let's show him snake," said Lindy. She pulled the tape to its full length and put the end in Will's hand. Then she started jerking it up and down. Randall jerked back. Pretty soon the tape measure was snapping in the air, and Will was laughing along with his brother.

One emergency diverted, thought Lindy. If only the others were as easy.

She made a few calls from her cell phone while the boys chased each other through the half-constructed booths. When the Portasans arrived, the three of them oversaw their placement at the end of the church parking lot, then followed the truck to the back of the house to where the other rest stop would be located.

Lindy expected T.J. to stick his head out of the window, but he didn't appear.

She signed the delivery form and said, "Lunch time."

"McDonald's," the boys squealed.

They drove to McDonald's, where they ordered their second Happy Meals of the week.

"You know, there are other places to eat in New Jersey."

They looked like they didn't believe her.

"And if your Uncle Bill comes tomorrow, we'll have to eat someplace else."

"Burger King," said Will.

Lindy shook her head.

"Wendy's?"

"Nope."

"Taco Bell."

"I don't think we have a Taco Bell."

Randall's eyes widened. "You don't?"

"I'll think of something," said Lindy. She gathered up trash and boys, pushed the trash through the swinging doors of the orange receptacle and pushed the boys out the door and into the Volvo.

Rebo and company had arrived in their absence along with several committee members. Things were gearing up. With the marathon only a week away, the grounds were bustling with activity.

"Let's go find Rose," said Randall, and he and Will raced each other to the church.

"And where did you get those two youngsters?" asked Father Andrews coming up behind her.

"They belong to a friend of mine. His nephews. Their mother is visiting a sick relative. He has to work, so I thought they would have fun here."

Father Andrews' eyes twinkled. "A little taste of the old days, I imagine."

"A little, though two were enough, believe me." She considered for a moment. "But it is nice having all that unrestrained energy around for a few days."

Father Andrews laughed. "I wish I could harness it."

"Me, too."

They stood watching the activities in the yard, until Mary Elisabeth joined them. "The school just called. Melanie didn't show up for her classes today. She doesn't answer her phone. They're extremely unhappy."

Lindy unconsciously looked in the direction of their last night's adventure.

"I'm sure she would have called if she had an emergency," Mary Elisabeth continued. "She seems quite responsible in spite of her appearance. I hope she hasn't been in an accident or fallen ill somewhere."

"Wait a minute," said Lindy. "I might have seen her car in the parking lot. It was crowded, and I wasn't paying attention, but it could have been there."

All three of them went to look. Melanie's Dodge Dart was there, but there was no sign of Melanie. They checked in the church, but no one had seen her.

"That's odd," said Mary Elisabeth. "Where could she be?" Her eyes met Lindy's. "You don't think that Fallon is up to her tricks again?"

"You didn't give in to them, did you?" asked Lindy.

Mary Elisabeth pursed her lips. "Derrick came to talk to me yesterday. He tried to weasel his way back into my good graces."

"Did he succeed?" asked Father Andrews.

"I accepted his apology—for Fallon. He didn't exactly own up to his own behavior. He promised she wouldn't cause any more trouble. I felt I had to give them another chance."

"A selfish young man," said Father Andrews. "And just the kind of unfocused dilettante to attract a woman like Fallon."

Lindy looked at him in surprise.

He chuckled. "Surprised that a priest would know of such matters? I wasn't always a priest, my dear."

The drama group arrived a few minutes later. Rebo sent them off in search of Melanie, while he took Lindy aside. "I don't like the feel, smell or sound of this," he said. "You think Fallon has been at it again?"

"Not Vampirella, necessarily."

"You mean Derrick might have—oh, God. We've got to call those kids back. What if something awful has happened?"

"Oh, shit, are we ditzes or what?" said Rebo.

"What?"

"The springhouse. Did anybody look for her there?" They both started running at the same time.

They met Claudia at the edge of the cemetery. "No sign of her," she said. Her face was tense with worry.

"We're going to the springhouse."

"She's not there. I looked."

"Did you check inside?"

"No. It's padlocked."

"It can't be," said Lindy. "It's filled with dry ice."

Rebo began to run.

Lindy gave Claudia a shove. "Go get T.J. If he locked it, ask him to bring the keys. Hurry."

Claudia raced to the house.

Lindy caught up with Rebo in front of the springhouse. The door was padlocked.

"Melanie," called Rebo. There was no answer. He called again. Nothing. He banged on the door. "Can you hear me?"

"She may not be inside. Maybe T.J. locked it." Even as she said it, Lindy knew how unlikely it was. T.J. had told her to keep the door open.

Rebo began scuffing through the leaves, peering at the ground.

"What are you looking for?"

"The crowbar. I dropped it when Rip Van Winkle came out of the woods last night. I forgot about it."

Lindy joined the search, pushing frantically through the leaves.

"Got it," said Rebo. He shook it free of dirt and bounded toward the door.

There was just enough space to slide the bar between the door and the latch. He grabbed the top of the bar with both hands and thrust his weight down. The lock popped off, padlock still attached.

"Wait!" T.J. was running toward them followed by Mary Elisabeth and Father Andrews with Janey clinging to his arm. They were followed by the entire drama group. "Let it air out before you go in. There might be a build up of carbon dioxide."

Rebo ignored him and pulled the door open. A blast of cold air hit them. The smell was fetid.

"I've got a flashlight,'" said T.J. and went ahead. The others crowded around the door.

"Stand back, everybody," said Lindy. "They'll need the daylight to see."

Almost immediately, Rebo came out carrying Melanie and laid her on the ground.

"Somebody call 911."

Jeff pulled a cell phone from his pocket and made the call.

"Is she dead?" Dina asked.

"No," said T.J., "but she would be if we hadn't found her when we did."

Melanie took a labored breath and exhaled between chattering teeth. Her whole body began to shiver.

"She's freezing." Janey pulled off her cardigan. Carl stripped off his jacket and handed it to her.

Janey used his arm to lower herself to the ground, then tucked the coat and sweater around Melanie's chest. She took her hands in hers, fumbled with them for a moment, then began to chafe them vigorously. Melanie made a startled noise.

Janey patted her shoulder. "There, there," she murmured. "It's all right. I know. It's okay now." She continued to utter soothing words until the sound of sirens rent the air. Jeff ran to direct them to the springhouse and returned, bringing Judd with him.

"What the heck happened?"

"Someone locked Melanie in the springhouse with the dry ice," said Lindy.

Judd scanned the door and the surrounding ground. He flicked on his flashlight and stepped into the springhouse. A minute later he came back out and shook his head. Then he turned to Lindy. "Did you find anything?"

"No." *No limerick*, thought Lindy. If Fallon had done this, she would have left the last poem. Lechery. Melanie and Derrick? But there was no limerick.

Judd knelt down by Melanie. "Can you hear me? Did Fallon do this?"

At first Melanie didn't respond, just squinted up at him. Lindy leaned closer listening for her answer.

"Didn't see," she gasped.

Judd stood up. "Mary Elisabeth. I'll have to pursue this. I'm sorry."

Mary Elisabeth nodded.

Rebo clenched his fists. "Better pursue the—Derrick Justin, while you're at it."

Judd gave him a considering look. "Why don't you and me have a little talk—over there." He took Rebo aside while the paramedics went to Melanie's aid.

"I'm all right now." Her voice was scratchy and barely above a whisper.

"Maybe so," said Mary Elisabeth, "but you're going to let them take you to the hospital. Just to check you over."

"The school."

"I'll call them and tell them you were in an accident."

The paramedics moved Janey aside and helped Melanie to her feet. "Can you walk to the ambulance? Exercise will help get oxygen to your bloodstream."

Melanie nodded and was led toward the path. She stopped at the drama group. "Ms. Horowitz is in charge of rehearsal until I get back. Do what she says."

Lindy blinked in surprise. Janey lifted her chin and led the teenagers to the church.

"Well, something good has come out of this nightmare," said Mary Elisabeth, her eyes following Janey. "At least we have that."

Chapter Twenty-three

"Lindy!"

Lindy heard Rose's voice and looked up the path to see Will and Randall running toward her. She met them halfway, just as Rose came to a stop behind them and clamped a hand on each of their shoulders. "They heard all the commotion and came running before I could get out of the tree."

"What happened?" panted Randall.

"Melanie had an accident. But she's okay. They just took her to the hospital to check her out." She saw Will frown. "But she wouldn't have gotten hurt if she hadn't been wandering around by herself." She gave both the boys a severe look.

"Because she was mad," said Will.

"What?"

"Because she had a fight with that man."

Lindy knelt down, her blood racing, part with anticipation, part with concern for what Will might have seen or heard.

"What man?"

"You know, that one," said Will.

Lindy shook her head.

Will shuffled at some leaves.

"The one Rebo calls The Asshole," said Randall, then lowered his head and giggled.

"Derrick? With the curly hair?"

"Uh-huh."

"When?"

"When you were waiting for the dry-ice man. Will had to pee, so I told him to go in the woods. He was afraid to go by himself."

"Was not."

"Were too."

"Excuse me?" said Rose.

The boys quit arguing, but Will made a face at his brother.

"I went all by myself," he said. "And they were arguing."

"Did you hear what they were arguing about?"

"Kinda. She said, 'I'll kill you first.' But then she couldn't remember her lines, so she just sputtered a lot. He laughed real nasty. Just like a real bad guy, and Melanie got really mad. Then the giant came and scared them away. Are they going to be in the play, too?"

Her lines? The play? Will thought they had been rehearsing. "Maybe," said Lindy as the horrible import of Melanie's threat sank into her mind.

"Scared you more," said Randall. "I was watching from the trees. You shoulda seen Will run."

"Did not."

"Did too. And he wasn't even as good as the chain saw murderer. He's really scary."

The same thing Lindy had thought when she discovered the drowned detective.

Will moved closer to her. She gave him a quick squeeze. "Rose, why don't you take the boys up to the house to get cleaned up. We have to go in a few minutes."

"Aw, do we have to?" asked Randall.

Rose made wrestling positions at him. He laughed and took off toward the house. Will hesitated, then took Rose's hand. Rose batted her eyelashes at Lindy and led him away.

Rebo, Judd and Father Andrews were in consultation at the back of the springhouse. She walked slowly toward them trying to overhear their conversation.

"I have to have more than surmises," said Judd. "I can't haul the man in just because he's an as—oh, hi, Lindy."

"Are you going to question Derrick?" she asked.

"I'll ask him where he was today. But if nobody saw him here, that's about all I can do. Unless you can tell me why he would do such a thing."

Lindy deliberated. She knew she should tell Judd about the argument, but she couldn't get the boys involved without consulting Bill. And it was clear from the way Rebo was looking at her that he hadn't told Judd about the drugs.

She shrugged.

"I did pick up a little information," Judd continued. "Overheard it at the station. You're not going to like it, though."

Lindy waited.

"The detective, Earl Koopes. The M.E. thinks he was dead when he went in."

"Heart attack?"

"Blow to the head. And from the position of the bruise, it wasn't an accident."

"Oh, God," she gasped. "Uh, sorry, Father Andrews."

"It's quite all right. Who better to call on in our time of need."

"Paul's going to have to ask some more questions," said Judd. "It's kind of a jurisdictional nightmare." He shoved his hands in his pockets. "Things are looking pretty bleak for my teen center."

There was nothing to say. He was right.

"Judd? Did they ever find out why Koopes was here?"

"Nope. At least not that they're telling me. Said there weren't any files on us. They're checking with his bank to see if they can trace a check, but the person could have paid in cash. It's a long shot."

She watched him walk back to the road, shoulders slumped, a disappointed man. She was tempted to run after him and tell him about Melanie's suspicions and what the boys had overheard, but it wouldn't do any good. As he said, he needed more to go on than surmises.

"Okay, so there was no note at the springhouse," Lindy said as she watched Rebo pace back and forth from where she was sitting on the church steps. "No one has seen Fallon today or yesterday. But Randall and Will saw Melanie and Derrick fighting this morning. That puts him on the scene. I don't want to get the boys involved, but Randall said the giant saw them, too. He must mean Adam Crabtree."

"So we'll go see Adam Crabtree. Get him to talk, so the boys won't have to."

"You saw him last night. He doesn't talk. Just tells stories."

Rebo's eyes lit up. "Then perhaps we can convince him to tell us a story."

"Okay, but it will have to wait until tomorrow. I have to take the boys home now. Bill is picking them up in an hour."

"Are you going to tell him?"

"I don't know. I'm afraid for the boys. Maybe they shouldn't come back."

"Just try telling them they have to miss the test run tomorrow night."

The boys got reluctantly into the Volvo, but were soon chatting enthusiastically about the hayride test.

"Bryan said we have to go on it. He wants our opinion on if it's scary enough," said Randall.

"Is the giant going to be in it?" asked Will.

"No," Lindy assured him. "Just Jake and the dummy and some other stuff."

"Yeah, Jake's the headless horseman," explained Randall. "He's gonna chase the wagon—on a real horse. But he isn't headless. Rose says his coat just comes up over his head and there are eye holes so he can see out."

Lindy hated to break it to them that they might not be coming back. So she didn't. She'd talk to Bill first.

She could hear Bruno barking as they drove up the driveway.

"Too bad Bruno can't come on the hayride," said Will, getting out of the car.

"You don't have to go," said Lindy. "I might not go, either."

"Are you scared?" Will asked hopefully.

She knelt down beside him while Randall ran into the house to play with Bruno. "None of it is real. It's just dummies and kids dressed up in costumes."

Will didn't look convinced.

"Some people like to be scared. They watch monster movies and go on haunted hayrides. Some people don't think it's fun to be scared. And that's okay, too."

"It is?"

"Sure."

Bruno and Randall barreled out the door and into the back yard.

Will's mouth quirked up and he ran after them.

The telephone rang. She hurried in and picked it up.

"I've been thinking," Glen began without preamble.

She kept silent. She didn't know what to say, afraid of saying the wrong thing. Her heart began beating erratically. She took a slow, controlled breath.

"Lindy, are you there?"

"Yes." It came out in a tight whisper.

"I—I'm under a lot of pressure at work. I don't need pressure from home."

Okay, maybe that was what this was all about. She began to breath easier. Searched around for something to say that would be sympathetic and not set him off.

"I don't mean to be pressuring you. I just enjoy talking to you."

There was silence.

"You're my husband after all. Maybe I should close up the house and come to Paris. Then things will get back to normal, and every phone call won't be so important." It was the wrong thing to say.

"Look, Lindy. I'm very busy. I wouldn't have time to spend with you. I need some space for a while."

"What do you call two thousand miles and separate houses?" It was a knee-jerk reaction and she cringed.

"That's just what I mean. These constant demands."

"God. Whatever I say, you twist into something else. I haven't demanded anything from you lately." She heard the tears behind her voice, but she couldn't stop herself. "I offered to give up my job, my home, do whatever wives do when their husbands' jobs change. You're the one who keeps saying no."

"I just think we should cool it for a while."

Lindy laughed, a brittle sound that she had to cut off before it turned to sobs. "You sound like we're going steady. We've been married for twenty years. Have two children. How do you think they'll respond to us 'cooling' it?" She stopped, horrified. More quietly she asked. "What are we talking about here? Are you saying you want to separate?"

Silence on the other end.

Her stomach flip-flopped. She was afraid she was going to be sick.

"Divorce? Do you want a divorce?" She waited for his answer knowing that her life was about to change forever.

"I can't talk to you when you're being like this," he said and hung up.

Lindy looked at the receiver. "Being like what? This is crazy."

Then she became aware of the three faces looking at her from the mud-room door. Will, Randall and Bruno, quiet, wary, expectant—only Bruno's tongue was hanging out. She managed to turn away before her face crumpled.

She didn't cry. She was too numb to react to what had just

happened—or not happened. To be left with no answer, just a dial tone. Her life was falling apart, and idiot that she was, she hadn't even seen it coming. And to make matters worse, she had been utterly humiliated in front of two little boys and a dog.

She sat the boys at the table and fed them cheese and crackers. They were uncharacteristically quiet; she wondered how much they had heard.

When she went to the fridge, she could hear them whispering, but they stopped when she returned with glasses of juice spritzed with seltzer.

"You're going out to dinner with your uncle," she told them. "So don't spoil your appetites."

"Are you coming?" asked Randall.

She shook her head and turned away.

It seemed like an eternity before she heard Bill's car coming up the drive. A few more minutes. She could make it a few more minutes. Just say good night and get them in the car.

"Okay, guys. Get your stuff together. You don't want to be late for dinner."

"I'd rather eat here. We'll go someplace icky," complained Randall.

She bit her lip so she wouldn't yell at him. "Be thankful . . ." she began. "Be thankful—" Bill knocked on the door.

She pasted on a smile and went to meet him.

"What's wrong?" he asked the minute she opened the door.

She shook her head.

"Hey, Uncle Bill, guess what?" Randall ran from the kitchen followed by Will and Bruno.

Oh, God, she didn't think she could endure another description of the hayride right now. She had to get them out of here.

"Guess what?"

Bill's look switched to Randall. "What?"

"Lindy's getting a divorce."

Lindy felt the blood drain from her head. She wondered if she were going to faint. Bill seemed suspended before her.

"Now she can marry you, Uncle Bill." Will beamed up at his uncle.

Lindy wasn't aware of Bill's reaction. She was staring at his loosened tie. It was gray and had tiny stripes of black running diagonally through it.

"Get in the car."

"But—"

"Get in the car, please."

Lindy knew she should say good-bye, say something to gloss over the situation, say something—anything. But her mind was blank, even if she had been able to find her voice.

"Is it true?"

She looked up at him, but could only shrug and go back to contemplating his tie. She felt him open his arms, and she walked into them. Felt safe when they closed gently around her.

"I'm sorry," he said.

She squeezed her eyes shut.

He laughed quietly, his breath caressing her hair. "At least the noble part of me is."

She shook her head. She didn't want him to go on. She didn't want him to say anything that would link him with the terrible emptiness she felt now. She didn't want that.

"Shh. I'm not going to jump in and try to make you forget Glen, as tempting as it would be. I'm here if you need me, but Lindy, I'm not interested in being the consolation prize."

That shocked her back into real time.

She opened her mouth to say that she would never think of him that way, but he placed a finger over her lips. Then he let go of her and walked to his car.

Lindy stood at the door long after they had gone. She didn't remember saying good-bye or waving to the boys. She felt cold and dead, and lonelier than she had ever felt in her life.

Chapter Twenty-four

Bill dropped the boys off the next morning at the usual time. He didn't get out of the car; he didn't wave good-bye. Lindy was not surprised. He was probably angry with them for what they had blurted out the night before. And embarrassed. She wondered where Will had gotten such an idea. Surely, nothing she had said. Something he had said? No, not possible.

"We're supposed to apologize," said Randall as soon as she opened the door. "Uncle Bill says what we said was rude. He didn't talk to us the whole way home. And he made Will cry."

"Did not." Will was still standing on the threshold, unsure of his welcome.

"Well, it is the kind of thing that you shouldn't say. And I accept your apology. I'm sorry he's mad."

"But why is he mad?" asked Randall. "Uncle Bill deserves someone good to love him. Grandma said so. And me and Will like you."

"And Grandma will be happy," said Will, finally stepping

inside. "She had dis—disposed of Uncle Bill ever getting married."

Disposed?

"Despaired, dummy," said Randall. "She despaired of Uncle Bill ever getting married again."

"Uh, guys, I don't think we should be talking about this," said Lindy, even though it was intriguing. She had wondered herself why Bill had never remarried.

"What does despair mean?" asked Will. He looked at his brother.

Randall looked at Lindy.

"It means 'to give up hope,'" she answered. "Are you two ready to go?"

"You're not mad at us?" asked Will.

"No, I'm not, but I don't think you should bring up the subject again." She paused. "And I'm sure Uncle Bill won't stay mad for very long." She had to cross her fingers when she said that. She was pretty sure he would forgive them. He had a quick fuse, but he never held a grudge.

Rebo was waiting for them at the church. "Yo Frick-Frack. Rose is fitting the headless horseman into his costume. She probably needs you to hold his head."

Will's eyes rounded.

"Oops. It's just Jake. He's already here. Actually, they're all here. Got a dispensation to skip school to play dress-up. Go figure."

Lindy walked the boys through the church. They found Rose in a back room, kneeling in front of a pair of legs in black pants. Above them was a chicken wire frame and inside was Jake Adamson.

"Hi, Mrs. H."

"Wow," exclaimed the boys.

Rose pushed to her feet and draped a frock coat over the frame.

"How's he gonna see?" asked Will.

"There are eye holes in the coat."

"I don't see them."

"That's because they're covered in black mesh so nobody can see in. I mean how scary is a headless horseman if you can see Jake's head inside?"

"Will they be in the way?" asked Lindy. "Rebo and I have something to do."

"Rebo told me. Go ahead, but I want every detail when you get back."

Rebo held the door of the Volvo for her and then jumped in the passenger side. "We could take the Beauty, but I think we should surprise His Massiveness. And the Beaut isn't exactly quiet. Holy Moly, you look like shit."

"I think Glen is having an affair."

"Shit." He frowned at her. "Well, hell, it's midlife crisis or something. At least you have the wannabe waiting in the wings." He started humming "Look for the Silver Lining."

"You're getting as bad as Biddy." She and Biddy could sing entire conversations using the lyrics of Broadway show tunes as sentences. It was usually fun.

"I learned it from Biddy. Nothing better than a little schmaltz to put things in perspective."

"I guess." She slowed down looking for the opening to Adam Crabtree's drive.

A car pulled out onto the pavement. As it passed them, she recognized the diminutive figure behind the wheel.

"That's Janey," she said.

"Musta run out of tea."

"She had two new bags on Monday."

"Maybe she's getting worse."

That was definitely a possibility. She had lost more weight since work on the marathon had begun. And with all the additional strife, she had flagged tremendously.

Lindy made the turn. This time she drove over the bridge and breathed a sigh of relief when her tires found the other side.

They stopped at the front door; knocked but got no answer.

"He can't be far away if Janey just left," said Lindy. "Maybe he's in the shed." She led Rebo through the gardens toward the herb shed.

"Whoa-ho," he said, looking into the green house.

"I know, imagine growing tomatoes in this weather."

"Those aren't tomato plants."

"They're not? They look like tomatoes."

"Lindimwit. Our Gentle Giant is growing Mara-hoochi."

"Grass?"

"In the language of the sixties."

"Good God, do you think we have more than one dope peddler on our hands?"

"Honey, this town could compete with any Harlem street corner. Ever think of moving to the City where it's safe?"

"It's beginning to look like an option," said Lindy, momentarily distracted from their discovery.

"Hey, life works out, you know that?"

She met his eyes. "Thanks."

Adam Crabtree stepped out of the shed at that moment, recognized them and retreated inside.

Lindy and Rebo rushed toward the shed.

"You really have to talk to us, Mr. Crabtree. Adam."

No answer.

"Okay, Scheherezade. The gig is up. Come out or we come in fighting."

Still no answer.

"That really worked," said Lindy.

Rebo shrugged and walked over to the door. Before he could open it, Adam Crabtree stepped out.

Rebo looked up. "Gulp," he said.

Crabtree's beard twitched. "David and Goliath," he intoned.

"Wrong story," said Rebo, recovering himself. "How about *The Goose That Laid the Golden Egg?*"

Crabtree walked past him. "Once there was a country

where all was beautiful. Trees grew lush and the water in the streams ran pure. The people prospered and began to worship the god of Possession."

Rebo rolled his eyes at Lindy and motioned her to follow.

"They ignored their forests, their air, their crystal springs. Then a plague descended on the people, and they began to waste away with terrible diseases. They searched the land over for the physician who could heal them. Spent all the money in their coffers to no avail. Their ailment was spiritual."

He stopped before the hothouse. "Then a man came among them." He turned suddenly, making Lindy and Rebo jump back. He scowled at them, thunder in his eyes. "Not a man, but a demon masquerading as a man. Not a physician, but a magician who could make things appear and disappear. He promised to make the people happy again. For a price."

Lindy stood half mesmerized by his voice, half impatient for him to get to the point.

"They paid. Paid until there was nothing to bargain with but their souls. They rued the day he had come into their midst, but were impotent to stop him. They watched their children wither away, while they stood helpless." He stooped down and began pulling weeds from the earth.

"That's it?" said Rebo. "Do we have to put in more quarters to hear the ending?"

"This story is unfinished." Adam stood up and pointed to the greenhouse. "Those plants sometimes help the terminally ill. And those. And those." He gestured to the drying stalks in the garden, then to the wild undergrowth that surrounded the yard. They were all common plants, but the way Crabtree spoke of them made Lindy see them in a new light.

"Can you make this story have a happy ending?" she asked finally.

"Do not tie yourself to happiness—or unhappiness. They are—"

"Two sides of the same reality," said Rebo. "Yeah, we got all that the first time. What we need here is names, witnesses. We need you to tell us what you know about Derrick Justin and the drugs he's selling."

"What you need," said Adam Crabtree in a voice that set Lindy's nerves vibrating, "is patience. Difficulty at the beginning teaches perseverance."

Without another word, he walked into a thicket of bushes and was gone.

"Talk about your dramatic exits," said Rebo. "I guess it would be futile to follow him."

Lindy frowned. "Yeah. I think he wants us to figure out the clues he dropped in his little fable."

"Fable, schmable." Rebo scratched his head. "Oh, hell."

They walked back to the car.

"Okay, so Derrick is the demon," said Lindy. "I was never a whiz at symbolism, but I got that part. Crabtree must know that he's selling drugs. That's what all that business about making them happy and selling their souls was about."

"But how does he know?" asked Rebo. "And why won't he tell?"

"Maybe for the same reason Melanie won't. He doesn't have proof, and he might be afraid they'll accuse him. He does have a controlled substance growing on his property."

The scene from *The Crucible* rose in her mind, Melanie asking why the people of Salem had condoned the witch-hunt. And Kenny saying because they were afraid. Melanie, Mary Elisabeth, Adam Crabtree, all afraid. The parallel was a little too close for comfort.

"I wish the man wasn't so damned arcane," said Rebo. "I think he was telling us a bunch of stuff, but I can't figure out what was filler and what was important."

"Yeah, like the bit about the magician making things appear and disappear. Was that alluding to what drugs do to the mind, or—or about Fallon and the limericks? What if the limericks were a diversionary tactic? To take our minds off the drug problem—or the murdered detective."

"Yeah. Derrick, the magician, makes trouble appear somewhere else so the real problem won't be noticed. I'll buy that. You think Derrick thought those up?"

"No," said Lindy. "They were definitely Fallon's doing. Janey recognized her handiwork, but I bet Derrick put her up to it. They started right after the detective was found. At first I didn't think the two could be related, because of the timing, but now I think they are—for the same reason."

"Holy Moly. You think he iced the detective?"

"Maybe." Suddenly Mary Elisabeth's speculation about Howard hiring the detective and her fear that Fallon and Derrick had killed him, didn't seem so outlandish. "But at least we can be sure that he was selling drugs."

"And using the marathon as a front."

"I'm afraid so. And look what happened on Monday. Mary Elisabeth gives them their walking papers. Tuesday the drugs, if there were drugs, had been moved from the springhouse. He meant to store the dry ice in the cellar, but when he got kicked off the property, he knew that T.J. would use the springhouse. So he had to get the drugs out that night."

"Damn, if I had gotten Melanie to talk a day sooner, we might have caught him in the act."

"I wonder . . ."

"So wonder out loud."

"Why come back and lock Melanie in the springhouse? Why not just cut his losses and open up shop somewhere else?"

"So you're with me about Derrick locking Melanie in the springhouse," said Rebo.

"Fallon would have left a limerick."

"Everyone thinks it *was* Fallon, even without the limerick."

"Maybe that's just what Derrick was counting on."

Rebo's eyes snapped wide. "Hold on a sec. I'm getting an idea."

Lindy waited. She was getting a few ideas of her own.

"Okay, so Derrick locks her in. No limerick. He doesn't want her found until—oh, shit. He tried to kill her."

"And let Fallon take the rap for it," said Lindy.

"Yeah, but—what if she spills the beans about his drug operation?"

"Maybe he figures he can bluster his way past that. Who's going to believe her? She's a liar, a prankster and totally nuts."

"Hmm." Rebo's voice got quiet. "Or maybe he plans another little prank on Fallon. A permanent one."

Lindy swallowed. "I didn't think about that. Criminy. We'll have to warn her."

"Uh, Lindy?"

"Yeah?"

"Do you think he knows Melanie talked to us?" He went on before she could answer. " 'Cause if he's willing to get rid of both of them, I wonder what he has planned for us."

Chapter Twenty-five

"Talk about a reality check," said Rebo. "Would you get a load at what's parked in the driveway?"

A buckboard wagon stood next to a double horse trailer. Rose, holding Will and Randall firmly by the hand, watched Cy Madden, Jr., back a gray draft horse down the ramp. He harnessed the horse to the wagon and led it to the back of the house. Then he returned and guided another horse out of the trailer.

Right. Time to stop speculating about murder and get back to work. Lindy got out of the car.

"That's Jake's horse," exclaimed Randall. "He's going to chase the wagon on it."

"Hmm," said Lindy. Randall had mentioned real horses, but she hadn't been paying attention. She went over to confer with Cy.

"Nesbitt's big," said Cy. "But he's steady. Jake's a fairly good horseman. That's why he got the part."

"But what about the wagon? I assumed it would be drawn by a tractor. What if the horse gets spooked with things chasing him and flying out from the trees?"

"He's a she. Her name's Marie and she's gentle as a lamb. And old as the hills. Can't get her to go faster than a walk even if you dangle a carrot in front of her. And as for rearing up on her hind legs, I don't think she even knows how it's done." Cy quirked his head. "Don't worry. I'll be driving the wagon. Used to do it over at the Platts' when I was a kid. Heck, it'll be just like the old days."

"If you say so," said Lindy, not convinced. At least they would know if that was true after tonight. The test was a good idea.

"When's lunch?" asked Randall.

"In a few minutes. First Rebo and I need to talk to Fallon."

"You mean that mean lady that keeps wanting The Asshole to fly? Bryan says she's gonna mess up everything." Randall screwed up his face, giving full vent to his opinion.

"Not if I can help it," said Lindy. "And watch your language, young man." She turned to Rose. "Ten more minutes?"

"Sure. We'll be behind the house figuring out how to get Jake and the chicken wire on the horse."

The boys took that as permission and ran after Cy, Rose two steps behind.

"Let's go look for the Vamp." Rebo pulled up short. "Uh-oh. You've got company."

Lindy looked up to see Bill walking toward them.

"I'll go intercept the Vampessa," said Rebo. "You go have fun."

"I don't think he's here for fun."

"Doesn't look like it."

"What am I going to tell him?"

"You're on your own. Gotta go." Rebo skirted Bill, sketching a hello and good-bye as he passed.

Lindy went to meet him.

"Called in sick," Bill said.

"Are you?"

"Sick? No, just—" He broke off. "Where are the boys?"

"Around back with Rose and Cy. Did you come to take them back to the City?"

He shrugged.

Thoughts of drugs and murder flew from her mind. She slipped her arm through his. "Bill, it's okay. Come on."

Will was sitting atop Nesbitt. Cy was holding the reins as he led them around in a circle. "These guys are natural riders," he said as she and Bill came to an abrupt halt.

Will flashed her a grin; then he saw Bill and his face fell. Lindy felt Bill tense beside her, and she felt a rush of empathy for him. Children could be cruel in their innocence.

Randall looked at him warily. "Do we have to go?"

Lindy held her breath.

"No," said Bill. "I came to see the headless horseman."

"Oh, boy!" Randall launched into a description of Jake's costume and how he was going to ride Nesbitt. Cy helped Will down and he ran to join them.

"I was just about to take the boys for lunch," said Lindy.

"McDonald's?" asked Bill, apprehension showing plainly in his face.

"We'll compromise," she said.

She took them to the local diner. "It has video games in the lobby" had won the boys over.

As soon as they ordered, the boys relieved Bill of his change and ran to the machines. He and Lindy sat in silence across from each other, both staring out the window at the roofs of parked cars. His discomfort was palpable, as she was sure hers was. She tried to think of something to say.

"Bill," she began.

"You're not the only person in my life," said Bill before she got any further. "I have friends. I even get laid occasionally."

She stared at him, stunned. He was more than just embarrassed, she realized. He was bitter. He had never spoken of his feelings for her. They had just danced around them for the year and a half they had known each other. Which was fine. That way she didn't have to contemplate what her own feelings were. And this wasn't the time to break the code.

"I just didn't want you to think I was sitting around pining for you."

"I don't. I—"

The waitress brought their food.

"I'll get the boys." He was gone before the plates hit the table.

While the boys polished off hamburgers, fries and chocolate milk shakes, Bill and Lindy picked at Greek salads.

She couldn't believe the turn her thoughts had taken, as she disemboweled a stuffed grape leaf. Her life was in shambles, rejected by her husband, the marathon barely afloat. And she was jealous. She stabbed at the grape leaf. Jealous. It was sick. They were friends, and she was jealous because he had other friends. No that wasn't it, she thought. *Be honest. You wonder what kind of women Bill sleeps with.*

Bill was intently destroying a square of feta cheese.

"You should have gotten a hamburger, Uncle Bill. They're good." Will's cheeks bulged with food. "You want a French fry?"

"You want to see the hanged man when we get back?" asked Randall. "He's going to swing over the wagon."

"Did you see me on the horse?" asked Will.

"I rode him first," said Randall.

Lindy could feel Bill watching her from across the table, but she avoided his eyes. The boys kept asking questions until finally lunch was over.

While Randall and Will took Bill on a tour of the hayride, Lindy went to find Rebo. Rose, Peter and Mieko were rummaging through the sets for the Follies.

"Lose something?" she asked.

"A fly harness," said Peter. "One of us has been here all morning. Either someone copped it right under our noses, or it happened after we left last night."

"Weren't you the last to leave?"

"Yeah, some of the groups came in to rehearse, but we were the last ones out. I locked up. And no, I didn't notice the harness then. But I would have noticed someone walking off with it."

"Well, it's gone," said Rose appearing from behind a pew. "I've found sweaters, a tap shoe, two English books and a pair of jeans." She held up the latter. "I wonder what they wore home?" She stood to her full height. "But no harness. And Rebo said to tell you he was on a Vampirella stakeout."

"Thanks. I'll go find him."

"If you find the Vamp, search her for the harness."

"She doesn't have a key to the church."

"Bet The Asshole does."

Lindy came outside just in time to see Fallon going into the house. Rebo was making a beeline after her.

She raced across the parking lot. "Do we have a plan?"

"Scare the shit out of her?"

"Works for me. Let's go."

They caught up to her in the kitchen. Fallon and Janey were faced off in front of the oven. The aroma of something Italian filled the room.

"I'm guarding Stella's lasagna," said Janey.

"Good idea," said Rebo, giving Fallon a nasty look. "Got a cup full of ipecac, Lucretia?" He indicated the Starbucks cup.

"Where's Derrick?"

"With T.J. in the cellar." Janey turned to Lindy. "T.J. found the opening to a tunnel this morning. He's attempting to clear it. And Derrick is down there getting in the way and making dire predictions about the tunnel collapsing."

Fallon started for the cellar door.

"Just a minute." Rebo grabbed her elbow, relieved her of the coffee cup and put it on the table. "We need to talk."

"Let go of me. Derrick's latte will get cold."

"Tough." He escorted her efficiently through the door and into the hall. Lindy followed them to the parlor.

"Have a seat," he said and pushed Fallon into the wing chair. He looked around the room. "Now where is that rope? Maybe you can show me how you tied up Father Andrews."

Fallon jumped from the chair.

Rebo pushed her back down again.

Lindy closed the door to the hallway and came to stand beside him.

"You can't bully me," Fallon said petulantly. "I haven't done anything."

"The hell you haven't."

"For starters," Lindy interrupted, "we're not here to bully you. We just want to ask some questions, and warn you. But I'll be damned if I'm going to do either until you start talking like an adult. Do you realize how stupid you sound? You're practically thirty, for crying out loud. Why don't you try acting your age for once?" She took a deep breath. "There. I feel so much better."

Rebo gave her a startled look.

"Warn me about what?"

Lindy pulled up an incidental chair and sat down. She looked closely at Fallon's eyes, then to Rebo for confirmation. He cast his eyes heavenward. Higher than a kite.

"Does Derrick give you the drugs you're taking?"

"I'm getting out of here right now."

"I don't think so," said Rebo.

"How dare you." Fallon swung a manicured hand at him.

He grabbed her by the wrist. "Give it a rest, Demonetta. He's using you, and when he's done, you're gonna be cut off. What are you going to do when your supply dries up?"

"He loves me."

"Yeah, him and the rest of the world." He flung her hand away in disgust.

Lindy broke in before the confrontation turned into a slugfest. "Did you lock Melanie in the springhouse?"

Fallon gave an exaggerated shrug.

Lindy gritted her teeth. "If you did, why didn't you leave a limerick?"

"I did." Fallon clapped her hand to her mouth, her eyes frozen above it. "I mean—"

"No use in denying it, we know you did—you did?" Rebo looked at Lindy, then back at Fallon, his eyes narrowing. He grasped each arm of the chair and leaned forward, trapping her there. "Melanie could have died in there."

"Who says?"

"When dry ice sublimates, it gives off carbon dioxide," explained Lindy. "And in a closed storage space—"

Fallon's eyes weren't focusing. They had obviously lost her.

"Did you mean to kill her?" Rebo pressed his face close to Fallon's.

She wriggled away from him. "Me? I didn't do it."

"Then tell us who did. If you don't cooperate, you might be next."

"You're going to kill me?"

"Not us, dingbat." Rebo drew away, thoroughly exasperated. "Your boyfriend."

"Why would Derrick want to kill me?"

"Oh, Jesus." Rebo threw up his hands.

"Because you saw him lock Melanie in the springhouse," Lindy guessed.

"He didn't know I was there. I waited until he was gone before I left the limerick. And she deserves it, too. Always hustling her butt around him. Derrick calls her ghetto trash. And laughs at her behind her back."

"That smile's just begging to be slapped off your face." Rebo cracked his knuckles. "Are you saying that you left the limerick?"

"Of course I did, stupid. Everybody knows it was me. You already caught me, thanks to Miz Horowitz, that shriveled-up old clit."

Lindy surged to her feet. "You are the most—God, I can't even think of a word vile enough for you. Where did you leave the limerick?"

"I slipped it under the door. What's with you two? Take a dumb pill or something?"

"Take this, Fallon. You're playing a dangerous game, and I'd be really careful about Derrick's intentions toward you." Lindy felt herself grinding her teeth.

"You just wish he had intentions toward you."

Lindy expelled a groan of disgust. "I give up. I did my duty. You're on your own." She spun around and stalked out of the room. She stopped just outside the door and pressed her back against the wall, hugging herself, shaking with anger.

She heard Fallon say, "Can I go now? Derrick's latte is getting cold." The door opened. Fallon smirked at her as she passed by on her way back to the kitchen.

Rebo stopped beside her and leaned against the wall. "You okay?"

"How did that get out of hand so fast?" Lindy asked.

"Because the bitch is a case. Cuckoo la froo in spades."

"I don't understand how someone could come from a loving home and end up like that. It's heartbreaking."

"Yeah, but focus. She left a limerick under the door to the springhouse."

"No one found it."

"So where is it?"

Lindy quirked a shoulder. "Does it matter?"

"Probably not, but don't you have the teeniest little desire to find out?" Rebo gave her his best Peter Lorre leer.

Lindy's lips twitched. "I sure do."

They searched the springhouse and environs and found no limerick. It was growing dark when they returned to the house. They met Bill and the boys on their way to the hayride.

"It's going to start as soon as it gets dark," said Randall. "Bryan's invited everybody. This is going to be cool."

Will didn't look convinced. Maybe Lindy should suggest they stay behind, even though she had been looking forward to it.

"Will's a chicken poop, Will's a chicken poop," chanted Randall.

"Am not." Will's bottom lip quivered.

Bill knelt down beside Randall and drew him close. Quietly he said, "Will's your little brother. He looks up to you, and he needs you to help him grow up."

"I was just kidding," whispered Randall.

"Does Will think it's funny?"

Randall looked beyond Bill to his brother. "Oh." He walked over to Will. "You want to sit by me on the hayride?"

Will nodded.

"Let's go pick out a seat." The boys raced to the wagon.

Bill caught Lindy smiling at him and looked away. She took his hand and they went to join the ride.

Chapter Twenty-six

Just about everyone was there. Evelyn and Mary Elisabeth had materialized after being absent all day. Stella was chatting with Cy and Judd. Bryan stood nearby with a clipboard, flashlight and stopwatch. He gave last-minute instructions to a group of teenagers, who checked their watches and ran off toward the woods. Peter said a few words to Bryan and went down the road after them. Rebo and Rose grinned at Lindy and made silly faces when Bill wasn't looking.

Melanie was absent, probably in the church with the drama group. Lindy doubted that they had been invited. T.J. would not give up his work for something so mundane as a haunted hayride. There was no Fallon and no Derrick. This might be fun after all.

"You missed lasagna," said Stella, coming over to her. "Can't believe you deserted me for sawdust and special sauce."

"We went to the diner."

"Humph," said Stella, then leaned over and whispered, "Who's the hunk?"

Lindy looked at Bill in spite of herself. He was tall, angular, lithe. Not a hunk, but definitely a nice specimen. She clamped down on the thought. "A friend of mine. Are we almost ready?"

"Just waiting for Father Andrews and Janey."

"Janey's coming?"

"Said it might be her last hayride. Oh, here they come."

Father Andrews, wearing a black all-weather coat, a checkered tam on his head, escorted Janey to the wagon. Judd and Bryan helped her up and arranged a throw rug around her.

"I wouldn't miss it for the world," she said.

Cy lifted up Will and Randall, and the others climbed aboard.

Bryan and Cy took their places on the driver's seat, and Bryan checked his watch. "Just a couple of minutes," he said. "I need to get a strict timing so we can tighten up anything that lags."

Seated between Lindy and Bill, Will and Randall squirmed with anticipation.

"Okay. Let the hayride begin!" Bryan flourished his clipboard in the air and the wagon lurched forward.

They clacked down the road, shoulder to shoulder, all watching the woods to be the first to see the surprises in store for them. Marie snorted and kept to a snail's pace.

As soon as they were into the trees, Will snuggled closer to Bill. Randall began a running commentary. "Pretty soon we're gonna get to the Serpent Swamp and the Monster's Glen."

Ahead of them a writhing curtain of snakes stretched across the road. Marie slowed. Cy cracked the reins, and she picked up her pace again. Soon they were being slapped in the face by cold fingers of plastic. Someone let out a screech. It was Rose getting into the spirit of things. Everyone laughed. Bryan consulted his watch and scribbled something on the clipboard.

"Look," cried Randall and pointed into the woods. "Cool."

Pockets of mist hovered close to the ground far into the

woods. At least Derrick's dry ice was being put to good use, thought Lindy. Witches, ghouls and gremlins rose through the fog, their masks glowing green in the darkness. In the back of the wagon, heads swiveled left and right to take it all in. Will whimpered.

"It's done with flashlights," Randall assured him. "Peter put gel over the ends to make them green."

One by one, the specters melted back into the ground. The wagon rounded a curve and a black-robed grim reaper jumped out at them, swinging his ax. A piercing howl rent the darkness. Will climbed into Bill's lap.

"It's just a tape-recorder," said Randall. He turned to the others. "Wait til you see what's next."

They were coming to the bridge. The sounds of hoofbeats echoed through the night air. And there was Jake galloping toward them. Then he shot past them, clinging to Nesbitt's side.

"Damn," said Bryan.

Cy slowed the wagon and came to a stop just as Jake pulled himself back into the saddle.

"Sorry," came a muffled apology from inside the chicken wire coat. "The frame was bouncing around so much I couldn't control him."

"Shoulder straps," called out Rose. "We'll fix it tomorrow."

Jake rode back the way he had come. Bryan wrote something down while Cy set Marie in motion again.

Randall was standing with excitement. Bill pulled him back down. "The River of Blood," he cried. He turned around in his seat. "Look left, everybody. It's the River of Blood."

Rigged between two trees and rising ten feet overhead was a waterfall, lit, no doubt by Peter, with red spotlights. Everyone made comments of approval.

"I'm kinda proud of that," said Bryan. "It recycles by using two electrically generated water wheels."

Lindy smiled. Between Randall and Bryan, it was nearly impossible not to give in to the total enjoyment of being scared out of your wits.

"Wait til you see this, Uncle Bill," said Randall. "Me and Will worked on it, didn't we, Will?"

"I stuffed the hands," said Will. His arms were around Bill's neck.

Ahead of them, yellow light swathed the road. The hanged man swung down in front of the wagon. Marie whinnied and shied.

"Easy, girl," soothed Cy.

Someone screamed as the dummy arced back across the wagon. Marie lurched forward, throwing them against their seats, and broke into a trot.

"Hey, that's not my dummy," yelled Bryan as Cy fought to bring the wagon to a stop.

Fallon stepped out of the woods, laughing and pointing at them.

Derrick Justin swung like a human metronome across the road.

"Damn," said Rose. "That's where the harness went to."

"Oh, my God," moaned Janey. Next to her, Mary Elisabeth stared open-mouthed.

"That must be what their surprise was," said Stella. "Damn those two."

Bryan jumped off the seat and ran toward the hanged man.

Bill shoved Will at Lindy. "Don't leave the wagon." He jumped to the ground and began running.

She stared after him. It wasn't like Bill to panic, but then he didn't know Fallon and Derrick, and didn't realize that this was just another one of their tricks.

Judd jumped down after him. Bill had caught up to Bryan. He shoved him toward Judd, then ran toward the tree, where he pushed the two boys who had worked the lever back into the woods.

Judd pulled Bryan toward the wagon. Behind them, Derrick had come to a stop, his feet a head length from the ground. The sound of Fallon's laughter turned into a shriek.

Judd pushed Bryan onto the seat next to Cy. "Get going, Cy. Now!" Judd slapped Marie's flank and she took off at a trot, but not before Lindy heard Fallon cry out, "It's a joke. Get up, Derrick. Show them. Derrick. De-r-r-ick!"

Cy snapped the reins, and Marie galloped for home. Lindy held on to the seat with one hand while she tried to hold on to Randall and Will with the other. They whizzed past the chain-saw murderer, who stopped in the road and stared after them.

"He's messed up the whole thing," said Randall. "It isn't fair."

"What happened?" asked Will. "Where's Uncle Bill?"

Janey moaned. The jolting of the wagon must have been harrowing for her.

"Cy, this is crazy!" yelled Stella, her words vibrating as her body floundered wildly against the bench. "Slow that animal down."

Another tableau flew by, the teenagers caught unawares by the speeding wagon.

Father Andrews began to pray.

"I want Uncle Bill," whimpered Will.

"He had to help Bryan fix the hangman," Lindy shouted over the rattling wheels. "He'll meet us at the house."

Rebo lurched across her and fell onto the seat next to the boys. He looked at her across the top of their heads.

She looked backed at him, and even in the dark, she knew that he had come to the same conclusion.

Derrick Justin was dead.

Marie finally slowed down when she reached the church. Jake's sister, Steffy, was waiting for them.

"Why are you back so early? It should have taken another ten minutes."

"There was some trouble with one of the machines," said Bryan, his voice shaking. "You guys might as well go home. I don't think we'll be able to finish the test tonight."

Lindy peeled Will from her neck. "Rose is going to take you to the house for some dessert, while I go get Bill. Be back in a minute."

Rose swung the boys to the ground. "Stella made brownies. Race you to the kitchen."

Lindy and Rebo jumped from the wagon. Evelyn was already running down the road toward the hanging man. They ran after her, but when they neared the hangman's tree, she had disappeared.

Bill saw them coming and sprinted toward them. He grabbed Lindy by the shoulders and wheeled her around. "Don't come any closer. You don't want to see."

He looked ghastly in the dark, with the amber spotlight that marked the dummy's path lighting him from behind.

"Is he dead?" asked Lindy.

"Very."

"How?"

Bill shuddered. "Not hanged." He turned to Rebo. "Keep her here. No closer. Either of you. Understand?"

"Yeah," answered Rebo.

They watched him walk slowly back to the body. It was still hanging above the road. No one had bothered to take him down.

Lindy turned to Rebo. "Not hanged?"

Rebo widened his eyes at her. "Not hanged."

They turned slowly back to the tableau in front of them. Judd was holding a struggling Fallon. Bill stood away from the body, looking off into the woods, his hands shoved into his pants pockets.

After a few minutes, Lindy heard the sirens. A few minutes after that, the tramping of feet through the woods. An entire team of policemen arrived, along with emergency services and a squad of men in white jumpsuits carrying metal canisters.

"What is it? What are they doing?" asked Lindy.

"I don't know. But we're not going any closer."

Lindy agreed. Already the air was permeated with a hideous odor. She didn't know how the others could bear to stand so close to the body.

The units spread out in all directions, down the road and into the trees. An eternity passed while they searched. Lindy and Rebo watched with their hands covering their noses. At last, there was a call from the dark; several men appeared from the trees. One of them was carrying something at arm's length.

"An evidence bag," said Rebo. "I wonder what they found?"

Judd slipped on a pair of rubber gloves and took the bag. He held it open, while one of the men focused the beam of his flashlight on it, and another man reached inside with long metal tweezers. Slowly he pulled them out again. A round white cylinder caught the light.

"Shit, shit and double shit," muttered Rebo.

They clung to each other as they watched Judd put on his glasses and peer at the bottom of the Starbucks cup. They knew what he was reading—the missing limerick.

After a few minutes, Bill walked toward them. "Can you check on the boys? I'll be here for a while longer."

"Of course," said Lindy. She was dying to ask questions, but knew Bill wouldn't talk. He was no longer a detective, but Judd had obviously enlisted his help. She wanted to apologize for getting him into this, but Rebo nudged her away.

They walked silently back to the house. The horse trailer was gone. Cy must have taken Nesbitt and Marie back to the stables. They went straight to the kitchen.

Mary Elisabeth and Father Andrews sat at the table. T.J., hair and clothes covered with dirt, leaned against the counter.

"He's really dead?" he asked.

"I'm afraid so," said Lindy.

"I've called Howard," said Mary Elisabeth. "He's on his way. We've sent all the students home. And Stella drove Janey. She didn't want to leave. She was worried about the boys seeing that—that horrible sight. Oh, my God. My God."

"The boys are with your friends in the parlor," said Father Andrews.

"Thank you, Father," she said, but she couldn't meet his eyes. For the first time since she had known him, Father Andrews looked old.

They went into the parlor. The boys were asleep on the sofa, one at each end. The much abused afghan covered them. Rose, Peter and Mieko were sitting head to head by the cold fireplace.

"They'll have to cancel, won't they?"

"Most likely," said Lindy. "Damn Derrick Justin and his bag of tricks."

"We can stay over," suggested Rose.

"Thanks, but I don't think much will be going on tomorrow. And there's nothing any of us can do. Go home and get some sleep. I'll let you know what's going to happen."

"Why don't I take Frick-Frack to your house?" said Rebo. "I can stay with them until you get back."

"Thanks. I'd like them to be away from here."

Peter and Rebo carried the boys to the Black Beauty. Lindy said good night and went back to the kitchen to wait for Bill. A few minutes later, Howard arrived, looking tired and frightened. There were scratches across his cheek.

As soon as he entered the kitchen, Mary Elisabeth ran to him and threw herself into his arms. They clung to each other, not talking, while the others pretended not to see.

T.J. pushed away from the counter and went back to his digging. Bill and Judd returned to the house, and Judd took Mary Elisabeth and Howard outside.

Bill went to the sink and scrubbed his hands and face. He sat down at the table and pushed a strand of hair from his forehead. "They're taking Fallon in for questioning."

"Oh, no," said Lindy.

Father Andrews got wearily to his feet. "I'll go with them."

Bill and Lindy were left alone in the kitchen. She poured him a cup of coffee, which he drank in silence. His cheekbones stood out against tight, pale skin.

"It was bad, wasn't it."

Bill nodded. "Where are the boys?"

"Rebo took them to my house."

"Thanks."

"Bill, I'm sorry."

"It isn't your fault."

"Can you tell me what they think happened?"

He rubbed the back of his neck. She went to stand behind him, removed his fingers and replaced them with her own. She started at the base of his skull, pressing into the knotted muscles, massaging down his neck and across his shoulders. She worked in silence until gradually he began to relax.

"He was poisoned from the looks of it. We—they won't know until the lab tests are back, but it was pretty obvious. It was really—messy. He wasn't hanged; he was wearing a fly harness."

"He stole it from the church. Mieko was using it in the Follies. Does Judd think that Fallon poisoned him? It will kill Howard."

"That's the father? I don't know. She was hysterical, carrying on about flying and what a joke it was. Ugh."

"They found another limerick, didn't they? Lechery."

Bill pushed his chair back. "Do you mind if we go get the boys? I want to make sure they're okay."

"Too late," said Rebo. "They've already been bathed, fed—again—storied and are asleep upstairs in Cliff's room. I'm staying in Annie's. That leaves the downstairs guest suite for you." He grinned at Lindy. "I'm a very heavy sleeper. Night-night."

"I'd better wake them up; they can sleep in the car."

"Bill, it's late and you're too tired to drive to the City. Let them sleep. There's a toothbrush, razor, clean towels, anything you need in the guest room."

She saw the look on his face and felt a momentary pang of sympathy and a longer one of something else. Damn Rebo and his innuendoes. "Just pretend you're at a hotel."

Chapter Twenty-seven

Lindy lay in bed the next morning, listening to the silence, trying hard not to imagine that swinging corpse. She had to get up. Volunteers would be arriving at the farm soon, oblivious to what had happened. Someone would need to meet them, explain the situation, assuage their fears—cancel the marathon?

She pushed back the covers. And now there was no way to prove that Derrick had been selling the drugs. The possibility of making him confess had died with him. She shuddered. What a disgusting, horrible way to die. And for Judd and Bill to have to deal with. At least they had managed to keep the teenagers from getting a close look. It had been quick thinking on Bill's part. But someone would still have to call their parents. And that someone would be her.

She forced herself into the shower, pulled on jeans and a sweatshirt and went down the hall. She hadn't heard any sounds from the boys during the night. Hopefully, they had slept blissfully unaware of what they had seen.

She stopped at Cliff's room. It was empty. She listened for sounds of the television downstairs. Nothing. She looked into Annie's room. Rebo was asleep, Randall curled beside him.

But Will wasn't there. Had he panicked when he awoke to find himself alone? He didn't know that Bill had returned last night. She raced downstairs and looked in the kitchen and the family room. She stopped at the door of the guest room and listened. Not a sound, but the door was ajar. She peeked in and sighed with relief. Will slept cuddled to Bill's chest, his head on his uncle's shoulder, Bill's arm wrapped around him.

Lindy rested her head on the door frame and watched them sleep. A feeling of warmth suffused her, as a jumble of memories and emotions mingled into one. Her home with a small boy and a man. Bill and the father he might have been. Regret for the things he had never been able to enjoy with his son. Anger at Glen for throwing all he had away.

She backed into the hallway. They would need breakfast. She checked the fridge for eggs. There were three left. There was no cereal in the cupboard. No oatmeal. No cinnamon rolls. None of the things she always had on hand when Cliff and Annie had been living at home.

There was a box of pancake mix she had bought on Cliff's last visit. It had never been opened. For some reason that made her incredibly sad, as if all her choices were slipping through her hands. She brought it down. At least there was milk. She had bought some for the boys. Syrup. Shit. You couldn't have pancakes without syrup. She went back to the cupboard and rummaged inside. Surely, she had bought syrup when she bought the pancake mix. Where was the damned syrup?

Frantically she searched the shelves, clutching the box of pancake mix to her chest. She heard someone behind her. Bill, dressed but groggy from sleep, took the box of pancake mix out of her hand.

"I can't find the syrup," she said.

"Lindy, it's all right."

"You don't understand. You can't have pancakes without syrup." Her voice sounded funny. Her body felt funny.

He pulled her close, while she shivered against him. "We'll get through this."

The murders. The marathon. Her crumbling marriage. Their relationship. "Will we?"

He rested his cheek against her hair. "Yes." He held her for another second, then said, "But don't make pancakes. I don't think I could sit through such a domestic little scene this morning."

"McDonald's? I think they make breakfast."

He laughed quietly and pushed her away.

As it turned out, it was Rebo who found the syrup and made pancakes for the boys. Lindy and Bill drove separate cars to the Van Cleef farm.

The parking lot was crowded with trucks and squad cars. They squeezed their cars close to the house and got out. Judd was sitting on the steps, slouched in sleep. He was wearing wrinkled clothes and a growth of beard. He opened his eyes at the sound of the car doors slamming and got stiffly to his feet.

"Tried to get them to park out of sight," he said apologetically. "Told me to stick to my own caseload and butt out of theirs." He looked down at his clothes. "Sorry, but I've been up all night. At the hospital."

"The hospital?" said Lindy. "What's happened? Mary Elisabeth? Howard?"

"Hold up a minute. It's Fallon. She tested positive for drugs. They took her in for observation and psychiatric evaluation." Judd shook his head. "Mary Elisabeth and Howard stayed there all night. They're in bad shape. Howard says he had no idea that she was using. But he did admit that she attacked him Monday night after her fight with Mary Elisabeth over the limericks."

"She caused those scratches on Howard's cheek?"

"Yeah. And when Howard told me about that, Mary

Elisabeth came clean about being attacked with the scissors. Looks like Fallon has gone over the edge."

Lindy covered her mouth with both hands. She thought she might be sick.

"I know, it's a shock."

Lindy shook her head. "It isn't that. Rebo and I confronted Fallon yesterday. We told her that we thought Derrick was selling drugs and she had better watch her back. Oh, God, do you think we were responsible for what happened?"

Judd's eyes opened wide and he blinked several times. "I know I'm tired, but did you just say you think Derrick was the new drug connection?"

Lindy swallowed. Her heart began to thud against her breastbone. She couldn't seem to take a deep breath. Surely Melanie would understand if she told Judd, now that Fallon was under arrest for murdering Derrick. She glanced at Bill. Not that he could help. She hadn't even told him about their suspicions. What should she say?

The telephone rang from inside the house.

"I'll be right back," said Judd. "Don't go anywhere. You have some explaining to do." He ran up the steps into the house.

Again she looked at Bill. This time he eyed her back. She could see the disappointment in his eyes. She had withheld information—again. He couldn't understand that. Bill was totally honest. He even had trouble bending the truth for a good cause.

Judd stepped onto the porch. The door banged shut behind him. "Yew," he said.

"Me?" asked Lindy, feeling another rush of guilt.

"Yew, not ipecac."

"Judd, what are you talking about?"

Judd yawned. "Sorry. Guess I'm tired. That was the lab. Toxicology report on Derrick Justin. He was poisoned"—he paused to pull his notebook out of his shirt pocket—"with *Taxus canadensis*." He stumbled over the pronunciation. "For us ordinary folks, American Yew."

"A plant?" asked Lindy. Every nerve fiber was tingling. "He was poisoned with a plant?"

"Yeah. Found residue in the cup."

"Does that acquit Fallon? I can't see her searching the bushes for a poison. She might break a nail."

"Me neither, but I know who might."

"Adam Crabtree."

"She could've gotten it from him, though I can't imagine Adam having much truck with the likes of her. Then again, you never know how men will react to a pretty face. I'm going to a take a drive over to his place and ask a few questions before Paul Whitman gets to him."

"Paul won't like that very much," said Bill.

"You're right. But at this point, I'm too far in the hole with him to care. And I have to move fast so I can clear this up before Mischief Night."

"Mischief Night? We can't go on with the marathon. We'll have to cancel." Lindy couldn't even imagine holding festivities where so gruesome a murder had been committed.

"We can't not go on with the marathon. Too much is at stake. We have to raise that money by the first of the year."

"Can't you get a postponement?"

"No, the terms of the bequest are airtight."

"But even if the property reverts back to Adam, surely he could sign a waiver, or just sign over the property to the town. He'll own it after all."

"He will. Eventually. But it could take months, maybe years, to get though probate. I need that teen center now." Judd pulled his keys out of his pocket. "I'm going on over to Adam's, but don't think I've forgotten what you said about Derrick selling drugs. We'll have a talk when I get back. Before I turn you over to the homicide investigation."

He took a look at her face and smiled. "Turn you over for questioning, though they might feel like arresting you for holding back information that could have led to a drug arrest." He blew air through his teeth, shook his head and left.

"You're something else," said Bill after Judd had driven away.

"Is that a compliment?"

"Not entirely. Maybe you should tell me what you've been withholding before you have to tell it to the cops."

She sat down on the steps. Bill sat down beside her.

"It's a really long story and I only know parts of it. Rebo and I were going to—well, we had a lead of sorts, but we didn't have time to pursue it."

"Goddammit, Lindy."

Lindy winced. "It's not like it sounds."

Bill raised an eyebrow.

"I promised not to tell."

Bill raised his other eyebrow.

"Okay. I concede." She took a breath while she organized her thoughts. "Let me try to put this in order. First, there was the drowned detective. We didn't know for several days that he was a detective and was probably investigating something or someone connected with the marathon or possibly the property itself. In the meantime, we discovered three of the kids smoking pot down by the springhouse. Melanie went ballistic." She frowned. "You haven't met her yet. She's the new English teacher. Janey, you met her last night, is dying of cancer and had to retire. Melanie is young and with it and really has a way with the kids. But she said the same thing had happened in her former school."

"What same thing?"

"The sudden influx of drugs. She was sure Derrick was responsible."

Bill frowned, and she explained how Derrick had brought Melanie to the community. "She feels responsible, but she didn't have proof. She confronted Derrick, but he threatened to implicate her. We searched the springhouse—"

"Before or after she was locked in?"

Had she told him about that? She must have. "Before. It had been padlocked the whole week, but when we got there it was open and empty. And Adam Crabtree showed up out of the blue and said it was gone."

"What was gone?"

"Whatever it was. He didn't know. Or wasn't telling. Rebo and I went to see him. He told us a story about a pestilence on the land and a magician that promised happiness. It was obviously symbolic of what was happening at the marathon. He wanted us to glean the meaning out of the story without having to tell us outright. Derrick Justin was the magician. We're pretty sure about that part. Adam must have seen something that he hasn't told, because that was really clear. But when we asked him how the story ended, he said it wasn't over yet. Do you think that means he was deciding whether to kill Derrick or not?"

"From everything I've heard so far, Crabtree isn't exactly what you'd call proactive. He does seem to show up at pivotal moments, first with the drowning victim and then at the springhouse. And he's an expert on local flora, but that doesn't mean he killed the man."

She sneaked a look at Bill. How did he know all this? Had he been kibitzing with Judd? "Maybe not," she continued. "He's growing marijuana in his greenhouse. I didn't recognize it at first. I thought it was tomato plants."

Bill grinned. "Uh-huh."

"He said it lessened the side effects of chemotherapy. He cures people with herbs, not kills them." She sighed. "It just doesn't make sense. It must be Fallon, right?"

If she was expecting an answer from Bill, she didn't get one.

"This is crazy. I just wanted to get through the Frightmare Follies and go back to work. I don't know why these things happen to me. I went through my whole life without even seeing a fatal car wreck. And now, in less than two years, there've been . . . how many bodies?"

"Five—seven counting these two."

She forced herself to look at him. "Is it me?"

"You're serious, aren't you?"

She nodded, then looked away.

He moved closer and put his arm around her. "It isn't you. I don't know what it is. But it isn't you."

"It isn't natural to find this many dead people."

"Not for a civilian. Maybe you should sign up for the police academy. God knows you have the experience." He shook her gently. "Buck up, girl. You've gathered a lot of information, and I don't believe anything you said to Fallon drove her to commit murder."

"You don't know her."

"No, but I've heard enough about her to wonder how she would ever think of, much less figure out how to distill, a poison. Why not just do a repeat of ipecac? It would be a lot easier."

"So it might be Adam?"

"It's possible, but let the homicide squad figure it out."

"But what if they figure it out wrong?"

"Don't even think it, and don't withhold any more information."

Lindy rested her elbows on her knees. What the hell was she going to do? She had already withheld information. She was still withholding information. But she couldn't get the boys involved with this. She looked out over the carnival grounds, the half-constructed booths, the tarps covering them. She imagined the festivities uniting the community, giving the teens a safe place to spend their free time, the hard work that had gone into the preparations. All for nothing.

"Good God, what's she doing here?"

Evelyn was walking out of the woods. She stopped when she saw Lindy, then came toward them. "Where's Judd?"

"He just left. What are you doing here?"

"I knew that things would be dumped on you. I thought you could use some help."

"Thanks. I could." She introduced Evelyn to Bill. "I guess we'd better call the committee heads for a meeting.

Let them know that we're canceling so they can make their calls."

"You're thinking of canceling?"

Lindy looked up in surprise. "We can't have children coming here when two men have been killed, probably murdered. No one would come even if we did go on with it. I certainly wouldn't bring my children."

"But wouldn't it be better to keep all the suspects together, until this thing is cleared up?"

Lindy felt Bill come to attention beside her. It was a small movement, but a shiver of apprehension skittered across her back. She studied Evelyn's face, but it just reflected concern.

She glanced at Bill for an indication of what she should do, but he was studying Evelyn. Had he picked up on the same thing in Evelyn's manner that always disturbed her? And her manner *was* disturbing, even though Lindy couldn't put her finger on what it was. Nonetheless, Evelyn was right. Everyone had access to yew. Hell it was growing right here by the front porch. Any one of them could have poisoned Derrick. What if Fallon hadn't killed him?

Her mind began running in two directions. Everyone had access to yew, but not everyone had access to the coffee cup. They needed time to figure this out.

"Maybe you're right," she said at last. "At least we should get the others' opinions. Would you mind making the calls? Bill and I haven't eaten yet."

"Sure. It's eleven o'clock. Would one o'clock be good?"

"That would be fine. Thanks."

"You want to eat?" said Bill. "That's a first."

She suggested they take the Volvo. She wanted to drive because she intended to stop by the hospital on her way to breakfast, and she didn't want to have to fight with Bill.

"They're not going to let you talk to her," he said as she pulled into the hospital's parking lot.

"I just want to clear some things through Mary Elisabeth. I know she isn't thinking about the marathon, but I don't feel I can make a unilateral decision."

"Sure you don't," said Bill. "Let's go."

But Mary Elisabeth and Howard had gone home. Lindy and Bill returned to the car.

"I'll drive." He took the keys. "You might be on a constant diet, but I'm not. And you need to eat something or you're going to collapse."

Lindy acquiesced. She was already shaky with fatigue, hunger and indecision.

They ate bagels and cream cheese sitting in the front seat of the car.

"Are you sure Glen is in Paris and not on his way home?"

Lindy forced down her bite of bagel. "Why?" she managed to say.

"Because I'm about to suggest that I go to the City long enough to pick up some things for me and the boys and stay here for the next few days. But I don't want to take the chance of being named corespondent in this mess if Glen decides to make a surprise visit."

She laughed in spite of his serious expression. "I don't think I've heard anybody called a corespondent since that Fred Astaire movie."

Bill, however, didn't think it was amusing.

"I appreciate it, really," said Lindy. "But what do we do with the boys? They might not be safe."

"You might not be safe, either."

"You don't think Fallon killed Derrick, do you?"

"I'm reserving judgment. But I was there, remember? Either she's a really good actress, or she was genuinely horrified at what had happened."

"She's a terrible actress."

"I was afraid of that."

Chapter Twenty-eight

The committee meeting lasted for a volatile hour. At the end they decided to postpone the decision until Monday.

Paul Whitman was waiting outside the dining room when they adjourned. He asked those present at the hayride to stay. One by one he took them into the sunporch and asked them to go over their activities of that afternoon.

Stella, Janey, Evelyn and Lindy reconvened in the kitchen once the detective had left. They sat in silence while the sounds of excavating drifted up from the cellar.

Stella walked over to the door to the staircase and slammed it shut. "You can't hear yourself think with all that noise. Not to mention the police all over the place and asking questions."

"They're just tying up loose ends," said Evelyn. "They have nothing but circumstantial evidence that Fallon killed Derrick. They need concrete proof or an eye witness. Sometimes people see things they don't realize they've seen. He was not accusing anyone."

"At least they finished with the physical investigation before the committee members arrived," said Stella. "Can you imagine if they had seen all those vans and squad cars?"

"Those poor children," said Janey. "They must have been so frightened."

"The boys think that Derrick was playing a joke and messed up the test," Lindy reassured her. "Bryan and the others were upset, but Judd and Bill kept them from getting too close."

"Good riddance, I say, not to put too fine a point on it." Stella wandered around the kitchen at a loss without something to feed the others. She stopped and looked at Evelyn. "Are you sure they don't suspect any of us?"

Why did it seem that Evelyn was always subtly taking charge of the situation? wondered Lindy, then brushed the thought aside. *You're just jealous,* she told herself. She became close to Mary Elisabeth while you were gone. Was here when you were not. She may even resent the fact that you waltzed right back in and became the cochairman.

"We've all been questioned. Let's compare notes." Stella sat back down. "They asked me where I was, who I saw, and if I remember Fallon carrying the coffee cup." She shrugged. "I was making a delivery while Janey watched the lasagna I had made for dinner. I never saw Fallon or Derrick that afternoon."

"They asked me the same," Evelyn volunteered. "I didn't see anything either."

Convenient, thought Lindy. She realized everyone was looking at her. "I did see Fallon with the coffee cup. She left it on the table while Rebo and I talked to her in the parlor. Janey?"

"What?"

"Do you remember the cup?"

Janey seemed befuddled. Another of her bad days, Lindy guessed. They were coming more frequently and no wonder.

"Yes," she said after a moment. "I do remember. Fallon left it on the table. When I was watching the lasagna."

"Lindy, really," said Stella.

"Did anyone come in?" Lindy persisted.

"No, I don't think so. I believe T.J. got a glass of water from the faucet. I'm sorry. I wasn't really paying attention. I didn't want the lasagna to dry out."

"The poison was probably already in the cup by then," said Stella.

Lindy didn't answer. She was thinking about T.J.—his fights with Derrick, his disgust with Fallon. He had just happened to come for a glass of water while the cup was unguarded.

"But how did she get him in the tree?" asked Janey, breaking into her thoughts. "And why? It just doesn't make sense."

"No, it doesn't," said Lindy. "Except that Fallon saw the rigging at the church on Monday. She tried to get Peter to fly Derrick then, but Peter refused. You know how she is when she wants something; she doesn't let up. Maybe Derrick was just humoring her."

"It seems like a lot of trouble just to please Fallon," said Stella.

"Yes, it does," admitted Lindy. Then she was struck by a new idea. Maybe Fallon had blackmailed him into that tree. Maybe her threat of knowing something the others didn't was directed at Derrick and not Mary Elisabeth and Howard.

"What have you got in that brain?" asked Stella, looking at her suspiciously.

Lindy mentally shook herself. "Nothing—unfortunately." She frowned. "So where was everyone after Fallon left the kitchen?"

"Right here. We all ate lasagna." Stella hesitated. "Except you and Melanie."

"I was with Rebo."

"And Melanie was rehearsing," said Janey.

"Are you sure?" asked Stella.

"Reasonably sure. She rehearses at the same time every afternoon."

"T.J.," said Stella. "I just remembered. He said he had work to do, so he took his plate upstairs."

"Did you hear him working?" asked Lindy.

"Come to think of it, no."

Janey stood up with an effort. "I need to see Adam."

Lindy felt a pang of sympathy. What a hell of a way to spend your last days on earth.

Stella cast a worried glance toward her. "I'll drive you," she offered.

"That isn't necessary; I'm fine. I just need to talk to Adam."

They watched her walk slowly toward the door, shoulders bent, her body so emaciated that a breeze might blow her away.

"She's deteriorating so fast," said Stella. "And there's nothing any of us can do."

No, there wasn't. But at least they could do something about making her last days good ones. Lindy stood up. "I'll be back in a while." She walked out the back door thinking about what Evelyn had said. Sometimes people saw things they didn't realize they had seen. Well, she would go over everything, starting with finding the detective. Maybe she had seen something that would help.

T.J. was bumping a wheelbarrow up the cellar stairs. He seemed unaffected by the horrible occurrences of the last two weeks. It didn't seem natural.

She walked across the backyard and into the summer kitchen. The day was sunny and crisp, the air clean and wholesome. A paradox, when her mood was as black as night. She stopped at the bridge and peered down into the water. Looked upstream as if she could conjure the imprint of what had happened to the detective and where.

She replayed the scene—Bruno, the body, Adam Crabtree. The man figured heavily in the whole situation and yet wasn't a participant. Just an observer. An observer. Someone who sees. Sees, but doesn't tell. Had he seen who killed the detective? Had *he* killed the detective?

She moved away and walked slowly down the road. She was stabbing at air and she knew it. But it didn't seem that Paul Whitman and Judd were doing any better. Why didn't someone admit to hiring the detective? That made less sense than anything else. But life didn't always make sense. If it did, she would still be happily married. She pushed that thought away. Not now. Concentrate on the problem at hand. At least she might be able to do something about solving the murders.

She stopped before she reached the hangman's tree, afraid of what she might find there. Yellow crime tape was still draped around the immediate vicinity. She took a cautious breath. Nothing but the smells of drying leaves and earth. She moved closer and stopped again, the back of her neck prickling. Something was moving in the woods. She quirked her head, listening, then turned around. Two squirrels ran across the road and into a tree. She exhaled, but walked briskly away.

A few yards farther down the road, she turned to recapture the sight of Derrick Justin swinging from the hangman's noose. How had he gotten in the tree? She couldn't imagine a violently ill man agreeing to do that, even if Fallon was threatening him. Had he climbed there and hooked himself to the harness before the poison took effect?

He must already have been dead when the boys released the platform. Was that Fallon's big surprise? Could she be so nuts that she would announce her intentions to murder Derrick? Lindy tried hard not to imagine his last minutes as the poison took effect. Unable to free himself while Fallon waited callously for him to die.

Or was it Fallon who got the real surprise? But if Fallon didn't kill him, who did?

Lindy backed away. Her hands went to her ears, as if they could stop her from hearing the name that came to her mind. Melanie. She had threatened him. If she had found the last limerick, she was the only one that could have put it on the bottom of the cup. Had she really been in rehearsal all afternoon?

She forced herself down the path to the springhouse, knowing she would find nothing. Her skin was alive with the sense of someone watching her. It was stupid to be out in the woods alone, but it was a little late to be having second thoughts now.

She knelt in the trampled grass. Found nothing. She stood up. A flash of brown moved in the woods. Her throat tightened on a scream. Not an animal. Fabric. Adam Crabtree's cassock? Was he watching her?

"Adam?" she called, her voice trembling. "If that's you spying on me, Janey is waiting for you at your cottage."

There was no answer and no more movement. She suddenly felt ridiculous. Maybe she hadn't seen anything but her own expectations. Nonetheless, she scurried back to the road and broke into a run. She sped past the cemetery and careened around the side of the church. She crashed into Evelyn and bit back a scream.

"Lindy!" Evelyn's mouth tightened with concern. "I was just looking for you. You look like you just ran into the headless horseman."

Lindy straightened up, embarrassed. "Running late," she managed, then stopped. Evelyn was wearing a beige turtleneck sweater and matching gabardine slacks. Beige. Lindy took a step back. Evelyn? "Lots of work to do. Uh, did you need me for something?"

"I wondered if we should call Judd. Make sure it's okay for the council to work on the hayride today. If anyone shows up," she added.

Lindy began inching toward the church entrance. She needed to ask Melanie some questions before anyone else did. She realized for the first time that she wanted to protect her. She believed in her. Her work at least. But could she condone murder, even if it were the murder of a drug dealer? Maybe not, but she could at least ask Melanie about the limerick before she talked to the police. "Good idea. Could you call him?" That should keep Evelyn out of the way long enough for her to talk to Melanie.

"Sure." Evelyn whipped out her cell phone and touched a button. She had Judd's number in her memory pad.

Damn. Now what? She'd just have to take her chances that Evelyn would stay on the phone long enough for her to get to Melanie. "I'll be back in a minute. Just want to check on the rehearsal."

She willed herself not to hurry up the steps, but once inside the church, she ran toward the stage. Only three of the teenagers were there. Melanie was slumped on her stool, looking at the floor.

"Where is everyone?"

Melanie shrugged. "I guess—" She didn't finish, but clasped her hands between her knees and hung her head.

"Look. I've got to ask you something." Lindy glanced toward the back door. "And quick before anyone comes. Be straight with me. Did you find a limerick the day you were locked in the springhouse?"

"What?"

Lindy leaned forward and whispered urgently. "Melanie. You have got to tell me. They found a limerick on the bottom of Derrick's coffee cup. Fallon said she left it under the springhouse door." She grabbed Melanie's arm. "Do you see what this means?"

Melanie's head jerked up. "Yes."

"Which? Did you find it or do you know what it means?"

"Both." Melanie's eyes widened, and for the first time Lindy saw the woman behind the tough facade. "I did find it. I didn't remember until now. I went inside. I know it was stupid, but I was so angry. I just needed to take another look. Then the door slammed shut and someone locked it. I could hear them on the other side. I banged on the door. But they wouldn't let me out." She shivered. "I backed away. There was just a slit of light coming from beneath the door, and I saw the paper slide through it." Her voice cracked. "It was so dark and cold and I couldn't get out."

Lindy touched Melanie's shoulder. She always seemed so in control. None of them had thought about how frightened she must have been that day. Only Janey had gone to comfort her. Janey whose job she had taken.

"What did you do with the limerick?"

"I picked it up but—" She looked down at her hands. "You didn't find it?"

"Judd looked, but he didn't have time to do much of a search. Rebo and I went back yesterday—nothing."

Melanie reached automatically into her jacket pockets. "It isn't here. I would have put it in my pocket. I don't remember. I couldn't breathe. Then everything got hazy. I don't even know how I got out of the springhouse."

And Melanie hadn't been holding it when she walked to the ambulance. Lindy was sure of that.

"They'll think I put it on Derrick's cup. They'll think I killed him." Her eyes met Lindy's. "Derrick has finally managed to destroy my work, and he isn't even here."

"But you didn't kill him." Lindy realized her statement had ended in a lift, making it a question.

"No. Oh, God. What am I going to do?"

"We'll figure out something," said Lindy. But she would need both Rebo and Bill to do it. She turned to go and saw the afterglow of sunlight as the church door closed.

Someone had been listening. She ran to the door and cracked it open. Evelyn was walking across the gravel toward the house, her cell phone to her ear.

Suddenly cars began filling the parking area. Rose, Peter and Mieko in a taxi from the train station, Bill from the city, Rebo and the boys from home. She pulled Bill aside and motioned to Rebo to join them, but before he reached them, another car turned into the drive and came to a stop in front of the church. The door opened and Paul Whitman stepped out.

They all stood frozen as Paul walked past them and into the church. Then, in one motion, they hurried after him and crowded through the doorway.

Paul stopped at Melanie. Melanie stood up. Her cast of three watched helplessly as Paul Whitman escorted her up the aisle. Rebo shot her an anxious glance as they passed. Randall and Will pressed close to Bill. Rose and Peter looked at Rebo. Mieko looked at no one; her eyes were mere slits and her elbows dug into her sides.

"Just want to ask some questions," Paul said to the group as he led Melanie outside. They followed him out into the late afternoon sun.

Kenny Stackhowser was coming out of the side lot.

"You're late," said Melanie.

"What are they doing?" asked Kenny. He stepped forward, but Rebo grabbed his arm. "At ease, bulldog. Don't make it worse."

"Are they arresting Melanie, Uncle Bill?" asked Randall.

Paul turned around. "No, son, Melanie is just helping the police with some information. She's doing her duty as a good citizen."

Lindy wasn't sure if that was really for the boys' sake or for Melanie's. And then she remembered that the boys had seen Melanie arguing with Derrick. If they had to make a statement, it would throw suspicion from Fallon to Melanie.

How had she involved them in all of this? Bill would have to take them home. After they were gone, she would tell Judd what they had overheard—if she had to.

"What happened?" Rebo's voice held a note of accusation.

"When is she coming back?" asked Kenny.

Lindy shrugged at both questions. She was watching Bill. He looked worried. "I asked her about the limerick. She found it, but she doesn't remember what happened to it. Someone overheard us and must have called Paul." She held up a hand, stopping their questions. "And someone followed me when I went back over the hayride route."

"You what?" Bill's voice boomed in the air. The boys jumped. "Go stand over there." He motioned them to the hawthorn bushes.

"What did we do?" Randall asked.

"Nothing," he said, suddenly gentle. "I just need to talk to Lindy. Man to man."

Randall giggled.

Will looked at Lindy. "You're in trouble," he whispered.

"I know," she said.

"What the—" Bill glanced toward the boys, then continued in a subdued voice. "What were you doing out there? Alone?"

"Trying to jog my memory. I kept feeling someone watching me. I thought it was Adam Crabtree, because I saw a flash of brown. But it wasn't. I think it was Evelyn, and I think she's the one that overheard Melanie and me talking. She was on her cell phone when I came outside to see."

"She ratted on Melanie?" asked Rebo.

"Hmm," said Bill and walked away.

"But I've got to talk to Melanie. It can't wait," said Kenny. He was chewing the cuticle of his middle finger. His eyes darted from side to side as if he expected to be hauled off to the police station along with his teacher.

Lindy was aware of Bill saying something to Rose, then Rose going to stand by Will and Randall. Bill walked toward the house without a backward glance.

"I've got to talk to Melanie," said Kenny. "Now."

"Well, you can't," said Rebo. "So talk to us."

Kenny's eyes flitted around the group. He started on another finger. He bit his lower lip. Then his hand went to his pocket. "Let's take a drive."

Lindy looked a question at Rebo. Bill and Evelyn were standing near the farmhouse. Bill was talking. Evelyn was smiling. What was he up to?

"Come on," urged Kenny. He led them to the church parking strip and stopped in front of a blue BMW. "It belongs to my mother's husband. I borrowed it."

"Oh, shit," said Rebo.

"Just get in, okay?"

They did. Rebo and Lindy squeezed together in the passenger seat because Kenny wouldn't let them sit in the back. Lindy saw Bill look up when they drove away.

Kenny turned left on the main road, past the picketers.

Brown, thought Lindy despondently. They were all dressed in brown.

Kenny took the north fork toward Adam Crabtree's, but instead of turning left, he pulled onto a dirt road off to the right. He killed the engine and motioned to Rebo and Lindy to get out.

They watched Kenny open the door to the backseat and pull a blanket off the floor.

"Hell of a time for a picnic, honcho," said Rebo. Then his eyes widened. "Well, if it ain't genie in a bottle."

Val uncurled from where she had been lying on the floor, and Kenny hauled her out of the car.

"I had to sneak her out of her house," he said. "And we've got to get back before her mother comes home." He glanced at his watch. "Which gives us about ten minutes. Damn."

"Where's Melanie?" asked Val. "I'll only talk to Melanie. Kenny, what's going on?"

"They've arrested her."

"Don't jump the gun, Kenny. They're just questioning her."

"Yeah, right, and we know what happens next. The Porters'll pay some scheister to get Fallon off and they'll pin it on Melanie."

God, to be so young and so hopeless, thought Lindy.

"It's all my fault." Val's expression was so pitiful that Lindy automatically put an arm around her. The girl jerked away.

"Yeah, it is. You've really fucked it for all of us, you know that?"

"Kenny, that's enough," said Lindy. She turned to Val. "If you know something, you have to tell us."

"No." Kenny pushed the girl behind him. "First we have to make some ground rules. You gotta remember she was going to tell this to Melanie. Melanie doesn't know anything about this. If you turn it into something that will work against her, I'll—"

"You'll *manger merde* and die, my man. You know, you might have half a chance if you'd learn to recognize who your friends are. Now you've wasted two of your ten minutes. Talk fast, my little stowaway."

Val stepped from behind Kenny. "What should I do?"

Kenny chewed on his cuticle. "Tell them."

"Derrick gave me the stuff. He *gave* it to me. I didn't try to score or anything. He just came up one day and said I looked like someone who had real designer taste. He pulled out this vial and pressed it into my hand." She looked away. "I didn't use it at first. I mean, I'd already gotten busted and well, the play was pretty cool, and I didn't want to f—screw up, so I just kept it.

"But Derrick kept asking me how it was. Telling me he was relying on my opinion. You know, flattering me and making me feel like—I thought he was hot for me, you know? He said he was just hanging around Fallon until something better came along. He made me think I was that something. Then he said we could really live it up big, if I could just get a base in the drama group."

"A base?" asked Lindy.

"They were planning to use the group to push for them," said Kenny. "You fucking betrayed us, bitch."

"I know. I'm sorry. I'm sorry. I wish I was dead."

"No, you don't," said Lindy. She wrapped her arm around Val's shoulders. Val tried to pull away, but this time Lindy held tight. "You've screwed up pretty big time, but you can redeem yourself." Val shook her head. Two tears slid down her cheeks. "You can, but you'll have to tell the police what you told us."

"No. I can't. They're going to send me away. I don't want to go there. I want to stay at home and be in the play."

Val was working herself into a fit of hysterics. Lindy shook her. "Talk to Judd. You can trust him. He'll call your parents and let them know you're okay and that you're helping him. Maybe he can figure out a compromise so that you can stay."

Val sniffed and wiped her eyes. She looked toward Kenny. "I'm sorry I messed it up for everybody."

"You should be." He turned to Lindy. "Are you sure this will work? So help me, if you—"

"Can it," said Rebo. "Take us back to the farm and we'll take care of Val. You get this hot little item back home before your mother's husband finds out. Then you can get your butt to rehearsal."

They didn't have to take Val downtown. Judd was parked in front of the church when they returned.

"I didn't see the car you're driving," he said to Kenny. "Must still be in your driveway at home." He turned to Val. "And you're up the crick."

"Wait," said Lindy. "She has information. She was coming to tell you."

Judd's eyebrows rippled across his forehead. "That right? Then why don't you and me take a little trip down to my office. You can even ride up front with me, in case anybody sees you."

"Everything, Val," Lindy prompted as Judd helped the girl into the front seat.

Rebo turned to Kenny. "Beat it, unload the beemer, then get your butt back here." He turned to Lindy. "Let's go find the wannabe. I bet he found out a whole bunch of shit while we were gone. I think it's time to reconnoiter."

Chapter Twenty-nine

"Just chatting," Bill said.

"That's it?" asked Rebo. "You were chatting?"

Bill gave him a blank look. "Just chatting."

"Oh, great." Rebo threw up his hands and stalked away.

"You went hurrying after her just for a chat?" Lindy gave him her most "oh yeah, sure" look.

"We talked about the weather and her duties for the marathon." Bill was watching Rebo's retreating figure.

"If she was the one following me through the woods?"

"No." He turned back to Lindy. "And I suggest that you don't ask her either. How long have you known her?"

"Since the marathon started," said Lindy. "About a week and a half. Why?"

"Just curious."

"She's new in town. She lives in the same apartment complex as Mary Elisabeth."

Bill nodded slowly. "And did she move in before Mary Elisabeth did or after?"

"Mary Elisabeth left Howard at the end of the summer. Evelyn came in the beginning of September." She expelled a long breath. "After Mary Elisabeth. Bill, why are you asking this? Do you think it's significant? Do you think Evelyn is involved?"

"I don't know. Just give her a wide berth, okay?"

Lindy frowned at him. He had assumed his opaque face. He wanted information but wasn't going to give any back. He was cutting her out. She felt a jolt of disappointment.

Had Bill discovered something that linked Evelyn to the two murders? Was it possible? She rummaged in her mind. Came up with zip. So how had Bill managed it in such a short time? Because he had been a cop, still thought like one. But if that was the case, why hadn't Judd and Paul picked up on it? Or had they?

"How about dinner?" asked Bill.

"What?"

"The boys will be getting hungry."

"I've been thinking," said Lindy. "Will and Randall shouldn't be here. It isn't safe."

"I shouldn't be here either, but I can't leave you in the midst of all of this." His closed expression was gone and Lindy almost wished it back. This one was much too meaningful.

Her breath caught. She had never seen that look before. She felt overwhelmed by it. Bill was looking past her to a point over her shoulder. Waiting for her to—what? Agree with him and send him and the boys back to the City? Or to tell him that she needed him and wanted him to stay? And how many layers of meaning would that have?

She was only now realizing his depth of feeling for her. And hers for him. She had recognized their mutual attraction: intellectually, emotionally and, she had to admit, physically. But he had always been too polite to act on it. And she had blithely pretended it didn't exist. She hadn't been fair, but she was too selfish to give up his friendship just because they had wandered into uncharted territory.

She should send him away. Not let him get caught up in the disaster of her life. She could never think of him as the consolation prize. But if she asked him to stay, it would look that way. God, what should she do?

"We could starve to death while you're coming to a decision," he said. Then he smiled. He knew exactly what she had been thinking and was willing to risk it. "I'll go find the boys."

"Okay. I just have to get the Follies notes out of my bag in the office and give them to Rebo. We'll get him started and then he can take it from there."

She retrieved her bag and met Bill in the church. It was virtually empty. Not even a skeleton was in sight.

"What's going on?" she asked Rebo.

"News has gotten out about Derrick. People are afraid to come."

Lindy sank down on the nearest pew, utterly defeated. Rebo slumped next to her. A few more participants straggled in and sat down without speaking.

Miss Carole Anne came from behind the sets wringing her hands. "I'm sorry, Lindy, but everyone was afraid for the children. It's all over town about the murder and Derrick Justin being suspected of dealing drugs. Everyone is shocked and afraid. It was a group decision not to let the children appear. I'm so sorry."

On stage, one Macbeth witch stood ready to go. She was a thick-set woman with long gray hair that she had let down over her shoulders. "I'm ready to start. The others will come back if you don't cave in. At least the two other witches will. They'd never give me the satisfaction of appearing on stage without them."

The door opened, and a man accompanied by two young skeletons walked in. "I've changed my mind," he said. "I talked to my girls, explained some of what happened. I think it's about time this community opened its eyes and made a stand." He pushed his girls forward. "I'm going to be here every second. No one even goes to the bathroom by themselves. But my family is not backing down."

Rebo shrugged at Lindy. "Well, hell. It's a start. Go have dinner."

"I can't leave you like this."

"Sure you can. Just give me your notes." He raised his voice to the room. "On stage please. Eddie Poe, are you here? Good. Be ready to go on. Peter. Lights to half."

The lights dimmed. Lindy pulled out her legal pad. A slip of paper drifted to the floor. Bill picked it up and slid it into his jacket pocket.

Rebo took the pad. "Save me some dinner. I'm chaperoning." He kowtowed them out.

Bill cooked while Lindy called Mary Elisabeth. There was no answer at her apartment, so she tried Howard. Mary Elisabeth picked up.

"I'm glad you called." She sounded exhausted.

"I just wanted to let you know we're all concerned about you and if there's anything we can do . . ." Of course there was nothing anyone could do, except to find Fallon innocent, undo the hurt between husband and wife, take away all the suspicion and fear, turn Fallon into a perfect, loving daughter . . . She brought her attention back to what Mary Elisabeth was saying.

"I'm staying here with Howard for a few days. They're keeping Fallon at the hospital until tomorrow; then they'll let her come home. She'll have a full-time nurse, of course, one that I'm sure is trained in police procedure as well as nursing. But it's the best the lawyers could do."

"Are you sure that's wise?" asked Lindy.

"No. But Fallon swears she didn't kill Derrick. She said that it was Melanie. I don't want it to be either one of them, but I suppose the truth must come out. She is my daughter after all. I'll have to stand by her whatever happens."

This was a new attitude from Mary Elisabeth. And after all that Fallon had done.

"It's for Howard's sake, really. I can't bear to see him endure such pain alone."

Lindy told her what had been happening with the marathon. The postponement of the vote to cancel. How no one had showed up at the rehearsal and how Melanie had been taken to the police station and had not returned. She wanted to ask Mary Elisabeth about Fallon's drug use, if she had been party to Derrick's plan to use the drama club, if she knew who killed the detective. But she was afraid of causing her friend more pain.

Mary Elisabeth took the problem out of her hands.

"She's an addict." The words leapt across the phone line and fell into space.

"I know," said Lindy.

"Derrick gave it to her. He was a drug pusher, and he fooled this whole town. He deserved that hideous death, but Lindy, Fallon swears she didn't kill him. I think she did love him as far as she was capable of loving any person, but there's no excuse for what they did. She's sick, emotionally as well as physically. Even if she is acquitted of these horrible charges, she'll have to be institutionalized. I don't know how Howard will bear it." Her voice cracked and there was silence over the line. Then Lindy heard muffled crying. She must have put her hand over the receiver.

"He will, if he has you to help him," said Lindy, but she could hardly form the words. At what price would Mary Elisabeth save their relationship? If it could be saved after all that had happened. But if theirs could, couldn't her own? She and Glen didn't even have a tragedy to contend with.

Randall was motioning her to the table. He and Will had finished setting it, and Bill was dishing out something that smelled wonderful.

"I wasn't supposed to talk about this. But I don't know what else to do. Can't you please help us?"

Lindy's attention snapped back to the phone. "Me?"

"Lindy, please. I don't know who else to turn to."

"I—" Lindy looked over to the kitchen table where the

boys and Bill sat waiting for her. The image of a happy family. But it was just borrowed. The boys would return home, and Bill would go back to his work. It was a fantasy, and she was crazy to let herself be beguiled by it. "I'll try," she said and hung up.

She sat down across from Bill.

He looked up and narrowed his eyes. "Let me guess. Fallon swears she didn't"—he glanced at the boys—"*do* it, and Mary Elisabeth wants you to find out who did."

"She's my friend," Lindy mumbled. She knew he disapproved and it hurt, even if he was right. She picked up her fork and forced herself to eat. Complimented him on his cooking and felt guilty that she was too numb to appreciate it. She listened to the boys' nonstop narrative of their day. Smiled in the right places, she hoped. Cleared the table while Bill got them ready for bed. All the time wondering how she could possibly help the Porters without hurting Melanie and alienating Bill.

Bill returned as she was putting the last plate into the dishwasher. She didn't look at him. She felt suddenly awkward. Expectant. Too aware of his proximity. Heat suffused her face. She felt herself slipping from one disaster to another. Where was Rebo?

Bill sat down at the table and motioned her to the chair across from him. He knew how close she was to giving in—no, to using him. Using him to help her forget the horror of two murders and her disaffection from Glen. Good God, what was happening to her?

She sat down and told him what Mary Elisabeth had said.

He pushed a piece of paper toward her. The paper that had fallen from her bag at the church.

"When was the last time you opened that bag?" he asked.

Lindy thought back. "At the last Follies rehearsal. Saturday."

"That's almost a week." He tapped his finger on the paper. "Read it."

She read it twice trying to make sense of it. "Nosiness?" she said at last. "That's not a deadly sin."

"It sounds like someone is trying to warn you."

"A threat?"

"I don't know. But maybe you should heed their—let's call it advice."

"Hi, honeys, I'm home." Rebo bustled through the doorway, a smile of anticipation on his face. It quickly changed to disappointment. "This is boring. What's for dinner?" He ambled toward the stove and lifted the lid of the pan. "Hmm, smells good, Lindigestion. I didn't know you could cook."

"Bill cooked."

Rebo gave Bill an appraising look. Then he gave him the once-over. "You wanna get married?"

"Maybe some other time."

Rebo helped himself to a plate of sautéed chicken, vegetables and rice, and sat down between Bill and Lindy. He looked from one to the other.

"What happened at rehearsal?" asked Lindy.

"A few more people straggled in." He paused for a moment while he concentrated on his food. "We spent most of the time making a plan."

"What kind of plan?"

"Well, those who showed up insisted that the show must go on. So they went home to make some calls. I doubt if it will work, but at least they'll feel like they tried. What have you guys been up to? Something bad, I hope?"

"I got this," said Lindy. She pushed the limerick across the table to him.

Rebo frowned and picked it up. "I thought we already did these. Aren't there only seven sins?" Without waiting for an answer, he read:

"There's an eighth sin made just for you
It's nosiness to give you a clue
People who spy
May get stuck in the eye
Don't let this happen to you"

Rebo burst out laughing. "Whoever wrote this sure has your number. But hell, poked in the eye? This is the dumbest one yet. It doesn't even sound like a limerick, more like a sick Valentine or a fortune cookie. Maybe they'll let Vampessa sign up for a remedial English course while she's in the slammer."

"You think Fallon wrote it?" asked Lindy.

"She wrote the others. And who else around here qualifies as such a bad poet?" Rebo looked from Lindy to Bill. "Uh-oh. He's got on his cop face," he said, tilting his head toward Bill.

"I'm thinking," said Bill, but his face was expressionless, and Lindy felt a ripple of unease. "Just be careful, will you? Both of you?"

Lindy nodded, and knowing they'd get nothing more from him, she changed the subject. "I talked to Mary Elisabeth. You were right about Fallon having a drug problem. And I'm sure she knew about Derrick's plans for the drama group. But she accused Melanie of killing him."

"That little witch. Give me two minutes alone with her and I bet she'll change her tune."

Bill pushed back his chair and stood up. "Can't you two ever let the proper authorities do their jobs?"

Rebo looked nonplused. "You mean like in a union house?"

"Yeah," said Bill.

"Nah. Guess it comes from working in a profession where you retire when you grow up. Everyone treats us like kids, even our union. So you learn to take care of yourselves. And each other." He slanted a glance at Bill. "Can you sit down? You're giving me the willies."

Bill growled low in his throat, but he sat down.

Lindy leaned over and poured Rebo a glass of wine, mainly to hide her smile. There had been a time when he hadn't felt that way about loyalty. And there was a time when he would never even have acknowledged Bill, much less bantered with him. She raised her glass. "So I guess all we can do is bungle along and hope they make an arrest by Tuesday."

Rebo stopped with his glass halfway to his mouth. "You mean they haven't arrested Fallon?"

"Not officially, anyway," said Lindy. "She's going home with a special nurse."

"Damn. I'm beginning to feel a setup here." He glared at Bill. "That's how it works, right? The rich people hire all these lawyers, who find a loophole so they can nail an alternative. And that little bitch has already pointed the finger at Melanie. She won't have a chance."

He sounded like Jeff, but he was right, thought Lindy. Mary Elisabeth and Howard were wonderful people, but she had no doubt that they would do anything in their power to help their daughter. She looked at Bill, waiting for him to deny it.

But he didn't. Silence fell over the table. It was so quiet that Lindy heard the furnace click on in the basement. Finally, Bill leaned back in his chair.

"I don't know these people or their morals," he said. "But if the investigation doesn't turn up more than what they found at the crime scene, it will be circumstantial at best. They'll be asking a lot of questions in the next few days. I'm surprised they weren't more visible today."

"Paul questioned us already."

"I know."

"And we compared notes afterwards." She saw the scowl forming on his face and hurried on. "We know the poison was in the coffee. Fallon could have put it in his cup before she came. Janey only remembers T.J. coming in to get a drink of water while the cup was on the table."

"Yeah, T.J. could have done it," interrupted Rebo, relieved to find another suspect. "He and Derrick were always fighting over the property." He looked at Bill for a reaction. He didn't get one. "Or Janey. She was alone in the kitchen. Or afterwards. He might have put it down to go to the bathroom or something. Hell, anybody could have done the voodoo with the Yewhoo."

"Everybody but us, T.J., and Melanie was in the kitchen, eating lasagna. And no one saw Derrick before that." She cast him an apologetic look. "I know, it keeps coming back to Melanie or Fallon." She looked up and caught Bill's eye. "Doesn't it?"

"Not necessarily," he said. "Your reasoning isn't bad, except for one thing. You trust your friends. No one saw Derrick—according to them. Obviously, the killer wouldn't say that he had seen his victim."

Lindy sat back, deflated. "I just can't believe any of them would commit murder."

"I rest my case."

Chapter Thirty

A patrolman escorted Lindy from her parking place in the mall lot the next morning. The picketers were more subdued, perhaps because of the presence of a uniform. But she felt their stares even though she studiously avoided looking at them.

As soon as the patrolman had seen her across the street, he said, "I hope you're the last. I'm only supposed to stay on duty until ten, and it's already past that. We don't really expect any trouble, but if anybody leaves, make sure they do so in groups. We'll be making spot checks during the day."

She had convinced Bill and the boys to stay home and play with Bruno. Bruno was ecstatic; Bill was not. And now that she had seen the state of things with the Gospel church, she knew she had made the right decision. It would be traumatic for the boys to pass those angry protesters.

Rebo had promised them he would come back after the Follies rehearsal to help them make Halloween costumes, and Bill would take over for him at the marathon.

She hoped that he wasn't being overly optimistic and there really would be a Follies rehearsal. At least there was plenty of activity on the grounds. The sounds of hammering and skill saws filled the air. Stella shouted orders to a group of volunteers, directing traffic and deliveries like a drum major. There seemed to be more people than usual. Then she saw Mr. Morrison wave from a blue pickup that was hauling a ramp past the Portosans to the hayride route. Two men ran alongside the ramp, guiding it through the maze of construction that had sprouted over the tarmac next to the church. Parents were everywhere. Helping out, watching, lending support.

It was a festive atmosphere in spite of the picketers across the street. And in spite of the deaths that had occurred in the last two weeks. Lindy crossed her fingers. Now, if the Follies participants just showed up for rehearsal and nothing else happened, they would be in the homestretch. Only three more days to go and it would be over.

She went immediately to the church. She paused at the door, listening, trying to steel herself for an empty sanctuary. Not a sound came from inside. Disappointed, she stepped into darkness.

And then an eerie blue light emanated from the front of the pews; the Day-Glo tombstones appeared before her. She jumped when the opening notes of *Danse Macabre* filled the air and bony fluorescent arms began to writhe from behind the cardboard graves.

As the lights gradually rose, she made out the silhouettes of others sitting in the pews. The church was filled. She took a long, deep breath and exhaled away some of her tension along with the air.

Rebo appeared at her side, snapping his fingers and doing a jig. "They showed. Can you believe it?"

"Incredible," she said. She looked over the pews and recognized parents, teachers, senior citizens and local businessmen. This was what a community was about, she thought. Not houses and school systems and quaint stores. It was standing together for something you believed in.

She sat down on the nearest pew and watched the skeletons pop up from the graves and begin to dance across the floor. She listened to the recitation of "The Telltale Heart." She had more immediate problems to deal with, but she stayed in place as the familiarity of the theater calmed and strengthened her.

Mieko dropped from the rafters, spreading a black cape above the center aisle. From all parts of the sanctuary, little bats joined her, flapping bat wings and swirling. At the end of the dance, she enfolded them in her cape as the side drapes fell to either side of her. Immediately they were drawn back again. Mieko turned and opened her wings. The children had disappeared, and even though it was a hokey trick, Lindy applauded with the rest of the audience.

She laughed aloud when the men's kick line made their entrance, wearing flouncy cancan skirts over sweatpants and sneakers. Rebo walked backward up the aisle, his eye trained on the makeshift stage. He plopped down beside her.

"It's going great," she whispered.

"They're all on the wrong feet," he said.

"That's the beauty of it."

"If you say so."

The back doors crashed open. Lindy, Rebo and half the audience turned around. On stage, the Police Athletic League dominoed into each other.

The Gospel of Galilee Church hovered in the doorway. "The devil's work!" cried the man in front, his hands raised like a diva taking her bow. His voice was a deep bass, and his words reverberated through the hall. He marched forward, his congregation following silently behind him. "You have defiled a holy place. Called the Lord's vengeance upon you."

The house lights popped on, instantly dispelling the drama of his words.

Lindy's jaw dropped open. This was the charismatic Brother Bartholomew? His voice was by far the biggest thing about him. He couldn't have been more than five feet six, and skinny beneath an ill-fitting brown polyester suit. He walked with a hitch.

Rebo jumped up. Lindy latched onto his arm and held him back. Judd and several other policemen rushed down the aisle to confront him. Brother Bart's flock pressed close around him, except, Lindy noticed with satisfaction, three small children who had seen the skeletons sitting in a back pew and had stopped to admire their costumes.

Judd blocked the preacher's way, but it was the shining pate of Father Andrews that drew everyone's attention as he stepped into the empty pulpit.

"Look up!" he commanded. His head and hand shot toward the ceiling and everyone looked up.

"Do you see fire and brimstone falling on this place?"

A murmur ran through Brother Bart's people, and they cowered together.

"I see evil murder!" Brother Bart's tone was threatening. It sent a shiver down Lindy's spine.

"The *Lord* smites evil," returned Father Andrews in equally ominous tones.

That was a stretch even for Father Andrews, thought Lindy. Someone very human had "smote" Derrick Justin and the Suffern detective.

"And," interrupted Judd, getting into the act, "the city of New York frowns on those who skip without paying three months back rent. Not to mention the items missing from the Presbyterian Community Center."

More murmurs from the Gospel members. Brother Bart turned to repress it. "See how the devil has turned their tongues to lies!" he commanded. His followers shrank back. Another child slipped away.

Brother Bart's head jerked from the group to the retreating boy. "Women, see to your children." Two women scurried toward the pew to reclaim the truants. The first woman dragged two boys back to the preacher. But the second mother, a thin, tow-haired girl who couldn't have been more than twenty, cast a wistful look at the skeleton costumes before she reluctantly pulled her child away.

Brother Bart shook his fist. "These children have been

tempted by the devil. You must pray for their souls and cast out the evil."

"No."

There was a gasp from the group. All turned toward the source of that small, lilting, "no". It was the young mother who held her daughter close at her side. The crowd parted, leaving the preacher and the girl alone in the aisle.

"You dare defy the Lord?"

"I—" She glanced nervously at the others. "I," she tried again. Then she looked past Brother Bart to where Father Andrews stood in the pulpit. "I don't defy the Lord." She turned to Brother Bart and said in a small voice, "You are not the Lord."

"You defy me then?" Brother Bart's voice boomed across the space, and her little girl began to cry. The mother scooped her into her arms.

The girl's crying set off a chain reaction, and soon all the children were crying. For the briefest moment Lindy felt sorry for Brother Bart, surrounded by screeching children and distracted mothers.

But her compassion died when he stretched out his arms. "Give me the child."

The woman shrank back, shielding the girl from him.

"I don't think we're in Jersey anymore, Lindo," whispered Rebo.

An old man with a bulbous red nose stepped forward. "Where's our money?" he asked. "We took up a collection for the rent we owed."

Judd stepped in between the two men. "We'll accompany you people back across the highway." He motioned to other members of the force, who quickly surrounded the Gospel Church members. "And then I'm going to ask the town to rescind your permit to picket." He gestured toward the door.

Brother Bart sputtered, looked from Judd to Father Andrews to his parishioners. Then he lifted his chin and walked slowly toward the door. The others followed, accompanied by the local police force, flounced skirts and all.

Father Andrews stepped down from the pulpit and applause broke out around the hall. He walked up the aisle, a spring to his step. Lindy and Rebo motioned him over.

"How did you make such a precipitant appearance?" she asked.

"The church grapevine works in mysterious ways," said Father Andrews and winked at her.

"You knew he was going to disrupt the rehearsal?"

"I heard that he was planning something, so I got here early to be ready for him." He took a deep breath. "How dare that man use the wrath of God to intimidate those people? And ones who need the comfort of His love more than most. That poor young girl and her child, probably not even married. And the others so needy and so downtrodden. It makes me truly angry. The Gospel of Galilee Church, indeed. It's pure Old Testament scare tactics." He looked toward the back door, bit his lip and walked out of the church.

"Where do you think he's going?" asked Lindy.

"To do a little sheepherding." Rebo flashed a grin. "The padre ain't bad in the scheme of things. Oh good, my PAL's are returning." The police officers came back inside and headed for the stage. Rebo fell in behind them. "Okay, men. Once more with feeling."

Lindy spent the rest of the morning overseeing the construction of booths and making calls to the participants reminding them of the schedule of events. On the fifth call she learned that Lisa Conway had delivered twin boys early that morning. She wouldn't be able to play Madame Glosky after all. No one could come up with suggestions for her replacement.

Around noon, she was surprised to see Bill and the boys walking through the entrance.

"McDonald's?" Lindy raised her eyebrows at the bags the boys were holding.

"I also stopped by the deli." Bill held up a paper bag.

They settled themselves at one of the tables that had been set up in the parking strip and unpacked Styrofoam containers.

Rebo joined them seconds later. "Madame Glosky, huh?" He pulled a bottle of springwater toward him and began to cant over it. "I zee a br-r-right future ahead of you. Ah! Sehr gut." He looked up and grinned. "Hah bah dah?"

"You?" asked Lindy.

"Why not? The seer-spouting madame will just have to take a couple of hours off to commune with the spirits while I do the Follies. Frick and Frack can help me with my costume."

"Oh, boy. Can we?" asked Randall.

"Are you going to wear a dress?" Will giggled.

"With ruffles," said Rebo.

"Can we start on it now?" asked Randall. "Maybe we can—you know." He gave Rebo a conspiratorial look.

"We have to go back to the City," said Bill.

The boys' faces fell.

"I thought you were stay—" Lindy swallowed her surprise.

"I have to make arrangements for my sub for next week. And I need to do some others things." Bill glanced at the boys. "We'll come back for the marathon."

Lindy thought she must feel the way the boys looked. Dejected. Disappointed. She had gotten used to having them—him—around.

Bill began gathering up the trash. "You'll be all right. Just stick to the marathon and leave the rest to the police force." He looked intently at Lindy. "Please." He stuffed the remains of lunch into the bag. "Come on, guys."

Randall and Will got slowly out of their chairs. Randall cast an anxious look at Rebo. Rebo gave him a quick thumbs up before Bill led the two boys away.

"That was abrupt," she said.

Rebo snatched up the water bottle and peered into it. "I see confusion," he intoned. "I see—"

"Never mind," said Lindy. "What are you plotting with Randall? I saw that look."

"The boys are afraid they won't be able to go trick or treating since there're no houses in Manhattan."

"They can go in Bill's apartment building."

"I told them I'd ask you if they could go out here. I promised to take them."

"It's fine with me, but I don't know if Bill will go for it. He may want to take them himself. I think he's feeling a little like a fifth wheel these days."

"The wannabe? He should be used to it by now. Well, gotta go. Have to make sure that Melanie's out of the slammer for rehearsal." He strolled away, leaving Lindy flushed with consternation. Had she done this? Did everyone see Bill as Rebo did? It was so hurtful and completely unfair. He wasn't like that at all.

She didn't notice Judd come up behind her. She let out a squeak of surprise when he sat down.

"Sorry. Didn't mean to startle you." He scowled at her from across the table. "I just came from Mary Elisabeth and Howard's."

"How's Fallon?"

"Off the stuff and nastier than ever. I guess they don't have the evidence to arrest her, and she's putting the screws to Melanie. Accused her of being Derrick's partner in crime."

"That's ridiculous."

"Maybe, but the school board got wind of it and have put her on leave until this is cleared up."

"Oh, no. Her poor students. First Janey and now Melanie. They'll feel deserted."

"Yeah, and at a time like this. At least there is some good news. Val's parents are letting her finish the play before they pack her off. I didn't make an official report of what actually happened. Just said that she stated that Derrick had approached her about selling drugs."

"Do you think the other kids will forgive her?"

"If Melanie's around to do her tough love thing."

"You like her, don't you?"

"Yeah. Even if she does have green hair."

Stella and Evelyn were in the kitchen. A pile of tissues sat on the table at Stella's elbow. Her eyes were red from crying. Evelyn leaned against the counter. For once, she looked relieved to see Lindy.

"Stella, what's wrong?" Lindy rushed to her side, fighting off a sense of panic.

"Janey just called a few minutes ago," said Stella. "She's not coming in today. She sounded pretty bad. I offered to bring her some lunch, but she said she just wanted to be alone." Stella's voice cracked, and her eyes teared up. "She's so much worse. To be dying and having your last days clouded over by these awful murders. I wish there was something we could do."

Evelyn moved away from the counter. She seemed distracted. Probably having second thoughts about having volunteered for the committee, thought Lindy.

"And she's so worried about Melanie." Stella reached for a tissue and blew her nose. "I just don't understand. Why take Melanie when they'd already arrested Fallon?"

"Fallon hasn't been charged officially," said Evelyn.

"She hasn't? Why not? How do you know?" asked Stella.

Lindy wondered the same thing, but before she could ask, T.J. appeared in the doorway to the back stairs and went to the coffee pot. He was dirtier than ever.

"Dead end," he exclaimed. He threw up his hands, sending particles of dirt into the air, then took his cup to the table and dropped into a chair next to Stella. "Too damned much rubble. I can't get through without equipment and there's no way to get equipment into the cellar without tearing up the foundation."

They all lapsed into their own thoughts, the silence punctuated by an occasional sigh from T.J.

At some point Lindy began studying each of them. What if it hadn't been Fallon or Melanie? What if Derrick had another partner and had been killed by him? She looked hard at T.J. At Stella. At Evelyn. It was just too ludicrous. Then she heard Bill's voice in her head. Maybe it wasn't ludicrous at all. She reached in her bag for her notebook.

"What are you doing?" Evelyn asked.

"Making some notes."

"About the marathon?"

"Sort of."

Evelyn reached over Lindy's shoulder and closed her notebook. "Stay out of it," she said and walked from the room.

Chapter Thirty-one

Janey finally appeared in time to run the rehearsal of *The Crucible*. The change in her over the last few days had deflated Lindy's mood more than all the other problems put together. She watched from a front pew, ready to come to the rescue in case Janey collapsed, which seemed very likely.

Rebo, Mieko, Rose and Peter left at four o'clock. She had hoped Rebo would stay over. She felt like having company, but he wanted to pick up some things in the City for his role of Madame Glosky.

As soon as she opened the mud room door, Bruno darted past her to the car. He jumped against it, braced his paws on the window, then looked back at her.

"Just me, I'm afraid. We've been deserted."

He padded back to the house, gave her an accusatory look and went to stand by his food bowl.

Lindy dumped a can of food into his bowl and watched him gobble it down. She was too tired to eat, but too restless to sit still. She was afraid of having too much time to think. And she didn't want to be at home in case Glen called. Not that he would. She knew from experience that when Glen didn't want to face something, he just ignored it. It was Lindy who was doing the worrying, feeling the uncertainty. He was probably out with his new—damn. This was just what she didn't want to do.

Lindy reached for Bruno's leash. He jumped at her feet and finally sat long enough for her to snap the leash in place. Then they started down the road to the nearby bridle path. She managed to force Glen from her mind, but he was immediately replaced by thoughts of the marathon.

They were almost ready. The grounds had been transformed into a village of brightly colored booths and game areas. Judd had promised to ask for a withdrawal of the Gospel Church's right to picket. The Follies cast had returned. Melanie hadn't, but Judd had assured her that she would. Only two more days. But she wouldn't breathe easy until it was over. And then she'd have to deal with her failing marriage. And what was she going to do about Bill?

She broke into a jog, pushing away her thoughts, concentrating on the rhythm of her body. Bruno trotted happily beside her.

When they returned home an hour later, the message machine was dark. *See*, she said to herself. *I told you he wouldn't call.*

But the phone was ringing when she stepped out of the shower a few minutes later.

She grabbed a towel and ran across the bedroom to snatch up the receiver.

"Thank God you're home," said Howard Porter. "Fallon's gone."

"Gone? Where? What happened to the nurse who was watching her?"

"She went to the bathroom, and when she came out, Fallon had disappeared. We searched the house and the yard. We even called the neighbors. Then we discovered the Trans Am missing. I'm afraid to call the police. What if they find her and she resists them? She might get hurt or—or she might hurt herself. Oh, God. You've got to help me."

Lindy was already pulling clothes out of the bureau. "Howard. Don't panic. Do you have any idea of where she might go?"

"I don't know. This morning she started asking for Derrick. She accused us of not letting him visit her. She thinks he's still alive. She's—she's really not rational."

"Do you think she would go to the Van Cleef farm, looking for him?"

"Oh, my God. I didn't think of that. What am I going to do?"

"Call Judd and tell him to meet us at the farm. Then call T.J. and tell him to watch out for her. I'll meet you there."

She finished dressing as she ran down the stairs. Bruno streaked past her. She pushed her feet into her running shoes and grabbed her car keys off the peg in the mud room. Bruno pressed his nose to the door.

"You're right, boy. I could use the company. Let's go."

She heard the telephone ringing as she started the Volvo. It might be Howard—or it might be Glen. She backed quickly down the drive.

She made it to the Van Cleef farm in less than ten minutes, slowing only when going down the main street of town. There was a light on in the farmhouse. Fallon's Trans Am was parked haphazardly near the front steps. There were no other cars. She must have beaten Howard and Judd there.

She stopped behind the Trans Am, then looked at Bruno. "Come on, but stay by me. Heel," she commanded. Bruno bounded out of the backseat and disappeared around the side of the house.

She opened the front door and called out; there was no answer. She stepped into the hallway and called more loudly. T.J. stumbled up from behind the telephone table, holding his head. Lindy rushed to help him.

"The little bitch brained me," he said and grabbed the newel post to steady himself. "She was already here when Howard called. She said she was looking for Derrick. She had a cup from Starbucks. She's totally nuts; she kept saying that Derrick was waiting for his latte. When I tried to stop her, she threw the lamp at me." He pointed to the shattered glass and lamp base at his feet. "That lamp was an original Tiffany. It's worth thousands."

"Where is she now?"

"She ran out the front door." He swayed on his feet.

"Sit down until Judd gets here. Tell him I'm out looking for her."

"I'm going with you. She's dangerous." He lurched toward the table and opened the top drawer. He pulled out a flashlight and led the way into the night.

They looked around the house, shined the light along the shrubbery, into the hidden corners of the booths, searched through the church, but found no sign of Fallon.

"The hangman's tree," said Lindy. The very thought made her blood congeal. Where were Judd and Howard? She took off toward the outdoor kitchen.

T.J. staggered after her, holding his head with one hand and the flashlight with the other. The rising moon cast strange shadows on the ground; the stone fireplace loomed out of the darkness.

They entered the woods, and Lindy slowed down, looking for movement, listening for a sound. T.J. hurried ahead, the cone of light bouncing over the broken road. They passed the horse bridge and the River of Blood, whose machinery stood silent among the trees.

The night air was rent with a peal of laughter and Fallon's coy call of, "Derrick, I know you're up there. Come down, Derrick. I've got your latte."

T.J.'s free hand clamped over Lindy's arm. They stole forward and came to an abrupt halt when T.J.'s flashlight outlined Fallon's silhouette.

She was looking up into the hangman's tree but turned when the light hit her. She stared at them like a startled animal. Then she slipped away into the darkness.

"Stop playing games, Fallon," called T.J. He rushed forward.

It took only a heartbeat before Lindy followed him. "We only want to talk to you, Fallon. Please come back."

Fallon didn't answer. They stood listening, trying to discover where she had gone. There was no wind, and the trees were still. They should have heard her moving through the brush, but only a dull thudding sound reached their ears.

"She's climbing the tree," whispered Lindy.

Laughter echoed from above them. T.J. jerked the light upward. Fallon grinned down at them from the hangman's platform. She was hugging the stuffed hanged man to her chest.

"You want to see us fly?" She laughed wildly.

"No!" yelled Lindy, then quickly modulated her voice. "Not quite yet," she said soothingly. She looked frantically to T.J. He was edging toward the tree, keeping the light focused on the platform.

"I made him fly," said Fallon. "He didn't want to, but I made him." She started swaying, clutching the dummy in her arms. "I know a secret," she sang. "I know *his* secret and I made him fly."

She flailed her arms and the dummy fell to the wooden floor. She looked down at it. "I'll tell if you don't fly." She nudged it with her foot. "I'll tell. I know something you don't know." The nasal singsong made the bile rise in Lindy's throat. She watched, mesmerized, as Fallon swayed on the platform. Suddenly, she cocked her head and the energy seemed to drain from her. "Derrick's dead," she said in a normal voice. "Melanie killed him."

A night bird cried out, and there was a rustling in the branches.

Fallon looked up. "Derrick?"

"Why did Melanie kill Derrick?" asked Lindy.

Fallon keened a high-pitched moan. "Because he killed the detective and threw him in the brook. I hope they lock her away for a long, long time." She gathered up the dummy and held it in one arm. "I want to fly. Derrick always lets me fly." She stretched her free arm out in the air and swayed forward.

"No!" screamed Lindy, then froze as a shadow swooped down and enveloped Fallon in darkness.

T.J. gasped and bobbled the flashlight. For a second the light went out. Then it popped on again, shining into the tree. Adam Crabtree held Fallon in his arms, white beard mingled with her auburn hair. He stepped out of the light and they heard him descend the wooden rungs of the ladder. In a few seconds, he reappeared in front of them with Fallon cradled against his chest.

"How—" began Lindy.

"Sitting on the ridge, listening to the night. Heard the commotion." He walked past them in the direction of the house, Lindy and T.J. following behind.

Once inside, he laid Fallon on the sofa and covered her with the afghan. They heard car engines come to a stop outside. A few seconds later, Howard, Mary Elisabeth and Judd came through the parlor, followed closely by Paul Whitman. Minutes later, more policemen arrived and the Porters' personal physician, who examined Fallon and announced that she was incapable of answering questions. Paul allowed him to take her to the hospital accompanied by two guards and her parents.

When they were gone, he pulled up a chair and sat down. He motioned the others to do the same, pulled a pen from his breast pocket and flipped open a black notebook. "Okay. The three of you can tell me what's been going on here."

Lindy and T.J. went through the series of events from Fallon's arrival at the farmhouse to Adam Crabtree's rescuing her from the tree.

"She said that Derrick killed the detective." Lindy looked down at her hands, feeling the full weight of what she was about to reveal. "She also said that Melanie killed Derrick."

"Not Melanie," said Adam. It was the first time he had spoken.

"You know who did?" asked Paul.

"No."

Paul shifted impatiently. "But you have an idea who did?"

"Ideas exist in the mind, not in reality," said Adam.

Judd, who had stayed in the background until now, moved closer. "Look, Paul. It's obvious that Fallon's gone off the deep end. She killed Derrick. She just can't face up to the horror of it. So she's transferred her guilt to somebody she doesn't like. It's basic psychology."

"That's enough," said Paul with a warning look.

"Come on, Paul. Let it rest. You'll never get a conviction. They'll have her declared mentally incompetent. Can't you let it end there? She confessed that Derrick killed the detective. The case is wrapped up."

"She also said that Melanie killed Derrick Justin. You can't allow one part of her statement and not the other. You're arguing in circles, Judd."

Judd dropped onto the sofa and cradled his chin in his hands. "I only need two more days," he said dejectedly.

Paul asked a few more questions, which Lindy and T.J. answered as best they could. When pressed, Adam said he had "heard the ruckus and came to see." Practically a direct quote from the night at the springhouse, thought Lindy with disgust. Then he said he refused to "speculate about what-ifs and maybes," stood up and walked out into the night.

"Well, I guess that about rounds it up," said Paul. He said good night to T.J. and accompanied Judd and Lindy outside.

Lindy was getting into the Volvo when she suddenly remembered Bruno. She jumped out.

"What?" asked Judd.

"Bruno," she exclaimed. "I forgot all about him."

Paul yawned. "You can stay and look for him. Judd will help you. I have a report to fill out."

It only took a few minutes of whistling and cajoling before Bruno came bounding out of the woods. He was soaking wet and covered with burrs.

"Bruno. How could you?" asked Lindy. Thoroughly exhausted, she opened the back door and let him climb in. She said good night to Judd and drove home.

The blinking message light was the first thing she saw. She stared at it for a few seconds before deciding what to do. *Oh, hell,* she thought. Might as well get the worst over all at once. She played back the message.

"Lindy. It's Bill. Call me as soon as you get home. It's important."

She was already dialing when the message ended. Bill picked up on the first ring. Lindy sank onto a kitchen chair and pulled off her sneakers. Bruno flopped down beside her.

"Have you been at the marathon all day?" he asked.

"No, but I had to go back again." She told him about Fallon.

Bill didn't bother to muffle the expletive that exploded across the phone line.

"Don't yell. I'm too tired." She wondered if she had the energy to get to the sink for a glass of water.

"So what does Paul think?" he asked. Lindy was wondering when he and Paul Whitman had become first-name acquaintances.

"He was vague. They don't know how much of Fallon's statement to believe. I hope that I didn't get Melanie in trouble by telling them what she said."

Another expletive; then he laughed.

"Now what?"

"I'm proud of you for coming clean—for once."

"I'm not."

"I know. But truth is truth whatever the outcome."

"Is it? I wonder what Adam Crabtree would have to say about that."

"I called for a reason," said Bill.

"Afraid I might think you were asking me for a date?" Lindy froze and covered her eyes with her fingers. Why the hell had she said that? She heard Bill sigh.

"You're right," he said. "I deserved that. But now that I'm paid back, listen to me, okay?"

"Okay," she said meekly. What she really wanted to do was apologize, but the time had passed. "I'm listening."

"This might be unnecessary after tonight's developments, but I'm going to say it anyway. Please keep your distance from Evelyn."

"Evelyn? Why do you keep saying that?"

"Could you just for once take my advice without asking a million questions?"

"That was only two. You're not going to tell me, are you?"

"That was three and no, I'm not. But I am coming back tomorrow—if that's okay with you."

Her heartbeat quickened, not from the prospect of seeing Bill, but from unease. "You're worried about something."

"I was. Probably no need now. But I'm coming out just the same."

"Are you bringing the boys?"

"They'll never forgive me if I don't." He hung up.

Lindy pushed herself off the chair and took a look at the muddy floor beneath Bruno. Bruno thumped his tail.

"Oh, what the hell. You can sleep on a towel." The two of them trudged upstairs to bed.

Chapter Thirty-two

Lindy rounded the curve approaching the Van Cleef farmhouse the next morning and slammed on the brakes, barely missing the car stopped in front of her. A line of cars inched down the road toward the mall. She could see the picket signs waving above their roofs.

At the front of the line, a car honked, then another and another. Her pulse quickened. She pleaded silently that it was just an ordinary traffic jam, not a sign of real trouble. The line of cars crept forward until she could see two patrol cars parked on the shoulder of the road. There were twice as many picketers as the day before. So much for Judd's promise to get rid of them.

Steeling herself for the worst, she eased her foot down on the gas. And did a double take. The Gospel Church picketers were facing a second group across the police car. A group dressed in ordinary clothing and carrying a different array of signs: *A Safe Mischief Night*, *Family Friendly Spooks,* and *Honk if you're going to the marathon*.

She pulled alongside the new group and recognized the father from the Friday night rehearsal. He pumped his sign in the air when he saw her. Dismayed, she honked, then turned into the mall parking lot.

Optimism sparked inside her. The town was fighting back. She gave a thumbs-up sign to the pro-marathon picketers as she hurried across the road. Brother Bart's group hurled dire predictions. They were drowned out by cheers and whistles.

She burst through the kitchen door to find Janey and Stella at the table. Evelyn stood at the sink, looking out the window.

"Did you see that?" Lindy exclaimed. "How did they round up all those people?"

"Don't you ever read the local newspaper?" asked Stella and tossed her the copy she was holding. "Page three."

Lindy opened the paper and read the editorial that was titled, *Keeping the Fun in Halloween.* It came out firmly on the side of the marathon, mentioned the death of a local drug dealer, and used Derrick's murder to argue its support for safe entertainment. It was followed by letters to the editor. All were pro-marathon. She sat down and almost missed the chair as she read the letter that thanked the "avenging angel who had rid them of the parasite who preyed on the community's children."

Lindy looked up, dumbfounded. "Amazing."

"The paper has been flooded with letters and phone calls since the news about Derrick leaked out. They bumped the regular editorial and put this in at the last minute," said Stella. "I'd say it was amazing, all right."

"I just hope the two groups don't come to blows," said Lindy. She handed the paper back to Stella and turned to Janey. "How did you feel about the *Crucible* rehearsal yesterday?"

Janey attempted a smile. "Melanie's done a wonderful job with them. She'll make a good addition to the staff."

"Except that I've been let go," said Melanie, moving into the room. She wore a denim shirt, jeans and no makeup.

Janey returned her teacup to the table. The cup rattled against the surface. "You don't mean it."

"Well, they asked me to take a temporary leave of absence. But I know what that means."

"When did you eat or sleep last? Have a blueberry muffin," said Stella, pushing the plate toward her.

"Thanks. I'm not very hungry."

"Nonsense. You can't think on an empty stomach." Stella eyed Lindy. "Well?"

"Well, what?"

"How are we going to clear Melanie's name?"

Melanie looked up, surprised. Janey leaned forward, waiting for Lindy's answer. Evelyn turned from the sink. Her expression was unreadable, and Lindy felt a flutter of wariness. Why had Bill warned her to stay away from her? And where was he? She glanced at the clock. Eleven-thirty.

"There's nothing you can do," said Melanie.

Stella prompted Lindy with a look.

She had to say something. But she didn't want to say anything in front of Evelyn until she talked to Bill. Damn.

Another, more impatient look from Stella.

"We'll think of something," Lindy said weakly. "Just let me get a few things squared away." She fled outside.

She went directly to the church. Only Peter was there, standing at the front with Bryan Morrison. "They all went to lunch," he said. "I'm just showing Bryan some of the finer points of rigging."

Lindy saluted and walked back down the aisle, smiling. She never ceased to be amazed at how Jeremy's company embraced whatever they were doing. Peter wasn't obligated to spend time with Bryan or work on the hayride. Mieko didn't have to help the boys with their homework or sit in the rafters waiting to play Bat Queen to a bunch of children. Rose didn't have to reconstruct the amateur costumes or turn the church into something fit for the Met. And Rebo. He was the most incredible of all. Director, sidekick, baby-sitter, Madam Glosky.

For the thousandth time, Lindy thanked the stars that she had these people. They would be there for her, too, if the time came when she was alone again. But she wouldn't think about that now. Not until this was over.

She stopped at the top of the steps, searching the grounds. Hoping that Bill had arrived. Games were set up. Signs hung at the front of the booths, and boxes of prizes were stacked inside. Electric cables crisscrossed the gravel, and electric floodlights marked the perimeter. At the far side, Madame Glosky's tent was a study in whimsy, its blue and white stripes swagged with red, pink and yellow drapery.

At last she saw Bill, being tugged along by Randall and Will.

"I was beginning to think you weren't coming," said Lindy, trying for a light tone.

"Me, too," said Randall. "We were supposed to come earlier, but Uncle Bill had to work on the Internet. Then he made a bunch of phone calls."

"I thought we were never gonna leave," agreed Will.

"I think Bryan is waiting for us," said Bill. "See you later." He scuttled them away.

She watched them walk toward the hayride route, wondering if she and Bill would ever feel comfortable together again.

She tried to meet with Janey and Stella, but whenever it looked as though they could talk privately, Evelyn suddenly appeared. It happened very naturally, but Bill's warning rang in her head. It was beginning to spook her.

It was six o'clock before Bill reappeared. The building crew had left for the day. Rebo and gang had packed up and returned to the City. Bill and Lindy walked together to the parking lot, the boys running ahead as soon as they crossed the road. The picketers had gone home, and the lot was empty. The sun was setting over the angular mallscape. They stopped by Lindy's car.

Lindy sighed. "One more day and it will all be over."

"I want you to tell me that you're going home and staying there."

She turned to search his face. "What are you worried about? Fallon won't get away again. They've hospitalized her. And if you're concerned about Melanie—I'm sure she didn't kill Derrick. I just wish I could think of some way to prove it. I've racked my brain all day and couldn't come up with a thing. You don't think she's guilty, do you?"

"I just don't want you to get caught in the crossfire if anything goes down."

"Goes down? Bill, you're scaring me. What could possibly go down now? The marathon's tomorrow."

"Probably nothing. I just don't like leaving you alone."

She wanted to say, *Then don't. Don't leave me alone.* But he might misconstrue her meaning. *She* might misconstrue her meaning.

"I'll be okay," she said. She turned away and looked out at the sunset, a golden ball dipping into red above the black silhouette of the mall. "It's beautiful, isn't it? In spite of the buildings."

She felt his finger touch her neck and draw a line down her spine.

She shivered and started to face him. His hand went to her shoulder.

"Don't turn around," he said softly.

This wasn't about the marathon. Alarm bells sounded in her head. She pushed them away and laughed unsteadily. "Is this a stickup?"

"Kind of. I want to say something."

Again she tried to face him.

"No." She heard his intake of breath and the slow exhale. She tried not to panic. She concentrated on Will and Randall, chasing each other on the tarmac.

"I love you. I just thought I should take a number in case things between you and Glen don't work out."

For a moment she couldn't talk. Couldn't think.

She heard his soft laughter. "I'd feel really bad if you fell in love with somebody else, and I hadn't at least declared myself. There. It's done. Life goes on."

"Bill." But she didn't know what she wanted to say. She didn't dare turn to him. She was afraid of what might happen. "I don't know what's going on with Glen, but he's my husband. We have children. Can't you and I go on being what we were before all this happened? At least until I get my life sorted out?"

Now he turned her around. "This *is* what we were before." He smiled and chucked her on the chin. "Nothing has changed."

Nothing? She stared at him in disbelief. He had just told her that he loved her, and nothing had changed? "How can you compartmentalize your life like that?"

Bill shrugged. "You learn it when you're a cop. It works okay."

"You deserve better."

"I don't want better." He looked over her head. "Come on you two. We've got a long ride back."

Randall and Will swooped down on them, yelping and screeching. "We're coming back in the morning, right, Uncle Bill? We have to meet Rebo at ten. We promised."

"He's going to help us make our costumes," said Will. He looked uncertainly at Lindy. "Did he ask you? Is it okay?"

"Yes, of course," she said. "It's fine."

"What's this about?" asked Bill.

"The boys want to trick or treat out here."

"Can we, Uncle Bill?" asked Randall.

"Please?" added Will.

"We'll talk about it later. Now let's get going."

The boys jumped into the backseat.

"Bill," Lindy began.

He gave a small shake of his head, then leaned over and kissed her cheek the way he always did. Then he opened her car door and shut it behind her. "See you tomorrow. Please stay out of trouble tonight."

He followed her out of the lot. At the opposite side of town, he continued straight toward the highway, and Lindy turned left onto the road that led home. Her head was reeling. Bill had just said he loved her—to her back—in a mall parking lot.

She had never expected to hear those words from Bill. But they were said, and now she had to consider what her own feelings were. Was it possible to love two men at once?

Chapter Thirty-three

She still hadn't figured out the answer the next morning, even though she had spent most of the night thinking instead of sleeping.

She dreaded going to the marathon; she dreaded having to face Bill. But her spirits leapt when she saw his Honda in the parking lot.

She hurried across the road, past the delivery trucks that clogged the entrance, and went straight to the church. The sanctuary was empty, but she heard voices from the sewing room in back.

Rebo looked up when she opened the door. He threw his arms wide, preventing her entrance. "Out. Out," he exclaimed.

She peered around his shoulder at colorful satin spread across the work table. Randall and Will threw themselves across it.

"I guess it's a surprise," she said and backed out the door. "Where is Uncle Bill?" she asked from the hallway.

"Talking to the giant," said Will.

"Adam Crabtree?" But she didn't wait for an answer. She went to find Bill. She lost her courage halfway across the drive. What on earth would they say to each other? She was relieved to see the Madden truck parked at the pumpkin-painting booth. She showed them where to pile the pumpkins, then stopped to referee an argument between two exhibitors who had claimed the same space.

She directed an ambulance to the back of the house, out of sight where medical services had taken over a toolshed. The ambulance would be able to get directly to the paved road without disrupting the activities. She hoped it wouldn't be necessary.

She finally made her way through the crowd of workers, but slowed to a stop when she saw Bill returning from the direction of the summer kitchen. Memories of their last meeting rushed back at her. She swallowed as she watched him walk slowly toward her. He looked as if he hadn't had much sleep either.

What a pair we are, she thought wryly.

"He told me a story," said Bill, not looking at her directly. "He knows something, but he isn't sharing."

Lindy blinked in confusion. Bill had said that nothing had changed between them. Evidently, nothing had to him. He was the same Bill he had always been.

"Things seem to be going well," he said. "What time does the marathon start?"

"Four o'clock. If anyone comes," she said.

"Go do whatever you need to do. I'll entertain myself."

She risked a surreptitious look. It was obvious that he wasn't going to talk about last night. And it was just as obvious that he was up to something, and he wasn't going to talk about that either. Well, fine. She had too much to do as it was.

It was after three when Lindy looked up from posting a list of work schedules. Rebo, garbed in layers of satin and a gauzy veil, strode across the games area. He was flanked by two small gypsies in bright red satin head scarves identical to Madame Glosky's. Everyone stopped working and applauded as they made their way toward Lindy, Rebo whirling in a cloud of red and black ruffles, the boys bowing in all directions.

"That's some outfit," she said when Rebo curtseyed before her. He had painted cleavage above the ruffled bodice which had been enhanced, probably by the same bird seed that had made the dummy's hands. "And your two courtiers are something else."

"We're not courtiers," said Will.

"We're gypsies," said Randall. "We're going to stand outside Reb—Madame Glosky's tent and escort the suckers inside."

Rebo flipped his veil over his forehead and grinned. "Want to be the first to have your fortune told?"

"Thanks. But I don't think I want to know."

"Cheer up, Lindepression. I bet Madame Glosky can see good things ahead." He leaned close to her ear. "Maybe even great sex."

She pushed him away.

"Where's the wannabe? Maybe he'll want *his* fortune told."

"Rebo," Lindy urged, glancing toward Randall and Will.

"Who's the wannabe?" asked Randall.

"Nobody," said Lindy. She turned to Rebo. "That could really hurt somebody's feelings if it got back to them."

"Oh, yeah. Sorry." Rebo looked mildly chagrined, but it was gone in a second. "Time to take up residence in the palatial tent." He made an elaborate curtsey and ushered the boys across the gravel.

A few minutes later a hush fell over the site. They were ready, and all attention was focused toward the entrance and the ticket kiosks that stood at each side. Lindy checked her watch. Two minutes to four. Would anybody come?

And there they were—a mother and three girls dressed in ballerina costumes. They were soon followed by others. By four-thirty, the games area was crowded with children and parents. At five-thirty, Bryan stopped by to say they were starting the first hayride.

"All the dry ice is out of the springhouse and I padlocked it again, like you said, Mrs. H." Bryan radiated excitement. "Gotta get going. Wish me luck."

"Good luck," Lindy called after him.

Just before six, she slipped past the crowd gathered around the front doors of the church and went inside. Peter sat behind the light board testing the cues, Mieko beside him. The entire cast, including Val, was on stage where Melanie was leading them through a series of facial and vocal exercises, while Rose made last-minute adjustments to their costumes.

Lindy sat down next to Janey in the front pew. "How's it going?" she whispered.

"Very well. They're in good hands. I know that now."

Lindy swallowed the tightness in her throat. This might be the last time Janey saw a school play. There must be so many things that she was seeing, knowing it would be her last. Lindy gave her an impulsive hug and turned away.

A few minutes later, the doors opened and the church filled with people. They were led to seats by candelabra-wielding ushers, dressed in hooded monks' robes.

Lindy took a last look over the audience as the houselights dimmed and *The Crucible* began. She couldn't help but make the comparison of her own village with that of seventeenth-century Salem. A community torn apart by fear and distrust. But there was hope for this community. The marathon was an unparalleled success. The town had rallied to its support. Melanie's "at risk" kids had a full house. And they were good.

By the time Kenny made his final speech as John Proctor and gave his life to protect his friends, Lindy was completely involved in the play. The lights went out, and there was a moment of silence before the audience broke into noisy applause. The cast took their bows, then called Melanie onto the stage. The applause was clamorous and Melanie had to hold up her hands for silence.

"I thank you all for your warm reception, and I want to thank these kids for their hard work." Applause broke out again, and she waited for it to die out. "But most of all I want to thank Janey Horowitz for standing behind me when things looked bleak. And for guiding us all to the evening you have just seen." She motioned to Janey. Amidst more applause, Kenny and Carl stepped down and helped her from the pew. When she was on stage, Melanie leaned over and kissed her cheek. The cast crowded around her as the houselights came on.

Lindy wiped away tears of gratitude and sadness and pushed through the crowd to where Melanie and Janey stood together, surrounded by the drama group.

"That was wonderful," she said.

"Yes, it was," agreed Janey. "I'm very proud of you all." She squeezed Melanie's hand. "It's getting late, and I have to go. Congratulations."

"Thanks," said Melanie. She hugged the English teacher and turned to accept the congratulations of another group of people.

Lindy walked beside Janey into the night. Janey paused at the church steps and looked out over the festivities.

Taking it all in, thought Lindy.

"I'd like to walk over to the bonfire and then have a cup of tea before I leave. Would you walk with me?"

"I'd be honored to," said Lindy.

"It's been a good life," said Janey. "Don't mourn for me."

Lindy focused on the lights of the games area, blinking the blur from her eyes.

They walked slowly through the crowd. Stopped to watch children painting faces on Cy Madden's pumpkins. Laughed as Rebo ushered four giggling girls into Madame Glosky's tent. Took in every sound as they walked down the path to the bonfire.

Adam Crabtree's voice filled the air. The fire blazed high behind him, catching the folds of a patchwork velvet coat in its light. Janey paused to listen, her eyes intent. "Adam," she murmured. Her lips curved in a faint smile.

After a few moments, she turned toward the house. Lindy followed her into the kitchen and put on water for tea. She heard Janey sigh. A contented sigh, she thought. She was glad she had been part of this last walk through the marathon. Janey wouldn't see another.

"I hired the detective."

Lindy held the teakettle in her hand ready to pour. She stared at Janey, not comprehending.

Janey glanced at her cup and the wicker basket of tea balanced on the rim. Lindy poured the water over the leaves and returned the kettle to the stove.

"You hired the detective?"

"Yes. Judd was not the only one who was concerned about the rise of drug use among my students. It started just about the same time that Fallon returned, bringing Derrick Justin with her. And Derrick brought Melanie. At first I thought it was mere coincidence. But one night I happened to see Derrick talking with a young man I had once had in my English class. He graduated several years ago. Not to college but into a more unsavory school."

"Did you tell Judd?"

"Of course not. It was just speculation and suspicion on my part. Derrick could merely have been asking directions. So I hired Mr. Koopes to investigate him—and Melanie. I thought they might be working together, but I couldn't figure out how Fallon fit into the picture."

Janey lifted the strainer and waited for the tea to drip into the cup. Then she placed it on the table. She took a sip. "Then Derrick killed the poor man."

"That's what Fallon said."

"Adam saw him do it. The ridge behind his house looks down on the brook. He spends most nights outside communing with nature. He's a fine man, but a solitary man."

"He didn't want to get involved," said Lindy.

"That isn't entirely true, though it is sometimes difficult to understand what motivates him." Janey rubbed her forehead, then reached into her purse. She brought out a white envelope and laid it on the table. "I killed Derrick Justin. My confession is in that envelope."

Lindy looked at Janey, not believing; the envelope creating a wall between them.

"But I wanted to tell you in person. So that you could explain to Mary Elisabeth and Howard that I did not mean to hurt them in any way. Nor Fallon, in spite of the pain she has caused. Please, make them understand that."

"Janey—" Lindy pleaded.

Janey shook her head. "Let me finish. I don't have much time left. I made a preparation of yew and carried it in my purse, waiting for the chance to poison him. When Fallon left the coffee in the kitchen that day, it seemed the perfect opportunity. So while you were in the parlor with her, I added it to his coffee. I had no idea what they were planning for the hayride. I would never have done it then, if I had known the children would witness it."

"But the limerick."

"I taped it to the cup, not Fallon. I couldn't help myself. Derrick seduced this town, fawned on them, stroked their egos, lusted after their children." Janey smiled self-consciously. "Lechery. It seemed the perfect symbolic gesture." She paused to sip some tea, then looked at Lindy. "I don't regret what I did. I couldn't leave them unprotected. So I took the law into my own hands. I'm guilty before God."

"Why didn't you kill me, too?" Melanie stood in the doorway, breathing hard, her eyes wild. Bill and Judd were standing behind her.

Janey looked up. She didn't seem at all surprised to see her. "I wasn't sure of you, at first. But when I found the limerick clutched in your hand at the springhouse, I understood. I took it. I didn't want you to be the subject of rumors the way I had been. I know now that you'll take good care of my children." Janey lifted her cup in a solitary toast and drank down the rest of the tea.

Melanie's eyes widened, and she lunged across the table just as Evelyn and Adam Crabtree came through the door. "No!" she screamed and knocked the cup from Janey's hand. The cup shattered against the counter. "She's taken poison." Melanie pushed herself from the tabletop and rushed to where Janey was sitting.

"I'll get the ambulance," said Lindy and headed for the door. Adam Crabtree stopped her. "Janey has her own journey to make."

"No," cried Lindy, twisting away.

"I'll take her home," said Adam.

Janey shook her head. "I didn't expect such a full house." She smiled at Adam. "Thank you, but I can't involve you in this. Judd can drive me to the hospital. They can pump my stomach. It's Carolina jasmine, not yew. We have plenty of time." She sighed in defeat. "I'd rather just go home."

"I'm afraid I can't allow that, Janey." Judd's face was etched with sadness. "I'm sorry."

Janey sighed. "Let's go then. Judd, you take the envelope. It explains everything." He swiveled his head from Melanie to Lindy, but took the envelope and helped Janey up.

They watched silently until the back door closed behind them.

"I poured the water for her tea," said Lindy. "I almost killed her." Bill wrapped an arm around her.

"No," said Adam, his voice subdued.

Lindy propelled herself away from Bill and turned on Adam. "You saw Derrick kill the detective. Why didn't you tell Judd? He could have prevented all of this."

"Not before the marathon was destroyed. His teen center a forgotten dream." Adam's voice was strong but held none of the theatricality with which he had always spoken before. "I'm not a reliable witness."

"None of this had to have happened. Even if the property had rescinded to you, you could have given it back. Why didn't you just give the land to the town? Why?"

Adam said nothing. It was Evelyn who spoke.

"The answer is obvious, Lindy. He isn't the only living Van Cleef. And a lawsuit could have tied up the property for years."

"There are other relatives?"

"One," said Evelyn. "Mr. Crabtree has a daughter."

Lindy's eyes widened, and she stared at Evelyn.

There was a moment of total silence; then Evelyn burst out laughing. "Not me, if that's what you're thinking." She turned to Adam. "He has a daughter. And the daughter isn't very nice is she, Mr. Crabtree? She's already tried to have him committed because of his eccentric lifestyle. That's why you turned down the inheritance, isn't it? She stood to be become a very rich woman. Involving her would have been an unnecessary complication for the committee. Maybe even a tragic one."

Adam inclined his head toward Evelyn and walked out the door without a word. Melanie sank into a chair.

"How do you know these things?" asked Lindy.

Evelyn gave her a considered look. "I had hoped to leave without having to admit this, but I suppose you deserve an explanation." She reached inside her jacket and pulled out a leather wallet. She flipped it open. "DEA. We've been investigating Derrick Justin and his several aliases for a number of years now. It's been impossible to get enough hard evidence to arrest him. He's not as dumb and self-centered as he appears, or appeared, at any rate. We would have liked to nab the whole ring, but . . ." She shrugged. "I shouldn't complain. Death is the only cure for a drug dealer. They're not exactly an endangered species." She turned to Bill. "Thanks for not blowing my cover. I know it was difficult." She cut her eyes toward Lindy and smiled.

"What are you going to do about Janey?" asked Lindy.

"She's already received the death penalty. Who am I to stand in the way?"

She sounded frighteningly like Adam Crabtree, and Lindy shivered.

"I'll appropriate her confession from Judd. I might be able to prevent it from becoming public knowledge. I'm not sure. But we won't take action on it until it's—uh, too late."

"But what about Adam?"

"Storytelling and herbal teas are not within my jurisdiction. There is one thing, however, that still needs to be done."

Lindy stiffened.

"I would like to stay on and fulfill my duties as Cleanup Chairperson. It's an appropriate job description, don't you think?"

Chapter Thirty-four

Lindy awoke late in the morning to an empty house. Rebo, Bill and the boys had already left for the farm and taken Bruno with them.

Well, the marathon didn't need her this morning. Her job was over. She could spend the whole day in bed if she wanted to.

She went to the farm.

True to her word, Evelyn was directing cleanup operations. "You didn't have to show up so early," she said, taking a good look at Lindy. "Things are proceeding nicely."

She was right. The Morrisons' pickup truck was already filled with black garbage bags. Most of the booths had been dismantled; their canvas roofs were folded and stacked, awaiting pickup by the rental service. Coils of electrical cables dotted the drive.

"Nobody knows what went down last night," said Evelyn, her eyes scanning the activity. "They also don't know anything about me. And it should stay that way."

Lindy nodded and went into the house. T.J. was alone in the kitchen, perfectly clean and pressed and slumped over a cup of coffee. He looked up when she entered, then went back to contemplating his cup.

"We'll be out of your hair before the sun sets," she told him. She poured herself a cup and sat down.

T.J. sighed.

"Don't say that you're going to miss us."

"No. I won't say that. It's time I got the restoration back on schedule. It looks like there will be enough money in the coffers after all."

"And that doesn't make you happy?"

"Oh, sure, but I was hoping to find the exit for my tunnel. It will take months to clear the rubble at this end."

"I'm sure something will turn up eventually," she said.

"Yeah," he said. "Eventually."

Lindy and Bill sat on the porch, watching the last of the lumber being hauled away and enjoying the afternoon sunshine. Randall and Will ran out from the woods, Bruno jumping at their side. All three of them were covered with mud and dirt.

"What the—where have you been?" asked Bill.

"You gotta come see, Uncle Bill. We found it." Randall was hopping from foot to foot with excitement.

Bill surged to his feet. "What did you find?"

"T.J.'s tunnel!" said Will. "We told Bruno to show us where he found the body—" He slapped a dirty hand over his mouth. "Oops."

Bill narrowed his eyes at Lindy.

She cast a disparaging look at Bruno. "Now you start obeying."

"My tunnel? Where?" They all looked up to see T.J. hanging out of a second-story window.

"Underneath the bridge," called Randall. "You wanta see it?"

"I'll be right down."

"Didn't I tell you not to go near the water?" asked Bill.

The boys shuffled guiltily. Will's bottom lip was sticking out in an effort not to cry.

"We just wanted to see," said Randall.

"That's not the point. It's dangerous."

"No, it isn't. It's covered with bricks."

"How did they manage to find a tunnel when the police searched the area only a few days before?" asked Lindy.

Bill shrugged. "I guess they weren't looking for a tunnel."

T.J. came out, carrying an armload of flashlights and handed them around. "Let's go."

The boys led them to the bridge while Bruno chased back and forth in front of them. Bill grabbed both of them by the wrists when they reached the bank. He held on to them as they skittered down the side of the bank.

"See." Randall pointed to the roots twisted around the bridge supports.

T.J. pushed ahead and shined the light where Randall was pointing. "I don't see anything."

"You have to crawl around that big mess of roots," said Randall. "It's kinda slimy."

T.J. edged his way around the curtain of roots and squeezed out of sight. Randall broke away from Bill and followed him. Bill pushed Will toward Lindy and he, too, disappeared.

Will looked at Lindy. Lindy looked at him. Then she took his hand and they followed the others. They climbed downward using the roots for footholds until they came to a rock shelf. It was slippery with mud and debris. Lindy clutched Will by the back of his sweatshirt as he slipped and slid toward a set of rough-hewn steps that descended into darkness. She switched on her flashlight.

"It really is a tunnel," she said and her words echoed back at her.

"Come on," said Will. He pulled her down the steps and into a narrow passageway. It was low, about five feet high, and she walked crablike behind him. She could see T.J.'s light bouncing along the brick walls ahead of them and hear his running commentary on how slaves were smuggled into Canada.

Bill heard them coming, and he and Randall stopped to wait for them. T.J. kept moving, engrossed in his narrative, not realizing that he had lost his audience.

"Seems sturdy enough," Bill said, his words ringing hollow against the stone floor.

T.J.'s voice echoed back to them "Damn—amn—mn—mn."

"He's found something," said Randall, his voice quivering with excitement.

Was it possible? wondered Lindy. Had he actually found evidence of the underground railroad?

"Stay close to me and Lindy." Bill took Randall by the hand and led the way.

They found T.J. standing upright and open-mouthed in a larger chamber, his face uplit from the flashlight like one of the hayride ghouls. They all trained their lights in the direction of his and stared at the wonder before them.

"Wow," said Randall.

"What is it?" asked Will.

"A still," said Bill. Lindy could tell by the slight waver in his voice that he was trying not to laugh.

She looked at the jungle of rusted coils, vats and burners. Broken jugs littered the floor at its base. Not an underground railroad for escaped slaves but a bootlegger's hideout.

"Circa 1920s," said T.J.

Bill clapped him on the shoulder. "Don't feel bad, T.J., This tunnel may not have helped emancipate the slaves, but I bet it made a lot of people really happy."

T.J. expelled his breath. "Doesn't mean I won't find anything. And now with the success of the marathon, I've plenty of time."

"We'll leave you to it then," said Bill and guided Lindy and his nephews back to the stream.

That night Rebo and the boys went trick-or-treating. Bill and Lindy walked slowly down the road as Madame Glosky and her two gypsy companions ran up and down driveways to ring doorbells. Rebo was having as much fun as Randall and Will.

"I can't believe that it's finally over," said Lindy. "But at what cost? Earl Koopes. Derrick. Fallon. She'll get the best of care, but poor Howard and Mary Elisabeth. How will they ever get through this?"

Bill didn't answer. He must have realized that Lindy just needed to talk. And she knew he was listening. Knowing that was better than any answer he could have given.

"Judd said I wouldn't believe what went on behind the beautiful facades in this town. It makes you think, you know?"

Bill took her arm and they stood in silence as the boys descended on another house.

"What will happen to Janey?"

"I think that's an academic question, if you'll forgive the pun," he said quietly.

"She won't last much longer, will she?"

"No."

"I'm glad she didn't die, even if it would have been easier for her. I poured the water for her tea. I would have been culpable."

"No, you wouldn't. Don't even start thinking along those lines." She felt his fingers tighten and release on her arm. "You have other things to think about."

She nodded. She knew she did, but she didn't want to have to think about them yet.

"I'm not deserting you."

She looked at him in confusion.

"I—" He paused. "I think I should make myself scarce for a while. Give you time to see things clearly—without undue influence, so to speak."

"I don't understand," said Lindy, even as she did begin to understand. He was leaving her, too.

"I'll be there for you if you need me. You know that. But I don't think we should see each other for a while."

"Why?" she blurted out. "Why can't we just be like we were?"

"I'm not sure that it's enough." Bill turned her toward him. "That's not what I mean exactly. I want you to be a part of my life. I'll accept whatever part that is going to be. But if I stick around now, you'll always associate me with your divorce. Every time you look at me, you'll think of the past. And I want to have a future with you. Whatever it is."

Burning built up in her stomach. Emptiness, cold and relentless, flooded the rest of her. First Glen, now Bill. She wanted to make a logical argument to prevent him from leaving, or beg him not to desert her. She could have said a hundred things, but what she said was, "Fine."

They didn't speak again. He didn't kiss her cheek when the boys climbed into the car and they drove away. She thanked Rebo and gave him a check. He left shortly afterwards to catch the end of the Christopher Street celebrations.

She wandered back into the house, numb with exhaustion and heartache. She didn't bother to go upstairs to bed, but climbed between the sheets in the guest room where Bill had slept. And thinking of the president who had confessed to adultery in his heart, she fell asleep.

Lindy went to the hospital the next day. Melanie was standing by Janey's bed. Janey was so frail that her body barely made a wrinkle in the covers. She tried to smile when Lindy leaned over to kiss her cheek. Her skin was cool and paper thin.

"I'm turning in my resignation to the school board," said Melanie. "Because of me—" She cleared her throat. "Because of me, a drug dealer was unleashed on an unsuspecting community, and—"

"You're taking too much credit, dear," said Janey, though her voice was barely audible. "Derrick wasn't the first. He certainly won't be the last." She patted a place beside her on the bed, and Melanie gingerly sat down. "He used you, but you can have your revenge. You can stay in the system and fight people like him. I need to know that my children are safe. They're a big responsibility, and they won't thank you for it until twenty years later. You'll probably never find out what good you did for most of them, but I trust you to take care of them."

Melanie bit her lip to keep it from trembling. Lindy blinked furiously.

"Now, you two don't be sad. I've lived a good life. And Evelyn tells me I won't go to jail. That's more than I could hope for."

Her eyes closed, and they could tell she had fallen asleep. They tiptoed from the room and stopped in the hallway.

"She's right, you know," said Lindy.

"I know." Melanie met her eyes. Then she went back inside and closed the door.

The following week, Melanie accepted the school board's offer of a permanent position. Evelyn moved from her apartment, leaving no forwarding address. The new teen center officially moved into the church annex. And Lindy returned to work.

Biddy and Jeremy were tanned and happy from their week in Mexico. Lindy was glad for them. Biddy did what she always did when Lindy was depressed. Took her shopping. Now there were bags and bags of unopened packages lined up in the guest room. She hadn't returned to her room upstairs. There was more than enough space for her on the first floor.

Cliff picked up Bruno and she waved good-bye to them, feeling a little pang of nostalgia when she saw Bruno riding in the front seat. She had managed not to let Cliff see her worry.

Glen called once to say that he wouldn't be home for Christmas. Lindy had tried to confront him, but he had been evasive and hung up shortly after.

"He doesn't want a divorce, but he doesn't want me, either," Lindy told Biddy one night when they were having dinner in the City.

"Men," said Biddy. "They never want a divorce until they're ready to get married again. Then that's all they can talk about. You'd better get a life."

She already had a life, thought Lindy. She just had to figure out what to do with it.

Five weeks after the Mischief Night Marathon, Janey Horowitz died of natural causes. If you could call cancer natural. No autopsy was performed. The funeral was held on a cloudy, sleet-driven December afternoon.

Lindy dressed in a black wool suit. It was a size six, and she hadn't worn it in years. She had once thought she would never fit into it again. Had been watching calories and carbohydrates ever since. Now it hung loosely from her waist.

What a hell of a way to lose weight, she thought sadly. Nothing like having your life in upheaval to kick-start a diet.

A crowd of people huddled beneath black umbrellas outside the large Catholic church downtown. Lindy squeezed through them and up the steps of the church to where an usher escorted her to a seat next to Stella. The sanctuary was filled with people. Friends, neighbors, parents, students, past students with their children—no relatives. Janey was the last of her line.

After the service, the casket was borne outside by Howard Porter, Judd Dillman and six young pallbearers. Bryan Morrison, Jake Adamson, Tolliver Ames, Kenny Stackhowser, Darien Ghandami and Jeff Linden walked in perfect unison. Brought together at last by the woman who had loved them all.

The funeral procession snaked its way to the cemetery where Janey would be laid to rest. Heads bent against the slicing rain, mourners trudged up the hill to where her coffin was covered with scores of flowers. Flowers and wreaths filled the tent and spilled out onto the lawn. Janey's English class handed out daffodils until the somber hillside was covered with spots of color, like points of light in the gloom.

Father Andrews stood near the casket, hands folded in front of him, his head bowed. For a frantic moment, Lindy worried that he had fallen asleep on his feet. But he raised his head, looked to the gray skies and began the eulogy. She could feel waves of sadness wash over the mourners; she flinched at every sob that broke out among them.

Father Andrews said a last prayer, his voice raspy with emotion. The coffin was lowered into the ground, and the crowd began to disperse quietly to their cars. Others filed by the casket. One by one they dropped their flowers onto the ones already blanketing the coffin.

Lindy felt someone come to stand beside her, then slip his arm through hers.

"It's just me," said Bill.

"I know. I'm glad."

Bareheaded in a dark dress coat, his mere presence seemed to give her strength. They watched Stella and her children drop their flowers into the ground. Then Evelyn.

"She came back for the funeral," said Lindy, and somehow that fact seemed the saddest of all.

Melanie knelt at the open ground, said something only Janey could hear and let her flower fall from her hand. Mary Elisabeth and Howard, arm in arm, paused behind her.

"They're back together?" asked Bill.

Lindy nodded. She didn't look at him. He didn't say anything else, but she knew what he was thinking. She took her place in line and dropped her flower on a casket that could no longer be seen. "Good-bye, Janey," she said.

They walked back across the sodden grass toward their cars, Bill guiding her by the elbow. The sun made a brief appearance from behind the clouds.

"It's enough," he said.

"What?"

"Whatever it is that we are."

Lindy smiled, but she couldn't keep her lip from trembling. "Janey would like that syntax." She had to turn away. "He isn't coming back." There was still surprise in her voice, she noted, even though she had accepted the fact weeks ago.

"I'm sorry."

She risked a glance at him.

"Well, the honorable side of me is sorry—the rest of me is rejoicing."

"I'm—" She couldn't finish.

"Hurt—angry—confused. I understand. There's no hurry. We'll just be us for now."

They stopped at the Volvo and Lindy turned to face him. Then she looked past his shoulder.

"Holy shit," she said.

"What?"

"Look. Over the tent. That cloud. It has a silver lining."

Bill turned to look. When he turned back, he was grinning. "If that's not a sign, I don't know what is." He glanced heavenward and started to laugh.

Lindy tried to keep a straight face. It was a funeral, for crying out loud. But she couldn't help it; it bubbled up from some dark recess within her. "Janey would be so thrilled. Symbolism that even I can understand." And she laughed, too.

Please turn the page for an exciting sneak peek of

Shelley Freydont's newest

Lindy Haggerty mystery

A MERRY LITTLE MURDER

coming next month in hardcover!

Lindy was depressed when she and Biddy entered the Rickshaw Café the next morning.

Rose and Jeremy were waiting for them at a table by the panoramic window. Lindy sat down and peered out at the deserted beach. Beyond it, a gray sea swelled beneath an even grayer sky. White caps erupted from the waves, then turned to foam as the waves broke on the shore. It had been cold, but sunny, when they arrived at the hotel the day before. Now, it looked like a storm was coming in.

Perfect, she thought. Neither the Christmas decorations nor the piped-in disco version of "Silver Bells" could dispel her mood. It had been like this every morning since Glen had announced that he wasn't coming home for the holidays. And later, that he wouldn't be coming home at all. He had left her in limbo, not asking outright for a divorce, but making it perfectly clear that he no longer wanted to be a part of her life.

"Madame?"

Lindy realized the waiter was attempting to take her order.

"Toasted bagel," she said without thinking and went back to her ruminations.

And Bill would be arriving sometime that morning. It had seemed like a good idea to invite him to join her for the week. In a few days he would be leaving for Connecticut to spend Christmas with his family, and the company would be on tour by the time he returned to his teaching duties at John Jay College in January. Anyway, it wasn't like she was seducing him. He would have his own room. They were friends. Well, maybe more than friends. Suddenly, she was nervous about spending the next five days with him. What if he pushed her to make a commitment to him? What if he became disgusted with her indecision? What if Glen came back after all?

"So the scuttlebutt is—" Rose lifted a fork of scrambled eggs to her mouth, and Lindy realized that their breakfast had arrived. "That Enrico is unveiling a new line of ball gowns this morning in the vendors' room."

Lindy dragged her attention back to the conversation and breakfast. Biddy was watching her with a worried look. So was Jeremy. Rose arched an eyebrow over a piece of toast.

"Even after what happened last night?" Lindy asked, making an effort to change the focus from her back to Rose.

"Last night was nothing compared to the scene that drove him away in the first place. No one thought that he would ever come back. The man has incredible chutzpah." Rose paused to cut a piece of ham. "He and Luis were setting up a booth in the vendors' room last night, mannequin and everything. No slapping everything on a hanger and shoving them onto a clothes rack like the rest of the poor slobs. But that's all anybody got to see. They hung black drapes around the whole thing before they unpacked the gowns—hermetically sealed from the curious world.

"The hotel security guards finally kicked everybody out around two o'clock. I just happened to be coming out of the Pagoda Bar. Enrico was trying to convince them to let Luis, the Long-Suffering, sit and guard the dresses through the night. Wouldn't want anybody getting a peek before the big day."

"Or do to him want he did to Felicia Falcone last night," said Lindy.

"I'm sorry I missed it," said Biddy. "I'm hanging around from now on."

Jeremy frowned at her over his coffee cup.

Biddy smiled at him, then champed down on her jelly donut and chewed with gusto.

Lindy looked down at her toasted bagel and wondered if a plate of scrambled eggs or a donut would entice her appetite back to normal. "It's a gorgeous dress," she said. "And that turquoise, incredibly rich. The other dresses were so over the top, no subtlety anywhere. And those cutaway midriffs and slit skirts, ugh. I always thought of ballroom dancing as the ultimate romantic activity, but—"

Rose and Biddy both gave her a look. Jeremy bit his lip and looked out the window.

"Well, besides *that*, but you know what I mean. This is all so, I don't know, circusy."

"It is getting more and more out there," agreed Rose. "That's what happens when you make everything a competition. But there are still a few tasteful couples on the floor if you know where to look. I'll point them out tonight."

"I wonder what's happening on the Boardwalk," said Jeremy, rising from his chair to get a better view from the picture window.

"What is it?" asked Biddy.

Jeremy shrugged. "Beached fish, maybe."

Rose pointed to Lindy's bagel. "Hurry up and finish. I want to get a ringside seat at the unveiling."

Lindy pushed her plate away. "I'm ready."

"Oops. Round three," said Rose under her breath and nodded toward the door.

Dawn stood just inside the restaurant. She spotted them and rushed toward the table. "Have you seen Katja or Shane this morning?" Without waiting for an answer, she sped on.

"No one has seen them. Katja never came back to the suite last night. I thought she might have spent the night with some of the girls from the studio, but they haven't seen her either. And Shane doesn't answer his phone. He's missing ten Pro Am heats this morning."

Rose skewed her mouth toward Lindy and Biddy. "Understudy," she whispered.

"Rusty can't possibly take on any more dances and he doesn't know the routines. Mrs. Perkins refused to go on without Shane. She's threatening to leave and wants her money back. Do you know how much that will cost me?"

The three of them shook their heads.

"The woman's in nineteen heats plus two Showcases. At forty dollars a heat and sixty each for the showcases. You do the numbers."

Lindy started multiplying. Almost a thousand dollars, not including hotel and meals.

From the window, Jeremy said, "Oh, shit."

"I'll wring his pretty little neck when he does show up." Dawn stopped to take a frantic look around. "I can imagine what everybody is saying. I bet Junie is just having a big guffaw over this. Damn him."

Rose immediately sobered and said in an uncharacteristically gentle voice, "Maybe Shane's with Junie."

Biddy got up from the table and joined Jeremy.

Dawn finally stopped talking. A look of pain suffused her face. "Junie's in the ballroom." She sniffed, took a deep breath, and brought herself back to speed. "And Enrico is demanding his dress back. How should I know what Katja did with it? I can't even find her. I can't believe she would do this. I've given her everything. She's like a daughter to me. If you see either of them, tell them to come to the ballroom immediately."

"What color did you say that dress was?" asked Biddy.

"Turquoise," Rose and Lindy said in unison.

"Oh, shit," repeated Jeremy. He and Biddy turned to face the others. "There's something turquoise lying in the sand."

"Katja!" screamed Dawn. "Katja!" She spun around and ran toward the door, bumping into a couple just entering the restaurant.

Rose pushed back her chair and took off after her. Biddy, Jeremy, and Lindy exchanged looks, then they, too, rushed to the door.

They took the stairs down one flight to the Casino level, which opened onto the boardwalk. Dawn was ahead of them, running as fast as her four-inch platform mules would allow. They caught up to her at the exit door.

Rose grabbed her. "It might not be—"

Dawn pushed her away and threw herself against the door. Cold air blasted them from outside and wind whistled through the opening. Dawn staggered backward. She grabbed the handle and held on. Then suddenly she was outside and Rose was right behind her.

"Oh, shit," said Jeremy. He hunched over and pushed through the door.

Biddy looked at Lindy. "Here we go again." And she followed Jeremy.

Lindy hesitated. Bill might show up at any minute, and he wouldn't be happy if he found her standing over a body. But then again maybe it was just a beached fish. Wearing a turquoise dress? Not likely. Well, she wouldn't know until she saw for herself. She followed the others onto the boardwalk.

She immediately began to shiver. The temperature must have dropped ten degrees since yesterday morning. A fine mist hung in the air. She hugged herself and looked down the boardwalk. To her left stood the pier, closed for the season. Next to it a set of steps led down to the beach. A bundled figure stood on the sand, surrounded by blue shopping bags and hundreds of sea gulls. Is that what Jeremy had seen? A blue shopping bag?

Across from her, chair taxis were lined against the railing, but there were no cab men. She turned to the right. A hundred feet away, a concrete ramp zigzagged down to the beach. A group of people huddled together at the edge of the wooden walkway, peering over the rail.

Lindy heard a scream and saw Jeremy and Rose pulling Dawn away from the ramp. She started to run. The wood was slick with mist and her feet nearly slid out from under her.

She squeezed through the crowd until she could grasp the railing. She looked down—and gagged. Partially hidden in the corner between the ramp and the boardwalk was the turquoise skirt of Katja's ball gown. It was covered with sand and seaweed, and the wet, discolored fabric clung to her legs. The dress was open down the back, where someone had cut the zipper free. She was still wearing her dance shoes.

ABOUT THE AUTHOR

Shelley Freydont has toured internationally as a professional dancer with Twyla Tharp Dance and American Ballroom Theater. She has also choreographed for and appeared in films, television, and on Broadway. She now lives in New Jersey with her husband and two children. Shelley loves to hear from readers and you may write to her c/o Zebra Books. Please include a self-addressed stamped envelope if you wish a response.